SEA STORIES

SEA STORIES

Edited by
Patricia J. Robertson

Illustrated by
Reginald Gray

First published 1981 by
Octopus Books Limited
59 Grosvenor Street
London W1

ISBN 0 7064 1572 8

Printed in the United States of America

Contents

KIDNAPPED AT SEA
W. H. G. Kingston

Peter Lefray is sent from his home in Ireland, in disgrace, and goes to sea. After reaching North America, he signs on as crew with the schooner Foam, *but is persuaded by the kindly Captain Searle of the brig* Susannah *to sail with him instead.*

The 'Susannah' was a fine brig, of about three hundred tons burden. She had a raised poop, but no top-gallant forecastle, so the crew were berthed in the fore-peak, in the very nose, as it were, of the vessel. I had engaged to serve as a boy before the mast. Indeed, perfectly unknown as I was, with slight pretensions to a knowledge of seamanship, I could not hope to obtain any other berth.

The crew were composed of about equal numbers of Americans – that is, subjects of the United States – and of Englishmen, with two blacks and a mulatto, a Spaniard, and a Portuguese. The first officer, Mr Dobree, was a great dandy, and evidently considered himself much too good for his post; while the second mate, Mr Jones, was a rough and ready seaman, thoroughly up to his work.

I was welcomed by my new shipmates in the forepeak with many rough but no unkind jokes; and as I had many stories to tell of my adventures in the backwoods, before we turned in for the night, I had made myself quite at home with them.

At daybreak on the next morning all hands were roused out to weigh anchor. The second mate's rough voice had scarcely done sounding in my ear before I was on deck, and with the rest was running round between the capstan-bars. 'Loose the topsails,' next sang out the captain.

I sprung aloft to aid in executing the order. Though a young seaman may not have knowledge, he may, at all events, exhibit activity in obeying orders, and thus gain his superior's approbation. The anchor was quickly run up to the bows, the topsails were sheeted home, and with a light breeze from the northward, we stood towards the mouth of the Mississippi.

As we passed close to the spot where, on the previous day, the 'Foam' lay at anchor, I looked for her. She was nowhere to be seen. She must have got under weigh and put to sea at night. 'She's gone, Peter, you observe,' remarked Captain Searle, as some piece of duty called me near him. 'I am glad you are not on board her; and I hope neither you nor I may ever fall in with her again.'

From New Orleans to Belize, at the mouth of the Mississippi, is about one hundred miles, and this distance, with the aid of the current and a favourable breeze, we accomplished by dusk, when we prepared once more to breast old ocean's waves. These last hundred miles of the father of rivers were very uninteresting, the banks being low, swampy, and dismal in the extreme, pregnant with ague and fevers. Although I rejoiced to be on the free ocean, I yet could scarcely help feeling regret at leaving, probably for ever, the noble stream on whose bosom I had so long floated – on whose swelling and forest-shaded banks I had travelled so far – whom I had seen in its infancy, if an infant it may ever be considered, in its proud manhood, and now at the termination of its mighty course.

These thoughts quickly vanished, however, as I felt the lively vessel lift to the swelling wave, and smelt the salt pure breeze from off the sea. Though the sea-breeze was very reviving after the hot pestilential air of New Orleans, yet as it came directly in our teeth, our captain wished it from some other quarter. We were enabled, however, to work off the shore, and as during the night the land-breeze came pretty strong, by daybreak the next morning we were fairly at sea.

Before the sun had got up the wind had gone down, and it soon became what seamen call a flat calm. The sea, as the hot rays of the sun shone on it, was, as it were, like molten lead; the sails flapped lazily against the mast; the brig's sides, as she every now and then gave an unwilling roll, threw off with a loud splash the bright drops of water which they lapped up from the imperceptibly heaving bosom of the deep. The hot sun struck down on our heads with terrific force, while the pitch bubbled up out of the seams of the deck; and Bill Tasker, the wit of the crew, declared he could hear it squeak into the bargain. An awning was spread over the deck in some way to shelter us, or we should have been roasted alive. Bill, to prove the excess of the heat, fried a slice of salt junk on a piece of tin, and peppering it well, declared it was delicious. The only person who seemed not only not to suffer from the heat, but to enjoy it, was the black cook, and he, while not employed in his culinary operations, spent the best part of the day basking on the bowsprit-end.

The crew were engaged in their usual occupations of knotting yarns, making sinnet, etc., while the aforesaid Bill Tasker was instructing me – for whom he had taken an especial fancy – in the mysteries of knotting and splicing; but we all of us, in spite of ourselves, went about our work in a listless, careless way, nor had the officers even sufficient energy to make us more lively. Certainly it was hot. There had been no sail in sight that I know of all the day, when, as I by chance happened to cast my eyes over the bulwarks, they fell on the topsails of a schooner, just rising above the line of the horizon.

'A sail on the starboard bow!' I sung out to the man who was nominally keeping a look-out forward. He reported the same to the first mate.

'Where away is she?' I heard the captain enquire, as he came directly afterwards on deck.

'To the southward, sir; she seems to be creeping up towards us with a breeze of some sort or other,' answered Mr Dobree. 'Here, lad,' he continued, beckoning to me, 'go aloft, and see what you can make of her; your eyes are as sharp as any on board, if I mistake not, and a little running will do you no harm.'

I was soon at the masthead, and in two minutes returned, and reported her to be a large topsail schooner, heading north-north-east, with the wind about south-east.

'I can't help thinking sir, from her look, that this is the same craft that was lying off New Orleans two days ago,' I added, touching my hat to the captain. I don't remember exactly what made me suppose this, but such I know was my idea at the time.

'What, your friend Captain Hawk's craft, the 'Foam,' you mean, I suppose,' he observed. 'But how can that be? She was bound to the

Havanah, and this vessel is standing away from it.'

'I can't say positively, sir; but if you would take the glass and have a look at her, I don't think you would say she is very unlike her, at all events,' I replied.

'It's very extraordinary if such is the case,' said the captain, looking rather more as if he thought I might be right than before.

'Give me the glass, and I'll judge for myself; though it's impossible to say for a certainty what she may be at this distance,' Saying this he took the telescope, and in spite of the heat, went aloft.

When he came down again I observed that he looked graver than usual. He instantly gave orders to furl the awning, and to be ready to make sail as soon as the breeze should reach us. 'The youngster is right, Mr Dobree,' he said, turning to the mate, and probably not aware that I overheard him.

'It's that picarooning craft, the "Foam"; and Mr Hawk, as he calls himself, is after some of his old tricks. I had my suspicions of him when I saw him off New Orleans; but I did not think he would venture to attack us.'

'He's bold enough to attack any one sir,' said the mate; 'but we flatter ourselves that we shall be able to give a very good account of him, if he begins to play off any of his tricks on us.'

'We'll do our best, Mr Dobree,' said the captain; 'for if we do not, we shall have but a Flemish account to render of our cargo, let alone our lives.'

I do not know if I before stated that the 'Susannah' carried four guns – two long and two carronades; and as we had a supply of small arms and cutlasses, we were tolerably able to defend ourselves.

The captain walked the deck for some time in silence, during which period the stranger had perceptibly approached us. He then again went aloft, and scrutinised her attentively. On coming down he stopped at the break of the poop, and, waving his hand, let us know that he wished to address us. 'My lads,' he began, 'I don't altogether like the look of that fellow out yonder, who has been taking so much pains to get up to us. He may be honest, but I tell you I don't think so; and if he attempts to molest us, I'm sure you'll one and all do your duty in defending the brig and the property on board her entrusted to you. I need not tell you that pirates generally trust to the saying, that dead men tell no tales; and that, if that fellow is one, and gets the better of us, our lives won't be worth much to any of us.'

'Don't fear for us, sir; we're ready for him whatever he may be,' sung out the whole crew with one voice.

The stranger brought along the breeze with him, but as yet our sails had not felt a particle of its influence. At length, when he was little more than a mile off, a few cat's-paws were seen playing on the water; they came, and vanished again as rapidly, and the sea was as smooth as before. In time they came oftener and with more power; and at length our topsails and top-gallant sails were seen slowly to bulge out as the steadier breeze filled them.

The wind came, as I have said, from the south-east which was directly in our teeth in our proper course to the Havanah. The stranger had thus the weather-gauge of us; and a glance at the map will show that we were completely embayed, as had we stood to the eastward, we should have run on the Florida coast, while on the other tack we must have run right down to meet him. We might possibly reach some port; but the probabilities were that he would overtake us before we could do so, and the appearance of fear would encourage him to follow us. We had therefore only the choice of running back to Belize, or of fighting our way onward. Captain Searle decided on the latter alternative; and bracing the yards sharply up on the starboard tack, we stood to the eastward, intending, whatever course the stranger pursued, to go about again at the proper time.

The schooner, on seeing this, also closely hugged the wind and stood after us. There could now be no longer any doubt about his intentions. We, however, showed the stars and stripes of the United States, but he hoisted no ensign in return. It was very soon evident that he sailed faster than we did, and he was then rapidly coming within range of our guns. Our captain ordered us, however, on no account to fire, unless we were struck, as he was unwilling to sacrifice the lives of any one unnecessarily, even of our enemies.

Every stitch of canvas the brig could carry was cracked on her; all would not do. The stranger walked up to us hand over hand. Seeing that there was not the slightest chance of escaping by fight, Captain Searle ordered the foresail and top-gallant sails to be clewed up, and, under our topsails and fore-and-aft sails, resolved to wait the coming up of the enemy, if such the stranger might prove.

On came the schooner, without firing or showing any unfriendly disposition. As she drew near, I felt more and more convinced that she must be the 'Foam.' She had a peculiarly long cut-water and a very straight sheer, which, as she came up to windward of us and presented nearly her broadside, was discernible. As she heeled over to the now freshening breeze, I fancied that I could even discern, through the glass, Captain Hawk walking the quarter-deck. When she got about a quarter of a mile to windward of us she hove to and lowered a boat, into which several people jumped and pulled towards us. At the same time up went the Spanish ensign at her peak.

Captain Searle looked puzzled. 'I cannot make it out, Dobree,' he observed. 'I still doubt if that fellow is honest, and am half inclined to make sail again, and while he bears down to pick up his boat, we may get to windward of him.'

'If he isn't honest he'll not trouble himself about his boat, but will try to run alongside us, and let her come up when she can, ' answered the mate. 'There is no trusting to what such craft as that fellow may do.'

'Oh, we'll take care he does not play off any tricks upon us,' said the captain; and we waited the approach of the boat.

As she drew near, she was seen to contain eight men. Four were pulling, one sat in the bows, and the other three in the stern-sheets. If they were armed it could not be discovered. When they got within hail, the captain asked them what they wanted.

They pointed to their mouths, and one answered in Spanish 'Aqua, aqua, por amor de Dios.'

'They want water, sir, they say,' observed the first mate, who prided himself on his knowledge of Spanish.

'That's the reason, then, that they were in such a hurry to speak to us,' said the captain. 'But still, does it not strike you as odd that a vessel should be in want of water in these seas?'

'Her water-butts might have leaked out, and some of these Spanish gentry, sir, are very careless about taking enough water to sea,' replied the mate, who was biased by the pleasure he anticipated of being able to sport his Spanish.

'Get a water-cask up on deck, and we'll have it ready to give these fellows, whatever they may be,' said our humane captain. 'Have some pannikins ready to serve it out to them. Thirst is a dreadful thing, and one would not keep a fellow-creature in that state a moment longer than one could help.'

I do not know what the second mate thought of the strangers, but I remember several of the crew saying that they did not like their looks; and I saw him place a cutlass close to the gun nearest the starboard gangway, while he kept eyeing them in no very affectionate manner. Notwithstanding the heat of the weather, the men in the stern-sheets wore cloaks. On observing this, Bill Tasker said he supposed it was to hide the shabby jackets they wore under them. The other men were dressed in blue shirts, and their sleeves rolled up to the shoulder, with the red sash usually worn by Spaniards round their waist, in which was stuck the deadly *cuchillo*, or cut-and-thrust knife, in a sheath, carried by most Lusitanian and Iberian seamen, and their descendants of the New World.

They pulled up at once alongside, and before any one attempted to stop them they had hooked on, the man in the bows climbing up on deck, followed by his companions in cloaks, and two of the seamen. The other two remained in the boat, pointing at their mouths, as a sign that they wanted water.

Seamen, from the sufferings and dangers to which they are exposed, are proverbially kind to those in distress. Our men, therefore, seemed to vie with each other who should first hold the pannikins of water to the mouths of the strangers, while a tub, with the fluid, was also lowered into the boat alongside. They eagerly rushed at the water, and drank up all that was offered them, but I could not help remarking that they did not look like men suffering from thirst. However, a most extraordinary effect was produced on two of them, for they fell down on the deck, and rolled about as if in intense agony. This drew the attention of all hands on them; and as we had no surgeon on board, the captain began to ransack his medical knowledge to find remedies for them.

While he was turning over the pages of his medical guide to find some similar case of illness and its remedy described, the schooner was edging down towards us. As she approached, I observed only a few men on board; and they, as the people in the boat had done, were pointing at their mouths, as if they were suffering from want of water. The boat was on the lee side.

I think I said that there were some sails, and two or three cloaks,

13

apparently thrown by chance, at the bottom of the boat. While all hands were engaged in attending to the strangers, and for some minutes no one had looked towards the schooner, on a sudden I heard a loud grating sound – there was the wild triumphant cry of a hundred fierce voices. The seemingly exhausted men leapt to their feet – the helmsman and our captain lay prostrate by blows dealt by our treacherous foes – the second mate and several of the men were knocked down; and before any of us had time to attempt even any defence of the brig, a set of desperadoes, of all colours and nations, were swarming down on her decks from the rigging of the schooner; while others who had been concealed in the boats sprang on board on the lee side. Never was a surprise more complete, or treachery more vile. In an instant we were helplessly in the power of as lawless a band of pirates as ever infested those seas. The captain and mates were first pinioned – the men were sharing the same treatment. I was at the time forward, when, on looking aft, who should I see but Captain Hawk himself, walking the deck of the brig as if he were her rightful commander. He took off his hat with mock courtesy to poor Captain Searle, as he passed him. 'Ah! my dear sir, the fortune of war makes you my prisoner today,' he said, in a sneering tone; 'another day, if my people do not insist on your walking the plank, you may hope, perhaps, to have the satisfaction of beholding me dangling at a yard-arm. By the bye, I owe you this turn; for you shipped on board your craft a lad who had engaged to sail with me; and I must have him forthwith back again, with a few other articles of your cargo which I happen to require.' As he said this, his eye fell on me, and he beckoned me towards him. I saw that there was no use hanging back, so I boldly advanced. 'You are a pretty fellow, to desert your colours,' he continued, laughing. 'You deserve to be treated as a deserter. However, I will have compassion on your youth, if you will swear to be faithful to me in future.'

'I never joined your vessel, so I am not a deserter. I cannot swear to serve a man of whose character I know nothing, except that he has taken forcible possession of a peaceable trader.' I said this without hesitation or the least sign of fear. The truth is, I felt too desperate to allow myself to consider what I said or did.

'You are a brave young bantam,' he answered, laughingly. 'And though all the rest may hang or walk the plank, we will save you to afford us sport; so set your mind at rest on that point.'

A set of desperadoes swarmed over the decks.

'Thank you for my life; for I've no wish to lose it, I can assure you,' I replied: 'but don't suppose I am going to spend it in your service, I shall do my best to get away from you as soon as possible.'

'Then we must tie you by a lanyard to the leg,' he answered, without at all appearing angry. 'Here, Mark Anthony,' – he beckoned to a tall, ill-looking black who had been busy in securing the rest of the crew, – 'take charge of this youngster, and render an account of him to me by and by, without a hair of his head injured, mind you.'

'Yes, sare,' said the Roman general, who I afterwards found was a runaway slave from Kentucky. 'I'll not singe his whiskers even. Come here, Massa.' And, seizing me by the shoulder, he dragged me forward away from the rest of the people. 'What's your name?' asked my black keeper as he made me sit down on the bits of the bowsprit. 'Peter, at your service, Mr Mark Anthony," said I in as fearless a voice as I could command; for having once taken a line of conduct which seemed to answer well, I determined to persevere in it.

'Den, Massa Peter, you sit dere quiet,' he said with a grin. 'I no break your skull, because Captain Hawk break mine if I do. I no let anybody else hurt you for same reason.'

From his look and voice I certainly did not flatter myself that he refrained from throwing me overboard from any love he bore me; but, on the contrary, that he would have been much more gratefully employed in making me walk the plank, or in tricing me up to the fore-yard.

Meantime the pirates were busily employed in ransacking the vessel, and in transferring everything of value to them, which they could find, from her to their own schooner. The captain and mates were threatened with instant death if they did not deliver up all the money they had on board; and even the crew were compelled to hand over to our captors the small sums they possessed. To make them do this, they were knocked about and beaten unmercifully, and even those who possessed watches and rings were deprived of them, as well as of any clothes which appeared worth taking.

I had often read the history of pirates and of their bold exploits, until I almost fancied that I should like to become one, or at all events that I should like to encounter them; but I can assure my friends that the reality was very different from the fiction, and as the hideous black was standing over me, ready every moment to knock out my brains, and my companions were suffering all sorts of ill-treatment, I most heartily wished that such gentry as pirates had not been allowed to exist.

Though I tried to look as indifferent as possible, the black would have observed me trembling, had he not been watching to see what his friends were about, no doubt eager to obtain his share of the plunder. The work the pirates were engaged in went on for some time, until even they had tolerably satiated their eagerness for booty; and I then fully expected to see them either heave my shipmates overboard as food for the sharks alongside, or hang them at the yard-arms, and then set the ship on fire, as Mark Anthony insinuated, for my satisfaction, that they would do. Instead of this, to my surprise, Captain Hawk went up to Captain Searle, and said, 'I sent a message by that youngster there to you to look out for yourself, and I never threaten in vain. He goes with me. I want a good navigator; and as your second mate seems a likely sort of person, I shall take him also. The rest of you may go free; but remember, that if any of you attempt to betray me, or to appear as witnesses against me, you will dearly pay for it.'

Our poor captain, who was almost ruined and heartbroken by the pillage of his ship, said nothing, but bowed his head on his breast, looking as if he would as soon have been killed outright. The unfortunate mate, Abraham Jones, seemed horrified at hearing what his fate was to be; but he knew enough about the pirates to be aware that it would have been worse than useless to attempt to escape accompanying them. He, however, took the precaution of calling on the crew of the 'Susannah' to bear witness that he was compelled through bodily fear and by force to join the pirates; and he made the best show of resistance that under the circumstances he could venture to do.

From what I saw of him, I do not think that he had so great an objection to joining them as some men might have had. Indeed, I confess that I was very wrong in doing so; and I feel that a person ought rather to sacrifice his life than consent to commit a crime, even though driven to it with a dagger at his throat. However, both Jones and I fancied that the only chance of saving our own lives, and those of our shipmates, was by our going on board the schooner.

'Remember, Captain Searle, if we get into any misfortune through you, these two will be the first to suffer; and then again, I say, look out for yourself,' exclaimed the chief pirate, as he quitted the deck of the 'Susannah.'

His people then hove her guns overboard, and removed the small arms on board their own craft, to which the mate and I were also transferred. They also cut the standing and running rigging, which would effectually prevent her from making sail for a long time to come.

The first mate was next released, and was ordered to stand on the poop, on pain of being shot down if he attempted to move while the schooner was near. Her boat was then hoisted in, she was cast off from the brig, and with a cheer of triumph from her crew, she stood away from the 'Susannah.'

The first mate wisely did as he was ordered, and it was not until we had got to such a distance, that there was little fear of his being hit, that I saw him jump down to release his companions. It was with a sense of misery and degradation I have never before experienced, that I watched until we lost sight of the unfortunate 'Susannah.'

★　★　★　★

After many adventures at sea, Peter eventually returns to Ireland where he was happily reunited with his father.

DISASTER
Paul Gallico

The S.S. *Poseidon* was as high as an apartment building, and as wide as a football field. Set down in New York she would have stretched from 42nd Street to 46th Street – four city blocks – or in London from Charing Cross station to the Savoy. A third of her 81,000 gross tonnage was below the waterline, crammed with propulsion and refrigeration machinery, boilers, pumps, reduction gear, dynamos, oil, ballast tanks and cargo space.

At this particular time the *Poseidon* was light, riding too high out of the water, improperly ballasted and technically unseaworthy. The Captain had been led into this trap through a series of strokes of ill luck and timing and a bad decision on his part based upon strictly commercial considerations.

The International Consortium that had purchased the liner had converted her for a freight-cruise combination, sailing out of Lisbon, visiting some fifteen countries in Africa and South America in a period of thirty days. They had tripled her cargo space by knocking out the tourist and cabin classes fore and aft, along with much of the crew quarters, limiting passenger space to first-class while retaining her original speed of thirty-one knots. The amount of freight carried enabled them to bring the cruise price of these accommodations within the reach of those who had never before been able to afford such a holiday.

When she had steamed into La Guaira, Venezuela, the next to last leg of her highly successful maiden voyage, Christmas cruise, her cargo holds were all but empty having discharged at Georgetown, British Guiana, and her oil bunkers only a third full. She was due to replenish these with Venezuelan oil and take on a full shipment of freight.

Unfortunately at La Guaira they ran into a wildcat dock strike. After waiting thirty-six hours, the *Poseidon* was compelled by her tight schedule – she was due to leave again from Lisbon on December 30th on a New Year's cruise – to sail with her cargo holds empty and no replacement of fuel.

She had sufficient to reach Lisbon but it was the Captain's decision not to compensate for the missing oil from her double bottom tanks with water ballast that made his ship dangerously tender and landed him in his fix.

To have filled this space with salt water as he should have done, meant that the time required to flush and clean them in Lisbon would have wrecked the turn-around schedule already tightened by the delay.

For the record the Consortium sent him a cable, 'Use your own judgement.' For his private information they bombarded him with coded messages that he was inviting financial catastrophe for them. Five hundred arriving passengers would be living at company expense in Lisbon hotels, not to mention the ill will that would be engendered when they missed their promised New Year's Eve party at sea. The cables pointedly referred to a high pressure area over the Middle Atlantic with forecasts of continuing fair weather. It was the Captain's first big command: he gambled.

At Curaçao, the last port of call, collected reports from all weather stations along his route indicated high pressure area holding firm. It confirmed his decision to sail with his ship as she was.

Once at sea and encountering the mysterious swells, the jaws of the trap closed. To have tried to flood the tanks of a ship of low stability while she was rolling would have been to court immediate disaster.

He did what he could to secure his vessel: battened down, strung lifelines, emptied the swimming-pools, placed his crew on double watch alert and kept his radio room crackling, looking for the storm that he was certain lay in his path, in spite of the reassuring weather forecasts. For in his experience, limited to the Eastern Mediterranean, swells indicated the passage of a great disturbance or one to be encountered. Since up to then he had sailed through nothing but smooth water the trouble must lie ahead. The Captain's mind was centred upon locating that missing storm and avoiding it if he could.

At two o'clock that afternoon he was let off the hook. Sparks brought him a message broadcast from the seismographic station on the Azores to the effect that there had been a mild, rolling, sub-sea earthquake of no great duration registered both there and in the Canaries, resulting in the build-up of the swell affecting vessels to the south. This dismissed the fears of unreported storm centres. Almost simultaneously came a radio message from a Spanish freighter, the *Santo Domingo* out of Barcelona, to whom they had spoken earlier in the day. She was now a hundred and twenty miles north-east of the *Poseidon,* had steamed out of the shock area and reported an end to the disturbance, of the sea. By six o'clock that evening, even at reduced speed, the *Poseidon* could be expected to sail out of the range of the swells.

The Captain thereupon ordered an unalarming, watered-down version of the reason for the ship's behaviour to be broadcast to the passengers with a promise that before nightfall it would have abated.

Shortly after six o'clock the swells abruptly ceased and the *Poseidon,* after overcoming the inertia set up by her rolling, sailed level on a flat, glassy, breathless sea. The relieved Captain lifted restrictions on the kitchens and cabin service, directed a few junior officers to appear at dinner to provide a sprinkling of white uniforms and gold braid, while still holding the rest of his crew and staff on alert. For he was not wholly happy nor his mind entirely at ease. But when the perfect conditons continued to prevail, he ordered maximum possible speed ahead.

The frame of the old liner began to shudder and shake as her four turbines, each propelling a thirty-two-ton screw, thrust her onwards into the gathering dark at some thirty-one knots. Glasses and drinking-water bottles rattled in their racks, things loose vibrated. The great effort the old giantess was making was only too apparent.

To the majority of those who had been miserably ill the pardon came too late. The relief arriving so close to the evening meal inspired very few to come to dinner. At half-past eight there were only a few more than had been present for lunch scattered about the huge dining-saloon. Manny

Rosen's Strong Stomach Club was present, augmented by a full complement at the grab-bag table with the appearance of Mr Kyrenos the Third Engineer and Mrs Rogo.

Linda Rogo was as usual overdressed in a long, white, silk sheath gown so tight that it showed the indentation of her buttocks and the line of her underpants. From the tremendous cleavage it was probably an inheritance from the wardrobe of her starlet days, which caused Manny Rosen to whisper to his wife, 'What's holdin' them in?'

Linda was a pretty, girlie-doll blonde with a small mouth which she exaggerated into a bee-stung pout. She somewhat resembled Marilyn Monroe except for the bite of personality. She affected a blue-eyed, baby stare but the eyes were ice cold. She had let everyone know that she had been a Hollywood starlet, appeared in a Broadway play and had given up a theatrical career to marry Rogo. She never let her husband forget it either.

Frank Scott said to her, 'So glad you were able to come tonight, Mrs Rogo. The table wasn't the same without you.'

Linda flirted her head and cooed, 'Oh, Reverend, do you really mean it:' Then dropping her voice, but still sufficiently audible, she said to her husband, 'You didn't want me to come.'

Rogo looked innocently aggrieved as he always did when Linda abused him and answered, 'Aw now, baby, I just didn't want you to be sick.'

The shivering of the ship was more noticeable in the restaurant and Muller's glass, touching a carafe, rang like a tuning fork. He clutched at the rim so quickly that Rosen, who was facing him at his neighbouring table for two, was startled and said. 'What happened?'

Muller said, 'Old seagoing superstition. You let a sailor die if you don't stop a glass from ringing.' He added, 'I'm irreligious but superstitious.' In a moment he had them all clutching at their glasses to stop the tinkling.

This the last night but one had brought out the third best evening frocks of the women. Miss Kinsale was in her short, grey taffeta – she had brought three for the voyage: black for best, a green and a grey which she wore alternately. Belle Rosen was in a black lace, short dress with high-heeled shoes and the inevitable diamond clips and mink cape. Jane Shelby and Susan appeared in a knee-length mother and daughter set of chiffon in contrasting shades of lilac. The men, with the exception of Scott, wore dinner jackets. The Minister was in a dark-blue suit and the flamboyant Princeton orange and black tie. Martin's dinner-jacket was tartan plaid in blue and green. In spite of the perfect fit of Rogo's clothes, his stocky body made him look like a bouncer in a night club. The two stewards Acre and Peters as usual were in their stiff shirts and white mess-jackets. Across the room The Beamer and his girl were at his table, beginning to drink their evening meal. Pamela's mother was still ill.

Robin Shelby ordered, 'I'll have the Lobster Newburg.'

'No you won't!' said his mother. 'Not at night.'

Her husband said, 'Turkey hash is practically obligatory the day after Christmas.'

Miss Kinsale asked for Salmon Timbales, and hoped they would be like the fishcakes she was used to at home. The Rosens opted for the Devilled Chicken; the Rogos never ate anything but steak or hamburgers.

Stewards with their food trays made their way through the aisles of deserted tables of the nearly empty dining-room and in between the shaking of the ship as she drove through the early evening, one could hear the occasional clink of fork and plate. It was rather a silent meal, for denied the covering hum and clatter of a full restaurant, the diners kept their voices and laughter down.

In the engine room the temporary double watch, their voices drowned out by the thunder of their machinery revolving at top speed, hovered over bearings, dials and gauges and wondered how long the Skipper intended to keep her driving at that pace. One of the oilers was sent to fetch a couple of dozen cokes. The boiler-room crew kept an equally anxious eye on temperature gauges and fuel consumption.

Topside in the radio room on the sun deck, the night wireless operator was getting off a backlog of messages.

On the bridge the Captain, thanking his stars that he had got off so lightly, nevertheless was still apprehensive. He had discarded as unnecessary as well as dangerous the idea of taking on water ballast under way, even in a calm ocean through which his ship was sailing normally again. Should there be a hurricane warning, there would still be ample time to do so to enable his ship to ride out a storm. But from all reports, high-pressure zones were holding. Once again he made the decision not to ballast. If he pushed his engines to their capacity, he would be able to make up some of the lost time and bring her in no more than a day late already provided for. Yet no skipper is ever truly comfortable when his vessel is going all out. He operated therefore with the sixth sense of the veteran seaman: weather good, forecast holding, sea track clear, nerve ends uncomfortable.

With nightfall the sky had become overcast and the surface of the flattened sea had an oily quality which was distasteful to the Master as though a leaden-coloured skin had formed over it. When his ship entered the zone of total darkness he sent a second man up into the crow's nest and posted two young officers permanently at the radar screen whose revolving arm lit up not a single blip on a fifty-mile range.

The executive, who was second-in-command and a more stolid person, could not imagine what was bugging the Skipper or keeping him striding nervously. Thrice he had asked whether the second lookout had been posted. Each time he passed the radar screen he glanced into it. He was like a man driving a car who, checking his rear vision mirror before making a turn, does not quite believe it when he sees there is no one behind him.

From time to time he went out on to the port bridge wing which projected out over the water and looked down upon the oily sea reflecting the speeding string of lights of his ship keeping pace with him on its surface. The news of the minor quake had made him conscious of what lay below. His charts showed that the submerged mountain peaks of the Mid Atlantic Ridge, extending in a gigantic letter 'S' ten thousand miles from Iceland to the edge of the Antarctic, at that point were a mile and a half beneath his keel.

The charts, however, were not specific seismic maps and hence indicated neither the three volcanoes believed to be active pointing in line towards the top of South America, nor reflected the huge fault known to exist in the Ridge in that area.

At exactly eight minutes past nine, this fault already weakened by the preliminary tremor, now without warning shifted violently and slipped a hundred or so feet, sucking down with it some billions of tons of water.

If the *Poseidon* had not been shuddering so from the power she was generating, the bridge might have felt the sudden jolt of earthquake shock echoing upwards, though its force was downwards. Indeed, the

Captain and his executive did glance at one another sharply for an instant, because of something they thought they felt in the soles of their feet. But when the *Poseidon* continued to surge forward, they relaxed and by then it was too late.

For a moment they experienced that sickening feeling at the pit of the stomach when an elevator lift drops too quickly, as the ship, sucked into the trough of the sea's sudden depression, lurched downward and began to heel. At the same time there was some babbling from the telephone to the crow's-nest and the Third Officer at the radar screen gave an unbelieving shout of 'Sir!' as, eyes popping from his head, he pointed to the blips which showed them about to run into a solid obstacle that had not been there a minute before.

The Captain tried to run in from the end of the bridge wing, but it was already going up hill. He heard the clang of the engine-room telegraph as the executive reached the levers and the order, 'Right full rudder! All engines full astern!' the almost automatic reaction to an obstacle dead ahead.

And so when the S.S. *Poseidon* met the gigantic, up curling, seismic wave created by the rock slip, she was more than three-quarters broadside, heeling farther from the turn. Top heavy and out of trim, she did not even hang for an instant at the point of no return, but was rolled over, bottom up, as swiftly and easily as an eight-hundred ton trawler in a North Atlantic storm.

The first intimation the scattering of passengers in the dining-saloon had of impending catastrophe was the sudden drop of the thick carpeted floor from beneath their feet. Chairs and tables tilted them forward or sideways, revealing a dizzying abyss before they were catapulted downwards into it.

Simultaneously the ship screamed.

The scream, long-drawn-out and high-pitched, was compounded of the agony of humans in mortal fear and pain, the shattering of glass and breaking crockery, the clashing, cymbal sound of metal trays and pots and pans mingled with the crashing of dishes, cups, knives, forks and spoons hurled, some with deadly missile effect, from the dining room tables.

The scream mounted to a crescendo as every object in the ship not fastened was carried away in that sickening whip that laid her on her side.

The Poseidon rolled over like a trawler.

Service doors from the kitchens and pantries swung open and the metallic protest of copper cauldrons, steamers, Dutch ovens and cooking utensils bounding and rebounding down the canting floor, added to the deafening chaos of sound through which penetrated one high, animal cry of anguish which preceded a cook's dying from scalding.

The Beamer and his girl came tumbling down the 118-foot width of the two-storey dining-saloon, turning over and over in slow motion like clowns in a contortionist act, breaking their descent clutching at chairs and tables that had suddenly assumed the vertical. They fell from starboard down to port and then, as the ship completed its revolution, slid another twenty feet, the height of the room, to land dazed, bruised but uninjured in a tangle of arms and legs with the Rosens, Muller, and Mike and Linda Rogo.

It was that first drop varying from fifty to over a hundred feet, the full breadth of the ship, that either crippled or killed those passengers and serving stewards who had the misfortune to be near the centre or the far starboard side of the ship as she careened over to port.

The more fortunate ones were those at the side tables to port. Muller, Belle and Manny Rosen were simply spilled out of their chairs. The Shelbys and the occupants of the grab-bag table had not much farther to go and were able to break their descent by holding on for a moment to their seats. Manny Rosen landed upon the rectangle of the window with nothing between him and the green sea but the thick glass.

But so swift and continuous was the capsizing that before the pressure of the water could fracture it, the *Poseidon's* entire superstructure came thundering down, burying itself in the sea. The port windows now starboard were raised up and cleared themselves. Manny, clutching wildly at Belle, found himself sliding head-first along with the Rogos, the Shelbys and the others, down the slanting side of the vessel to land on the glass-covered ceiling amidst a mass of broken china, trays, cutlery and food. The topmost branches of the Christmas tree which had come tumbling out of its tub, the ornamental star affixed to its peak unbroken, fell upon them.

The moment of sealed-in quiet that followed the death cry of the ship contained more of horror and menace than the nerve-shattering clamour, for it uncovered the small, helpless noises of the injured and dying: murmurs, moans, pleadings, the occasional tinkling drop of some errant utensil that had lagged behind and the rolling about in the pantries of pots that had not yet managed to come to rest.

During the instant just as it appeared that the ship was about to blow herself apart before the final plunge, Mike Rogo was heard to say, 'Someone get off my leg, will you?'

Thereupon there occurred an appalling explosion initiating a series of detonations as three of her boilers blew up.

If the first outcry of the stricken vessel had been a shriek, her second following the explosions was a shattering, ear-rending roar as her innards broke away.

The remaining boilers came loose first. Their pathway to the sea lay through two of the three giant stacks of the liner and they went down with the noise of a thousand men hammering upon sheet iron.

The engine room came apart more slowly, as the heavy turbines, dynamos, generators and pumps hanging downwards, imposed an intolerable strain upon the steel that clamped them to the floor. With the grinding outcry of tortured metal they began to crash down the ship-high rectangular shaft over the engine room and through the glass roof to join the boilers at the bottom of the sea.

Some of these, instead of dislodging completely, fractured to slide sideways and tangle with yet other break-away parts to jam together in a mass of tangled steel, torn piping and uncovered armatures. The S.S. *Poseidon* seemed to be retching up her bowels in mortal agony.

She did this to such an awful continuity of sounds: splintering wood, a whine of tearing metal, thunderclaps, surgings, hissings, great boomings accompanied by suckings and bubblings that the survivors still crumpled in heaps upon the ceiling-floor, could descend no further down the paths of terror.

They could only lie there stunned and deafened by the grinding, rumbling and thunderous poom-boom as of some great war drum, clangour of metal striking upon metal and the shouting of steam loosed as though from the anteroom of hell.

Once a great muddy cascade of water shot into the dining-saloon as though expelled from a cannon. But it ceased as abruptly as it had come, ran off into the opening made by the top of the grand staircase and which now, upside-down, had become a watery pit.

Then all the lights went out.

Yet, by some mystery of buoyancy connected with air trapped in the spaces now emptied of cargo, boilers and heavy machinery, the *Poseidon* still remained afloat with her new waterline lapping against the hull just below where the former ceiling of the dining-saloon had become the floor. The clouds overhead parted, letting through enough tropical night light to cast a faint glow through the reversed sidelights, now high above like clerestory windows in a chapel, upon the desolation of the saloon and the people therein waiting to die.

The convulsions of the ship diminished, except for isolated thuds, bumps and clankings, sudden roars that were stilled as quickly as they had commenced, the bursting of the hatchcovers, the rushing sound of water entering some compartment, until again there was that almost intolerable quiet through which now once more moans of pain and cries for help became audible.

Those on the bridge and topsides quarters died immediately. The Captain, his officers, helmsman, quatermaster and the watch were either slung into the port wing, or jammed up against the side of the enclosure, wedged and pinned there by centrifugal force, or crippled by the fall. None of them had been able even to get close or reach for emergency switches to close all watertight doors. They were drowning before they knew what was hapening to them.

★ ★ ★ ★

A few of the passengers who were in the dining room managed to make their way to the upside-down hull of the ship and were eventually rescued by salvagers.

FIRST DAYS AT SEA
Richard Gordon

Doctor Simon Sparrow decides that the only way to escape from the humdrum routine of general practice (and from the amorous advances of various patients) is to become a ship's doctor. He signs on with the SS Lotus and reports for duty. For the three days the ship is a hive of inactivity.

The *Lotus* sailed, to the surprise of her crew, three days later. We spent the time tethered to the quay, loading heavy packing-cases from railway trucks. It was an interesting performance. The cases were raised to the level of the ship's deck, drawn horizontally inwards, and lowered into the holds. This was done with the derricks and steam winches, each set manned by a gang of Liverpool dockers, who went about their work with the leisurely decorum of the House of Lords considering an unimportant Bill on a hot afternoon.

There was a docker at each winch, and the rest of them worked either down the hold or on the quay. Each gang was controlled by a man in a long overcoat and a bowler hat, who directed their activities with the economy of gesture of an experienced bidder at an auction. The twitch of a little finger, an inclination of the head, the drop of an eyelid, and four tons of crated machinery went spinning through the air and down the hatch as cleanly as a holed-out golf ball.

The stowage of the cargo was supervised by the Mates, under the directions of Archer. He had his bunk covered with cargo manifests, bills of lading, and plans of the ship with the different merchandise coloured in with crayon.

'The Second gets the thin end of it,' he said. 'He's always cargo officer.

Too much work in it for me.'

'But it looks fairly simple. Don't you just go on putting the stuff in until the ship's full?'

'Haven't you ever packed a case for a holiday? The things you want first always seem to be at the bottom. If that happened in the ship there'd be trouble. You can't tip everything out.'

'I see what you mean.'

'Besides, there's the trim of the ship to think about. There's more in cargo than meets the eye.'

He looked at his plan. 'Nos. 1 and 4 are full, but there's plenty of room in 2 and 3. We'll be here a week yet, you can bet on that.'

But orders, based on some deep calculation in the Fathom Line offices, came for us to sail. Twenty-four hours later, in the morning, the *Lotus* left.

An air of excitement spread through the ship before sailing, as everyone began to go about their jobs more briskly. I was greatly stimulated by the promising departure, for I had become thoroughly used to living alongside the wharf in the past few days and occasionally doubted that we would ever sail at all. The dockers who had made free with our decks were turned down the gangway, leaving behind them a litter of newspapers, cigarette packets, and matches trampled into the rusty steel. The wide hatches were covered with heavy slabs of wood, and square tarpaulins lashed over them. At the head of the gangway the quartermaster fixed a blackboard announcing confidently THE S.S. LOTUS WILL SAIL AT 10 O'CLOCK FOR SANTOS NO SHORE LEAVE, and a thin black stream of smoke shot powerfully upwards from the funnel. Our bleak masts were enlivened with flags: the red ensign trailed over our stern, the Company's house-flag – a red F topped by an anchor on a white square – was hoisted at the mainmast, and from the foremast the blue-and-white P announced our intentions to the waterside.

'That at least is a flag I recognize,' I said to Trail. 'The Blue Peter.'

'Yes, we'll soon be on our way, Doc. It's a bloody nuisance. I was just getting a nice little piece lined up last night. It's always the same.'

'I shall be glad to get to sea, I must say. I've seen enough of Liverpool.'

'You'll get your bellyful of sea all right, don't you worry. Shouldn't get too excited, though. They may change their minds and send us into Cardiff when we get out in the Irish Sea. Not a bad place, Cardiff, though

I prefer Middlesbrough myself. The pubs are better.'

Shortly afterwards Trail reappeared on deck with his cap on, looking very determined and ten years older.

'Got to do the testing,' he explained brusquely. 'Tugs'll be here any minute now.'

I heard him ring the bridge telegraphs and sound the whistle, which blew a long silent plume of steam into the air for some seconds before it struck its note. The customs officers gave us a final suspicious look and made for the shore, their threatening bags of rummage tools over their shoulders. Men in yellow raincoats and misshapen trilbys hurried aboard with desperate last letters addressed to Captain Hogg, and rushed away again anxiously looking at their watches. A Mr Swithinbank, a pale youth with steel spectacles from the Liverpool office, came breathlessly down the deck after me, with a paper in his hand.

'Here's the Bill of Health, Doctor,' he said. 'Cripes! For a moment I thought I'd lost you! You can't sail without it.'

'Thank you very much,' I said, taking the document reverently.

'Are you all right?' he asked quickly, making for the gangway. 'Medical stores O.K.? Too late now, anyway. Have a good voyage. Cheery-bye!'

'Good-bye,' I shouted after him helplessly. 'We seem a bit short of sulphonamides.'

'Bring us a ham from Brazil if you remember it,' he called over his shoulder. 'Don't forget the poor starving English.'

He hurried away between the railway waggons and lorries on the quay. It was almost ten. Two sailors, who had somehow managed to drink themselves to a standstill at that hour, staggered up the gangway and collapsed on the deck.

'Take 'em below,' Hornbeam shouted to the Bos'n, with the air of a man handling a familiar situation. 'They'll be logged tomorrow morning. Has Smiley turned up yet?'

'No sign, Mr Hornbeam.'

'I dunno,' Hornbeam said resignedly. 'If you docked a ship in Hell you'd still get deserters. Get my watch turned-to, Bos'n. I'm going to stations.'

'Aye aye, sir.'

Two tugs nuzzled under our bow and stern, their skippers standing impassively at the wheel in their oilskins like waiting taxi-drivers. The pilot came aboard – an alarmingly unnautical figure in a tweed overcoat and bowler hat carrying an umbrella and a black Gladstone bag. I watched Trail knock on the Captain's door, salute, and announce 'Tugs alongside and pilot aboard sir.' He stepped aside as Captain Hogg appeared, resplendent in gold braid, and mounted solemnly to the bridge. The gangway came up, the two tugs plucked the ship away from the quay, and the ropes fell into the water with long splashes. The *Lotus* became suddenly changed into an entity, a being in her own right, instead of a rusty appendage of a dirty Liverpool wharf.

I leant over the rail with Easter, watching the steadily widening gap of water between us and the shore. I had never been on a moving ship before, apart from a brief passage from Margate to Southend in a paddle steamer, and I felt excited and apprehensive. I found the belief that we should now all be transported by the *Lotus* from Liverpool to the Tropics too outlandish to take seriously.

'Well, we're off,' was all I could think to say.

'Yes, sir. In an hour or so we'll be well out in the River.'

'You know, Easter, to me it seems almost impossible for this little ship to take us all the way to South America.'

'Sometimes, sir,' he answered gloomily, 'I think it's a bloody miracle she moves at all.'

We shook with a gentle ague as the engines picked up speed, slipped down the channel of thick Mersey water, passed the tolling buoys and the Bar light, out into the Irish Sea; in the afternoon a sharp sea-wind blew down the deck and the Welsh mountains were huddling on the horizon. I pranced delightedly round the ship, which was now musical with the wind, looking at everything like a schoolboy in the Science Museum.

I had a letter in my pocket from Wendy, which I purposely kept unopened until we were under way. It was a short prim note, wishing me a good voyage, hoping my headaches were better, and mentioning that I was not to think of ourselves as betrothed any longer. It appeared that she had become enamoured of the son of the local draper. I tore the letter up and scattered it over the side: the pieces spread on the sea and were left behind. I laughed. I felt a cad, a devilish cad. But now, surely, I was allowed to be: I was a sailor. A wife in every port for me! I thought. Watch out, my girls, watch out! A rollicking sailor lad, indeed! With a

I watched the gap between the shore and ship widen.

snatch of sea-shanty on my lips I went below for a cup of tea, aware that I was perhaps not quite myself.

* * * *

My elation lasted less than a day. The next morning I was sick.

The *Lotus* creaked and groaned her way through the water like an old lady in a bargain sale. She climbed to the top of a wave, paused for breath, shook herself, and slid helplessly into the trough of the next. I lay on my bunk and watched the sprightly horizon jumping round the porthole, trying to think about eminently terrestrial objects, such as the Albert Hall.

Easter put his head round the door. In his hands he had a cup of tea and a small roseless watering-can, of the type preserved for the conveyance of tepid water in English country hotels.

'Good morning, Doctor,' he said briefly. 'Will you be in for breakfast?'

I rolled my head on the pillow.

'Not feeling too good, Doctor?'

'I think I'm going to die.'

He nodded, gravely assessing the clinical findings.

'Throwing up much?' he asked pleasantly.

'Everything.'

'If I may take the liberty, a good meal is what you want. Plate of fried eggs and bacon and you'll be as right as rain. Works like a charm. Hold it a moment, Doctor, I'll fetch a bowl.'

I held the bowl like a mother with a newborn infant.

'Feeling better now you've got all that up?' he asked solicitously.

'A bit.'

A thought struck him.

'Wouldn't like a bit of cold beef and a few pickles, would you? They'd do just as well.'

'No, no, no! I don't want anything. Nothing at all. I just want to be left alone.'

'Very good, Doctor. Just as you say. Perhaps you might feel like a bit of lunch?'

'I doubt it very much.'

He left me in ecstatic solitude. I lay rigidly on the bunk, concentrating on the words stencilled, by order of the Ministry of Transport, immediately above me: CERTIFIED TO ACCOMMODATE ONE SEAMAN. Seaman, indeed! All I wanted to see was a tree.

It was essential to keep my mind fixed on something beyond the clouds of nausea spiralling round me, so I started to count the rivets in the deckhead. I had reached ninety-eight when Hornbeam came in. He was smoking a pipe.

'Hello, Doc! I hear you're off colour. What's the trouble?'

'I'm seasick.'

He looked surprised.

'Yes, I suppose she is pitching a bit,' he admitted, glancing through the porthole. 'Do you mind if I use one of your matches?'

He blew mouthfuls of smoke into the cabin.

'Better out than in,' he said, as I put the bowl down again.

'I suppose so.'

'You know what, Doc? I'm going to give you a genuine cure for seasickness. I can't often treat a doctor, but this is just the thing. Do you want to try it?'

'What is it?'

'A pint of sea-water. It's an old sailor's cure. When I was an apprentice it was the only thing that stopped me on my first voyage. If we were sick we got kicked down the bridge ladder and given a pint glass just out of the sea-bucket by the Mate. Shall I get you some?'

I raised my hand.

'I think I'd rather not have anything at all at the moment, thank you.'

'As you like, doc. I'm only making a suggestion. Have you tried covering one eye?'

'It wasn't much good.'

'No, I don't believe it is. Damn! Can I have another match? My pipe's gone out again.'

'Would you mind lighting it outside? It's a bit – a bit strong at the moment.'

'Oh, sorry! I didn't think of that.'

I called weakly after him at the door.

'How long is this likely to go on for?'

He calculated for a few seconds.

'Not very long. I should say we'd be in calm water in five or six days.'

'Five or six days!'

I groaned.

I lay and tried hard to analyse my condition, like the dying surgeon, John Hunter. It was, of course, a ridiculously simple malady when one looked at it with scientific detachment. The endolymph in my semicircular canals was stimulating the endings of my cochlear nerve, which transmitted influences to the brain and initiated the reflex arc of vomiting. It should be easy for a little will-power to inhibit the reflex. After all, the brain was the master . . . I exercised the will-power.

'Morning!' Trail said from the doorway. 'When you've got your head out of that bowl I'll tell you a sure-fire cure for seasickness.'

I fell back on the pillow. I had given up. When the angel of death arrived I would shake him cordially by the hand.

Trail came over to the bunk. He put his hands in his trouser pockets and pulled out two bottles of stout.

'Guinness,' he said proudly. 'Drink these and you'll be fine by lunchtime. Works like magic.'

'Oh God!' I said. 'Oh God, oh God!'

Trail looked puzzled.

'What's the matter? Don't you like stout? Here, take it easy! That one nearly went over my uniform.'

He left me wondering submissively how long it would be before Easter came back and started talking about lunch. And it was bound to be Irish stew.'

★　★　★　★

After three days the sea and I achieved a compromise. The sun came out, the wind dropped and lost its malice, the water was tidied up like a room after a wild party. For myself, I learned to lean against the sway of the ship, and I felt well enough to risk lunch in the saloon.

It was my first meal at sea. I sat with the Captain, the Chief Engineer, Hornbeam and Archer, and the Chief Steward, a thin little mouse-faced man called Whimble. As soon as the bell rang we converged on the dining saloon with the briskness of seaside boarders: Captain Hogg disliked anyone being late.

I was on the Captain's right hand, the Mate on his left. The Chief

Engineer faced the Captain, and the other two sat themselves between.

'Ah, Doctor!' Captain Hogg said, jovially enough. 'Decided to join us at last, have you?'

'Yes, sir.'

He unfolded his napkin and tucked it under his chin with deliberation.

'Seasickness,' he said slowly, 'is entirely mental. You imagine it.'

I shrugged my shoulders.

'Well,' I said, in my professional tone, 'there are more complicated reasons than that. I admit there may be a psychological element. But there is obviously some fault with the balancing apparatus in the ears, and probably with the gastric nerves.'

The Captain broke a roll.

'No.' He said it decisively. 'It is entirely mental.'

He started drinking soup loudly.

No one spoke until he had finished.

'Mr McDougall,' he said, slipping half a roll into his mouth, 'have you got that book you were going to lend me at supper last night?'

The Chief looked up. He was a thin, wrinkled Scot with a face dominated by a thick strip of sandy eyebrow, from which his eyes looked out like a couple of Highland gamekeepers inspecting poachers through the undergrowth.

'Aye,' he said. 'You mean *The Squeaker*?'

The Captain nodded.

'That's it. I like a bit of Peter Cheyney.'

'But surely,' I said immediately. '*The Squeaker* was by Edgar Wallace? It was written over twenty years ago.'

'No,' the Captain said. 'It was Peter Cheyney.'

'You know, sir, I'm perfectly . . .'

'Peter Cheyney,' he said, with the emphasis of a full stop. He then fell upon a plate of mutton chops, which disappeared into his mouth like a rush-hour crowd going down an escalator.

We continued eating in silence.

Captain Hogg finished his chops and brought his knife and fork together with a flourish.

'Mr Whimble,' he said.

'Sir!'

The Chief Steward jumped, and choked over a chop bone.

'I have, I suppose, tasted worse chops than these. In a fifth-rate café on the Mexican coast possibly. Why don't you throw the cook over the side? If he'd served filth like this to the Captain when I was an apprentice the fellow would have had his bottom kicked round the deck.'

'I'm sorry, Captain,' Whimble mumbled. 'I'll see to it.'

'I should think so. You never get cooking like you used to. All they think about these days are vitamins and calories and such stuff. What good's that to a man? Fad, that's all it is. You don't need vitamins or calories,' he said with disgust. 'Eh, Doctor?'

'Well, they are really two quite different factors. And vitamins are terribly important.'

'Bosh! I'm not a doctor – I don't pretend to be. But if you get a good bellyful of meat and spuds every day you'll be all right.'

'You must have vitamins,' I insisted, but feebly.

'Vitamins are bosh, Doctor. Bosh!'

I began to see that opinions were forbidden, even professional ones. Our mealtimes were going to be rollicking.

THE MARY CELESTE
Jean Morris

At one o'clock in the afternoon of Wednesday, 5th December, 1872, the brigantine *Dei Gratia,* twenty days out from New York on the Gibraltar run, sighted another brigantine, seventy-eight miles East of the Azores. There was something very wrong with her. She was heading unsteadily West, making one and a half or two knots; her upper foretopsail and foretopsail were gone, her lower foretopsail hanging by its four corners, her mainsail down; though she was on the starboard tack, her jib was trimmed on the port side, and she was coming into the wind and falling off again as if there were no hand on the helm.

Thinking she must be in distress, Captain Morehouse of the *Dei Gratia* sent his first mate, Oliver Deveau, to board her. Oliver Deveau, a capable and observant young man, was shocked at what he found. She had been abandoned; there was not a soul aboard. And she was a ship they all knew; Captain Morehouse had dined with her master twenty-nine days before, in New York. She was the *Mary Celeste,* 282 tons, Captain Benjamin R. Briggs, outward bound from New York to Genoa with a cargo of crude alcohol, eight days in front of the *Dei Gratia.* She had carried ten souls, and one of them a two-year-old child: Captain Briggs, his wife Sarah, their daughter Sophia, first mate Albert Richardson, second mate Andrew Gilling, cook Edward Head, and four seamen from the north of Germany, Volkert Lorensen, his brother Boz, Arian Martens, and Gottlieb Goodschall.

Not one of them was ever heard of again.

★ ★ ★ ★

By four in the afternoon of that 5th of December, Captain Morehouse had put a crew of three men on board the *Mary Celeste:* Oliver Deveau and two seamen, Charles Lund and Augustus Anderson. They were all he could spare, though they were barely enough to work the ship. Deveau's first action was to check the depth of water in the ship, and in doing this he remarked that the sounding rod which was used for this purpose was lying on the deck. The well showed three and a half feet of water, and it took them until nine at night to pump her dry and get under way. But it was three days before they could repair the damage to the rigging enough to make any headway. Just short of Gibraltar they were separated from the *Dei Gratia* by a storm and overran the harbour; but early in the morning of the 13th December – which was an unlucky Friday – twelve hours after the *Dei Gratia,* the *Mary Celeste* made Gibraltar. During those days at sea, though they were busy days, Deveau mentioned later that they had no time to wash down the decks, the three men saw every detail of the ship's condition.

There was water in the main cabin; but not, they all agreed, more than they would have expected from a ship that had wallowed out of control in the stormy Atlantic; just as the depth of water in the well seemed to them reasonable leakage in a wooden vessel. There were no signs of violence, but many signs of great hurry. The captain's bed had not been made. In the crew's quarters there were clothes and boots and even pipes scattered about. Toys and a child's clothes lay in the Captain's cabin, and on one of the beds was the impress of a child's body. In spite of the cramped quarters aboard, Mrs Briggs had had her comforts about her. There were two boxes of clothes 'of the superior sort'; a sewing-machine stowed under the sofa, and a work-bag with needles and thread and buttons; a dressing-case, a writing-desk, and some religious books (Captain Briggs was known to have been a devoutly Christian man). In the centre of the cabin was a rosewood harmonium, and near it a 'little child's high chair.'

Captain Morehouse sent three men to board the Mary Celeste

There was a quantity of food, neatly stored in an open box: sugar, flour, tea, dried herring, rice, a nutmeg, beans, and pots of preserved fruits. In the mate's cabin was the ship's Log Book, which had been made up to 24th November, ten days before the meeting of the *Mary Celeste* and the *Dei Gratia*. There was also the Log Slate, where observations made by the officer of the watch on the bridge would be entered, to be written up in the Log Book later; and on the Log Slate were the last recorded messages from the *Mary Celeste*. These read: *8 a.m., 25th November 1872: Eastern point bears SSW, 6 miles distant*. And then: *Fanny, My Dear Wife, Frances N.R.* The first mate's wife was Fanny Richardson. Were those words the draft of a letter started in an idle moment, or a last desperate effort at a last desperate message?

The *Eastern point* was the island of Santa Maria in the Azores, 78 miles West of the meeting with the *Dei Gratia*. Apart from the Log Book and the Log Slate, all the ship's papers were missing, together with the chronometer and sextant – everything a ship's master would automatically seize on abandoning ship.

Elsewhere there was damage, but not more than might reasonably have been sustained by a derelict in ten days of Atlantic rough weather. The compass was destroyed and the binnacle stove in, and two of the smaller hatch covers were off. The cargo was in good condition and had not shifted (indeed, this cargo finally reached its destination in Genoa in April 1873, and was then stated to be in excellent condition). The anchor and chains were on board, so that there could be no thought that the ship had dragged her mooring, and Deveau noticed no unusual stains on the deck. The rigging had been damaged, apparently by weather, and the helm was not lashed – the final sign of hurry, for no captain will leave his ship, with sail set, and the helm swinging, unless the emergency is very grave indeed.

There was one other small item: under the Captain's berth Deveau found a sword. He saw nothing remarkable about that, and put it back where he found it. Swords were part of ceremonial dress then, and if the blade was rusty the ship had taken in a great deal of water.

And finally, there was no life-boat. The *Mary Celeste* had davits at the stern, but these had plainly not been in use, for a spar was found lashed across the davits to keep them steady. Instead, the boat (a yawl, as afterwards appeared) had been lashed across the main hatch between two fenders. It was gone, and opposite the main hatch the ship's rails were found lying on the deck.

It was this missing boat, and Captain Brigg's sword, that were to cause trouble.

★   ★   ★   ★

In Gibraltar, the case of the *Mary Celeste* was taken in charge by the British Vice-Admiralty Court. There was the enquiry into the loss of the crew, and also the question of the salvage money due to the *Dei Gratia*. The Surveyor of Shipping spent five hours meticulously examining the ship, and an experienced diver examined the hull. Their reports are admirably full, conscientious, and sensible; but they were not published until seventy years later. And there now arrives on the scene a Mr Solly Flood, who held the positions of Queen's Proctor of Admiralty and Attorney-General of Gibraltar, of whom the United States Consul in Gibraltar later remarked mildly that he was a man having 'a very vivid imagination'. It seems also that he was not a seaman, for he refused to believe, what Captain Morehouse and Oliver Deveau appeared to think possible, that the *Mary Celeste* could have run 78 miles of the Atlantic as a derelict. Therefore, reasoned Mr Solly Flood, she had *not* been abandoned on the 25th November, the day of the last recording log reading; instead, some tragedy had occurred aboard her on that day that was too terrible to be admitted.

What tragedy? This is where Captain Brigg's sword comes in. Mr Solly Flood was convinced that the marks on the blade, which Oliver Deveau had calmly taken for rust, were blood. In his view, the crew had murdered Captain Briggs and his family and officers, and escaped in the boat.

This would have been a possible theory – at least it accounted for the marks of hurry and the lack of the yawl – if any marks of violence could have been found on the sword or in the ship. Mr Solly Flood was so convinced of the truth of his own theory that he engaged a Dr J. Patron of Gibraltar to examine not only the sword but the whole of the ship for bloodstains.

Dr Patron's report was full and decisive: 'I feel myself authorized to conclude that there is no blood either in the stains observed on the deck of the *Mary Celeste* or on those found on the blade of the sword I have examined.'

Whereupon Mr Solly Flood refused to let anyone see the report. We can only guess that he was reluctant to admit that his imagination had been too vivid.

Meantime, the maritime Press, denied authorized reports, printed their own imaginings – spots of blood on the sword and the deck, a completely false suggestion of a scheme to defraud insurance companies. The proceedings of the Court continued, far too slowly to satisfy those concerned; eventually the salvage claims were paid, the sad personal belongings returned to New York, letters written by the U.S. Consul to the German Government about the seamen of that nationality, and sooner or later the orphaned families stopped hoping that their men-folk would come home again. And in 1885 the *Mary Celeste* herself came to an end, wrecked and left to break up on a reef off the coast of Haiti.

But her mystery went marching on.

★ ★ ★ ★

Everyone knows the story of the *Mary Celeste,* of course. She was found abandoned at sea. But if you enquire closely, you will find that everyone knows a slightly different story.

For one thing, she is mostly known, incorrectly, as the *Marie Celeste.* Where did that mistake come from? And then some will tell you that it was not the *Dei Gratia* who found her East of the Azores, but the Spanish authorities who found her 'near the Straits of Gibraltar' (and turned her over to an English Court?). This version says that there was a half-eaten dinner, or perhaps breakfast, on the Captain's table, and his watch still ticking on the nail above his berth. Others say that there were mugs of tea still warm, or that the galley stove, though raked out, was hot; that there was a chess-board with a game half-played on it, the pieces undisturbed in spite of the gale that had only moderated on the morning of the 5th December; or that the ship's cat, undisturbed, was fast asleep on a bunk.

More people than Mr Solly Flood had vivid imaginations.

But in all these imaginative stories, there was one common factor, one false statement; this was that on the abandoned ship the boat was intact.

If the boat was intact, the crew could not have abandoned ship willingly. So what had happened to them? It was a question ready-made for vivid imaginations.

A criminal conspiracy between Captain Briggs and Captain Morehouse was an early suggestion, indignantly refuted by those who knew them. In 1904, the solution was that a giant octopus had seized the crew and 'sunk slowly into the deep again.' This story places the *Mary Celeste's* finding near Gibraltar, and moreover increases the number of the crew to twenty – making the octopus even bigger and more dexterous. Pirates, of course, were an easy solution – except that by 1872 international action had cleared pirates from the seas. The novelist H. A. Vachell suggested that a submarine explosion had released a gas which turned everyone who inhaled it into a suicidal lunatic. The crew of the *Mary Celeste,* leaning over the rail in curiosity, one by one went mad and threw themselves into the sea. Not even the writer seems to have taken this suggestion seriously. Two more stories of the same kind, however, seem to have been advanced in dead seriousness. One deduces from the fact that the upper rigging was damaged that there must have been aerial activity over the ship, and states that the crew were kidnapped from flying saucers. Another, claiming to find its truth in the measurements of the Great Pyramid of Gizeh in Egypt, states that the crew (who included two angels) were dematerialized over the sunken continent of Atlantis.

There were several more rational explanations; such as, in several versions, a long string of deaths aboard, either from accident or murder, ending with two survivors plunging into the sea locked in mortal combat, or one survivor throwing himself overboard in madness or remorse. They might be possible, if not very likely, if they were not all refuted by the obvious ignorance of the writers of the true facts of the *Mary Celeste's* condition when found. They repeat the same inventions – the hot stove, the half-eaten meal; and in particular they repeat that the ship's boat was still on board. Some of these stories inevitably reflected on the integrity of Captain Briggs, or of Captain Morehouse, and at least twice members of Captain Brigg's family had to refute publicly stories which injured his memory.

One of the most ingenious, and in itself a mystery, because the author was never identified – was the so-called story of John Pemberton, which first appeared in 1926. John Pemberton was said to be a Liverpool sailor, then aged eighty, who had been cook on the *Mary Celeste.* The cook on the *Mary Celeste,* as the records show, was Edward Head; but the records, says Pemberton, were false. His story is long and confused, but it reduces both the *Mary Celeste* and the *Dei Gratia* to ill-found ships, and their captains to unpopular captains ready for any shady trick to get a crew and a cargo – or, in the case of Captain Morehouse, some salvage money, Captain Morehouse lends Captain Briggs three men of his crew until he can sign on more in the Azores; on the voyage to the Azores, Mrs Briggs is killed by accident, the Captain kills himself in a fit of madness, and one of the crew is murdered; the rest desert at the Azores, except for the three from *Dei Gratia,* who make their rendezvous with Captain Morehouse, who then decides to fake the derelict to pick up the salvage money.

It was an ingenious piece of fiction, accounting for many curious details but quite astray in others. Bizarrely, it insisted that little Sophia Briggs never existed, and that the baby in question was Mrs Briggs's cottage piano, which, breaking loose in a gale, crushed her to death, and then was thrown overboard. The real Mrs Briggs's real harmonium was returned to her family from Gibraltar, and both Captain Briggs and Captain Morehouse were men of high reputation, who not only would never have stooped to such crimes but were too highly regarded in their profession to need to do so.

And even 'John Pemberton', ingenious as he was in many ways, did not read the original reports of the *Mary Celeste,* and therefore, like the rest of the imaginative writers, did not know the one vital fact that reduces the story from an insoluble mystery to an ordinary sad sea-problem:

The yawl was missing.

Since the yawl was missing, the crew could have abandoned ship in her; since the crew could have abandoned ship, there never was any need to invoke sea-monsters, flying-saucers, or criminal conspiracies. The only problems are – what was the emergency that made the crew put out in the yawl, and why did they not return to the ship?

Captain Winchester, past-owner of the *Mary Celeste* said of Captain Briggs: 'He was a courageous officer and good seaman who would not, I think, desert his ship except to save life. The Mate Richardson was an experienced and courageous officer in whom I had great confidence.'

After so many years, and so much pondering, the words of the man who first boarded the *Mary Celeste* are as valuable as any. Oliver Deveau said:

'My idea is that the crew got alarmed, and thinking she would go down abandoned her. The only explanation of the abandonment that I can give is that there was a panic from the belief that the vessel had more water in her than she had.'

It has been suggested that the ship was hit by a water-spout, whose low-pressure centre could have sucked the bilge-water into the pump and made it appear as if the ship was holed and filling. Or it may have been that there was an alarm that the cargo of alcohol was leaking and liable to explode. If a small amount of alcohol had leaked from the casks into the bilges and been drawn into the pump, a spark, perhaps from a lantern, perhaps from a pipe, could have set off a terrifying but harmless fire, which would have burnt itself out without leaving any trace on the metal of the pump. Whatever the cause of the panic, the crew took to the boat in a great hurry, with Mrs Briggs and the little girl, the Captain pausing only to take his ship's papers and navigating instruments, and not even daring to lash the helm. And then?

As the *Dei Gratia* was to discover, under the sail she carried the *Mary Celeste* would run before the wind. Perhaps there had been no time to rig a tow-rope; perhaps, in the tangle of ropes from the damaged rigging found by Oliver Deveau, there were the unrecognizable remains of a tow-rope that had snapped under the strain of a sudden squall. Once let the *Mary Celeste's* sails fill, and no amount of pulling would have brought the tiny yawl up with her again. Ten souls would have been swept into the Atlantic, eight hundred miles from landfall.

They were never heard of again; but that winter one hundred sailing vessels were reported missing from New England ports alone.

One last mystery to solve: what started the story that the *Mary Celeste* was found abandoned with her boat intact?

After 1873 public interest in the *Mary Celeste* vanished. But a few years later a struggling young doctor was living in Portsmouth who had found that he could make a little money by writing stories. He had, it seemed, a trick of getting them to sound real. Searching about for a subject, he recalled reading about an abandoned ship, and expanded his memory into a splendidly lurid story. He remembered the name of the ship wrongly – which is why so many writers after him called her the *Marie Celeste* – and either he had forgotten that the yawl was missing or he wanted it aboard to improve his story. The story is called *J. Habakuk*

Jephson's Statement. It gives the *Marie Celeste* a sinister passenger, one Septiminus Goring, who takes her to the coast of Black Africa in pursuit of his own plans to found an African Empire. No one who reads the story can take it for anything but a flight of imagination. Unfortunately, this young doctor's trick of realism was in it, so that when he said that the *Marie Celeste's* yawl was still on deck when she was found everyone believed him. His name was Arthur Conan Doyle. Four years later he wrote another story about a detective called Sherlock Holmes; and to this day some people think that Sherlock Holmes was a real man.

MATTERS MARINE
Lillian Beckwith

Hector had decided to sell his boat *Wayfarer* so that he could buy a bigger one with more accommodation for passengers, for Bruach was being discovered by a steadily increasing number of campers and coach tourists and the crofters were confidently predicting that the coming season would be a bumper one. Some days after his advertisement had appeared in a Highland paper Hector turned up at my cottage with a sheaf of letters he had received in reply.

'It's a grand day,' he proffered with beguilement in his blue eyes and a diffidence in his voice that was no doubt induced by the fact that it was at least six weeks since our last meeting and that I had, on that occasion, soundly unbraided him for daring to borrow my one and only toothbrush. He had been bewildered and hurt by my attack and had been quick to assure me that he had put the brush back most carefully in its tumbler beside the water bucket where it was always kept. What he hadn't been able to reassure me about was why, when I came to use the toothbrush, its bristles should have been fuzzy with black hair that was exactly the same shade and texture as his own.

'Why, Hector!' I greeted him now with genuine cordiality, for no one could help loving him whatever he did. 'where on earth have you been all this time? I don't seem to have seen you for ages.'

'Ach, I'm just where the tide left me when last you saw me,' he said with a gloomy smile. I told him to sit down but he remained standing, shuffling from one foot to another and gnawing along the length of a grubby forefinger.

'Behag was tellin' me,' he began, and then pushing up his peaked cap he rubbed an exploratory hand among the sparse hair it constrained, 'I was wonderin',' he started again, this time pulling at his ear, 'maybe would you do me a few wee letters on tsat machine you have? I'm tsinkin' it would be quicker.'

I looked up from the sewing machine on which I was running up a pair of gay new curtains. 'Of course I'll do them,' I agreed. 'Do you want them right away?'

'Ach, no.' With renewed confidence he drew up a chair and sat down beside me. 'You can finish what you're doin' first,' he told me magnanimously.

I turned back to the machine.

'Will I work the handle for you,' he offered when he had watched me long enough to be sure the task required very little exertion. I said that I would prefer to do it myself and while I put on a new reel of cotton and re-threaded the needle he toyed delightedly with the material, rubbing it between his stained fingers and examining the bright red peonies with which it was patterned. 'Tses is nice flowers,' he confided, 'I mind they used to call tsem "chrissie-annies" in Glasgow when I was tsere.'

When I commenced sewing again Hector bent over me anxiously. Now despite the fact that I need to wear spectacles for close work I flatter myself that I can run up a straight seam as neatly as anyone, but Hector, who admittedly had perfect eyesight, was so dubious of my skill that every few inches if he considered there was the slightest deviation he would give an audible 'tech' of concern and an enthusiastic twitch as the material, which resulted in the sewing of a pronounced 'V'. I must confess I was too amused to curb his enthusiasm though by the time I had reacehd the end of the seam the stitching resembled a wavering flight of birds. I thought it might be more satisfactory if I finished the curtains when I was alone but he was insistent that the work should not be put aside just for his 'few wee letters'. I suspected that he was thoroughly enjoying guiding what he no doubt believed to be my very erratic hand, and he seemed greatly disappointed when we had finished and I announced that I must press the curtains before they were hung so that he would have to wait until his next visit before he could admire the full effect of his collaboration.

I put away the sewing machine and brought out the typewriter. 'Now,' I invited, when there was a sheet of paper in the machine, 'tell me what you want to say.'

He began to chew his finger again. 'Well, what will I tell tsem?' he demanded perplexedly.

'What do you want to tell them?' I retaliated.

He put the letters down on the table beside me. 'Well, tsat one wants to know is tse engine forrard or aft. You could tell him it's aft.' He brought up one of his knees and attempted to rub his chin on it. 'Tsere's anusser wants to know where is tse wheelhouse. You can tell tsem it's aft too.' He sat back limp and exhausted. I glanced quickly through the letters.

'They all want to know the price you're asking. You'll need to give them an idea of that,' I told him.

Hector looked momentarily discomfited. He did not want me or anyone else in the village to know the price he had set on *Wayfarer*. 'Well, now I'll not be knowin' what to ask for her,' he prevaricated. 'Behag's saying' one tsing and tse cailleach's sayin' anusser.'

'We'll leave that blank then, and you can fill it in when you and Behag had decided,' I suggested.

'Aye. aye. Tsat'll be tse way of it.' He cheered up instantly.

I drew up a list of questions and asked Hector for the answers. 'Now,' I told him. 'We'll just set down all this information in each letter and then they'll know as much about the boat as you can tell them. Is that all right?'

'Tsat's fine,' said Hector.

'Shall I just begin, "Dear Sir, In reply to your letter of such and such a date, here is the information you ask for . . ."?'

'We cannot say "Dear Sir",' cut in Hector with shocked disapproval. 'Not when you're writin' to folks about a boat.'

'Why not?' I asked with surprise. 'You don't know these people, so you should begin with "Dear Sir".'

'It's no' friendly,' he argued.

'It's perfectly correct,' I insisted.

'Ach, no,' he said, fidgeting with embarrassment of having to argue with me. 'As like as not tsey won't even read it if you say tsat.'

'Why ever shouldn't they, Hector?' I demanded, my voice edged with asperity.

Hector frowned. 'Well, if ever I get a letter and it begins with "Dear Sir" then I throw it straightway into the fire because I know it'll be a nasty one,' he explained.

Together we pondered the assortment of letters, deciphering names and addressing them in as friendly a manner as Hector wished and also, at his insistence, we informed the prospective buyers chattily that in Bruach it had been a very coarse winter; that the potatoes would surely be very late going into the ground this year and that the Department of Agriculture bull had arrived earlier than expected. Hector then professed himself completely satisfied. 'I'll put a P.S. at tse end tellin' tsem tse price,' he said with true Gaelic finesse.

A month went by; a month of exhilarating dawns which heralded days that stretched themselves to hold more and more hours of gentle sunshine. The seared wintry grass of the crofts took on a more comely appearance and wherever one's glance rested there were bursting buds and courting birds and all the lovely lilting things of spring. Old men in creased dark clothes came out of their wintry hiding places and leaned against the walls of the houses, sampling the quality of the sunlight and pronouncing upon the condition of the cattle, upon the prospects of the fishing, or, if encouraged, upon the fate of the world. The children left off their tackety boots and thick handknit socks and skipped to school barefooted with the same friskness as the young lambs bleating on the hills, while on the dry, heathery moors the local incendiarists, with whom every village in the Islands seems to be afflicted, wantonly satisfied their urges so that there was rarely a day when one did not see the spreading blue tendrils of heather smoke creeping steadily or tillering and racing menacingly according to the whim of the wind.

For all of us the days were full of the outdoors: cutting peats, turning them, lifting and finally stacking them; burning the unruly patches of sedge that no scythe could master; gathering up the stones which always seemed to stray on to the crofts during the winter of neglect; teaching new calves to drink from a pail while one stroked the sun-warmed curls of its back and endured the caress of a milky tongue. For the women there was in addition the annual blanket washing, perhaps in a zinc bath of water carried laboriously pailful by pailful from the well, perhaps in a cauldron over a wood fire beside the burn. We worked dedicatedly, cramming the days with toil, and when dusk approached and we could feel we had earned a respite we walked to our homes with the clean cool wind from the hill fanning our glowing faces and our bodies heavy with that good weariness that comes from physical labour in the open air.

It was after just such a day that I went out to my last chore of the evening. The sun had not long set in a splendour of vermilion and turquoise and the sky was still streaked as though it had been clawed by grey fingernails. Busy ripples flecked with silver raced across the loch and tumbled with Dresden tinkles on to the pebbles of the shore. The hills looked smug and withdrawn behind a faint veil of mist while across the water the brightest of the lighthouses was already beginning to show as a dim spark on the horizon. My line of newly washed blankets, now dry and wind softened, stirred lazily and as I unpegged each one I did it lingeringly and with a feeling of ecstasy as though I might be dipping a flag in salute to the glory of the night.

'Here! Come an' get me a drink of water. My hands is all sticky!' Erchy's voice, uneasy with authority, came from the direction of the house. Obediently, I gathered up the blankets and went indoors. Erchy was holding a large brush in front of him, its bristles sticky with glistening tar. His hands too were liberally coated. 'I'm that thirsty I'm like to faint,' he told me.

I dumped the blankets on the table well out of his way and poured out a large mug of water. He drank it with audible relish but when I offered to make tea for him he declined it.

'I didn't take my dinner yet,' he explained. (In Bruach one always 'took' one's meals.)

'Then you must be hungry. Let me give you a scone or something.'

'I daren't wait,' he insisted. 'See, I promised the cailleach I'd see to the cow for her tonight as she's goin' ceilidhin' over with Katy. She'll be makin' a swear at me already for bein' as late as I am.' He leaned his elbow on the dresser. 'She wasn't lettin' me come down here today at all but I told her I'd get the boat tarred while she was good and dry.'

'Tar!' I repeated with a grimace of disgust. 'Why is it you always put so much tar on your boats? Why don't you paint them in nice bright colours instead of just slathering them with dirty black tar?'

Erchy appeared slightly outraged. 'Tar keeps out the water better than paint,' he defended. 'Any splits in the planks or any places where she might be takin' in the water, once they're filled with tar they'll keep out the sea for as long as the season lasts,' he explained.

'I'd like to think there was something more than a gob of tar between me and the sea,' I murmured.

'Ach!' snorted Erchy.

'Anyway it doesn't alter the fact that it's unsightly stuff,' I told him.

'Damty sure it is,' agreed Erchy amiably. 'Here,' he demanded. 'D'you mind Tarry Ruari?'

I shook my head. 'No,' I replied. 'I've seen the house where he lived but he was dead when I came here.'

'You've seen his house? Then you'll know the way it's tarred all over – the roof and the walls – all black?'

I remembered Ruari's house as a stained hovel of a place near a boggy slope of the burn and recalled Morag describing it as being 'very delaborated'.

'Yes,' I admitted, 'it did look as if it might have been tarred.'

'Now that's a man went mad with tar,' said Erchy with complete seriousness. 'He tarred his wee boat inside and out over and over again until she was that heavy he could hardly pull her up the beach. Then he started tarring his house – outside at first and then on the inside. He even tarred the furniture. By God! but you never saw such a place in your life. Folks here just used to laugh at him at first but then the nurse went there one day and found he'd tarred the blankets on his bed. They came and took him away then.'

'Good gracious!' I ejaculated. 'Was he married?'

'Oh, no,' explained Erchy simply. 'Just daft.'

He moved vaguely towards the door. 'I'd best be goin',' he said. 'Thanks for the drink. I was badly needin' it.'

'I'm sorry it wasn't something more sustaining,' I told him with spurious apology.

Erchy turned quickly. 'Indeed but I wouldn't have thanked you for it just now, then.'

'No?' I mocked.

'Damty sure I wouldn't. If you'd handed me a bottle of whisky I would have given it back to you without a thought for it.'

'I'd like to see you refuse whisky,' I said.

'Well, you will someday at that.'

I smiled disbelievingly.

'You know,' he went on, 'I reckon that's the reason folks like me don't go bad with the drink like they do in Glasgow and them places. You see what I mean?'

I waited, not at all sure that I did.

'What I'm sayin' is, take me at the cattle sale. I've plenty of money on me so I get drunk as hell on it for maybe two or three days. Well, then I come to the end of it and I don't want anything but to get out on to the hill. I make an excuse to go after the sheep and I'm away first light without my breakfast and only a wee potach in my pocket. When I get thirsty I put my head down into one of the burns – the colder the better – and I can tell you it's sweet! When I've had one drink I'm lookin' forward to tastin' the water in the next place and the next. By the time I come back again I feel as though I never want to take a drop of whisky again in my life.'

'But it doesn't last?' I queried.

'No, thank God,' said Erchy fervently. He appeared to muse for a few moments before he spoke again. 'Did I tell you I'm a big sheep man now?' he asked, changing the subject completely.

'No,' I said. 'Since when?'

'I found them up on the hill one time when I was away like I've been tellin' you.'

'Found them?' I echoed.

'Aye, as true as I'm here.'

'How long have they been lost?'

'Well, it was about five years ago now that I was takin' some old ewes that I had to the sale and one of them went lame on the way so I drove her off to the side of the road and left her there. There was no sign of her by the time I got back so I never gave her another thought except that she'd probably go off somewhere quiet and die. The beast was only worth a few bob then, anyway. Well, like I was sayin', I was up there on the hill and in a wee corrie all by themselves I came on an old ewe first an' there was my markings on her. I had the dog with me so I caught the rest of them an' they had no markings on them at all so I knew they must be mine. She would have been in lamb when I left her,' he explained, 'an' it must have been a ram lamb.'

'It's strange no one has noticed them before,' I said.

'Ach, no, not where they was,' he told me. 'Nobody goes much round the back of the Beinn there, an' the corrie they was in you wouldn't see from the path. That old ewe's a hardy, though,' he muttered appreciatively, 'she hadn't as much fleece left on her as you'd need to bait a hook.' He made another vague move towards the door but in his reminiscent mood I knew he would linger for another half-hour at least before he finally detached himself from the cottage, so I began preparing my evening meal.

'It must be very pleasant to come across a flock of sheep you didn't know you had,' I remarked as I grated cheese into a basin.

Erchy watched me curiously, 'Aye,' he admitted. He came back to the table. 'What's that you're makin'?'

'Oh, just a cheese sauce,' I told him.

'I mind fine when my sister was at home – she's a cook in Edinburgh, you know, and she has to make these fancy things there – she found some cheese in the cupboard that had gone dry. Ach, I can eat the stuff in the winter all right but not in the summer when there's plenty of crowdie,' he explained hurriedly. 'She handed me one of those grater things and told me to get on and grate it for her. Hell, by the time I'd finished all my fingernails had gone into the basin, too. When I showed her she was mad at me so I told her she wasn't to make me do it for her again,' he finished with remembered triumph. I opened a bottle and poured a little of its contents into the pan. Erchy sniffed.

'That's beer!' he accused. 'I thought you didn't like it?'

'I don't like to drink it,' I said. 'But I do sometimes use it in sauces.'

'I wouldn't fancy beer like that,' he said, shaking his head. 'Now, if it was whisky . . .'

'There you go again,' I taunted. 'You're obsessed with whisky.'

'No, not me,' he denied. 'I like to have a good drink when I have one but that's only when I have the money. I'm not like these folks from Rudha that has a bottle sent out on the bus two or three times every week.'

'Tell me, Erchy,' I asked, for he had touched on a subject that had been puzzling me for a long time, 'how do they manage to afford bottles of whisky two or three times a week? They're only crofters and some of them even draw Public Assistance, yet they seem to be able to buy drink and cigarettes as much as ever they want to. They don't seem to go short of anything.'

'No, an' I'm damty sure they never will,' said Erchy, looking mysterious.

'What's their secret?' I cajoled.

'Well, it was durin' the war,' Erchy began. 'There must have been a big wreck some place out here an' there was lots of stuff came ashore one night. The Rudha folks got word of it an' they was all waitin' to grab it. Trunks packed with money, folks say there was, an' they hid it all away. There was plenty of corpses too, scattered all over the shore, so when they'd taken as much stuff as they wanted for themselves the Rudha people told us an' then they told the pollis. Ach, it was a dirty trick,' said Erchy with disgust creeping into his tones. 'Anyway, the pollis didn't come out straight away so as soon as it got dark me an' Tearlach went over there to see would we find anythin'. All we found was bolls of flour, plenty of them, and corpses, dozens of them too, all over the shore. An' the moon was shinin' on them so that they gleamed an' the tide was washin' round some of them makin' their limbs move so that you'd think they were tryin' to get up. God! We got that scared we just lifted a boll of flour on to each other's back an' we ran home with it as fast as we could go. Indeed I don't believe we stopped for breath until we got to within sight of Anna's house, an' we never went back there neither.'

The path to Rudha was four miles of narrow sheep track along the shoulder of the hill, below which the land slid steeply to the jagged rocks of the shore. Even in broad daylight the uninitiated take one look and either turn back or tackle it quakingly on all fours.

'An then the pollis came,' continued Erchy, 'an' they took away the corpses but they left the bolls of flour. The rest of the folks here just went then and helped themselves.' He sighed. 'That's all Bruach ever got out of it – a few bolls of flour, except for Tearlach's dog that got a good feed off one of the legs of the corpses,' he added reflectively.

I put on the tablecloth. 'Your mother will be giving you up for lost,' I reminded him.

'Aye,' he said, without much interest and, still havering in the doorway, he turned to look out into the night. 'Did Hector tell you he has a buyer for his boat?' he asked over his shoulder.

'No,' I replied with some surprise. 'Has he really? Who?'

'Ach, some fellow down Oban way, I believe,' answered Erchy, turning round again and leaning against the edge of the door. 'He's asked me will I sail down there with him on Friday if the weather stays this way.'

'And are you going?'

'Aye. I might just as well. Seein' we're goin' we're takin' Johnny Comic to the dentist. The poor man's near crazy with the toothache.'

'That's rather a job to tackle, isn't it?' I asked. 'Johnny's never been away from here before, has he?'

'No, an' he's that scared of comin' with us I believe we'll have to put a rope on him first.'

'You'll never get him into a dentist's chair,' I warned, suspecting that Johnny's one idea would be to play hide-and-seek with his companions until they could delay their return no longer.

'Ach, Tom-Tom's comin' to hold him,' said Erchy. 'An' there'll be the two of us if we're needed.' I stared at him in surprise. 'Aye, you can look like that,' he told me, 'but gentle as Johnny is he's a strong man when it comes to strugglin' an' he'll struggle well enough if he thinks he's goin' to have somethin' done to him.' He edged half of himself outside the door and started to pull it to behind him. 'Is there anythin' you'll be wantin' us to bring back for you? We'll likely be doin' some shoppin'.'

There was always at the back of my mind a list of things which I intended to ask people to get for me should there be some prospect of their visiting the mainland. Now, confronted with Erchy's sudden question, I could recall only the relatively unimportant fact that when the previous autumn I had wanted to make use of some small green tomatoes – the grudging produce of a dozen troublesomely acquired and carefully nurtured plants – I had no vinegar to make them into chutney. It was no use even asking the grocer if he stocked it, for the crofters though lavish in their use of salt were as yet not conditioned to, or perhaps aware of, the other condiments. One never saw a bottle of sauce on a Bruach table.

'Would you bring me a bottle of vinegar?' I asked, still vainly struggling to recall some more needful item on my mental list.

'Vinegar?' repeated Erchy in a puzzled voice, and then, as enlightenment slowly dawned, he went on: 'Aye, I mind now what you mean. Vinegar's the stuff they put on chips in Glasgow, isn't it?'

He was outside the door by now and letting in a gently chill breeze that was brining up the gooseflesh on my sun-tanned arms.

'Hector's supposed to be bringin' back a few chickens for Morag,' he informed me. 'You'll not be wantin' any yourself, will you?'

'That is a good idea,' I responded with enthusiasm. The only chickens one could get in Bruach were the hard progeny of the inveterate fowls that scratched around every house and corn-stack, flaunting their mongrel feathers with the aplomb of peasants attired in their national costume. I had once tried to get pure-bred chickens sent up to me simply to find out if they laid better, but the length of the train journey coupled with the capriciousness of the local carrier had ensured that none of the chickens had survived. I asked Erchy to bring me a dozen day-old chicks – Black Leghorns if they were available.

'I'll do that,' he promised, and then perhaps because he remembered he was going in a leaky old boat on an unpredictable sea, or perhaps because he recalled a previous experience of high life in Oban, he added a cautionary, 'If the Lord spares me.' He sounded a trifle embarrassed. 'I'm away. Good night,' he called, and shut the door.

'Good night!' I rejoined and sat down at last to eat my supper.

There was a clouding over of the sky in the late afternoon of the following day and the next morning the sun, which had shone unrestrainedly for so long, only cocked a sleepy eye before retiring beneath a canopy of grey cloud. It looked as if the spell of fine weather was coming to an end. Friday morning dawned wet and windy with the sea flouncing angrily against the rocks and with grey sweeps of rain being hurried across the bay. When I went up to the village shop to buy paraffin I espied Erchy, Hector and Tom-Tom leaning in various attitudes of disconsolation against the gable of the latter's house. All were gazing with equal gloom at *Wayfarer* who was plunging and rearing at her mooring.

'You're not going off today, then?' I observed.

'No damty fear,' replied Erchy. 'That sea is goin' to get bigger before it gets smaller.'

'There's some big enough lumps out there already,' said Tom-Tom. 'I don't fancy it myself.'

'We're safer where we are,' agreed Hector with glum acceptance.

'Well, here's one who's mightly pleased we're not settin' foot on the sea,' said Erchy with a wink and a nod towards a hunched figure which squatted miserably beside him. 'Is that not so, Johnny?' he shouted, and in answer the figure raised a face that would normally be described as being of 'ashen hue'. However, when one has become a burner of peat as opposed to coal it is a description one can no longer use, for 'ashen' would imply the complexion of a Red Indian.

'Poor Johnny Comic,' I said. 'Is his toothache still as bad as ever?'

'No,' denied Erchy. 'You cannot have toothache an' be scared out of your life at the same time. You can only feel one or the other.'

We were joined by Morag who was also on her way to get paraffin.

'So my brave boys has decided it's too rough for them,' she said by way of greeting, and the men turned away, discomfited by the derision in her voice. I picked up my can and moved away. Morag walked alongside me, a smug grin on her face.

'It doesn't look very nice out there, does it?' I remarked.

'Ach,' she said disdainfully. 'They're not much of sailors nowadays. I've seen my father go out in seas three times as big as I'm seein' out there an' their boats not half the size either.' She turned and gestured towards the bay. 'I've known myself be out in more sea than there is now.'

'Morag,' I demanded. 'Have you ever been out in a sea big enough to frighten you?'

'Only once that I mind,' she confessed with a slight grimace of shame.

'Was it rough then?'

'Ach, it was all yon big green beasts that you an see through. Comin' straight at us they was till you thought with every one of them that the boat would never ride the next. My father made me lie down under one of the thwarts so that I wouldn't get thrown out.' She sighed. 'Aye, we were caught badly that day an' I believe I was as frightened as I've ever been. Mind you,' she added hastily, 'frightened though I was, I was never what you'd call inebriated with fear.' She chuckled. 'I was younger then, though, an' I daresay I hadn't as much sense as I have now.'

With our cans filled with paraffin we started off for home again, stopping frequently for me to change my can from one aching arm to the other. Morag, who was carrying twice the amount of paraffin, did not put hers down for an instant and only watched my struggles with a tolerant smile. Hector and Erchy were still propping up the end of Tom-Tom's house but by this time they had been joined by Old

Murdock and Yawn who had doubtless come to offer cautionary advice although at this moment they were engaged in conversation with a young girl who stood, slim and straight, between the two bent old men, like an 'I' in parentheses.

'Yon's the lassie that's been stayin' with Mary Ann over the last few days,' said Morag in a low voice. 'You'll have seen her likely?'

'Only in the distance,' I admitted.

'She was askin' Hector last night would she get back to the mainland with him today an' he had to promise her he'd take her.'

'I should jolly well think he would have promised,' I muttered as we drew closer. She was quite the most beautiful creature I had ever seen, with huge brown, lustrous eyes, dark curly hair, exquisitely fine bones and a skin of such golden-ness that it looked on this dull day as though it was exuding sunshine. Even I felt momentarily stunned by her appearance. What she did to men I could only guess.

'But, Hector,' she was saying with wheedling fretfulness as we approached, 'you promised you'd take me. I would have gone on the bus this morning and caught the ferry if I'd thought your boat wouldn't be going. I've simply got to be back in the office in London on Monday morning or I'll get the sack.' Hector only hunched his shoulders harder against the wall and looked sulky.

'Ach, you'll not get the sack,' consoled Erchy. 'Tell them you got held up by the storm an' it'll be all right.'

'I can't tell them that,' she retorted.

'Why not?' demanded Erchy.

'They wouldn't understand.'

Erchy grunted his scepticism.

'It'll maybe get a bit calmer by this evening yet,' Yawn prophesied, and the girl who, despite the fact that her teeth were chattering, still managed to look ravishing, brightened up visibly.

'Will you take me across this evening then, if it gets calm?' she coaxed, with a look at the men that should have sent them hurrying to launch any number of boats.

'Ach, no,' said the usually impressionable Hector, shuffling uncomfortably. 'Tse tide will be all wrong by tsis evenin' for gettin' the dinghy off the shore.'

The girl's expression as she turned to me was one of chagrin.

'Please,' she begged. 'They don't seem to understand how terribly important it is for me to get back. It's a new job I've landed – quite a good one and I wasn't really due a holiday yet but they kindly let me have these few days. Will you try to explain to Hector for me?'

I shook my head, understanding her frustration but by now almost as out of touch with her world as were the rest of the group.

'Well,' said Erchy with decision. 'You say you cannot get back to London by Monday morning unless you leave here tonight. An' you cannot leave here tonight so you cannot do anythin' else but wait.'

'They'll not take it so badly if you just explain to them that it was the storm that kept you back,' soothed Yawn. 'An' the tide,' he added as an afterthought.

The lassie drooped with dejection. 'I've told you,' she reiterated. 'You can't explain to people in London about things like that. They'll never believe it,' she finished with a grim smile.

Yawn was visibly staggered. 'They wouldn't believe you?' he demanded.

The lassie shook her head.

'Well, lassie,' he advised her with great gravity. 'I'm tellin' you, you'd best never go back at all to a place like that. If they don' understand about storms and tides and things they must be a lot of savages just.'

'Miss Peckwitt and Morag! Is it yourselves?' Tom-Tom's wife appeared round the corner of the house. Come away in now and take a fly cuppie with me. I have it ready.'

We followed her inside, and the men, anxious to evade the lassie's continued importunings, lumbered after us.

'Honest to God,' grumbled Erchy, as he seated himself on the bench. 'Some people thinks it's us that makes the weather.'

'Aye, an' tse tides,' rejoined Hector. 'Some of tsese folks tsat come in my boat, tsey say to me, "Can I leave tsis picnic basket," or sometsing like tsat. "Will it be all right here on tse shore till we get back?" And tsen when I tell tsem no, tsey must take it up on tse rocks out of tse tide's way, tsey tsink I'm not bein' nice to tsem'.

He shook his head sadly.

'It just seems as though they don't understand about the tides,' said Erchy wonderingly.

'They know the theory but not the practice,' I said. 'They learn about tides ebbing and flowing but they're not taught that this means the water is always moving up to or away from the actual bit of beach they're sitting on.'

Hector gazed at me with serious surprise. 'Tsey shouldn't need to be taught tsings as simple as tsat,' he assured me. 'Tsey didn't teach ourselves.'

As I drank my tea I studied Hector covertly, for I had just witnessed him do a thing which I had always thought him incapable of doing and that was to remain impervious to the charms of a young and beautiful girl. I was curious to know the reason for it.

'Isn't that lassie a beauty?' I hazarded.

'Eh?' said Erchy stupidly.

Tom-Tom's wife thought for a moment. 'I don't believe she's so bad at that,' she conceded.

Hector looked up from his tea. 'Ach, what good is she when she's tsat tsin you could use her for darnin' a sock,' he observed with a grin, and looked at the other men for confirmation.

Tom-Tom's wife, who had once been described to me as being 'not fat but needin' an awful lot of room when she sat down', chuckled appreciatively. I stared at Hector. He had never struck me as being particularly figure conscious when selecting his female companions. What then, I wondered, was there about this girl that he should find her so uninteresting?

'She tsinks too much of herself, tsat one,' he explained, as though I had asked the question aloud. 'I was down on tse shore tse usser day,' he went on, 'and she comes along. She was after lifting tsese coloured stones from tse beach to take back wiss her and when she sees me she drops tse bag and she says: 'Oh, Hector, I'm so glad I've met a big, strong man to carry my stones for me. Tsey're awful heavy,' she says.'

'An' did you carry them for her?' questioned Morag with a wink at me.

'Indeed I did not,' responded Hector. 'I told her if she'd managed to carry tsem tsat far she must be stronger tsan she tsought she was, so she'd best carry tsem tse rest of tse way.' His blue eyes were impish as he looked at each of us in turn, expecting our approval. 'You know she was tsat vexed wiss me she hardly spoke to me all tse way home.'

'I don't understand it,' I said. 'I would have expected every man in the place to be following her. I'll bet she's used to plenty of attention in England.'

'Well, she'll no' get much of it here,' Erchy stated flatly.

'And yet she's what I'd describe as a real beauty queen,' I mused.

'I'm no' seein' it tsen,' scoffed Hector. He took a noisy gulp of tea. 'I believe she's only one of tsese foreigners anyway and she's queer.' He frowned down at his cup. 'I wouldn't want to take anytsin' to do wiss her anyway, for no religion has she at all but a bit of wood or stone.'

All weekend the clouds raced greyly above a shaggy sea but on Monday night there seemed to be a promise of calm in the night sky and on Tuesday morning I woke without the sound of rain on my windows or the wind bullying the roof. In Bruach one's life was so inextricably bound up with the weather that one got into the habit of waking with an ear cocked for the sound of wind much as, after an illness, one wakes to the expectation of pain. If there was no noise of storm in the morning one waited tensely, hesitating to believe the miracle and then when one had accepted it one would throw off the bedclothes and hasten to get started on the labours of a busy day.

By the time I returned from milking Bonny, *Wayfarer* had left her moorings and was already a dark speck on the horizon. Within a few days Nelly Elly, the postmistress, had received a telephone message from Erchy saying that Johnny had been taken to the dentist and that Hector had bought himself a new boat in which they now proposed to sail back. She reported that he had sounded quite sober. For two or three days there was no word from the men and so it was assumed that they were already on their way. Those of us who had binoculars went frequently to lean on our elbows on the stone dykes and stare out to sea, hoping to be the first to pick up a sight of the mariners and send the word round the village. For easily diverted people like myself it was an excuse to scan the outlying islands, trying to identify their varied peaks or, nearer home, to focus the glasses on the constant industry of the sea birds; on cormorants fishing greedily; on busy, bobbing guillemots and on the swift dipping flight of terns over the sea, contrasting their activity with the motionlessness of a stately heron standing beside the mouth of the burn, and then, ruefully, with my own idleness.

But a week went by without any sign of the boat and when on the following Tuesday morning the mist rolled in from the sea, thick as a sponge, and hid everything beyond the boundaries of the crofts, we knew we could not expect to see them for some time. I wondered if Morag and Behag, Hector's wife, were worrying about the lack of news and felt I ought to go along and ceilidh with them for the evening. When I pushed open the door of Morag's cottage there came the sound of many voices. 'Come away in,' called Morag happily. Come in and see the rascals.'

Erchy, Tom-Tom and Hector, their faces shining in the lamplight, were seated at the table enjoying a meal of salt herring and potatoes. There was a partly full whisky bottle on the table and a couple of empties down in the hearth. The men looked mightily pleased with themselves.

'How on earth did you get home on a day like this?' I asked them.

'We came in Hector's new boat. How would you think?' replied Erchy waggishly.

'Did you have a compass?'

'We did not, then. What would we be wantin' with one of them things, anyway?'

'But isn't the mist as thick on the water as it is here on the land?' I wanted to know.

'Twice as thick,' pronounced Erchy. 'We kept catchin' the boat right bangs. Hector said they was only hard pieces of water but I believe we hit every rock between here and Oban.' He broke open a large floury-looking potato and stuffed almost the whole of it into his mouth. He turned to Hector. 'She's a good strong boat you have there,' he told him, with an accompanying slap on the back. 'She must be or she'd be in bits by now.'

Hector smiled bashfully at the herring he was holding in his two hands.

'Seriously,' I taxed them. How did you manage to navigate if you don't have a compass?'

'Ach, well, we was just goin' round in circles to begin wiss,' explained Hector. 'Every time tse mist lifted we saw tse same bit of coast one side of us or tse usser. We was keepin' close in, you see, trying would we creep round tse shore.'

'Aye,' Erchy took up the tale, 'and then I remembered how my father had told me about bein' caught in the mist on the sea once. He tore up a newspaper he had in the boat and scattered bits of it on the water as he

He scattered newspaper into the water as he went.

went so he'd know if he was goin' in circles. We did the same just. We did that all the way and it got us home here, safe as hell.'

It sounded like a story I had heard before and ought to have more sense than to believe. 'Is that true?' I asked doubtfully.

'As true as I'm here,' asserted Erchy, and to this day I do not know whether he was pulling my leg.

'You didn't tell us yet how Johnny got on at the dentist's with his teeths,' said Behag quietly from the bench where she was sitting patiently with three alert kittens and the irrepressible Fiona all helping her to knit a fair-isle sweater.

The three men gave a concerted hoot of laughter. 'You should have been there to see it,' Erchy said. 'Johnny went and sat in the chair like a lamb and we didn't think he was goin' to give any trouble at all, but the dentist took one look at him an' decided he'd best give him gas. That was all right and he took the tooth out after a bit of a struggle, but then he must have taken the gag out too soon or somethin'. Anyway, he had his thumb right inside Johnny's mouth when suddenly Johnny's teeths clamps down on it. My, you should have heard the dentist shoutin'. He started swearin' at his assitant an' the assistant swore back and told him what a fool he was to his face. He got his thumb out at last, but by God! he was in a state, I can tell you. Then Johnny comes to, an' feelin' his bad tooth's out an' not hurtin' him any more, his face lights up and he jumps up from the chair an' rushes at the dentist shoutin' "By God! By God!"' Here they were all overcome with laughter. 'The poor wee dentist mannie didn't know Johnny only wanted to shake hands with him and thank him for gettin' his sore tooth sorted for him,' resumed Erchy. 'He was terrified! He thought Johnny was after him to do him some hurt an' there he was runnin' round and round the surgery holding his thumb with Johnny chasin' after him still shoutin' "By God! By God!" like he always does when he's excited. "Get him out of here!" the dentist yells at us. Screamin' he was too. "Get the bugger out of here before he kills me." Well me and Tom-Tom manages to get hold of Johnny and drag him out. Poor man was that puzzled about it all so I went back an' told the dentist that Johnny had meant him no harm, it was only that he was wantin' to thank him.' Erchy disgorged a mouthful of herring bones on to his plate. 'But he wouldn't listen to me. "Don't you ever let him come here again," says he. "I might never be able to pull another tooth the way my hand is now." '

'Poor man,' ejaculated Morag half-heartedly, but I did not know to whom she was referring.

'Did you bring any chickens?' I asked after a pause.

'Aye, so we did.'

'Black Leghorns?'

'Aye.'

'Black Leghorns!' shrilled Morag with an acerbity that was mellowed by the tot of whisky she had just swallowed. 'Drunk Leghorns more likely!'

'Drunk?' I echoed with a smile.

'Aye, drunk,' affirmed Morag, lifting the lids of two cardboard boxes near the fire.

'Aye,' Erchy started to explain. 'You see we got them three days ago when we first thought we was startin' back. Well, then we met up with some lads we knew and we had a good drink with them so we didn't wake up in time to get goin' the next day. The lads came again the next night so we stayed and had another good drink. We'd forgotten about the chickens, you see.'

'I didn't forget tsem,' repudiated Hector who was begining to doze in his chair. 'I gave tsem a wee taste of oatmeal I scraped up from tse linings of my pockets.'

Morag snorted. 'For all the good that would be to them you might just as well have left it here,' she told him.

'Well as I was saying',' resumed Erchy, 'we didn't think about the chickens until sometime last evenin' when Hector says all of a sudden: "My God! What about them chickens?" So we fetched them out of the wheelhouse where they'd been all the time and we had a look at them. They didn't look bad and they was makin' plenty of noise but they was huddled together just as though they was feelin' the cold.'

'Sure they was feelin' the cold,' interpolated Morag. 'The poor wee creatures.'

'What did you do then?' I encouraged.

'We didn't know what to do,' said Erchy. 'We had no coal on the boat to put on a fire and no other way of warming them, until Hector said we should try would we warm them with our own breath. So that's what we did. We took it in turns just to go and give them a good breathin' on every now and then. Is that not the way of it, Hector?'

Hector again roused himself to confirm his own brilliance.

'But how did they get drunk?' I persisted.

'Ach, well you know how it is, Miss Peckwitt. These lads we met, they came down again and they'd brought a few bottles with them, so we started drinkin' again. We minded not to forget the chickens though an' we kept openin' the lids of their boxes and givin' them a good warmin' with our breaths. I remember thinkin' one time that they looked to be gettin' sleepy. Their eyes were closin' and they started staggerin' and lyin' down with their legs stretched out. I thought they must be dyin' all right but Hector said no, they was lyin' down because they were goin' to sleep as they should.' He laughed. 'Ach, I think we was both pretty drunk then.'

'I would have expected Johnny Comic to have mothered them like a hen,' I said.

'He didn't know a thing about them,' said Erchy. 'As soon as he stepped back on the boat he rolled himself in his oilskin and lay in the bunk there and he stirred only to eat one of the hard-boiled eggs Kirsty had given him when he came away. Honest, she gave him three dozen of them!'

'They're no' lyin' down any more,' said Morag, taking another peep into the boxes. 'They're no' very strong but they're up on their feets.'

'Am I not after tellin' you it was just drunk they was. Drunk on too much whisky fumes,' said Tom-Tom who, since finishing his meal, had sat smiling foolishly at the coloured plates on the dresser as though he was watching a chorus of dancers.

'The poor wee things,' said Morag again. 'Day-old chicks and so drunk I'm thinkin' they'll not reach a day older before they're dead.'

But she was wrong. 'The poor wee things' not only survived but thrived exceedingly well. They seemed to be immune from all the maladies that can affect young chickens and not even Morag had ever known such wonderful layers.

GOODBYE TO AMERICA
Joshua Slocum

Joshua Slocum was the first man to sail single-handed around the world. This extract describes his voyage from America to the Azores.

I now stowed all my goods securely, for the boisterous Atlantic was before me, and I sent the top mast down, knowing that the *Spray* would be the wholesomer with it on deck. Then I gave the lanyards a pull and hitched them afresh, and saw that the gammon (the lashing of the bow-sprit) was secure, also that the boat was lashed, for even in summer one may meet with bad weather in the crossing.

In fact, many weeks of bad weather had prevailed. On 1st July, however, after a rude gale, the wind came out nor'west and clear, propitious for a good run. On the following day, the head sea having gone down, I sailed from Yarmouth, and let go my last hold on America. The log of my first day on the Atlantic in the *Spray* reads briefly: '9.30am sailed from Yarmouth. 4.30pm passed Cape Sable; distance, three cables from the land. The sloop making eight knots. Fresh breeze N.W.' Before the sun went down I was taking my supper of strawberries and tea in smooth water under the lee of the east-coast land, along which the *Spray* was now leisurely skirting.

At noon on 3rd July Ironbound Island was abeam. The *Spray* was again at her best. A large schooner came out of Liverpool, Nova Scotia, this morning, steering eastward. The *Spray* put her hull down astern in five hours. At 6.45pm I was in close under Chebucto Head light, near

Halifax harbour. I set my flag and squared away, taking my departure from George's Island before dark to sail east of Sable Island. There are many beacon lights along the coast. Sambro, the Rock of Lamentations, carries a noble light, which, however, the liner *Atlantic*, on the night of her terrible disaster, did not see. I watched light after light sink astern as I sailed into the unbounded sea, until Sambro, the last of them all, was below the horizon. The *Spray* was then alone, and sailing on, she held her course. 4th July, at 6am I put in double reefs, and at 8.30am turned out all reefs. At 9.40pm I raised the sheen only of the light on the west end of Sable Island, which may also be called the Island of Tragedies. The fog, which until this moment had held off, now lowered over the sea like a pall. I was in a world of fog, shut off from the universe. I did not see any more of the light. By the lead, which I cast often, I found that a little after midnight I was passing the east point of the island, and should soon be clear of dangers of land and shoals. The wind was holding free, though it was from the foggy point, south–south–west. It is said that within a few years Sable Island has been reduced from forty miles in length to twenty, and that of three lighthouses built on it since 1880, two have been washed away and the third will soon be engulfed.

On the evening of 5th July the *Spray*, after having steered all day over a lumpy sea, took it into her head to go without the helmsman's aid. I had been steering southeast by south, but the wind hauling forward a bit, she dropped into a smooth lane, heading southeast, and making about eight knots her very best work. I crowded on sail to cross the track of the liners without loss of time, and to reach as soon as possible the friendly Gulf Stream. The fog lifting before night, I was afforded a look at the sun just as it was touching the sea. I watched it go down and out of sight. Then I turned my face eastward, and there, apparently at the very end of the bowsprit, was the smiling full moon rising out of the sea. Neptune himself coming over the bows could not have startled me more. 'Good evening, sir,' I cried; 'I'm glad to see you.' Many a long talk since then I have had with the man in the moon; he had my confidence on the voyage.

About midnight the fog shut down again denser than ever before. One could almost 'stand on it'. It continued so for a number of days, the wind increasing to a gale. The waves rose high, but I had a good ship. Still, in the dismal fog I felt myself drifting into loneliness, an insect on a straw in the midst of the elements. I lashed the helm, and my vessel held her course, and while she sailed I slept.

During these days a feeling of awe crept over me. My memory worked with startling power. The ominous, the insignificant, the great, the small, the wonderful, the commonplace – all appeared before my mental vision in magical succession. Pages of my history were recalled which had been so long forgotten that they seemed to belong to a previous existence. I heard all the voices of the past laughing, crying, telling what I had heard them tell in many corners of the earth.

The loneliness of my state wore off when the gale was high and I found much work to do. When fine weather returned, then came the sense of solitude, which I could not shake off. I used my voice often, at first giving some order about the affairs of a ship, for I had been told that from disuse I should lose my speech. At the meridian altitude of the sun I called aloud, 'Eight bells', after the custom on a ship at sea. Again from my cabin I cried to an imaginary man at the helm, 'How does she head there?' and again, 'Is she on her course?' But getting no reply, I was reminded the more palpably of my condition. My voice sounded hollow on the empty air, and I dropped the practice. However, it was not long before the thought came to me that when I was a lad I used to sing; why not try that now, where it would disturb no one? My musical talent had never bred envy in others, but out on the Atlantic, to realize what it meant, you should have heard me sing. You should have seen the porpoises leap when I pitched my voice for the waves and the sea and all that was in it. Old turtles, with large eyes, poked their heads up out of the sea as I sang 'Johnny Boker', and 'We'll Pay Darby Doyl for his Boots', and the like. But the porpoises were, on the whole, vastly more appreciative than the turtles; they jumped a deal higher. One day when I was humming a favourite chant, I think it was 'Babylon's a-Fallin', a porpoise jumped higher than the bowsprit. Had the *Spray* been going a little faster she would have scooped him in. The sea-birds sailed around rather shy.

10th July, eight days at sea, the *Spray* was twelve hundred miles east of Cape Sable. One hundred and fifty miles a day for so small a vessel must be considered good sailing. It was the greatest run the *Spray* ever made before or since in so few days. On the evening of 14th July, in better humour than ever before, all hands cried, 'Sail ho!' The sail was a barkantine, three points on the weather bow, hull down. Then came the night. My ship was sailing along now without attention to the helm. The wind was south; she was heading east. Her sails were trimmed like the sail of the nautilus. They drew steadily all night. I went frequently on deck, but found all well. A merry breeze kept on from the south. Early in the morning of the 15th the *Spray* was close aboard the stranger, which proved to be *La Vaguisa* of Vigo, twenty-three days from Philadelphia, bound for Vigo. A lookout from his masthead had spied the *Spray* the evening before. The captain, when I came near enough, threw a line to me and sent a bottle of wine across slung by the neck, and very good wine it was. He also sent his card, which bore the name of Juan Gantes. I think he was a good man, as Spaniards go. But when I asked him to report me 'all well' (the *Spray* passing him in a lively manner), he hauled his shoulders much above his head; and when his mate, who knew of my expedition, told him that I was alone, he crossed himself and made for his cabin. I did not see him again. By sundown he was as far astern as he had been ahead the evening before.

There was now less and less monotony. On 16th July the wind was northwest and clear, the sea smooth, and a large bark, hull down, came in sight on the lee bow, and at 2.30pm I spoke to the stranger. She was the bark *Java* of Glasgow, from Peru for Queenstown for orders. Her old captain was bearish, but I met a bear once in Alaska that looked pleasanter. At least, the bear seemed pleased to meet me, but this grizzly old man! Well, I suppose my hail disturbed his siesta, and my little sloop passing his great ship had somewhat the effect on him that a red rag has upon a bull. I had the advantage over heavy ships, by long odds, in the light winds of this and the two previous days. The wind was light; his ship was heavy and foul, making poor headway, while the *Spray*, with a great mainsail bellying even to light winds, was just skipping along as nimbly as one could wish. 'How long has it been calm about here?' roared the captain of the *Java*, as I came within hail of him. 'Dunno, cap'n,' I shouted back as loud as I could bawl. 'I haven't been here long.' At this the mate on the forecastle wore a broad grim. 'I left Cape Sable fourteen days ago,' I added. (I was now well across towards the Azores.) 'Mate,' he roared to his chief officer – 'mate, come here and listen to the Yankee's yarn. Haul down the flag, mate, haul down the flag!' In the best of humour, after all, the *Java* surrendered to the *Spray*.

The acute pain of solitude experienced at first never returned. I had

A large bark came into sight on the lee bow.

penetrated a mystery, and, by the way, I had sailed through a fog. I had met Neptune in his wrath, but he found that I had not treated him with contempt, and so he suffered me to go on and explore.

In the log for 18th July there is this entry: 'Fine weather, wind south-southwest. Porpoises gamboling all about. The S.S. *Olympia* passed at 11.30am, long W. 34° 50'.'

'It lacks now three minutes of the half hour,' shouted the captain, as he gave me the longitude and the time. I admired the businesslike air of the *Olympia*; but I have the feeling still that the captain was just a little too precise in his reckoning. That may be all well enough, however, where there is plenty of sea-room. But over confidence, I believe, was the cause of the disaster to the liner *Atlantic*, and many more like her. The captain knew too well where he was. There were no porpoises at all skipping along with the *Olympia*! Porpoises always prefer sailing-ships. The captain was a young man, I observed, and had before him, I hope, a good record.

Land ho! On the morning of 19th July a mystic dome like a mountain of silver stood alone in the sea ahead. Although the land was completely hidden by the white, glistening haze that shone in the sun like polished silver, I felt quite sure that it was Flores Island. At 4.30pm it was abeam. The haze in the meantime had disappeared. Flores is one hundred and seventy-four miles from Fayal, and although it is a high island, it remained many years undiscovered after the principal group of the islands had been colonized.

Early on the morning of 20th July I saw Pico looming above the clouds on the starboard bow. Lower lands burst forth as the sun burned away the morning fog, and island after island came into view. As I approached nearer, cultivated fields appeared, 'and oh, how green the corn!' Only those who have seen the Azores from the deck of a vessel realize the beauty of the mid-ocean picture.

At 4.30pm I cast anchor at Fayal, exactly eighteen days from Cape Sable. The American consul, in a smart boat, came alongside before the *Spray* reached the breakwater, and a young naval officer, who feared for the safety of my vessel, boarded and offered his services as pilot. The youngster, I have no good reason to doubt, could have handled a man-of-war, but the *Spray* was too small for the amount of uniform he wore. However, after fouling all the craft in port and sinking a lighter, she was moored without much damage to herself. This wonderful pilot expected a 'gratification', I understand, but whether for the reason that his government, and not I, would have to pay the cost of raising the lighter, or because he did not sink the *Spray*, I could never make out. But I forgive him.

It was the season for fruit when I arrived at the Azores, and there was soon more of all kinds of it put on board than I knew what to do with. Islanders are always the kindest people in the world, and I met none anywhere kinder than the good hearts of this place. The people of the Azores are not a very rich community. The burden of taxes is heavy, with scant privileges in return, the air they breathe being about the only thing that is not taxed. The mother-country does not even allow them a port of entry for a foreign mail service. A packet passing never so close with mails for Horta must deliver them first in Lisbon, ostensibly to be fumigated, but really for the tariff from the packet. My own letters posted at Horta reached the United States six days behind my letter from Gibraltar, mailed thirteen days later.

The day after my arrival at Horta was the feast of a great saint. Boats loaded with people came from other islands to celebrate at Horta, the capital, or Jerusalem of the Azores. The deck of the *Spray* was crowded from morning until night with men, women, and children. On the day after the feast a kind-hearted native harnessed a team and drove me a day over the beautiful roads all about Fayal. 'Because,' said he, in broken English, 'when I was in America and couldn't speak a word of English, I found it hard until I met someone who seemed to have time to listen to my story, and I promised my good saint then that if ever a stranger came to my country, I would try to make him happy.' Unfortunately, this gentleman brought along an interpreter, that I might 'learn more of the country.' The fellow was nearly the death of me, talking of ships and voyages, and of the boats he had steered, the last thing in the world I wished to hear. He had sailed out of New Bedford, so he said, for 'that Joe Wing they call "John".' My friend and host found hardly a chance to edge in a word. Before we parted my host dined me with a cheer that would have gladdened the heart of a prince, but he was quite alone in his house. 'My wife and children all rest there,' said he, pointing to the churchyard across the way. 'I moved to this house from far off,' he added, 'to be near the spot, where I pray every morning.'

I remained four days at Fayal, and that was two days more than I had intended to stay. It was the kindness of the islanders and their touching simplicity which detained me. A damsel, as innocent as an angel, came alongside one day, and said she would embark on the *Spray* if I would land her at Lisbon. She could cook flying-fish, she thought, but her forte was dressing *bacalhao*. Her brother Antonio, who served as interpreter, hinted that, anyhow, he would like to make the trip. Antonio's heart went out to one John Wilson, and he was ready to sail for America by way of the two capes to meet his friend. 'Do you know John Wilson of Boston?' he cried. 'I knew a John Wilson,' I said, 'but not of Boston.' 'He had one daughter and one son,' said Antonio, by way of identifying his friend. If this reaches the right John Wilson, I am told to say that 'Antonio of Pico remembers him.'

THE RETURN TO ITHAKA
Iain Finlayson

You are determined to have an account of my travels, Lord Alcinous, no matter how painful it may be for me to recall them. The list of my woes is a long one, but I will tell you my story. My fame and my fate by now are common knowledge among men, and even the gods know of my misery.

I am Odysseus, son of Laertes and king of Ithaka. I was born and raised on that lonely isle that faces westward towards the setting sun, and I am homesick for that barren, rocky kingdom. It is a hard land that raises heroes who struggle for survival. Yet Ithaka calls back her sons, however far from home they may have settled, no matter how rich and soft they may have become in foreign lands. I have travelled for weary years trying to return to Ithaka, to my homeland and to the wife and son I left so long ago to wage war on the city of Troy.

After a long and bitter siege, Troy fell to us and we embarked in our great curved ships intending to sail for our homes with all speed. The wind that filled our sails to carry us from Troy drove us first to Ismarus, the city of the Cicones. I killed the defenders of the town and looted it. I was all for clearing off immediately, but my crew couldn't get enough of stuffing themselves with the city's food and wine and they carried on feasting. And so, while they were drinking and roasting fat sheep and cattle by the shore, those that were left of the Cicones raised the alarm among their kith and kin up in the hills and by dawn they were upon us, thick as autumn leaves, pitching in with bronze spears and chariots, so that we had to fight all day. At nightfall, they broke our ranks and six of my warriors from each of my twelve ships were killed. The rest of us managed to get away, but that wasn't the end of our troubles. More like the beginning of them.

Zeus, chief of the gods, commands the clouds and with malice towards me whistled up a terrific blast of wind from the north. He covered land and sea with a thick blanket of low cloud, closing us in darkness like a great shadow. The gale battered our ships sideways, tearing the sails to shreds. We were deathly scared, but we rowed mightily against the storm to reach land. For two days and two nights we cowered in harbour, but the third day dawned calm and we hauled up our sails again and trusted to the wind and our helmsmen to keep us straight on course. We'd have reached home if the sea swell, the current and the North wind hadn't driven us drifting past Cythera. We suffered nine days of that, until on the tenth day we reached the land of the Lotus-eaters, people that live on vegetables.

I sent three men off on a scouting party. They met up with some of the Lotus-eaters who were very friendly – at least, they didn't try to kill the men – and gave the scouts some lotus to taste. No sooner had they eaten the sweet fruit than they lost all thought of reporting back to the ships. All they wanted was to stay where they were, eating lotus for the rest of their lives completely forgetful of anything else. I had to drag them back to the ships by force and clap them in irons for their own good. It was pitiful to see them weep, but I had the rest of my crew to think about, and I ordered everyone back on board with the warning that they were on no account to eat any fruit or vegetables they might have found. We cast off immediately and sailed off, beating the white surf with our oars, sick at heart.

Our next port of call was the land of the Cyclopes. We came on it unexpectedly, beaching without warning in the soft breakers that rolled up to the coast. It had been a long, moonless night of thick fog that even the sharpest-sighted among us could not penetrate. We slept for a few hours on the beach, and when red-streaked dawn broke we separated into groups and set off with our curved bows and long spears to hunt mountain goats for breakfast. Each of the crews from my twelve ships bagged nine goats, a good haul, and we passed the whole day roasting the rich supply of meat and drinking good vintage wine. In the distance we could see smoke from the fires of the Cyclopes and hear the bleating of their sheep and goats. That night we again slept soundly by our beach camp and rose to greet another rosy dawn.

'Good friends,' I cried, addressing the men, 'I want you to wait for me while I take my own ship and crew to find out what sort of men live here – whether they are brutal, lawless savages, or god-fearing men of goodwill who will give us a welcome.'

My men took their places at the oars and we churned the grey sea until we reached the nearest point of the mainland where we came upon the mouth of a great cave. To judge by the goat and sheep pens and the great wall of stone sunk deep between mighty oaks and tall pines, this was the den of a giant, and this was no mild vegetable-eater. This was a monster that heeded neither the laws of gods nor of men. Deciding to take a close look, I chose twelve of my best men and we equipped ourselves with goatskins of wine and leather wallets full of food.

The cave, when we reached it, was deserted. But there were baskets crammed with cheeses, pens alive with lambs and kids, buckets and bowls brimming with whey. My men were all for making off with as much food and livestock as they could and getting back to the ship at the double. But I obstinately refused to leave. I wanted to know what sort of man – or beast – owned the cave, and I had hopes that we'd be given gifts to take away with us. We settled down to light a fire and cooked one of the penned animals. We helped ourselves to cheeses, ate a good dinner and waited for our host to return. At last we heard him, shepherding his flocks back to the cave for the night. He threw down the huge bundle of wood he was carrying with such a clatter that we retreated, terrified, into a deep niche at the back of the cave. Sheep poured in through the mouth of the cave and the huge shadow of the giant blotted out the daylight as he entered. He picked up a mighty slab of stone which he slammed across the entrance, closing us all inside together.

He sat down to milk his ewe and goats and then lit his fire. It was then as he turned and caught sight of us that we saw that he had only one, huge eye in his head. His voice boomed as he demanded who we were and what we wanted. I answered, 'We are soldiers of the great lord

Agamemnon, returning from the city of Troy which we sacked after destroying its armies. We have been carried off our course by contrary winds, and we are here as your guests. We beg you to remember the laws of hospitality and your duty to the gods. We are at your mercy, driven by Zeus who is the god of travellers, mightiest father of the gods, and sworn to take vengeance on any who abuse the rights of those he protects.' The monster paid no attention. He cast his pitiless eye over us and said, with a sneer,

'Stranger, you are a fool. We Cyclopes care nothing for the gods. We are stronger than they, so do you think I fear trouble from Zeus? Now, where did you anchor your ship? Nearby, or further up the coast? I'd like to see such a brave little boat.'

I know deceit and honeyed words when I hear them, and I can give as good as I get. I answered him, saying,

'The sea god Poseidon wrecked my ship by driving it up to the headland and dashing it on the rocks. My friends and I escaped with our lives. We are stranded travellers, and we ask for shelter and aid.'

The brute said nothing, but simply reached out and grabbed a couple of my men, dashing their heads against the floor. Their brains and blood soaked the earth as they were pulled apart limb by limb and stuffed into the giant's great maw. Having filled his belly, the Cyclops washed down his meal with milk and stretched out among his flocks to sleep. I was about to plunge my sword right through his liver, but stopped short. For if I killed the monster, how would we ever move the rock that stopped up the entrance? The Cyclops alone could shift it, and until he did we were trapped. So we just sat there, waiting for daylight, groaning and utterly helpless.

At dawn, the Cyclops lit his fire and milked his flock. After he had again snatched up two more of my men and filled his gut with human flesh, he turned his flocks out of the cave and replaced the massive stone against the mouth of our prison. Closed in, with murder in my heart, I beat my brains for a plan. I'd noticed the Cyclops' staff of green olive wood, a pole that seemed to us as big as a ship's mast. We cut off a piece about six feet in length and sharpened it to a point which we hardened by stabbing it into the heart of the fire. We hid the stake under a pile of animal dung and waited for the Cyclops to return.

He murdered another two of my men for his evening meal and when he had devoured them I approached the Cyclops with some of our wine, offering it in a deep bowl and saying,

'Here, you ugly brute. Try this and find out the sort of mellow vintage we were prepared to give you in return for your help in setting us back on our way. But you're just a savage, a loathsome monster who deserves to live alone, unvisited by decent men.'

The Cyclops drained the bowl and bawled for more. When the fool had poured three more draughts of good wine down his throat, he asked my name and promised me a gift.

'Cyclops,' I shouted, 'my name is Nobody.'

'Well, Nobody,' bellowed the giant, 'my gift is this. Of all your company, I will eat you last.' He let out a great boom of laughter and toppled over in a stupor, drunk, to lie face up on the ground. Immediately we manhandled the pole and made its tip red-hot in the fire. Just as it was about to burst into flame, we swung it up, round, and plunged its sharp tip dead centre into the Cyclops' eye. The giant gave a shriek that rang like the crack of doom around the walls. He pulled out the stake and hurled it from his eye. Drenched in blood that ran like a river from the gaping wound, he screamed mightily to rouse his neighbours who gathered outside the cave to find out the cause of the uproar.

'What's the trouble, Polyphemus? It's the middle of the night. Why are you making all that row? Are you being robbed or murdered?' From the cave came Polyphemus' howls of agony.

'Oh, Nobody has tricked me! Nobody is killing me!'

'Well,' the Cyclopes answered, 'if nobody is bothering you, you must be mad, and there's nothing anyone can do about it!'

Polyphemus blundered sightlessly around the cave for a while, moaning and groaning, while I kept out of his way and tried to think of an escape plan. Suddenly I had an idea! We tied together some of the fat sheep and clung upside down with our hands and feet, gripping their fleece. They would be shepherded out as usual, at dawn. Even Polyphemus in his pain could not ignore their bleating cries. It worked. The Cyclops never noticed the trick, and once outside the cave we were on our feet and running to the ship, driving the sheep before us. The least the giant owed us was a few sheep! We were safely at sea, but not out of earshot of the Cyclops when I shouted recklessly.

'Polyphemus, if anyone ever asks you how you were blinded, tell him your eye was put out by Odysseus, destroyer of cities, son of Laertes, king of Ithaka.'

Polyphemus moaned and raised his clenched fists to heaven, invoking his father Poseidon, god of the sea, crying out for vengeance against me and my men.

'Hear me, Poseidon, and recognise me as your son. Grant that Odysseus may never reach Ithaka or, if it is his fate to reach his native land, grant that his homecoming shall be long delayed, that all his comrades will perish, and that his house be sorely plagued.'

I laughed, and at the sound of my voice the Cyclops picked up an enormous boulder which he hurled with such force that it missed our steering oar by inches and created a wave strong enough to carry us to the far shore and the rest of my fleet. That was a stroke of luck, the last I had for a long time. Stubborn pride had set the hand of another god against me and every man of my crew.

Things went without incident for a while. We were lucky to be entertained royally by Aeolus, lord of the floating isle of Aeolia, whom Zeus had appointed Warden of the Winds. I gave the old gentleman news of the fall of Troy and in return he kindly gave me a leather bag, the skin of an enormous ox in fact, in which he had put enough wind energy to blow us home. To take us from Aeolia, Aeolus raised a westerly breeze that carried us along for nine days, and on the tenth day we sighted Ithaka, actually came near enough to shore to see people going about their daily business. Sheer exhaustion forced me to sleep at last, safe (as I thought) in sight of my homeland. Fool that I was! Word had got about that the bag given to me by Aeolus was stuffed with a fortune in gold and silver. Some of my men undid the bag to take a look, and the winds billowed out, rushing and buffeting together, beating our ships headlong back out to sea. Truly, the gods are my enemies. In despair, I pulled my cloak over my head and lay back down where I'd been resting, not caring if I lived or died. We were driven back to Aeolia where I asked the Warden again for his help, but he was furiously angry and dismissed us empty-handed.

Miserably, we rowed on, until we fetched up at the island of Aeaea which I knew to be the home of the goddess Circe. Here we disembarked and rested on the shore for two days and nights, overcome by exhaustion. At sun up on the third day I armed myself with spear and sword and slipped away inland on a hunting expedition. From the top of the high hill I noticed a spiral of smoke in the distance and reckoned it must be coming from Circe's house. I thought of reconnoitering, but a fine stag crossed my path and I was fortunate enough to bring it down with the bronze head of my spear. Then I slung the great antlered beast round my neck and returned to the ship where we spent the full day feasting. We slept well that night, and at daybreak I told them of the wisps of smoke I had seen.

They weren't happy, but I split my forces into two parties, both armed to the teeth, and took command of one personally. The other I put in the charge of Eurylochus who took his twenty two men into the interior while we stayed behind to guard the ship. After a while Eurylochus came back alone in a fearful state of shock. It was all we could do to get him to make sense, but finally we managed to piece his story together. The group had come on a clearing in which there stood a fine palace from which they could hear the sound of a woman's voice singing as she sat weaving at her loom. They were at first alarmed by mountain lions and wolves that prowled around in the glade, but the creatures appeared to be friendly. Eurylochus and his men shouted to attract the woman's attention, and presently she appeared at the polished doors to welcome them inside her house. Eurylochus, suspecting something amiss, hung back and waited alone at a distance. He waited in vain, because not one of the men came out again. He heard songs of feasting, and then the grunting of pigs, and before long Circe opened her doors again and drove out a herd of swine, pig-headed and bristled, grunting like hogs, but weeping human tears. She penned these in sties and threw them some acorns and berries for food. So there, wallowing in the mud, were pigs with human minds, my men transformed by the magic herbs that Circe had put in their banquet.

I armed myself with a curved bow and strapped on my great bronze sword in its silver scabbard. Despite Eurylochus' protests, I turned my back on the ship and struck inland. And who should I meet with but Hermes, god of the golden wand. He casually greeted me and plucked a nearby herb with a black root and a white flower. He explained that this plant, which the gods call Moly, acted as an antidote to Circe's drug. He told me she mixed her magic in a sort of porridge that changed anyone who ate it into a beast. Hermes then advised me that Circe would strike me with her wand and that I should immediately draw my sword and lunge at her as if to kill her on the spot.

Hermes wandered off and I continued up to the palace where Circe greeted me kindly and all went as the god had told me it would. She shrieked when I drew my sword and begged very prettily for mercy. I made her give her word not to try any fancy business and she got up from her knees to fetch some ointment which she took outside and smeared over the pigs in her sties. The bristles dropped off, and my men were returned to their human shape. They recognised me at once and rushed over to embrace me and we all stood there weeping and laughing for a while. Even Circe was very touched by our reunion. In the end, we all stayed with her for a full year, feasting on meat and wine and taking it easy. But when the seasons began to repeat themselves, my men reminded me tactfully that we were still far from home and that we should soon be on our way, sailing for Ithaka in our black ship.

Circe very nobly said she had no intention of keeping us against our will, but her next words struck cold in my heart. She insisted that I should consult Teiresias, the blind seer, for advice about our voyage. Teiresias, I knew, had been dead for years and that his shade now haunted the cold halls of Hades, the kingdom of the dead. Circe was asking my black ship into Hell. My crew set up a howl of terror when I told them but I insisted and finally we sailed with a breeze blown up for us by Circe and journeyed to the deep-running River of Ocean at the ends of this world where the Cimmerians, perpetually fog bound, inhabit their city of Eternal Cloud. Here, at a spot named by Circe, we made our sacrifices and libations of milk and honey, sweet wine and water. To attract the ghosts, we slaughtered sheep and filled a deep trench with their blood for Teiresias to drink. We held at bay a multitude of fluttering wraiths that came silently clustering up from the shadows, but finally, ancient Teiresias approached bearing a staff of gold in one hand. He slaked his thirst and began to prophesy, warning us not to harm the cattle and well-fed sheep of the sun-god which were pastured on the island of Thrinacie. Should they be destroyed, all of us would surely die and I alone would reach my kingdom to find my palace and estates infested with scoundrels eating me out of house and home, and my lands devastated.

The tribes of the dead had assembled around us as the prophet spoke, tens of thousands, each wailing dimly, drawing close around us. We panicked, I admit, and made our way quickly back to the ship and the current that would carry us down the River of Ocean back to the good sunlight. From the halls of the dead, we emerged into the wide sea and made haste back to Circe's isle. She welcomed us and warned us of perils ahead, then we feasted and recovered our strength for a few days before setting sail once more. Circe's first warning was of the mysterious music and singing of the Sirens who so entranced seafarers that they lost their reason and added their bones to the heap of mouldering skeletons collected by those withered hags of the sea. I plugged the ears of my crew with wax, and had them bind me firmly with thongs to the mast as we approached the flowery meadows of the Sirens' isle. As soon as they sighted the ship, the Sirens began to sing their flowing song, an air so bewitching that I struggled like a madman to loose my bonds and longed to listen forever to the sweet notes of those evil creatures. We soon passed out of earshot but no sooner was that danger over than another was upon us.

Great plumes of spray, like smoke hung ahead in the air. A pounding, raging, seething surf roared in the distance between towering cliffs. The oars dropped from the shaking hands of my crew, bringing the ship to a standstill. I braced them to the danger ahead and told them we would have to try to race past the monster Scylla and the churning gaping mouth of the great, sucking underwater creature Charybdis. My idea was to hug the cliffs and, ignoring Circe's warning not to arm myself in any way, I seized a couple of spears and positioned myself on the forecastle deck to search the crevices of the cliffs for the creature Scylla.

We sailed into the straits, giving Charybdis a wide berth as she alternately sucked down the salt water in a whirling vortex and spewed it up again in a torrent that washed down on the tops of the crags. I'd almost forgotten about Scylla when she lunged to snatch six of my ablest hands from the ship, swinging them high in the air where their arms and legs dangled helplessly in her clutch. They shrieked and stretched their arms for aid as they were swept into the monster's ugly jaws. To stop now would have been fatal to us all, and there was no help for our companions in their cruel deaths. We raced on and came to the isle of Hyperion, the Sun-god, whose cattle browsed peaceably with his sheep on lush meadows.

My memory stirred and I recollected Teiresias' warning to leave these beasts unharmed, and I told the men to drive the ship with all speed past this land. They were frankly fed up and exhausted, unwilling to scull another yard and weary for rest and food. Even Eurylochus took their side, blaming me for being a tyrant and a hard man whose body never tired, whose spirit never flagged. The men promised me faithfully not to touch any cattle or sheep on the island, and so we anchored in a sheltered bay and made the best of our rations which were running low. Later, I went inland to pray to the gods in hopes that one of them might aid us, but all they did was put me to sleep. In my absence, Eurylochus set up a complaint about the lack of fresh meat and he persuaded some of the men to round up and slaughter a few of the broad-browed cattle and sturdy sheep. I woke and returned to camp to be greeted by the fine smell of roasting meat. There was no help for it, the beasts were dead and eaten, though I raged and fumed at the folly. Hyperion was furious and apparently went straight to Zeus to demand revenge and compensation. He even threatened to retreat to Hades and shine there intead of in the heavens. Zeus, the cloud-gatherer, persuaded him to keep the sun shining and promised to strike our ship with a thunderbolt and pound us to pieces once we were at sea.

Zeus positioned an ominous black cloud directly above us the moment we were at sea and out of sight of any land. The cloud's shadow darkend the sea and screaming wind bore down on us with hurricane force. The ship's mast tumbled towards the stern as Zeus released his mighty thunderbolts and shivered the ship with a tremendous bolt of lightning. My crew was tossed overboard and hung in the raging sea like seagulls on the waves. There would be no homecoming for them, the god made sure of that. I was the last man on board, moving from base to base until a giant wave tore the black ship's sides from the keel. With a leather thong, I manged to lash the broken mast to the keel and gripped with all my strength to these two pieces of timber. I was wind and sea tossed like a wineskin until the storm subsided a little only to be hurled by great winds in the direction of Scylla's rock and the dreadful mouth of Charybdis. For a whole night I was swept along and at dawn I found myself swirling around the lips of Charybdis who, at that moment, spouted up casting me towards a strong fig tree on which I took a firm

Zeus shivered the ship with a tremendous bolt.

grip. There I hung like a bat until the monster threw up my timbers to the surface of the sea, then I plunged down once more into the foam and straddled the great logs, paddling for dear life with my hands in an effort to break out of the currents. I thank the gods that they spared me, on this occasion at least, the horror of Scylla. I drifted for nine days and washed up on the tenth on the island of Ogygia, the country of the beautiful goddess Calypso who took me in, tended me, and restored me to health and strength. Seven years I stayed there until the goddess Athene, who had seen my son and my wife despairing that I should ever return to them, persuaded Zeus that I should continue my interrupted voyage. Zeus sent his son Hermes, messenger of the gods, to convey his words to Calypso. Over the endless waves rode Hermes to Ogygia where he told Calypso that she must let me go. In tears, she found me on the shore where I was sitting and gave me permission to fell some tall, stout trees, twenty in all, and construct a boat. Within five days I'd built myself a broad-bottomed, trading ship and with a glad heart I steered a course out to sea, navigating by the stars. I'd forgotten the enmity that Poseidon, god of the sea, still had for me and at the sight of my little craft nosing through the waves he was stirred to fresh anger.

Grasping his trident in his hands, mighty Poseidon whipped the seas and stirred the winds. Darkness raced across the sky and the gales buffeted together with tremendous force, raising a mountainous crest of water that bore down on me like a sweeping cloak, crashing down and whirling my vessel around. The steering oar jolted from my hands and I was blown like a feather overboard just as the mast snapped in two and the sail flapped high in the air like a bird. I fought, grasping for lungfuls of air, as the force of the waves threw me back time and again. Miraculously, the boat still tossed on the surface and even though the weight of my clothes threatened to keep me underwater, I managed to scramble aboard. Squatting amidships, I crouched helplessly as the heavy seas swirled me this way and that, round and around, hither and thither like a ball being tossed between the winds for sport. But I had a friend among the gods – Ino, daughter of Cadmus, who lived in the salt depths of the sea and who took pity on me. She rose from the water like a gull winging up from the sea and settled beside me in the boat. With her, she had brought a veil which she twisted round my waist as a protection against death by drowning and she cried out to me to swim. She herself plunged back into the deep, swallowed up by dark water and just as I was making up my mind whether I dared leave the boat, Poseidon hurled another monster wave full towards me. It hung for a moment, curled above my head, then hurtled down breaking the boat in pieces. There was no help for it – it was sink or swim, and I struck out into the heavy seas. I swam for two nights and two days in a heavy swell before glimpsing wooded land, a sight that put new heart in me. The wind had dropped, and all was calm and still. I ached to tread land once more, land now so close after so long at sea.

But suddenly in my ears sounded the angry pounding of surf on rock. Roaring against the inhospitable, craggy coast, the heavy seas swelled and broke, spewing their breakers, veiling the land in misty spray. There were no safe coves or bays that I could see, only sheer rock and jutting reefs. Had I tried to land, I might well have been dashed against the rocks by a swelling breaker, and had I tried to swim further down the coast on the chance of finding a natural harbour, chances are I'd have been swept back out to sea to be food for the fish. My problem was solved when a tremendous surge of water raced me forward towards the rocks, threatening to break every bone in my body. But divine inspiration came to my aid, and I flung out an arm to grasp hold of a rock as I flooded past. I clutched this anchor with both hands and clung there, swept by the tide race. Then my hands were torn from the rock by the force of the great wave's backward suction and I was flung far out to sea once more where I struggled to regain my breath and strength while the salt sea licked agonisingly at my torn flesh. I was by now far enough beyond the coastal breakers to swim outside their bone crushing force, and I crawled along in search of a gently shelving beach. Presently the current changed and I found myself at the mouth of a fast-running stream, calm enough for me to land on the good earth at last. For a while I crouched on my knees, my hands flat on the ground, while salt water poured from my mouth and nostrils. I untied Ino's veil from my waist and cast it behind me into the waters without a backward look as she had made me swear to do. The current swept it full out to sea and back to the goddess.

I made my way inland and finally, having come to your country, my Lord Alcinous, I slept the profound sleep of one delivered from the spite of the gods and the chill jaws of death. You have received me royally, my lord, and yet my tale is not ended. I have not reached Ithaka, my voyaging is not yet done. I have prayed to Athene, wise daughter of all powerful Zeus, and I have hopes that the enmity of the gods may no longer plague me. I will see my homeland at last.

★　★　★　★

Odysseus' tale at an end, Alcinous and his people, the Phaeacians, lavished gifts upon their guest and fitted out a stout ship that received the blessing of Zeus after he had been placated by the sacrifice of a bullock. No sooner had the crew struck the water with their oars than a dreamless sleep fell upon Odysseus. In the soft light of dawn, at the rising of the sun, brightest of all stars, the ship drew near to Ithaka and put in quietly at a safe harbour. With willing hands, the ship's company raised the brave Odysseus, still wrapped in sleep, and laid him on the shore.

When Odysseus awoke he failed to recognise the place where he lay. The goddess Athene had cast a mist over the land, disguising its long hill paths, its quiet coves, its jutting rocks and fair green trees. Thinking himself betrayed by friends who had promised to restore him safe to his homeland, Odysseus shuffled aimlessly along the edge of the pounding surf. But bright-eyed Athene disguised as a young shepherd, stepped forth to greet Odysseus. As the goddess spoke, she dispersed the mist and the sun flooded the land making it clear and plain to Odysseus that he stood at last in his own kingdom, in Ithaka, and joy filled the heart of the king as he bent to kiss the soil, the end of all his exploring.

ABOARD THE ARANGI
Jack London

Captain Van Horn, skipper of the vessel Arangi, *is one of the toughest captains sailing the tropical seas. Despite his harsh appearance, his heart goes out to a mongrel dog that he comes across on a trip to the cannibal island of Malaita and he takes him aboard, deciding to call him Jerry.*

The first watch, from eight to twelve, was the mate's; and Captain Van Horn, forced below by the driving wet of a heavy rain squall, took Jerry with him to sleep in the tiny stateroom. Jerry was weary from the manifold excitements of the most exciting day in his life; and he was asleep and kicking and growling in his sleep, ere Skipper, with a last look at him and a grin as he turned the lamp low, muttered aloud: 'It's that wild-dog, Jerry. Get him. Shake him. Shake him hard.'

So soundly did Jerry sleep, that when the rain, having robbed the atmosphere of its last breath of wind, ceased and left the stateroom a steaming, suffocating furnace, he did not know when Skipper, panting for air, his loin cloth and undershirt soaked with sweat, arose, tucked blanket and pillow under his arm, and went on deck.

Jerry only awakened when a huge three-inch cockroach nibbled at the sensitive and hairless skin between his toes. He awoke kicking the offended foot, and gazed at the cockroach that did not scuttle, but that walked dignifiedly away. He watched it join other cockroaches that paraded the floor. Never had he seen so many gathered together at one time, and never had he seen such large ones. They were all of a size, and they were everywhere. Long lines of them poured out of cracks in the walls and descended to join their fellows on the floor.

The thing was indecent – at least, in Jerry's mind, it was not to be tolerated. Mister Haggin, Derby, and Bob had never tolerated cockroaches, and their rules were his rules. The cockroach was the eternal tropic enemy. He sprang at the nearest, pouncing to crush it to the floor under his paws. But the think did what he had never known a cockroach to do. It arose in the air, strong-flighted as a bird. And as if at a signal, all the multitude of cockroaches took wings of flight and filled the room with their flutterings and circlings.

He attacked the winged host, leaping into the air, snapping at the flying vermin, trying to knock them down with his paws. Occasionally he succeeded and destroyed one; nor did the combat cease until all the cockroaches, as if at another signal, disappeared into the many cracks, leaving the room to him.

Quickly, his next thought was: Where is Skipper? He knew he was not in the room, though he stood up on his hind-legs and investigated the low bunk, his keen little nose quivering delightedly while he made little sniffs of delight as he smelled the recent presence of Skipper. And what made his nose quiver and sniff, likewise made his stump of a tail bob back and forth.

But where was Skipper? It was a thought in his brain that was as sharp and definite as a similar thought would be in a human brain. And it similarly proceded action. The door had been left hooked open, and Jerry trotted out into the cabin where half a hundred blacks made queer sleep-moanings, and sighings, and snorings. They were packed closely together, covering the floor as well as the long sweep of bunks, so that he was compelled to crawl over their naked legs. And there was no white god about to protect him. He knew it, but was unafraid.

Having made sure that Skipper was not in the cabin, Jerry prepared for the perilous ascent of the steep steps that were almost a ladder, then recollected the lazarette. In he trotted and sniffed at the sleeping girl in the cotton shift who believed that Van Horn was going to eat her if he could succeed in fattening her.

Back at the ladder-steps, he looked up and waited in the hope that Skipper might appear from above and carry him up. Skipper had passed that way, he knew, and he knew for two reasons. It was the only way he could have passed, and Jerry's nose told him that he had passed. His first attempt to climb the steps began well. Not until a third of the way up, as the *Arangi* rolled in a sea and recovered with a jerk, did he slip and fall. Two or three boys awoke and watched him while they prepared and chewed betel nut and lime wrapped in green leaves.

Twice, barely started, Jerry slipped back, and more boys, awakened by their fellows, sat up and enjoyed his plight. In the fourth attempt he managed to gain half way up before he fell, coming down heavily on his side. This was hailed with low laughter and querulous chirpings that might well have come from the throats of huge birds. He regained his feet, absurdly bristled the hair on his shoulders and absurdly growled his high disdain of these lesser, two-legged things that came and went and obeyed the wills of great, white-skinned, two-legged gods such as Skipper and Mister Haggin.

Undeterred by his heavy fall, Jerry essayed the ladder again. A temporary easement of the *Arangi's* rolling gave him his opportunity, so that his forefeet were over the high combing of the companion when the next big roll came. He held on by main strength of his bent forelegs, then scrambled over and out on deck.

Amidships, squatting on the deck near the skylight, he investigated several of the boat's crew and Lerumie. He identified them circumspectly, going suddenly stiff-legged as Lerumie made a low, hissing, menacing noise. Aft, at the wheel, he found a black steering, and, near him, the mate keeping the watch. Just as the mate spoke to him and stooped to pat him, Jerry whiffed Skipper somewhere near at hand. With a conciliating, apologetic bob of his tail, he trotted on up wind and came upon Skipper on his back, rolled in a blanket so that only his head stuck out, and sound asleep.

First of all Jerry needs must joyfully sniff him and joyfully wag his tail. But Skipper did not awake, and a fine spray of rain, almost as thin as mist, made Jerry curl up and press closely into the angle formed by Skipper's head and shoulder. This did awake him, for he uttered 'Jerry' in a low, crooning voice, and Jerry responded with a touch of his cold damp nose to the other's cheek. And then Skipper went to sleep again. But not Jerry. He lifted the edge of the blanket with his nose and crawled across the shoulder until he was altogether inside. This roused Skipper, who, half-asleep, helped him to curl up.

Still Jerry was not satisfied, and he squirmed around until he lay in the hollow of Skipper's arm, his head resting on Skipper's shoulder, when, with a profound sigh of content, he fell asleep.

Several times the noises made by the boat's crew in trimming the sheets to the shifting draught of air roused Van Horn, and each time, remembering the puppy, he pressed him caressingly with his hollowed arm. And each time, in his sleep, Jerry stirred responsively and snuggled cosily to him.

For all that he was a remarkable puppy, Jerry had his limitations, and he could never know the effect produced on the hard-bitten captain by the soft warm contact of his velvet body. But it made the captain remember back across the years to his own girl babe asleep on his arm. And so poignantly did he remember, that he became wide awake, and many pictures, beginning with the girl babe, burned their torment in his brain. No white man in the Solomons knew what he carried about with him, waking and often sleeping; and it was because of these pictures that he had come to the Solomons in a vain effort to erase them.

First, memory-prodded by the soft puppy in his arm, he saw the girl and the mother in the little Harlem flat. Small, it was true, but tight-packed with the happiness of three that made it heaven.

He saw the girl's flaxen-yellow hair darken to her mother's gold as it lengthened into curls and ringlets until finally it became two thick long braids. From striving not to see these many pictures, he came even to dwelling upon them in the effort so to fill his consciousness as to keep out the one picture he did not want to see.

He remembered his work, the wrecking car, and the wrecking crew that had toiled under him, and he wondered what had become of Clancey, his right-hand man. Came the long day, when, routed from bed at three in the morning to dig a surface car out of the wrecked show windows of a drug store and get it back on the track, they had laboured all day clearing up a half-dozen smash-ups and arrived at the car house at nine at night just as another call came in.

'Glory be!' said Clancey, who lived in the next block from him. He could see him saying it and wiping the sweat from his grimy face. 'Glory be, 'tis a small matter at most, an' right in our neighbourhood – not a dozen blocks away. Soon as it's done we can beat it for home an' let the down-town boys take the car back to the shop.'

'We've only to jack her up for a moment,' he had answered.

'What is it?' Billy Jaffers, another of the crew, asked.

'Somebody run over – can't get them out,' he said, as they swung on board the wrecking-car and started.

He saw again all the incidents of the long run, not omitting the delay caused by hose-carts and a hook-and-ladder running to a cross-town fire, during which time he and Clancey had joked Jaffers over the dates with various fictitious damsels out of which he had been cheated by the night's extra work.

Came the long line of stalled street-cars, the crowd, the police holding it back, the two ambulances drawn up and waiting their freight, and the young policeman, whose beat it was, white and shaken, greeting him with: 'It's horrible, man, It's fair sickening. Two of them. We can't get them out. I tried. One was still living, I think.'

But he, strong man and hearty, used to such work, weary with the hard day and with a pleasant picture of the bright little flat waiting him a dozen blocks away when the job was done, spoke cheerfully, confidently, saying that he'd have them out in a jiffy, as he stooped and crawled under the car on hands and knees.

Again he saw himself as he pressed the switch of his electric torch and looked. Again he saw the twin braids of heavy golden hair ere his thumb relaxed from the switch, leaving him in darkness.

'Is the one alive yet?' the shaken policeman asked.

And the question was repeated, while he struggled for will power sufficient to press on the light.

He heard himself reply, 'I'll tell you in a minute.'

Again he saw himself look. For a long minute he looked.

'Both dead,' he answered quietly. 'Clancey, pass in a number three jack, and get under yourself with another at the other end of the truck.'

He lay on his back, staring straight up at one single star that rocked mistily through a thinning of cloud-stuff overhead. The old ache was in his throat, the old harsh dryness in mouth and eyes. And he knew – what no other man knew – why he was in the Solomons, skipper of the teak-built yacht *Arangi,* running niggers, risking his head, and drinking more Scotch whisky than was good for any man.

Not since that night had he looked with warm eyes on any woman. And he had been noted by other whites as notoriously cold toward pickaninnies white or black.

But, having visioned the ultimate horror of memory, Van Horn was soon able to fall asleep again, delightfully aware, as he drowsed off, of Jerry's head on his shoulder. Once, when Jerry, dreaming of the beach at Meringe and of Mister Haggin, Biddy, Terrence, and Michael, set up a low whimpering, Van Horn roused sufficiently to soothe him closer to him, and to mutter ominously: 'Any nigger that'd hurt that pup . . .'

At midnight when the mate touched him on the shoulder, in the moment of awakening and before he was awake Van Horn did two things automatically and swiftly. He darted his right hand down to the pistol at his hip, and muttered: 'Any nigger that'd hurt that pup . . .'

'That'll be Kopo Point abreast,' Borckman explained, as both men stared to windward at the high loom of the land. 'She hasn't made more than ten miles, and no promise of anything steady.'

'There's plenty of stuff making up there, if it'll ever come down,' Van Horn said, as both men transferred their gaze to the clouds drifting with many breaks across the dim stars.

Scarcely had the mate fetched a blanket from below and turned in on deck, than a brisk, steady breeze sprang up from off the land, sending the *Arangi* through the smooth water at a nine-knot clip. For a time Jerry tried to stand the watch with Skipper, but he soon curled up and dozed off, partly on the deck and partly on Skipper's bare feet.

When Skipper carried him to the blanket and rolled him in, he was quickly asleep again; and he was quickly awake, out of the blanket, and padding after along the deck as Skipper paced up and down. Here began another lesson, and in five minutes Jerry learned it was the will of Skipper that he should remain in the blanket, that everything was all right, and that Skipper would be up and down and near him all the time.

At four the mate took charge of the deck.

'Reeled off thirty miles,' Van Horn told him. 'But now it is baffling again. Keep an eye for squalls under the land. Better throw the halyards down on deck and make the watch stand by. Of course they'll sleep, but make them sleep on the halyards and sheets.'

Jerry roused to Skipper's entrance under the blanket, and, quite as if it were a long-established custom, curled in between his arm and side, and, after one happy sniff and one kiss of his cool little tongue, as Skipper pressed his cheek against him caressingly, dozed off to sleep.

Half an hour later, to all intents and purposes, so far as Jerry could or could not comprehend, the world might well have seemed suddenly coming to an end. What awoke him was the flying leap of Skipper that sent the blanket one way and Jerry the other. The deck of the *Arangi* had become a wall, down which Jerry slipped through the roaring dark. Every rope and shroud was thrumming and screeching in resistance to the fierce weight of the squall.

'Stand by main halyards! – Jump!' he could hear Skipper shouting loudly; also he heard the high note of the mainsheet screaming across the sheaves as Van Horn, bending braces in the dark, was swiftly slacking the sheet through his scorching palms with a single turn on the cleat.

While all this, along with many other noises, squealings of boat-boys and shouts of Borckman, was impacting on Jerry's ear-drums, he was still sliding down the steep deck of his new and unstable world. But he did not bring up against the rail where his fragile ribs might well have been broken. Instead, the warm ocean water, pouring inboard across the buried rail in a flood of pale phosphorescent fire, cushioned his fall. A raffle of trailing ropes entangled him as he struck out to swim.

And he swam, not to save his life, not with the fear of death upon him. There was but one idea in his mind. *Where was Skipper?* Not that he had any thought of trying to save Skipper, nor that he might be of assistance to him. It was the heart of love that drives one always toward the beloved. As the mother in catastrophe tries to gain her babe, as the Greek who, dying, remembered sweet Argos, as soldiers on a stricken field pass with the names of their women upon their lips, so Jerry, in this wreck of a world, yearned toward Skipper.

The squall ceased as abruptly as it had struck. The *Arangi* righted with a jerk to an even keel, leaving Jerry stranded in the starboard scuppers. He trotted across the level deck to Skipper, who, standing erect on wide-spread legs, the bight of the mainsheet still in his hand, was exclaiming:

'Gott-fer-dang! Wind he go! Rain he no come!'

He felt Jerry's cool nose against his bare calf, heard his joyous sniff, and bent and caressed him. In the darkness he could not see, but his heart warmed with knowledge that Jerry's tail was surely bobbing.

Many of the frightened return boys had crowded on deck, and their plaintive, querulous voices sounded like the sleepy noises of a roost of birds. Borckman came and stood by Van Horn's shoulder, and both men, strung to their tones in the tenseness of apprehension, strove to penetrate the surrounding blackness with their eyes, while they listened with all their ears for any message of the elements from sea and air.

'Where's the rain?' Borckman demanded peevishly. 'Always wind first, the rain follows and kills the wind. There is no rain.'

Van Horn still stared and listened, and made no answer.

The anxiety of the two men was sensed by Jerry, who, too, was on his toes. He pressed his cool nose to Skipper's leg, and the rose-kiss of his tongue brought him the salt taste of sea-water.

Skipper bent suddenly, rolled Jerry with quick roughness into the blanket, and deposited him in the hollow between two sacks of yams lashed on deck aft of the mizzenmast. As an afterthought, he fastened the blanket with a piece of rope yarn, so that Jerry was as if tied in a sack.

Scarcely was this finished when the spanker smashed across overhead, the headsails thundered with a sudden filling, and the great mainsail, with all the scope in the boom-tackle caused by Van Horn's giving of the sheet, came across and fetched up to tautness on the tackle with a crash that shook the vessel and heeled her violently to port. This second knock-down had come from the opposite direction, and it was mightier than the first.

Jerry heard Skipper's voice ring out, first to the mate: 'Stand by main-halyards! Throw off the turns! I'll take care of the tackle!'; and, next, to some of the boat's crew: 'Batto! you fella slack spanker tackle quick fella! Ranga! you fella let go spanker sheet!'

Here Van Horn was swept off his legs by an avalanche of return boys who had cluttered the deck with the first squall. The squirming mass, of which he was part, slid down into the barbed wire of the port rail beneath the surface of the sea.

Jerry was so secure in his nook that he did not roll away. But when he heard Skipper's commands cease, and, seconds later, heard his cursings in the barbed wire, he set up a shrill yelping and clawed and scratched frantically at the blanket to get out. Something had happened to Skipper. He knew that. It was all that he knew, for he had no thought of himself in the chaos of the ruining world.

But he ceased his yelping to listen to a new noise – a thunderous slatting of canvas accompanied by shouts and cries. He sensed, and sensed wrongly, that it boded ill, for he did not know that it was the mainsail being lowered on the run after Skipper had slashed the boom-tackle across with his sheath-knife.

As the pandemonium grew, he added his own yelping to it until he felt a fumbling hand without the blanket. He stilled and sniffed. No, it was not Skipper. He sniffed again and recognized the person. It was Lerumie, the black whom had had seen rolled on the beach by Biddy only the previous morning, who, still more recently, had kicked him on his stub of a tail, and who not more than a week before he had seen throw a rock at Terrence.

The rope yarn had been parted, and Lerumie's fingers were feeling inside the blanket for him. Herry snarled his wickedest. The thing was sacrilege. He, as a white man's dog, was taboo to all blacks. He had early learned the law that no nigger must ever touch a white-god's dog. Yet Lerumie, who was all of evil, at this moment when the world crashed about their ears, was daring to touch him.

And when the fingers touched him, his teeth closed upon them. Next, he was clouted by the black's free hand with such force as to tear his clenched teeth down the fingers through skin and flesh until the fingers went clear.

Raging like a tiny fiend, Jerry found himself picked up by the neck, half-throttled, and flung through the air. And while flying through the air, he continued to squall his rage. He fell into the sea and went under, gulping a mouthful of salt water into his lungs, and came up strangling but swimming. Swimming was one of the things he did not have to think about. He had never had to learn to swim, any more than he had had to learn to breathe. In fact, he had been compelled to learn to walk; but he swam as a matter of course.

The wind screamed about him. Flying froth, driven on the wind's breath, filled his mouth and nostrils and beat into his eyes, stinging and blinding him. In the struggle to breathe he, all unlearned in the ways of the sea, lifted his muzzle high in the air to get out of the suffocating welter. As a result, off the horizontal, the churning of his legs no longer sustained him, and he went down and under perpendicularly. Again he emerged, strangling with more salt water in his windpipe. This time, without reasoning it out, merely moving along the line of least resistance, which was to him the line of greatest comfort, he straightened out in the sea and continued so to swim as to remain straightened out.

Through the darkness, as the squall spent itself, came the slatting of the

Jerry was picked up by the neck and flung through the air.

half-lowered mainsail, the shrill voices of the boat's crew, a curse of Borckman's, and, dominating all, Skipper's voice, shouting:
'Grab the leech, you fella boys! Hand on! Drag down strong fella! Come in mainsheet two blocks! Jump, damn you, jump!'

★ ★ ★ ★

At recognition of Skipper's voice, Jerry, floundering in the stiff and crisping sea that sprang up with the easement of the wind, yelped eagerly and yearningly, all his love for his new-found beloved eloquent in his throat. But quickly all sounds died away as the *Arangi* drifted from him. And then, in the loneliness of the dark, on the heaving breast of the sea that he recognized as one more of the eternal enemies, be began to whimper and cry plaintively like a lost child.

Further, by the dim, shadowy ways of intuition, he knew his weakness in that merciless sea with no heart of warmth, that threatened the unknowable thing, vaguely but terribly guessed, namely, death. As regarded himself, he did not comprehend death. He, who had never known the time when he was not alive, could not conceive of the time when he would cease to be alive.

Yet it was there, shouting its message of warning through every tissue cell, every nerve quickness and brain sensitivity of him – a totality of sensation that foreboded the ultimate catastrophe of life about which he knew nothing at all, but which, nevertheless, he *felt* to be the conclusive supreme disaster. Although he did not comprehend it, he apprehended it no less poignantly than do men who know and generalize far more deeply and widely than mere four-legged dogs.

As a man struggles in the throes of nightmare, so Jerry struggled in the vexed, salt-suffocating sea. And so he whimpered and cried, lost child, lost puppy-dog that he was, only half a year existent in the fair world sharp with joy and suffering. And he *wanted Skipper*. Skipper was a god.

On board the *Arangi*, relieved by the lowering of her mainsail, as the fierceness went out of the wind and the cloudburst of tropic rain began to fall, Van Horn and Borckman lurched toward each other in the blackness.

'A double squall,' said Van Horn. 'Hit us to starboard and to port.'
'Must a-split in half just before she hit us,' the mate concurred.

'And kept all the rain in the second half —'

Van Horn broke off with an oath.

'Hey! What's the matter along you fella boy?' he shouted to the man at the wheel.

For the ketch, under her spanker which had just then been flat-hauled, had come into the wind, emptying her after-sail and permitting her headsails to fill on the other tack. The *Arangi* was beginning to work back approximately over the course she had just traversed. And this meant that she was going back toward Jerry floundering in the sea. Thus, the balance, on which his life titubated, was inclined in his favour by the blunder of a black steersman.

Keeping the *Arangi* on the new tack, Van Horn set Borckman clearing the mess of ropes on deck, himself, squatting in the rain, undertaking to long-splice the tackle he had cut. As the rain thinned, so that the crackle of it on deck became less noisy, he was attracted by a sound from out over the water. He suspended the work of his hands to listen, and, when he recognized Jerry's wailing, sprang to his feet, galvanized into action.

'The pup's overboard!' he shouted to Borckman. 'Back you jib to wind'ard!'

He sprang aft, scattering a cluster of return boys right and left.

'Hey! You fella boat's crew! Come in spanker sheet! Flatten her down good fella!'

He darted a look into the binnacle and took a hurried compass bearing of the sounds Jerry was making.

'Hard down your wheel!' he ordered the helmsman, then leaped to the wheel and put it down himself, repeating over and over aloud, 'Nor'east by east a quarter, nor'east by east a quarter.'

Back and peering into the binnacle, he listened vainly for another wail from Jerry in the hope of verifying his first hasty bearing. But not long he waited. Despite the fact that by his manoeuvre the *Arangi* had been hove to, he knew that windage and sea-driftage would quickly send her away from the swimming puppy. He shouted Borckman to come aft and haul in the whaleboat, while he hurried below for his electric torch and a boat compass.

The ketch was so small that she was compelled to tow her one whaleboat astern on long double painters, and by the time the mate had it hauled in under the stern, Van Horn was back. He was undeterred by the barbed wire, lifting boy after boy of the boat's crew over it and dropping them sprawling into the boat, following himself, as the last, by swinging over on the spanker boom, and calling his last instructions as the painters were cast off.

'Get a riding light on deck, Borckman. Keep her hove to. Don't hoist the mainsail. Clean up the decks and bend the watch tackle on the main boom.'

He took the steering-sweep and encouraged the rowers with: 'Washee-washee, good fella, washee-washee!' – which is the *bêche-de-mer* for 'row hard.'

As he steered, he kept flashing the torch on the boat compass so that he could keep headed northeast by east a quarter east. Then he remembered that the boat compass, on such course, deviated two whole points from the *Arangi's* compass, and altered his own course accordingly.

Occasionally he bade the rowers cease, while he listened and called for Jerry. He had them row in circles, and work back and forth, up to windward and down to leeward, over the area of dark sea that he reasoned must contain the puppy.

'Now you fella boy listen ear belong you,' he said, toward the first. 'Maybe one fella boy hear'm pickaninny dog sing out, I give 'm that fella boy five fathom calico, two ten sticks tobacco.'

At the end of half an hour he was offering 'Two ten fathoms calico and ten ten sticks tobacco' to the boy who first heard 'pickaninny dog sing out.'

Jerry was in bad shape. Not accustomed to swimming, strangled by the salt water that lapped into his open mouth, he was getting loggy when first he chanced to see the flash of the captain's torch. This, however, he did not connect with Skipper, and so took no more notice of it than he did of the first stars showing in the sky. It never entered his mind that it might be a star nor even that it might not be a star. He continued to wail and to strangle with more salt water. But when he at length heard Skipper's voice he went immediately wild. He attempted to stand up and to rest his forepaws on Skipper's voice coming out of the darkness, as he would have rested his forepaws on Skipper's leg had he been near. The result was disastrous. Out of the horizontal, he sank down and under, coming up with a new spasm of strangling.

This lasted for a short time, during which the strangling prevented him from answering Skipper's cry, which continued to reach him. But when he could answer he burst forth in a joyous yelp. Skipper was coming to take him out of the stinging, biting sea that blinded his eyes and hurt him to breathe. Skipper was truly a god, his god, with a god's power to save.

Soon he heard the rhythmic clack of the oars on the thole-pins, and the joy in his own yelp was duplicated by the joy in Skipper's voice, which kept up a running encouragement, broken by objurgations to the rowers.

'All right, Jerry, old man. All right, Jerry. All right – Washee-washee, you fella boy! – Coming, Jerry, coming. Stick it out, old man. Stay with it – Washee-washee like hell! – Here we are, Jerry. Stay with it. Hang on, old boy, we'll get you – Easy . . . easy. 'Vast washee.'

And then, with amazing abruptness, Jerry saw the whaleboat dimly emerge from the gloom close upon him, was blinded by the stab of the torch full in his eyes, and, even as he yelped his joy, felt and recognized Skipper's hand clutching him by the slack of the neck and lifting him into the air.

He landed wet and soppily against Skipper's rain-wet chest, his tail bobbing frantically against Skipper's containing arm, his body wriggling, his tongue dabbing madly all over Skipper's chin and mouth and cheeks and nose. And Skipper did not know that he was himself wet, and that he was in the first shock of recurrent malaria precipitated by the wet and the excitement. He knew only that the puppy-dog, given him only the previous morning, was safe back in his arms.

While the boat's crew bent to the oars, he steered with the sweep between his arm and his side in order that he might hold Jerry with the other arm.

'You little son of a gun,' he crooned, and continued to croon, over and over. 'You little son of a gun.'

And Jerry responded with tongue-kisses, whimpering and crying as is the way of lost children immediately after they are found. Also, he shivered violently. But it was not from the cold. Rather was it due to his over-strung, sensitive nerves.

Again on board, Van Horn stated his reasoning to the mate.

'The pup didn't just calmly walk overboard. Nor was he washed overboard. I had him fast and triced in the blanket with a rope yarn.'

He walked over, the centre of the boat's crew and of the three-score return boys who were all on deck, and flashed his torch on the blanket still lying on the yams.

'That proves it. The rope-yarn's cut. The knot's still in it. Now what nigger is responsible?

He looked about at the circle of dark faces, flashing the light on them, and such was the accusation and anger in his eyes, that all eyes fell before his or looked away.

'If only the pup could speak,' he complained. 'He'd tell who it was.'

He bent suddenly down to Jerry, who was standing as close against his legs as he could, so close that his wet forepaws rested on Skipper's bare feet.

'You know 'm, Jerry, you known the black fella boy,' he said, his words quick and exciting, his hand moving in questing circles toward the blacks.

Jerry was all alive on the instant, jumping about, barking with short yelps of eagerness.

'I do believe the dog could lead me to him,' Van Horn confided to the mate. 'Come on, Jerry, find 'm, sick 'm, shake 'm down. Where is he, Jerry? Find 'm. Find 'm.'

All that Jerry knew was that Skipper wanted something. He must find something that Skipper wanted, and he was eager to serve. He pranced about aimlessly and willingly for a space, while Skipper's urging cries increased his excitement. Then he was struck by an idea, and a most definite idea it was. The circle of boys broke to let him through as he raced for'ard along the starboard side to the tight-lashed heap of trade-boxes. He put his nose into the opening where the wild-dog laired, and sniffed. Yes, the wild-dog was inside. Not only did he smell him, but he heard the menace of his snarl.

He looked up to Skipper questioningly. Was it that Skipper wanted him to go in after the wild-dog? But Skipper laughed and waved his hand to show that he wanted him to search in other places for something else.

He leaped away, sniffing in likely places where experience had taught him cockroaches and rats might be. Yet it quickly dawned on him that it was not such things Skipper was after. His heart was wild with desire to serve, and, without clear purpose, he began sniffing legs of black boys.

This brought livelier urgings and encouragements from Skipper, and made him almost frantic. That was it. He must identify the boat's crew and the return boys by their legs. He hurried the task, passing swiftly from boy to boy, until he came to Lerumie.

And then he forgot that Skipper wanted him to do something. All he knew was that it was Lerumie who had broken the taboo of his sacred person by laying hands on him, and that it was Lerumie who had thrown him overboard.

With a cry of rage, a flash of white teeth, and a bristle of short neck-hair, he sprang for the black. Lerumie fled down the deck, and Jerry pursued amid the laughter of all the blacks. Several times, in making the circuit of the deck, he managed to scratch the flying calves with his teeth. Then Lerumie took to the main rigging, leaving Jerry impotently to rage on the deck beneath him.

About this point the blacks grouped in a semi-circle at a respectful distance, with Van Horn to the fore beside Jerry. Van Horn centred his electric torch on the black in the rigging, and saw the long parallel scratches on the fingers of the hand that had invaded Jerry's blanket. He pointed them out significantly to Borckman, who stood outside the circle so that no black should be able to come at his back.

Skipper picked Jerry up and soothed his anger with:

'Good boy, Jerry. You marked and sealed him. Some dog, you, some big man-dog.'

He turned back to Lerumie, illuminating him as he clung in the rigging, and his voice was harsh and cold as he addressed him.

'What name belong along you fella boy?' he demanded.

'Me fella Lerumie,' came the chirping, quavering answer.

'You come along Pennduffryn?'

'Me come along Meringe.'

Captain Van Horn debated the while he fondled the puppy in his arms. After all, it was a return boy. In a day, in two days at most, he would have him landed and be quit of him.

'My word,' he harangued, 'me angry along you. Me angry big fella too much along you. Me angry along you any amount. What name you fella boy make 'm pickaninny dog belong along me walk about along water?'

Lerumie was unable to answer. He rolled his eyes helplessly, resigned to receive a whipping such as he had long since bitterly learned white masters were wont to administer.

Captain Van Horn repeated the question, and the black repeated the helpless rolling of his eyes.

'For two sticks tobacco I knock 'm seven bells outa you,' the skipper bullied. 'Now me give you strong fella talk too much. You look 'm eye belong you one time along this fella dog belong me, I knock 'm seven bells and whole starboard watch outa you. Savve?'

'Me savve,' Lerumie plaintively replied; and the episode was closed.

The return boys went below to sleep in the cabin. Borckman and the boat's crew hoisted the mainsail and put the *Arangi* on her course. And Skipper, under a dry blanket from below, lay down to sleep with Jerry, head on his shoulder, in the hollow of his arm.

INTO THE ENEMY CAMP
Robert Louis Stevenson

Jim Hawkins is cabin boy on board Hispaniola, *searching for treasure. The mate, Long John Silver, and some of the crew mutiny. Jim is injured in the fighting.*

Owing to the cant of the vessel, the masts hung far out over the water, and from my perch on the cross-trees I had nothing below me but the surface of the bay. Hands, who was not so far up, was, in consequence, nearer to the ship, and fell between me and the bulwarks. He rose once to the surface in a lather of foam and blood, and then sank again for good. As the water settled, I could see him lying huddled together on the clean, bright sand in the shadow of the vessel's side. A fish or two whipped past his body. Sometimes, by the quivering of the water, he appeared to move a little, as if he were trying to rise. But he was dead enough, for all that, both being shot and drowned, and was food for fish in the very place where he had designed my slaughter.

I was no sooner certain of this than I began to feel sick, faint, and terrified. The hot blood was running over my back and chest. The dirk, where it had pinned my shoulder to the mast, seemed to burn like a hot iron; yet it was not so much these real sufferings that distressed me, for these, it seemed to me, I could bear without a murmur; it was the horror I had upon my mind of falling from the cross-trees into that still green water, beside the body of the coxswain.

I clung with both hands till my nails ached, and I shut my eyes as if to cover up the peril. Gradually my mind came back again, my pulses quieted down to a more natural time, and I was once more in possession of myself.

It was my first thought to pluck forth the dirk; but either it stuck too hard or my nerve failed me; and I desisted with a violent shudder. Oddly enough, that very shudder did the business. The knife, in fact, had come the nearest in the world to missing me altogether; it held me by a mere pinch of skin, and this the shudder tore away. The blood ran down the faster, to be sure; but I was my own master again, and only tacked to the mast by my coat and shirt.

These last I broke through with a sudden jerk, and then regained the deck by the starboard shrouds. For nothing in the world would I have again ventured, shaken as I was, upon the overhanging port shrouds, from which Israel had so lately fallen.

I went below, and did what I could for my wound; it pained be a good deal, and still bled freely; but it was neither deep nor dangerous, nor did it greatly gall me when I used my arm. Then I looked around me, and as the ship was now, in a sense, my own, I began to think of clearing it from its last passenger – the dead man, O'Brien.

He had pitched, as I have said, against the bulwarks, where he lay like some horrible, ungainly sort of puppet; life-size, indeed, but how different from life's colour or life's comeliness! In that position, I could easily have my way with him; and as the habit of tragical adventures had worn off almost all my terror for the dead, I took him by the waist as if he had been a sack of bran, and, with one good heave, tumbled him overboard. He went in with a sounding plunge; the red cap came off, and remained floating on the surface; and as soon as the splash subsided, I could see him and Israel lying side by side, both wavering with the tremulous movement of the water. O'Brien, though still quite a young man, was very bald. There he lay, with that bald head across the knees of the man who had killed him, and the quick fishes steering over both.

I was now alone upon the ship; the tide had just turned. The sun was within so few degrees of setting that already the shadow of the pines upon the western shore began to reach right across the anchorage, and fall in patterns on the deck. The evening breeze had sprung up, and though it was well warded off by the hill with the two peaks upon the east, the cordage had begun to sing a little softly to itself and the idle sails to rattle to and fro.

I began to see a danger to the ship. The jibs I speedily doused and brought tumbling to the deck; but the mainsail was a harder matter. Of course, when the schooner canted over, the boom had swung out-board, and the cap of it and a foot or two of sail hung even under water. I thought this made it still more dangerous; yet the strain was so heavy that I half feared to meddle. At last, I got my knife and cut the halyards. The peak dropped instantly, a great belly of loose canvas floated broad upon the water; and since, pull as I liked, I could not budge the downhaul, that was the extent of what I could accomplish. For the rest, the *Hispaniola* must trust to luck, like myself.

By this time the whole anchorage had fallen into shadow – the last rays, I remember, falling through a glade of the wood, and shining bright as jewels, on the flowery mantle of the wreck. It began to be chill; the tide was rapidly fleeting seawards, the schooner settling more and more on her beam-ends.

I scrambled forward and looked over. It seemed shallow enough, and holding the cut hawser in both hands for a last security, I let myself drop softly overboard. The water scarcely reached my waist; the sand was firm and covered with ripple marks, and I waded ashore in great spirits, leaving the *Hispaniola* on her side, with her mainsail trailing wide upon the surface of the bay. About the same time the sun went fairly down, and the breeze whistled low in the dusk among the tossing pines.

At least, and at last, I was off the sea, nor had I returned thence empty-handed. There lay the schooner, clear at last from buccaneers and ready for our own men to board and get to sea again. I had nothing nearer my fancy than to get home to the stockade and boast of my achievements. Possibly I might be blamed a bit for my truantry, but the recapture of the *Hispaniola* was a clenching answer, and I hoped that even Captain Smollett would confess I had not lost my time.

So thinking, and in famous spirits, I began to set my face homeward for the block-house and my companions. I remembered that the most easterly of the rivers which drain into Captain Kidd's anchorage ran from the two-peaked hill upon my left; and I bent my course in that direction that I might pass the stream while it was small. The wood was pretty open, and keeping along the lower spurs, I had soon turned the corner of that hill, and waded to the mid-calf across the water-course.

This brought me near to where I had encountered Ben Gunn, the maroon; and I walked more circumspectly, keeping an eye on every side. The dusk had come nigh hand completely, and, as I opened out the cleft between the two peaks, I became aware of a wavering glow against the sky, where, as I judged, the man of the island was cooking his supper before a roaring fire. And yet I wondered, in my heart, that he should show himself so careless. For if I could see this radiance, might it not reach the eyes of Silver himself where he camped upon the shore among the marshes?

Gradually the night fell blacker; it was all I could do to guide myself even roughly towards my destination; the double hill behind me and the Spy-glass on my right hand loomed faint and fainter; the stars were few and pale; and in the low ground where I wandered I kept tripping among bushes and rolling into sandy pits.

Suddenly a kind of brightness fell about me. I looked up; a pale glimmer of moonbeams had alighted on the summit of the Spy-glass, and soon after I saw something broad and silvery moving low down behind the trees, and knew the moon had risen.

With this to help me, I passed rapidly over what remained to me of my journey; and, sometimes walking, sometimes running, impatiently drew near to the stockade. Yet, as I began to thread the grove that lies before it, I was not so thoughtless but that I slacked my pace and went a trifle warily. It would have been a poor end of my adventures to get shot down by my own party in mistake.

The moon was climbing higher and higher; its light began to fall here and there in masses through the more open districts of the wood; and right in front of me a glow of a different colour appeared among the trees. It was red and hot, and now and again it was a little darkened – as it were the embers of a bonfire smouldering.

For the life of me, I could not think what it might be.

At last I came right down upon the borders of the clearing. The western end was already steeped in moonshine; the rest, and the block-house itself, still lay in a black shadow, chequered with long, silvery streaks of light. On the other side of the house an immense fire had burned itself into clear embers and shed a steady, red reverberation, contrasted strongly with the mellow paleness of the moon. There was not a soul stirring, nor a sound beside the noises of the breeze.

I stopped, with much wonder in my heart, and perhaps a little terror also. It had not been our way to build great fires; we were, indeed, by the captain's orders, somewhat niggardly of firewood; and I began to fear that something had gone wrong while I was absent.

I stole round by the eastern end, keeping close in shadow, and at a convenient place, where the darkness was thickest, crossed the palisade as silently as possible.

To make assurance surer, I got upon my hands and knees, and crawled, without a sound, towards the corner of the house. As I drew nearer, my heart was suddenly and greatly lightened. It is not a pleasant noise in itself, and I have often complained of it at other times; but just then it was like music to hear my friends snoring together so loud and peaceful in their sleep. The sea-cry of the watch, that beautiful 'All's well', never fell more reassuringly on my ear.

In the meantime, there was no doubt of one thing; they kept an infamous bad watch. If it had been Silver and his lads that were now creeping in on them, not a soul would have seen daybreak. That was what it was, thought I, to have the captain wounded; and again I blamed myself sharply for leaving them in that danger with so few to mount guard.

By this time I had got to the door and stood up. All was dark within, so that I could distinguish nothing by the eye. As for sounds, there was the steady drone of the snorers, and a small occasional noise, a flickering or pecking that I could in no way account for.

With my arms before me I walked steadily in. I should lie down in my own place (I thought, with a silent chuckle) and enjoy their faces when they found me in the morning.

My foot struck something yielding – it was a sleeper's leg; and he turned and groaned, but without awakening.

And then, all of a sudden, a shrill voice broke forth out of the darkness:

'Pieces of eight! pieces of eight! pieces of eight! pieces of eight! pieces of eight!' and so forth, without pause or change, like the clacking of a tiny mill.

Silver's green parrot, Captain Flint! It was she whom I had heard pecking at a piece of bark; it was she, keeping better watch than any human being, who thus announced my arrival with her wearisome refrain.

I had no time left to recover. At the sharp, clipping tone of the parrot, the sleepers awoke and sprang up; and with a mighty oath, the voice of silver cried:

'Who goes:'

I turned to run, struck violently against one person, recoiled, and ran full into the arms of a second, who, for his part, closed upon me and held me tight.

'Bring a torch, Dick,' said Silver, when my capture was thus assured.

And one of the men left the log-house, and presently returned with a lighted brand.

★ ★ ★ ★

The red glare of the torch, lighting up the interior of the block-house, showed me the worst of my apprehensions realized. The pirates were in possession of the house and stores: there was the cask of cognac, there were the pork and bread, as before; and, what tenfold increased my horror, not a sign of any prisoner. I could only judge that all had perished, and my heart smote me sorely that I had not been there to perish with them.

There were six of the buccaneers, all told; not another man was left alive. Five of them were on their feet, flushed and swollen, suddenly called out of the first sleep of drunkenness. The sixth had only risen upon his elbow: he was deadly pale, and the bloodstained bandage round his head told that he had recently been wounded, and still more recently dressed. I remembered the man who had been shot and had run back among the woods in the great attack, and doubted not that this was he.

The parrot sat, preening her plumage, on Long John's shoulder. He himself, I thought, looked somewhat paler and more stern than I was used to. He still wore the fine broadcloth suit in which he had fulfilled his mission, but it was bitterly the worse for wear, daubed with clay and torn with the sharp briers of the wood.

'So,' said he, 'here's Jim Hawkins, shiver my timbers! dropped in, like, eh? Well, come, I take that friendly.'

And thereupon he sat down across the brandy cask, and began to fill a pipe.

'Give me a loan of the link, Dick,' said he; and then, when he had a good light, 'That'll do lad,' he added; 'stick the glim in the wood heap;

'Here's Jim Hawkins,' said Long John Silver.

and you, gentlemen, bring yourselves to! – you needn't stand up for Mr Hawkins; *he'll* excuse you, you may lay to that. And so, Jim' – stopping the tobacco – 'here you were, and quite a pleasant surprise for poor old John. I see you were smart when first I set my eyes on you; but this here gets away from me clean, it do.'

To all this, as may be well supposed, I made no answer. They had set me with my back against the wall; and I stood there, looking Silver in the face, pluckily enough, I hope, to all outward appearance, but with black despair in my heart.

Silver took a whiff or two of his pipe with great composure, and then ran on again.

'Now you see, Jim, so be as you *are* here,' says he, 'I'll give you a piece of my mind. I've always liked you, I have, for a lad of spirit, and the picter of my own self when I was young and handsome. I always wanted you to jine and take your share, and die a gentleman, and now, my cock, you've got to. Cap'n Smollett's a fine seaman, as I'll own up to any day, but stiff on discipline. "Dooty is dooty," says he, and right he is. Just you keep clear of the cap'n. The doctor himself is gone dead again you – "ungrateful scamp" was what he said; and the short and the long of the whole story is about here: you can't go back to your own lot, for they won't have you; and, without you start a third ship's company all by yourself, which might be lonely, you'll have to jine with Cap'n Silver.'

So far so good. My friends, then, were still alive, and though I partly believed the truth of Silver's statement, that the cabin party were incensed at me for my desertion, I was more relieved than distressed by what I heard.

'I don't say nothing as to your being in our hands,' continued Silver, 'though there you are, and you may lay to it. I'm all for argyment; I never seen good come out o' threatening. If you like the service, well, you'll jine; and if you don't, Jim, why, you're free to answer no – free and welcome, shipmate; and if fairer can be said, shiver my sides!'

'Am I to answer, then?' I asked, with a very tremulous voice. Through all this sneering talk, I was made to feel the threat of death that overhung me, and my cheeks burned and my heart beat painfully in my breast.

'Lad,' said Silver, 'no one's a-pressing of you. Take your bearings. None of us won't hurry you, mate; time goes so pleasant in your company, you see.'

'Well,' says I, growing a bit bolder, 'if I'm to choose, I declare I have a right to know what's what, and why you're here, and where my friends are.'

'Wot's wot?' repeated one of the buccaneers, in a deep growl. 'Ah, he'd be a lucky one as knowed that!'

'You'll, perhaps, batten down your hatches till you're spoken to, my friend,' cried Silver truculently to the speaker. And then, in his first gracious tones, he replied to me: 'Yesterday morning, Mr Hawkins,' said he, 'in the dog-watch, down came Dr Livesey with a flag of truce. Says he, "Cap'n Silver, you're sold out. Ship's gone." Well, maybe we'd been taking a glass, and a song to help it round. I won't say no. Leastways one of us had looked out. We looked out, and, by thunder: The old ship was gone. I never seen a pack o' fools look fishier; and you may lay to that, if I tells you that looked the fishiest. "Well," says the doctor, "let's bargain." We bargained, him and I, and here we are: stores, brandy, block-house, the firewood you was thoughtful enough to cut, and, in a manner of speaking, the whole blessed boat, from cross-trees to keelson. As for them, they've tramped; I don't know where's they are.'

He drew again quietly at his pipe.

'And lest you should take it into that head of yours,' he went on, 'that you was included in the treaty, here's the last word that was said: "How many are you," says I, "to leave?" "Four," says he – "four, and one of us wounded. As for that boy, I don't know where he is, confound him," says he, "nor I don't much care. We're about sick of him." These was his words.'

'Is that all?' I asked.

'Well, it's all that you've to hear, my son,' returned Silver.

'And now I am to choose?'

'And now you are to choose, and you may lay to that,' said Silver.

'Well,' said I, 'I am not such a fool but I know pretty well what I have to look for. Let the worst come to the worst, it's little I care. I've seen too many die since I fell in with you. But there's a thing or two I have to tell you,' I said, and by this time I was quite excited; 'and the first is this: here you are in a bad way: ship lost, treasure lost, men lost; your whole business gone to wreck; and if you want to know who did it – it was I! I was in the apple barrel the night we sighted land, and I heard you, John, and you, Dick Johnson, and Hands, who is now at the bottom of the sea, and told every word you said before the hour was out. And as for the schooner, it was I who cut her cable, and it was I that killed the men you had aboard of her, and it was I who brought her where you'll never see her more, not one of you. The laugh's on my side; I've had the top of this business from the first; I no more fear you than I fear a fly. Kill me, if you please, or spare me. But one thing I'll say, and no more; if you spare me, bygones are bygones, and when you fellows are in court for piracy, I'll save you all I can. It is for you to choose. Kill another, and do yourselves no good, or spare me and keep a witness to save you from the gallows.'

I stopped, for, I tell you, I was out of breath, and to my wonder, not a man of them moved, but all sat staring at me like as many sheep. And while they were still staring, I broke out again.

'And now, Mr Silver,' I said, 'I believe you're the best man here, and if things go the worst, I'll take it kind of you to let the doctor know the way I took it.'

'I'll bear it in mind,' said Silver, with an accent so curious that I could not, for the life of me, decide whether he were laughing at my request, or had been favourably affected by my courage.

'I'll put one to that,' cried the old mahogany-faced seaman – Morgan by name – whom I had seen in Long John's public-house upon the quays of Bristol. 'It was him that knowed Black Dog.'

'Well, and see here,' added the sea cook. 'I'll put another again to that, by thunder! for it was this same boy that faked the chart from Billy Bones. First and last, we've split upon Jim Hawkins!'

'Then here goes!' said Morgan, with an oath.

And he sprang up, drawing his knife as if he had been twenty.

'Avast there!' cried Silver. 'Who are you, Tom Morgan? Maybe you thought you was cap'n here, perhaps. By the powers, but I'll teach you better! Cross me, and you'll go where many a good man's gone before you, first and last, these thirty years back – some to the yard-arm, shiver my sides! and some by the board, and all to feed the fishes. There's never a man looked me between the eyes and seen a good day a'terwards, Tom Morgan, you may lay to that.'

Morgan paused; but a hoarse murmur rose from the others.

'Tom's right,' said one.

'I stood hazing long enough from one,' added another. 'I'll be hanged if I'll be hazed by you, John Silver.'

'Did any of you gentlemen want to have it out with *me*?' roared Silver, bending far forward from his position on the keg, with his pipe still glowing in his right hand. 'Put a name on what you're at; you ain't dumb, I reckon. Him that wants shall get it. Have I lived this many years, and a son of a rum-puncheon cock his hat athwart my hawse at the latter end of it? You know the way; you're all gentlemen o' fortune, by your account. Well, I'm ready. Take a cutlass, him that dares, and I'll see the colour of his inside, crutch and all, before that pipe's empty.'

Not a man stirred; not a man answered.

'That's your sort, is it?' he added, returning his pipe to his mouth. 'Well, you're a gay lot to look at, anyway. Not much worth to fight, you ain't. P'r'aps you can understand King George's English. I'm cap'n here by 'lection. I'm cap'n here because I'm the best man by a long sea-mile. You won't fight as gentlemen of fortune should; then, by thunder, you'll obey, and you may lay to it! I like that boy, now; I never seen a better boy than that. He's more a man than any pair of rats of you in this here house, and what I say is this: let me see him that'll lay a hand on him.'

There was a long pause after this. I stood straight up against the wall, my heart still going like a sledge-hammer, but with a ray of hope now shining in my bosom. Silver leant back against the wall, his arms crossed, his pipe in the corner of his mouth, as calm as though he had been in church; yet his eye kept wandering furtively, and he kept the tail of it on his unruly followers. They, on their part, drew gradually together towards the far end of the block-house, and the low hiss of their whispering sounded in my ear continuously like a stream. One after another they would look up, and the red light of the torch would fall for a second on their nervous faces; but it was not towards me, it was towards Silver that they turned their eyes.

'You seem to have a lot to say,' remarked Silver, spitting far into the air. 'Pipe up and let me hear it, or lay to.'

'Ax your pardon, sir,' returned one of the men; 'you're pretty free with some of the rules; maybe you'll kindly keep an eye upon the rest. This crew's dissatisfied; this crew don't vally bullying a marlin-spike; this crew has its rights like other crews, I'll make so free as that; and by your own rules, I take it we can talk together. I ax your pardon, sir, acknowledging that you to be capting at this present; but I claim my right, and steps outside for a council.'

And with an elaborate sea-salute, this fellow, a long, ill-looking, yellow-eyed man of five-and-thirty, stepped coolly towards the door and disappeared out of the house. One after another, the rest followed his example; each making a salute as he passed; each adding some apology. 'According to rules,' said one. 'Foc's'le council,' said Morgan. And so, with one remark or another, all marched out, and left Silver and me alone with the torch.

The sea cook instantly removed his pipe.

'Now, look you here, Jim Hawkins,' he said, in a steady whisper, that was no more than audible, 'you're within half a plank of death, and, what's a long sight worse, of torture. They're going to throw me off. But, you mark, I stand by you through thick and thin. I didn't mean to; no, not till you spoke up. I was about desperate to lose that much blunt, and be hanged into the bargain. But I see you was the right sort. I says to myself: You stand by Hawkins, John, and Hawkins'll stand by you. You're his last card, and, by the living thunder, John, he's yours! Back to back, says I. You save your witness, and he'll save your neck!'

I began dimly to understand.

'You mean all's lost?' I asked.

'Ay, by gum, I do!' he answered. 'Ship gone, neck gone – that's the size of it. Once I looked into that bay, Jim Hawkins, and seen no schooner – well, I'm tough, but I gave out. As for that lot and their council, mark me, they're outright fools and cowards. I'll save your life – if so be as I can – from them. But, see here, Jim – tit for tat – you save Long John from swinging.'

I was bewildered; it seemed a thing so hopeless he was asking – he, the old buccaneer, the ringleader throughout.

'What I can do, that I'll do,' I said.

'It's a bargain!' cried Long John. 'You speak up plucky, and, by thunder! I've a chance.'

He hobbled to the torch, where it stood propped among the firewood, and took a fresh light to his pipe.

'Understand me, Jim,' he said, returning. 'I've a head on my shoulders, I have. I'm on squire's side now. I know you've got that ship safe somewheres. How you done it, I don't know, but safe it is. I guess Hands and O'Brien turned soft. I never much believed in neither of them. Now you marks me. I ask no questions, nor I won't let others. I know when a

game's up, I do; and I know a lad that's staunch. Ah, you that's young –
you and me might have done a power of good together!'

He drew some cognac from the cask into a tin of cannikin.

'Will you taste, messmate?' he asked; and when I had refused: 'Well, I'll
take a drain myself, Jim,' said he. 'I need a caulker, for there's trouble on
hand. And, talking o' trouble, why did that doctor give me the chart,
Jim?'

My face expressed a wonder so unaffected that he saw the needlessness
of further questions.

'Ah, well, he did, though,' said he. 'And there's something under that,
no doubt – something, surely, under that, Jim – bad or good.'

And he took another swallow of the brandy, shaking his great fair head
like a man who looks forward to the worst.

THE ICEBERG
Jules Verne

In the 1860s three men, Professor Aronnax, his servant Conseil and a harpoonist were involved in the hunt for an unknown sea 'monster'. The monster turns out to be a man-made submarine commanded by Captain Nemo. The three men are abducted aboard the Nautilus *and are taken on an amazing underwater voyage of discovery.*

During the nights of the 13th and 14th of March the *Nautilus* returned to its southerly course. I fancied that, when on a level with Cape Horn, he would turn the helm westward, in order to beat the Pacific seas, and so complete the tour of the world. He did nothing of the kind, but continued on his way to the southern regions. Where was he going to? To the pole? It was madness! I began to think that the Captain's temerity justified Ned Land's fears. For some time past the Canadian had not spoken to me of his projects of flight; he was less communicative, almost silent. I could see that this lengthened imprisonment was weighing upon him, and I felt that rage was burning within him. When he met the Captain his eyes lit up with suppressed anger; and I feared that his natural violence would lead him into some extreme. That day, the 14th of March, Conseil and he came to me in my room. I inquired why.

'A simple question to ask you, sir,' replied the Canadian.

'Speak, Ned.'

'How many men are there on board the *Nautilus,* do you think?'

'I cannot tell, my friend.'

'I should say that its working does not require a large crew.'

'Certainly, under existing conditions, ten men, at the most, ought to be enough.'

'Well, why should there be any more?'

'Why?' I replied, looking fixedly at Ned Land, whose meaning was easy to guess. 'Because', I added, 'if my surmises are correct, and if I have well understood the Captain's existence, the *Nautilus* is not only a vessel: it is also a place of refuge for those who, like its commander, have broken every tie upon earth.'

'Perhaps so,' said Conseil; 'but, if any case, the *Nautilus* can only contain a certain number of men. Could not you, sir, estimate their maximum?'

'How, Conseil?'

'By calculation; given the size of the vessel, which you know, sir, and consequently, the quantity of air it contains, knowing also how much each man expends at a breath, and comparing these results with the fact that the *Nautilus* is obliged to go to the surface every twenty-four hours?'

Conseil had not finished the sentence before I saw what he was driving at.

'I understand,' said I; 'but that calculation, though simple enough, can give but a very uncertain result.'

'Never mind,' said Ned Land, urgently.

'Here it is then,' said I. 'In one hour each man consumes the oxygen contained in twenty gallons of air; and, in twenty-four that contained in 480 gallons. We must therefore find how many times 480 gallons of air the *Nautilus* contains.'

'Just so,' said Conseil. 'Or,' I continued, 'the size of the *Nautilus* being 1,500 tons; and one ton holding 200 gallons, it contains 300,000 gallons of air, which, divided by 480, gives a quotient of 625. Which means to say, strictly speaking, that the air contained in the *Nautilus* would suffice for 625 men for twenty-four hours.'

'Six hundred and twenty-five!' repeated Ned.

'But remember, that all of us, passengers, sailors and officers included, would not form a tenth part of that number.'

'Still too many for three men,' murmured Conseil.

The Canadian shook his head, passed his hand across his forehead, and left the room without answering.

'Will you allow me to make one observation, sir?' said Conseil. 'Poor Ned is longing for everything that he cannot have. His past life is always present to him; everything that we are forbidden he regrets. His head is full of old recollections. And we must understand him. What has he to do here? Nothing; he is not learned like you, sir; and has not the same taste for the beauties of the sea that we have. He would risk everything to be able to go once more into a tavern in his own country.'

Certainly the monotony on board must seem intolerable to the Canadian, accustomed as he was to a life of liberty and activity. Events were rare which could rouse him to any show of spirit; but that day an event did happen which recalled the bright days of the harpooner. About eleven in the morning, being on the surface of the ocean, the *Nautilus* fell in with a troop of whales – an encounter which did not astonish me, knowing that these creatures, hunted to the death, had taken refuge in high latitudes.

We were seated on the platform, with a quiet sea. The month of October in those latitudes gave us some lovely autumnal days. It was the Canadian – he could not be mistaken – who signalled a whale on the eastern horizon. Looking attentively one might see its black back rise and fall with the waves five miles from the *Nautilus*.

'Ah!' exclaimed Ned Land. 'If I was on board a whaler now such a meeting would give me pleasure. It is one of large size. See with what strength its blowholes throw up columns of air and steam! Confound it, why am I bound on these steel plates?'

'What, Ned,' said I, 'you have not forgotten your old ideas of fishing?'

'Can a whale-fisher ever forget his old trade, sir? Can he ever tire of the emotions caused by such a chase?'

'You have never fished in these seas, Ned?'

'Never, sir; in the northern only, and as much in Behring as in Davis Straits.'

'Then the southern whale is still unknown to you. It is the Greenland whale you have hunted up to this time, and that would not risk passing through the warm waters of the equator. Whales are localised, according to their kinds, in certain seas which they never leave. And if one of these creatures went from Behring to Davis Straits, it must be simply because there is a passage from one sea to the other, either on the American or the Asiatic side.'

'In that case, as I have never fished in these seas, I do not know the kind of whale frequenting them.'

'I have told you, Ned.'

'A greater reason for making their acquaintance,' said Conseil.

'Look! Look!' exclaimed the Canadian. 'They approach; they aggravate me; they know that I cannot get at them!'

Ned stamped his feet. His hand trembled as he grasped an imaginary harpoon.

'Are these cetacea as large as those of the northern seas?' asked he.

'Very nearly, Ned.'

'Because I have seen large whales, sir, whales measuring a hundred feet. I have even been told that those of Hullamoch and Umgallick, of the Aleutian Islands, are somethimes a hundred and fifty feet long.'

'That seems to me exaggeration. These creatures are only balaenopterons, provided with dorsal fins; and, like the cachalots, are generally much smaller than the Greenland whale.'

'Ah,' exclaimed the Canadian, whose eyes had never left the ocean, 'they are coming nearer; they are in the same water as the *Nautilus*!'

Then returning to the conversation, he said:

'You spoke of the cachalot as a small creature. I have heard of gigantic ones. They are intelligent cetacea. It is said of some that they cover themselves with seaweed and fucus, and then are taken for islands. People encamp upon them, and settle there; light a fire ——'

'And build houses,' said Conseil.

'Yes, joker,' said Ned Land. 'And one fine day the creature plunges, carrying with it all the inhabitants to the bottom of the sea.'

'Something like the travels of Sinbad the Sailor,' I replied laughing.

'Ah!' suddenly exclaimed Ned Lamb, 'It is not one whale: there are ten – there are twenty – it is a whole troop! And I not able to do anything! Hands and feet tied!'

'But, friend Ned,' said Conseil, 'why do you not ask Captain Nemo's permission to chase them?'

Conseil had not finished his sentence when Ned Land had lowered himself through the panel to seek the Captain. A few minutes afterwards the two appeared together on the platform.

Captain Nemo watched the troop of cetacea playing on the waters about a mile from the *Nautilus*.

'They are southern whales,' said he; 'there goes the fortune of a whole fleet of whalers.'

'Well, sir,' asked the Canadian, 'can I not chase them, if only to remind me of my old trade of harpooner?'

'And to what purpose?' replied Captain Nemo. 'Only to destroy! We have nothing to do with whale-oil on board.'

'But sir,' continued the Canadian, 'in the Red Sea you allowed us to follow the dugong.'

'Then it was to procure fresh meat for my crew. Here it would be killing for killing's sake. I know that is a privilege reserved for men, but I do not approve of such a murderous pastime. In destroying the southern whale (like the Greenland whale, an inoffensive creature), your traders do a culpable action, Master Land. They have already depopulated the whole of Baffin's Bay, and are annihilating a class of useful animals. Leave the unfortunate cetacea alone. They have plenty of natural enemies, cachalots, swordfish and sawfish, without *your* troubling them.'

The Captain was right. The barbarous and inconsiderate greed of these fishermen will one day cause the disappearance of the last whale in the ocean. Ned Land whistled 'Yankee-doodle' between his teeth, thrust his hands into his pockets and turned his back upon us. But Captain Nemo watched the troop of cetacea and, addressing me, said:

'I was right in saying that whales had natural enemies enough without counting man. These will have plenty to do before long. Do you see, M. Aronnax, about eight miles to leeward, those blackish moving points?'

'Yes, Captain,' I replied.

'Those are cachalots – terrible animals, which I have sometimes met in troops of two or three hundred. As to *those*, they are cruel mischievous creatures; they would be right in exterminating them.'

The Canadian turned quickly at the last words.

'Well, Captain,' said he, 'it is still time, in the interest of the whales.'

'It is useless to expose one's self, Professor. The *Nautilus* will disperse them. It is armed with a steel spur as good as Master Land's harpoon, I imagine.'

The Canadian did not put himself out enough to shrug his shoulders. Attack cetacea with blows of a spur! Who had ever heard of such a thing?

'Wait, M. Aronnax,' said Captain Nemo. 'We will show you something you have never yet seen. We have no pity for these ferocious creatures. They are nothing but mouth and teeth.'

Mouth and teeth! No one could better describe the macrocephalous cachalot, which is sometimes more than seventy-five feet long. Its enormous head occupies one-third of its entire body. Better armed than the whale, whose upper jaw is furnished only with whalebone, it is supplied with twenty-five large tusks, about eight inches long, cylindrical and conical at the top, each weighing two pounds. It is in the upper part of this enormous head, in great cavities divided by cartilages, that is to be found from six to eight hundred pounds of that precious oil called spermaceti. The cachalot is a disagreeable creature, more tadpole than fish, according to Fredol's description. It is badly formed, the whole of its left side being (if we may say it) a 'failure', and being only able to see with its right eye. But the formidable troop was nearing us. They had seen the whales and were preparing to attack them. One could judge before-hand that the cachalots would be victorious, not only because they were better built for attack than their inoffensive adversaries, but also because they could remain longer under water without coming to the surface. There was only just time to go to the help of the whales. The *Nautilus* went under water. Conseil, Ned Land and I took our places before the window in the saloon, and Captain Nemo joined the pilot in his cage to work his apparatus as an engine of destruction. Soon I felt the beatings of the screw quicken, and our speed increased. The battle between the cachalots and the whales had already begun when the *Nautilus* arrived. They did not at first show any fear at the sight of this new monster joining in the conflict. But they soon had to guard against its blows. What a battle! The *Nautilus* was nothing but a formidable harpoon, brandished by the hand of its captain. It hurled itself against the fleshy mass, passing through from one part to the other, leaving behind it two quivering halves of the animal. It could not feel the formidable blows from their tails upon its sides, nor the shock which it produced itself, much more. One cachalot killed, it ran at the next, tacked on the spot that it might not miss its prey, going forwards and backwards, answering to its helm, plunging when the cetacean dived into the deep waters, coming up with it when it returned to the surface, striking it front or sideways, cutting or tearing in all directions, and at any pace, piercing it with its terrible spur. What carnage! What a noise on the surface of the waves! What sharp hissing, and what snorting peculiar to these enraged animals! In the midst of these waters, generally so peaceful, their tails made perfect billows. For one hour this wholesale massacre continued, from which the cachalots could not escape. Several times ten or twelve united tried to crush the *Nautilus* by their weight. From the window we could see their enormous mouths studded with tusks, and their formidable eyes. Ned Land could not contain himself, he threatened and swore at them. We could feel them clinging to our vessel like dogs worrying a wild boar in a copse. But the *Nautilus*, working its screw, carried them here and there, or to the upper levels of the ocean, without caring for their enormous weight, nor the powerful strain on the vessel. At length the mass of cachalots broke up, the waves became quiet, and I felt that we were rising to the surface. The panel opened, and we hurried on to the platform. The sea was covered with mutilated bodies. A formidable explosion could not have divided and torn this fleshy mass with more violence. We were floating amid gigantic bodies, bluish on the back and white underneath, covered with enormous protuberances. Some terrified cachalots were flying towards the horizon. The waves were dyed red for several miles, and the *Nautilus* floated in a sea of blood. Captain Nemo joined us.

'Well, Master Land?' said he.

'Well, sir,' replied the Canadian, whose enthusiasm had somewhat calmed; 'it is a terrible spectacle, certainly. But I am not a butcher. I am a hunter, and I call this a butchery.'

'It is a massacre of mischievous creatures,' replied the Captain; 'and the *Nautilus* is not a butcher's knife.'

'I like my harpoon better,' said the Canadian.

'Every one to his own,' answered the Captain, looking fixedly at Ned Land.

I feared he would commit some act of violence, which would end in sad consequences. But his anger was turned by the sight of a whale which the *Nautilus* had just come up with. The creature had not quite escaped from the cachalot's teeth. I recognised the southern whale by its flat head, which is entirely black. Anatomically, it is distinguished from the white whale and the North Cape whale by the seven cervical vertebrae, and it has two more ribs than its congeners. The unfortunate cetacean was lying on its side, riddled with holes from the bites, and quite dead. From its mutilated fin still hung a young whale, which it could not save from the massacre. Its open mouth let the water flow in and out, murmuring like the waves breaking on the shore. Captain Nemo steered close to the corpse of the creature. Two of his men mounted its side, and I saw, not without surprise, that they were drawing from its breasts all the milk which they contained, that is to say, about two or three tons. The Captain offered me a cup of the milk, which was still warm. I could not help showing my repugnance to the drink; but he assured me that it was excellent, and not to be distinguished from cow's milk. I tasted it, and was of his opinion. It was a useful reserve to us, for in the shape of salt butter or cheese it would form an agreeable variety from our ordinary food. From that day I noticed with uneasiness that Ned Land's ill-will towards Captain Nemo increased, and I resolved to watch the Canadian's gestures closely.

★　★　★　★

The *Nautilus* was steadily pursuing its southerly course, following the fiftieth meridian with considerable speed. Did he wish to reach the pole? I did not think so, for every attempt to reach that point had hitherto failed. Again the season was far advanced, for in the antarctic regions, the 13th of March corresponds with the 13th of September of northern regions, which begin at the equinoctial season. On the 14th of March I saw floating ice in latitude 55°, merely pale bits of debris from twenty to twenty-five feet long, forming banks over which the sea curled. The *Nautilus* remained on the surface of the ocean. Ned Land, who had fished in the arctic seas, was familiar with its icebergs; but Conseil and I admired them for the first time. In the atmosphere towards the southern horizon stretched a white dazzling band. English whalers have given it the name of 'ice blink'. However thick the clouds may be, it is always visible, and announces the presence of an ice pack or bank. Accordingly, larger blocks soon appeared, whose brilliancy changed with the caprices of the fog. Some of these masses showed green veins, as if long undulating lines had been traced with sulphate of copper; others resembled enormous amethysts with the light shining through them. Some reflected the light of day upon a thousand crystal facets. Others shaded with vivid calcareous reflections resembled a perfect town of marble. The more we neared the south, the more these floating islands increased in both number and importance.

At the sixtieth degree of latitude, every pass had disappeared. But seeking carefully, Captain Nemo soon found a narrow opening, through which he boldly slipped, knowing, however, that it would close behind him. Thus, guided by this clever hand, the *Nautilus* passed through all the ice with precision which quite charmed Conseil; icebergs or mountains, ice-fields or smooth plains, seeming to have no limits, drift ice or floating ice packs, plains broken up, called *palchs* when they are circular, and streams when they are made up of long strips. The temperature was very low; the thermometer exposed to the air marked two or three degrees below zero, but we were warmly clad with fur, at the expense of the sea-bear and seal. The interior of the *Nautilus*, warmed regularly by its electric apparatus, defied the most intense cold. Besides, it would only have been necessary to go some yards beneath the waves to find a more bearable temperature. Two months earlier we should have had perpetual daylight in these latitudes; but already we had three or four hours night, and by and by there would be six months of darkness in these circumpolar regions. On the 15th of March we were in the latitude of New Shetland and South Orkney. The Captain told me that formerly numerous tribes of seals inhabited them; but that English and American whalers, in their rage for destruction, massacred both old and young; thus where there was once life and animation, they had left silence and death.

About eight o'clock in the morning of the 16th of March the *Nautilus*, following the fifty-fifth meridian, cut the antarctic polar circle. Ice surrounded us on all sides, and closed the horizon. But Captain Nemo went from one opening to another, still going higher. I cannot express my astonishment at the beauties of these new regions. The ice took most surprising forms. Here the grouping formed an oriental town, with innumerable mosques and minarets; there a fallen city thrown to the earth, as it were, by some convulsion of nature. The whole aspect was constantly changed by the oblique rays of the sun, or lost in the greyish fog amidst hurricanes of snow. Detonations and falls were heard on all sides, great overthrows of icebergs, which altered the whole landscape like a diorama. Often, seeing no exit, I thought we were definitely prisoners; but instinct guiding him at the slightest indication, Captain Nemo would discover a new pass. He was never mistaken when he saw the thin threads of bluish water trickling along the ice-fields; and I had no doubt that he had already ventured into the midst of these antarctic seas before. On the 16th of March, however, the ice-fields absolutely blocked our road. It was not the iceberg itself, as yet, but vast fields cemented by the cold. But this obstacle could not stop Captain Nemo: he hurled himself against it with frightful violence. The *Nautilus* entered the brittle mass like a wedge, and split it with frightful crackings. It was the battering ram of the ancients hurled by infinite strength. The ice, thrown high in the air, fell like hail around us. By its own power of impulsion our apparatus made a canal for itself; sometimes carried away by its own impetus it lodged on the ice-field, crushing it with its weight, and sometimes buried beneath it, dividing it by a simple pitching movement, producing large rents in it. Violent gales assailed us at this time, accompanied by thick fogs, through which, from one end of the platform to the other, we could see nothing. The wind blew sharply from all points of the compass, and the snow lay in such hard heaps that we had to break it with blows of a pickaxe. The temperature was always at five degrees below zero; every outward part of the *Nautilus* was covered with ice. A rigged vessel could never have worked its way there, for all the rigging would have been entangled in the blocked-up gorges. A vessel without sails, with electricity for its motive power and wanting no coal, could alone brave such high latitudes. At length, on the 17th March, after many useless assaults, the *Nautilus* was positively blocked. It was no longer either streams, packs or ice-fields, but an interminable and immovable barrier, formed by mountains soldered together.

'An iceberg!' said the Canadian to me.

I knew that to Ned Land, as well as to all other navigators who had preceded us, this was an inevitable obstacle. The sun appearing for an instant at noon, Captain Nemo took an observation as near as possible, which gave our situation at 51° 30' longitude and 67° 39' of S. latitude. We had advanced one degree more in this antarctic region. Of the liquid surface of the sea there was no longer a glimpse. Under the spur of the *Nautilus* lay stretched a vast plain, entangled with confused blocks. Here and there sharp points, and slender needles rising to a height of 200 feet; farther on a steep shore, hewn as it were with an axe, and clothed with greyish tints; huge mirrors, reflecting a few rays of sunshine, half drowned in the fog. And over this desolate face of nature a stern silence reigned, scarcely broken by the flapping of the wings of petrels and puffins. Everything was frozen – even the noise. The *Nautilus* was then obliged to stop in its adventurous course amid these fields of ice. In spite of our efforts, in spite of the powerful means employed to break up the ice, the *Nautilus* remained immovable. Generally, when we can proceed no farther, we have return still open to us; but here return was as impossible as advance, for every pass had closed behind us; and for the few moments when we were stationary, we were likely to be entirely blocked, which did, indeed, happen about two o'clock in the afternoon, the fresh ice forming around its sides with astonishing rapidity. I was obliged to admit that Captain Nemo was more than imprudent. I was on the platform at that moment. The Captain had been observing our situation for some time past, when he said to me:

'Well, sir, what do you think of this?'

'I think that we are caught, Captain.'

'So, M. Aronnax, you really think that the *Nautilus* cannot disengage itself?'

'With difficulty, Captain; for the season is already too far advanced for you to reckon on the breaking up of the ice.'

'Ah, sir!' said Captain Nemo, in an ironical tone, 'you will always be the same. You see nothing but difficulties and obstacles. I affirm that not only can the *Nautilus* disengage itself, but also that it can go farther still.'

'Farther to the south?' I asked, looking at the Captain.

'Yes, sir; it shall go to the pole.'

'To the pole!' I exclaimed, unable to repress a gesture of incredulity.

'Yes,' replied the Captain coldly, 'to the antarctic pole – to that unknown point from whence springs every meridian of the globe. *You* know whether I can do as I please with the *Nautilus!*'

Yes, I knew that. I knew that this man was bold, even to rashness. But to conquer those obstacles which bristled round the South Pole, rendering it more inaccessible than the North, which had not yet been reached by the boldest navigators, was it not a mad enterprise, one which only a maniac would have conceived? It then came into my head to ask Captain Nemo if he had ever discovered that pole which had never yet been trodden by a human creature.

'No, sir' he replied; 'but we will discover it together. Where others have failed, *I* will not fail. I have never yet led my *Nautilus* so far into southern seas; but, I repeat, it shall go farther yet.'

'I can well believe you, Captain,' said I in a slightly ironical tone. 'I believe you! Let us go ahead! There are no obstacles for us! Let us smash

The Nautilus *was obliged to stop amid the ice-fields.*

this iceberg! Let us blow it up; and if it resists, let us give the *Nautilus* wings to fly over it!'

'Over it, sir!' said Captain Nemo, quietly. 'No, not *over* it, but *under* it!'

'Under it!' I exclaimed, a sudden idea of the Captain's projects flashing upon my mind. I understood; the wonderful qualities of the *Nautilus* were going to serve us in this superhuman enterprise.

'I see we are beginning to understand one another, sir,' said the Captain, half smiling. 'You begin to see the possibility – I should say the success – of this attempt. That which is impossible for an ordinary vessel, is easy to the *Nautilus*. If a continent lies before the pole, it must stop before the continent; but if, on the contrary, the pole is washed by open sea, it will go even to the pole.'

'Certainly,' said I, carried away by the Captain's reasoning; 'if the surface of the sea is solidified by the ice, the lower depths are free by the providential law which has placed the maximum of density of the waters of the ocean one degree higher than freezing-point; and, if I am not mistaken, the portion of this iceberg which is above the water is as four to one to that which is below.'

'Very nearly, sir; for one foot of iceberg above the sea there are three below it. If these ice mountains are not more than 300 feet above the surface, they are not more than 900 beneath. And what are 900 feet to the *Nautilus*?'

'Nothing, sir.'

'It could even seek at greater depths that uniform temperature of sea water, and there brave with impunity the thirty or forty degrees of surface cold.'

'Just so, sir – just so,' I replied, getting animated.

'The only difficulty', continued Captain Nemo, 'is that of remaining several days without renewing our provision of air.'

'Is that all?' The *Nautilus* has vast reservoirs; we can fill them, and they will supply us with all the oxygen we want.'

'Well thought of, M. Aronnax,' replied the Captain, smiling. 'But not wishing to accuse me of rashness, I will first give you all my objections.'

'Have you any more to make?'

'Only one. It is possible, if the sea exists at the South Pole, that it may be covered; and, consequently, we shall be unable to come to the surface.'

'Good, sir! but do you forget that the *Nautilus* is armed with a powerful spur, and could we not send it diagonally against these fields of ice, which would open at the shock?'

'Ah, sir, you are full of ideas today.'

'Besides, Captain,' I added, enthusiastically, 'why should we not find the sea open at the South Pole as well as at the North? The frozen poles and the poles of the earth do not coincide, either in the southern or in the northern regions; and, until it is proved to the contrary, we may suppose either a continent or an ocean free from ice at these two points of the globe.'

'I think so too, M. Aronnax,' replied Captain Nemo. 'I only wish you to observe that, after having made so many objections to my project, you are now crushing me with arguments in its favour!'

The preparations for this audacious attempt now began. The powerful pumps of the *Nautilus* were working air into the reservoirs and storing it at high pressure. About four o'clock, Captain Nemo announced the closing of the panels on the platform. I threw one last look at the massive iceberg which we were going to cross. The weather was clear, the atmosphere pure enough, the cold very great, being twelve degrees below zero; but the wind having gone down, this temperature was not so unbearable. About ten men mounted the sides of the *Nautilus*, armed with pickaxes to break the ice around the vessel, which was soon free. The operation was quickly formed, for the fresh ice was still very thin. We all went below. The usual reservoirs were filled with the newly liberated water, and the *Nautilus* soon descended. I had taken my place with Conseil in the saloon; through the open window we could see the lower beds of the Southern Ocean. The thermometer went up, the needle of the compass deviated on the dial. At about 900 feet, as Captain Nemo had foreseen, we were floating beneath the undulating bottom of the iceberg. But the *Nautilus* went lower still – it went to the depth of four hundred fathoms. The temperature of the water at the surface showed twelve degrees, it was now only eleven; we had gained two. I need not say the temperature of the *Nautilus* was raised by its heating apparatus to a much higher degree; every manoeuvre was accomplished with wonderful precision.

'We shall pass it, if you please, sir,' said Conseil.

'I believe we shall,' I said in a tone of firm conviction.

In this open sea, the *Nautilus* has taken its course direct to the pole, without leaving the fifty-second meridian. From 67° 30' to 90°, twenty-two degrees and a half of latitude remained to travel; that is, about five hundred leagues. The *Nautilus* kept up a mean speed of twenty-six miles an hour – the speed of an express train. If that was kept up, in forty hours we should reach the pole.

For a part of the night the novelty of the situation kept us at the window. The sea was lit with the electric lantern; but it was deserted; fishes did not sojourn in these imprisoned waters: they found there a passage to take them from the antarctic ocean to the open polar sea. Our pace was rapid; we could feel it by the quivering of the long steel body. About two in the morning, I took some hours' repose, and Conseil did the same. In crossing the waist I did not meet Captain Nemo: I supposed him to be in the pilot's cage. The next morning, the 18th of March, I took my post once more in the saloon. The electric log told me that the speed of the *Nautilus* had been slackened. It was then going towards the surface; but prudently emptying its reservoirs very slowly. My heart beat fast. Were we going to emerge and regain the open polar atmosphere? No! A shock told me that the *Nautilus* had struck the bottom of the iceberg, still very thick, judging from the deadened sound. We had indeed 'struck', to use a sea expression, but in an inverse sense, and at a thousand feet deep. This would give three thousand feet of ice above us; one thousand being above the water-mark. The iceberg was then higher than at its borders – not a very reassuring fact. Several times that day the *Nautilus* tried again, and every time it struck the wall which lay like a ceiling above it. Sometimes it met with but 900 yards, only 200 of which rose above the surface. It was twice the height it was when the *Nautilus* had gone under the waves. I carefully noted the different depths, and thus obtained a submarine profile of the chain as it was developed under the water. That night no change had taken place in our situation. Still ice between four and five hundred yards in depth! It was evidently diminishing, but still what a thickness between us and the surface of the ocean! It was then eight. According to the daily custom on board the *Nautilus*, its air should have been renewed four hours ago; but I did not suffer much, although Captain Nemo had not yet made any demand upon his reserve of oxygen. My sleep was painful that night; hope and fear besieged me by turns: I rose several times. The groping of the *Nautilus* continued. About three in the morning, I noticed that the lower surface of the iceberg was only about fifty feet deep. One hundred and fifty feet now separated us from the surface of the waters. The iceberg was by degrees becoming an ice-field, the mountain a plain. My eyes never left the manometer. We were still rising diagonally to the surface, which sparkled under the electric rays. The iceberg was stretching both above and beneath into lengthening slopes; mile after mile it was getting thinner. At length, at six in the morning of that memorable day, the 19th day of March, the door of the saloon opened, and Captain Nemo appeared.

'The sea is open!' was all he said.

PROBLEM AT SEA
Agatha Christie

'Colonel Clapperton!' said General Forbes. He said it with an effect midway between a snort and a sniff.

Miss Ellie Henderson leaned forward, a strand of her soft grey hair blowing across her face. Her eyes, dark and snapping, gleamed with a wicked pleasure.

'Such a *soldierly*-looking man!' she said with malicious intent, and smoothed back the lock of hair to await the result.

'Soldierly!' exploded General Forbes. He tugged at his military mustache and his face became bright red.

'In the Guards, wasn't he?' murmured Miss Henderson, completing her work.

'Guards? Guards? Pack of nonsense. Fellow was on the music hall stage! Fact! Joined up and was out in France counting tins of plum and apple. Huns dropped a stray bomb and he went home with a flesh wound in the arm. Somehow or other got into Lady Carrington's hospital.'

'So that's how they met'.

'Fact! Fellow played the wounded hero. Lady Carrington had no sense and oceans of money. Old Carrington had been in munitions. She'd been a widow only six months. This fellow snaps her up. She wangled him a job at the War Office. *Colonel* Clapperton! Pah!' he snorted.

'And before the war he was on the music hall stage,' mused Miss Henderson, trying to reconcile the distinguished grey-haired Colonel Clapperton with a red-nosed comedian singing mirth-provoking songs.

'Fact!' said General Forbes. 'Heard it from old Bassington-ffrench. And he heard it from old Badger Cotterill who'd got it from Snooks Parker.'

Miss Henderson nodded brightly. 'That does seem to settle it!' she said.

A fleeting smile showed for a minute on the face of a small man sitting near them. Miss Henderson noticed the smile. She was observant. It had shown appreciation of the irony underlying her last remark – irony which the General never for a moment suspected.

The General himself did not notice the smiles. He glanced at his watch, rose and remarked: 'Exercise. Got to keep oneself fit on a boat,' and passed out through the open door onto the deck.

Miss Henderson glanced at the man who had smiled. It was a well-bred glance indicating that she was ready to enter into conversation with a fellow traveller.

'He is energetic – yes?' said the little man.

'He goes round the deck forty-eight times exactly,' said Miss Henderson. 'What an old gossip! And they say *we* are the scandal-loving sex.'

'What an impoliteness!'

'Frenchmen are always polite,' said Miss Henderson – there was the nuance of a question in her voice.

The little man responded promptly. 'Belgian, Mademoiselle.'

'Oh! Belgian.'

'Hercule Poirot. At your service.'

The name aroused some memory. Surely she had heard it before –?

'Are you enjoying this trip, M. Poirot?'

'Frankly, no. It was an imbecility to allow myself to be persuaded to come. I detest *la mer*. Never does it remain tranquil.'

'Well, you admit it's quite calm now.'

M. Poirot admitted this grudgingly. '*À ce moment,* yes. That is why I revive. I once more interest myself in what passes around me – your very adept handling of the General Forbes, for instance.'

'You mean –' Miss Henderson paused.

Hercule Poirot bowed. 'Your methods of extracting the scandalous matter. Admirable!'

Miss Henderson laughed in an unashamed manner. 'That touch about the Guards? I knew that would bring the old boy up spluttering and gasping.' She leaned forward confidentially. 'I admit I *like* scandal – the more ill-natured, the better!'

Poirot looked thoughtfully at her – her slim well-preserved figure, her keen dark eyes, her grey hair; a woman of forty-five who was content to look her age.

Ellie said abruptly: 'I have it! Aren't you the great detective?'

Poirot bowed. 'You are too amiable, Mademoiselle.'

'How thrilling,' said Miss Henderson. 'Are you "hot on the trail" as they say in books? Have we a criminal secretly in our midst? Or am I being indiscreet?'

'Not at all. Not at all. It pains me to disappoint your expectations, but I am simply here, like everyone else, to amuse myself.'

He said it in such a gloomy voice that Miss Henderson laughed.

'Oh! Well, you will be able to get ashore tomorrow at Alexandria. You have been to Egypt before?'

'Never, Mademoiselle.'

Miss Henderson rose somewhat abruptly.

'I think I shall join the General on his constitutional,' she announced.

Poirot sprang politely to his feet.

She gave him a little nod and passed out onto the deck.

A faint puzzled look showed for a moment in Poirot's eyes then, a little smile creasing his lips, he rose, put his head through the door and glanced down the deck. Miss Henderson was leaning against the rail talking to a tall, soldierly-looking man.

Poirot's smile deepened. He drew himself back into the smoking-room with the same exaggerated care with which a tortoise withdraws itself into its shell. For the moment he had the smoking-room to himself, though he rightly conjectured that that would not last long.

It did not. Mrs Clapperton, her carefully waved platinum head protected with a net, her massaged and dieted form dressed in a smart sports suit, came through the door from the bar with the purposeful air of a woman who has always been able to pay for anything she needed.

She said: 'John –? Oh! Good-morning, M. Poirot – have you seen John?'

'He's on the starboard deck, Madame. Shall I –?'

She arrested him with a gesture. 'I'll sit here a minute.' She sat down in a regal fashion in the chair opposite him. From the distance she had looked a possible twenty-eight. Now, in spite of her exquisitely made-up face, her delicately plucked eyebrows, she looked not her actual forty-nine years, but a possible fifty-five. Her eyes were a hard pale blue with tiny pupils.

'I was sorry not to have seen you at dinner last night,' she said. 'It was just a shade choppy, of course –'

'*Précisément,*' said Poirot with feeling.

'Luckily, I am an excellent sailor,' said Mrs Clapperton. 'I say luckily, because, with my weak heart, seasickness would probably be the death of me.'

'You have the weak heart, Madame?'

'Yes, I have to be *most* careful. I must *not* overtire myself! *All* the specialists say so!' Mrs Clapperton had embarked on the – to her – ever-fascinating topic of her health. 'John, poor darling, wears himself out trying to prevent me from doing too much. I live so intensely, if you know what I mean, M. Poirot?'

'Yes, yes.'

'He always says to me: "Try to be more of a vegetable, Adeline." But I can't. Life was meant to be *lived*, I feel. As a matter of fact I wore myself out as a girl in the war. My hospital – you've heard of my hospital? Of course I had nurses and matrons and all that – but *I* actually ran it.' She sighed.

'Your vitality is marvellous, dear lady,' said Poirot, with the slightly mechanical air of one responding to his cue.

Mrs Clapperton gave a girlish laugh.

"Everyone tells me how young I am! It's absurd. I never try to pretend I'm a day less than forty-three,' she continued with slightly mendacious candor, 'but a lot of people find it hard to believe. "You're so *alive*, Adeline," they say to me. But really, M. Poirot, what would one *be* if one wasn't alive?'

'Dead,' said Poirot.

Mrs Clapperton frowned. The reply was not to her liking. The man, she decided, was trying to be funny. She got up and said coldly: 'I must find John.'

As she stepped through the door she dropped her handbag. It opened and the contents flew far and wide. Poirot rushed gallantly to the rescue. It was some few minutes before the lipsticks, vanity boxes, cigarette case and lighter and other odds and ends were collected. Mrs Clapperton thanked him politely, then she swept down the deck and said, 'John –'

Colonel Clapperton was still deep in conversation with Miss Henderson. He swung round and came quickly to meet his wife. He bent over her protectively. Her deck chair – was it in the right place? Wouldn't it be better –? His manner was courteous – full of gentle consideration. Clearly an adored wife spoilt by an adoring husband.

Miss Ellie Henderson looked out at the horizon as though something about it rather disgusted her.

Standing in the smoking-room door, Poirot looked on.

A hoarse quavering voice behind him said:

'I'd take a hatchet to that woman if I were her husband.' The old gentleman known disrespectfully among the Younger Set on board as the Grandfather of All the Tea Planters, had just shuffled in. 'Boy!' he called. 'Get me a whisky peg.'

Poirot stooped to retrieve a torn scrap of notepaper, an overlooked item from the contents of Mrs Clapperton's bag. Part of a prescription, he noted, containing digitalin. He put it in his pocket, meaning to restore it to Mrs Clapperton later.

'Yes,' went on the aged passenger. 'Poisonous woman. I remember a woman like that in Poona. In '87 that was.'

'Did anyone take a hatchet to her?' inquired Poirot.

The old gentleman shook his head sadly.

'Worried her husband into his grave within the year. Clapperton ought to assert himself. Gives his wife her head too much.'

'She holds the purse strings,' said Poirot gravely.

'Ha ha!' chuckled the old gentleman. 'You've put the matter in a nutshell. Holds the purse strings. Ha, ha!'

Two girls burst into the smoking-room. One had a round face with freckles and dark hair streaming out in a windswept confusion, the other had freckles and curly chestnut hair.

'A rescue – a rescue!' cried Kitty Mooney. 'Pam and I are going to rescue Colonel Clapperton.'

'From his wife,' gasped Pamela Cregan.

'We think he's a *pet* . . .'

Two girls burst into the smoking room.

'And she's just awful – she won't let him do *anything*,' the two girls exclaimed.

'And if he isn't with her, he's usually grabbed by the Henderson woman . . .'

'Who's quite nice. But terribly *old* . . .'

They ran out, gasping in between giggles:

'A rescue – a rescue . . .'

That the rescue of Colonel Clapperton was no isolated sally, but a fixed project was made clear that same evening when the eighteen-year-old Pam Cregan came up to Hercule Poirot, and murmured: 'Watch us, M. Poirot. He's going to be cut out from under her nose and taken to walk in the moonlight on the boat deck.'

It was just at that moment that Colonel Clapperton was saying: 'I grant you the price of a Rolls Royce. But it's practically good for a lifetime. Now my car –'

'*My* car, I think, John.' Mrs Clapperton's voice was shrill and penetrating.

He showed no annoyance at her ungraciousness. Either he was used to it by this time, or else –

'Or else?' thought Poirot and let himself speculate.

'Certainly, my dear, *your* car,' Clapperton bowed to his wife and finished what he had been saying, perfectly unruffled.

'*Voilà ce qu'on appelle le pukka sahib*,' thought Poirot. 'But the General Forbes says that Clapperton is no gentleman at all. I wonder now.'

There was a suggestion of bridge. Mrs Clapperton, General Forbes and a hawk-eyed couple sat down to it. Miss Henderson had excused herself and gone out on deck.

'What about your husband?' asked General Forbes, hesitating.

'John won't play,' said Mrs Clapperton. 'Most tiresome of him.'

The four bridge players began shuffling the cards.

Pam and Kitty advanced on Colonel Clapperton. Each took an arm.

'You're coming with us!' said Pam. 'To the boat deck. There's a moon.'

'Don't be foolish, John,' said Mrs Clapperton. 'You'll catch a chill.'

'Not with us, he won't,' said Kitty. 'We're hot stuff!'

He went with them, laughing.

Poirot noticed that Mrs Clapperton said No Bid to her initial bid of Two Clubs.

He strolled out onto the promenade deck. Miss Henderson was standing by the rail. She looked round expectantly as he came to stand beside her and he saw the drop in her expression.

They chatted for a while. Then presently as he fell silent she asked: 'What are you thinking about?'

Poirot replied: 'I am wondering about my knowledge of English. Mrs Clapperton said: 'John won't play bridge.' Is not 'can't play' the usual term?'

'She takes it as a personal insult that he doesn't, I suppose,' said Ellie drily. 'The man was a fool ever to have married her.'

In the darkness Poirot smiled. 'You don't think its just possible that the marriage may be a success?' he asked diffidently.

'With a woman like that?'

Poirot shrugged his shoulders. 'Many odious women have devoted husbands. An enigma of Nature. You will admit that nothing she says or does appears to gall him.'

Miss Henderson was considering her reply when Mrs Clapperton's voice floated out through the smoking-room window.

'No – I don't think I will play another rubber. So stuffy. I think I'll go up and get some air on the boat deck.'

'Good-night,' said Miss Henderson. 'I'm going to bed.' She disappeared abruptly.

Poirot strolled forward to the lounge – deserted save for Colonel Clapperton and the two girls. He was doing card tricks for them, and noting the dexterity of his shuffling and handling of the cards, Poirot remembered the General's story of a career on the music hall stage.

'I see you enjoy the cards even though you do not play bridge,' he remarked.

'I've my reasons for not playing bridge,' said Clapperton, his charming smile breaking out. 'I'll show you. We'll play one hand.'

He dealt the cards rapidly, 'Pick up your hands. Well, what about it?' He laughed at the bewildered expression on Kitty's face. He laid down his hand and the others followed suit. Kitty held the entire club suit, M. Poirot the hearts, Pam the diamonds and Colonel Clapperton all the spades.

'You see?' he said. A man who can deal his partner and his adversaries any hand he pleases had better stand aloof from a friendly game! If the luck goes too much his way, ill-natured things might be said.'

'Oh!' gasped Kitty. 'How *could* you do that? It all looked perfectly ordinary.'

'The quickness of the hand deceives the eye,' said Poirot sententiously – and caught the sudden change in the Colonel's expression.

It was as though he realized that he had been off his guard for a moment or two.

Poirot smiled. The conjuror had shown himself through the mask of the *pukka sahib*.

The ship reached Alexandria at dawn the following morning.

As Poirot came up from breakfast he found the two girls all ready to go on shore. They were talking to Colonel Clapperton.

'We ought to get off now,' urged Kitty. 'The passport people will be going off the ship presently. You'll come with us, won't you? You wouldn't let us go ashore all by ourselves? Awful things might happen to us.'

'I certainly don't think you ought to go by yourselves,' said Clapperton, smiling. 'But I'm not sure my wife feels up to it.'

'That's too bad,' said Pam. 'But she can have a nice long rest.'

Colonel Clapperton looked a little irresolute. Evidently the desire to play truant was strong upon him. He noticed Poirot.

'Hullo, M. Poirot – you going ashore?'

'No, I think not,' M. Poirot replied.

'I'll – I'll – just have a word with Adeline,' decided Colonel Clapperton.

'We'll come with you,' said Pam. She flashed a wink at Poirot. 'Perhaps we can persuade her to come too,' she added gravely.

Colonel Clapperton seemed to welcome this suggestion. He looked decidedly relieved.

'Come along then, the pair of you,' he said lightly. They all three went along the passage of B deck together.

Poirot, whose cabin was just opposite the Clappertons, followed them out of curiosity.

Colonel Clapperton rapped a little nervously at the cabin door.

'Adeline, my dear, are you up?'

The sleepy voice of Mrs Clapperton from within replied: 'Oh, bother – what is it?'

'It's John. What about going ashore?'

'Certainly not.' The voice was shrill and decisive. 'I've had a very bad night. I shall stay in bed most of the day.'

Pam nipped in quickly, 'Oh, Mrs Clapperton, I'm so sorry. We did so want you to come with us. Are you sure you're not up to it?'

'I'm quite certain.' Mrs Clapperton's voice sounded even shriller.

The Colonel was turning the door-handle without result.

'What is it, John? The door's locked. I don't want to be disturbed by the stewards.'

'Sorry, my dear, sorry. Just wanted my Baedeker.'

'Well, you can't have it,' snapped Mrs Clapperton. 'I'm not going to get out of bed. Do go away, John, and let me have a little peace.'

'Certainly, certainly, my dear.' The Colonel backed away from the door. Pam and Kitty closed in on him.

'Let's start at once. Thank goodness your hat's on your head. Oh! gracious – your passport isn't in the cabin, is it?'

'As a matter of fact it's in my pocket –' began the Colonel.

Kitty squeezed his arm. 'Glory be!' she exclaimed. 'Now, come on.'

Leaning over the rail, Poirot watched the three of them leave the ship. He heard a faint intake of breath beside him and turned his head to see Miss Henderson. Her eyes were fastened on the three retreating figures.

'So they've gone ashore,' she said flatly.

'Yes. Are you going?'

She had a shade hat, he noticed, and a smart bag and shoes. There was a shore-going appearance about her. Nevertheless, after the most infinitesimal of pauses, she shook her head.

'No,' she said. 'I think I'll stay on board. I have a lot of letters to write.'

She turned and left him.

Puffing after his morning tour of forty-eight rounds of the deck, General Forbes took her place. 'Aha!' he exclaimed as his eyes noted the retreating figures of the Colonel and the two girls. 'So *that's* the game! Where's the Madam?'

Poirot explained that Mrs Clapperton was having a quiet day in bed.

'Don't you believe it!' The old warrior closed one knowing eye. 'She'll be up for tiffin – and if the poor devil's found to be absent without leave, there'll be ructions.'

But the General's prognostications were not fulfilled. Mrs Clapperton did not appear at lunch and by the time the Colonel and his attendant damsels returned to the ship at four o'clock, she had not shown herself.

Poirot was in his cabin and heard the husband's slightly guilty knock on his cabin door. Heard the knock repeated, the cabin door tried, and finally heard the Colonel's call to a steward.

'Look here, I can't get an answer. Have you a key?'

Poirot rose quickly from his bunk and came out into the passage.

The news went like wildfire round the ship. With horrified incredulity people heard that Mrs Clapperton had been found dead in her bunk – a native dagger driven through her heart. A string of amber beads was found on the floor of her cabin.

Rumour succeeded rumour. All bead sellers who had been allowed on board that day were being rounded up and questioned! A large sum in cash had disappeared from a drawer in the cabin! The notes had been traced! They had not been traced! Jewellery worth a fortune had been taken! No jewellery had been taken at all! A steward had been arrested and had confessed to the murder!

'What is the truth of it all?' demanded Miss Ellie Henderson, waylaying Poirot. Her face was pale and troubled.

'My dear lady, how should I know?'

'Of course you know,' said Miss Henderson.

It was late in the evening. Most people had retired to their cabins. Miss Henderson led Poirot to a couple of deck chairs on the sheltered side of the ship. 'Now tell me,' she commanded.

Poirot surveyed her thoughtfully. 'It's an interesting case,' he said.

'Is it true that she had some very valuable jewellery stolen?'

Poirot shook his head. 'No. No jewellery was taken. A small amount of loose cash that was in a drawer has disappeared, though.'

'I'll never feel safe on a ship again,' said Miss Henderson with a shiver. 'Any clue as to which of those coffee-coloured brutes did it?'

'No,' said Hercule Poirot. 'The whole thing is rather – strange.'

'What do you mean?' asked Ellie sharply.

Poirot spread out his hands. "*Eh bien* – take the facts. Mrs Clapperton had been dead at least five hours when she was found. Some money had disappeared. A string of beads was on the floor by her bed. The door was locked and the key was missing. The window – *window*, not port-hole – gives on the deck and was open.'

'Well?' asked the woman impatiently.

'Do you not think it is curious for a murder to be committed under those particular circumstances? Remember that the postcard sellers, money changers and bead sellers who are allowed on board are all well known to the police.'

'The stewards usually lock your cabin, all the same,' Ellie pointed out.

'Yes, to prevent any chance of petty pilfering. But this – was murder.'

'What are you thinking of, M. Poirot?' Her voice sounded breathless.

'I am thinking of the *locked door.*'

Miss Henderson considered this. 'I don't see anything in that. The man left by the door, locked it and took the key with him so as to avoid having the murder discovered too soon. Quite intelligent of him, for it wasn't discovered until four o'clock in the afternoon.'

'No, no, Mademoiselle, you don't appreciate the point I'm trying to make. I'm not worried as to how he got *out,* but as to how he got *in.*'

'The window of course.'

'C'est possible. But it would be a very narrow fit – and there were people passing up and down the deck all the time, remember.'

'Then through the door,' said Miss Henderson impatiently.

'But you forget, Mademoiselle. *Mrs Clapperton had locked the door on the inside.* She had done so before Colonel Clapperton had left the boat this morning. He actually tried it – so we *know* that is so.'

'Nonsense. It probably stuck – or he didn't turn the handle properly.'

'But it does not rest on his word. We actually heard *Mrs Clapperton herself say so.*'

'We?'

'Miss Mooney, Miss Cregan, Colonel Clapperton and myself.'

Ellie Henderson tapped a neatly shod foot. She did not speak for a moment or two. Then she said in a slightly irritable tone:

'Well – what exactly do you deduce from that? If Mrs Clapperton could lock the door she could unlock it too, I suppose.'

'Precisely, precisely.' Poirot turned a beaming face upon her. 'And you see where that leads us. *Mrs Clapperton unlocked the door and let the murderer in.* Now would she be likely to do that *for* a bead seller?'

Ellie objected: 'She might not have known who it was. He may have knocked – she got up and opened the door – and he forced his way in and killed her.'

Poirot shook his head. *'Au contraire.* She was lying peacefully in bed when she was stabbed.'

Miss Henderson stared at him. "What's your idea?" she asked abruptly.

Poirot smiled. 'Well, it looks, does it not, as though she *knew* the person she admitted . . .'

'You mean,' said Miss Henderson and her voice sounded a little harsh, *'that the murderer is a passenger on the ship?'*

Poirot nodded. 'It seems indicated.'

'And the string of beads left on the floor was a blind?'

'Precisely.'

'The theft of money also?'

'Exactly.'

There was a pause, then Miss Henderson said slowly: 'I thought Mrs Clapperton a very unpleasant woman and I don't think anyone on board really liked her – but there wasn't anyone who had any reason to kill her.'

'Except her husband, perhaps,' said Poirot.

'You don't really think –' She stopped.

'It is the opinion of every person on this ship that Colonel Clapperton would have been quite justified in "taking a hatchet to her." That was, I think, the expression used.'

Ellie Henderson looked at him – waiting.

'But I am bound to say,' went on Poirot, 'that I myself have not noted any signs of exasperation on the good Colonel's part. Also, what is more important, he had an alibi. He was with those two girls all day and did not return to the ship till four o'clock. By then, Mrs Clapperton had been dead many hours.'

There was another minute of silence. Ellie Henderson said softly: 'But you still think – a passenger on the ship?'

Poirot bowed his head.

Ellie Henderson laughed suddenly – a reckless defiant laugh. 'Your theory may be difficult to prove, M. Poirot. There are a good many passengers on this ship.'

Poirot bowed to her. 'I will use a phrase from one of your detective story writers. "I have my methods, Watson".'

The following evening, at dinner, every passenger found a typewritten slip by his plate requesting him to be in the main lounge at 8.30. When the company were assembled, the Captain stepped onto the raised platform

151

where the orchestra usually played and addressed them.

'Ladies and Gentlemen, you all know of the tragedy which took place yesterday. I am sure you all wish to co-operate in bringing the perpetrator of that foul crime to justice.' He paused and cleared his throat. 'We have on board with us M. Hercule Poirot who is probably known to you all as a man who has had wide experience in – er – such matters. I hope you will listen carefully to what he has to say.'

It was at this minute that Colonel Clapperton who had not been at dinner came in and sat down next to General Forbes. He looked like a man bewildered by sorrow – not at all like a man conscious of great relief. Either he was a very good actor or else he had been genuinely fond of his disagreeable wife.

'M. Hercule Poirot,' said the Captain and stepped down. Poirot took his place. He looked comically self-important as he beamed on his audience.

'Messieurs, Mesdames,' he began. 'It is most kind of you to be so indulgent as to listen to me. M. le Capitaine has told you that I have had a certain experience in these matters. I have, it is true, a little idea of my own about how to get to the bottom of this particular case.' He made a sign and a steward pushed forward and passed up to him a bulky, shapeless object wrapped in a sheet.

'What I am about to do may surprise you a little,' Poirot warned them. 'It may occur to you that I am eccentric, perhaps mad. Nevertheless I assure you that behind my madness there is – as you English say – a method'.

His eyes met those of Miss Henderson for just a minute. He began unwrapping the bulky object.

'I have here, *Messieurs* and *Mesdames,* an important witness to the truth of who killed Mrs Clapperton.' With a deft hand he whisked away the last enveloping cloth, and the object it concealed was revealed – an almost life-sized wooden doll, dressed in a velvet suit and lace collar.

'Now, Arthur,' said Poirot and his voice changed subtly – it was no longer foreign – it had instead a confident English, a slightly Cockney inflection. 'Can you tell me – I repeat – can you tell me – anything at all about the death of Mrs Clapperton?'

The doll's neck oscillated a little, its wooden lower jaw dropped and wavered and a shrill high-pitched woman's voice spoke:

'*What is it, John? The door's locked. I don't want to be disturbed by the stewards. . .*'

There was a cry – an overturned chair – a man stood swaying, his hand to his throat – trying to speak – trying . . . Then suddenly, his figure seemed to crumple up. He pitched headlong.

It was Colonel Clapperton.

Poirot and the ship's doctor rose from their knees by the prostrate figure.

'All over, I'm afraid. Heart,' said the doctor briefly.

Poirot nodded. 'The shock of having his trick seen through,' he said.

He turned to General Forbes. 'It was you, General, who gave me a valuable hint with your mention of the music hall stage. I puzzle – I think – and then it comes to me. Supposing that before the war Clapperton was a *ventriloquist*. In that case, it would be perfectly possible for three people to hear Mrs Clapperton speak from inside her cabin *when she was already dead . . .*'

Ellie Henderson was beside him. Her eyes were dark and full of pain. 'Did you know his heart was weak?' she asked.

'I guessed it . . . Mrs Clapperton talked of her own heart being affected, but she struck me as the type of woman who likes to be thought ill. Then I picked up a torn prescription with a very strong dose of digitalin in it. Digitalin is a heart medicine but it couldn't be Mrs Clapperton's because digitalin dilates the pupils of the eyes. I had never noticed such a phenomenon with her – but when I looked at his eyes I saw the signs at once.'

Ellie murmured: 'So you thought – it might end – this way?'

'The best way, don't you think, Mademoiselle?' he said gently.

He saw the tears rise in her eyes. She said: 'You've known. You've known all along. . . That I cared. . . But he didn't do it for *me* . . . It was those girls – youth – it made him feel his slavery. He wanted to be free before it was too late . . . Yes, I'm sure that's how it was . . . When did you guess – that it was he?'

'His self-control was too perfect,' said Poirot simply. 'No matter how galling his wife's conduct, it never seemed to touch him. That meant either that he was so used to it that it no longer stung him, or else – *eh bien* – I decided on the latter alternative . . . And I was right . . .

'And then there was his insistence on his conjuring ability – the

153

evening before the crime. He pretended to give himself away. But a man like Clapperton doesn't give himself away. There must be a reason. So long as people thought he had been a *conjuror* they weren't likely to think of his having been a *ventriloquist*.'

'And the voice we heard – Mrs Clapperton's voice?'

'One of the stewardesses had a voice not unlike hers. I induced her to hide behind the stage and taught her the words to say.'

'It was a trick – a cruel trick,' cried out Ellie.

'I do not approve of murder,' said Hercule Poirot.

ORDEAL
Angus Macdonald

On 6th November, 1942 the Ellerman liner City of Cairo, *five days out of Cape Town was torpedoed by a German U-boat. Many of the passengers and crew were either killed or went down with the ship. A few were lucky enough to take to the lifeboats. One of them was Quartermaster Angus Macdonald. This is his story.*

I was a quartermaster and had charge of No. 4 lifeboat. After seeing everything in order there and the boat lowered, I went over to the starboard side of the ship to where my mate, quartermaster Bob Ironside, was having difficulty in lowering his boat. I climbed inside the boat to clear a rope fouling the lowering gear, and was standing in the boat pushing it clear of the ship's side as it was being lowered, when a second torpedo exploded right underneath and blew the boat to bits. I remember a great flash, and then felt myself flying through space, then going down and down. When I came to I was floating in the water, and could see all sorts of wreckage around me in the dark. I could not get the light on my life-jacket to work, so I swam towards the largest bit of wreckage I could see in the darkness. This turned out to be No. 1 lifeboat and it was nearly submerged, it having been damaged by the second explosion. There were a few people clinging to the gunwale, which was down to water-level, and other people were sitting inside the flooded boat.

I climbed on board, and had a good look around to see if the boat was badly damaged. Some of the gear had floated away, and what was left was in a tangled mess. There were a few lascars, several women and children, and two European male passengers in the boat, and I explained to them that if some of them would go overboard and hang on to the gunwale or the wreckage near us for a few minutes we could bale out the boat and make it seaworthy. The women who were there acted immediately. They climbed outboard and, supported by the life-jackets every one was wearing, held on to an empty tank that was floating near by. I felt very proud of these women and children. One woman (whose name, if I remember rightly, was Lady Tibbs) had three children, and the four of them were the first to swim to the tank. One young woman was left in the boat with two babies in her arms.

We men then started to bale out the water. It was a long and arduous task, as just when we had the gunwale a few inches clear, the light swell running would roll in and swamp the boat again. Eventually we managed to bale out the boat, and then we started to pick up survivors who were floating on rafts or just swimming. As we worked we could see the *City of Cairo* still afloat, but well down in the water, until we heard someone say, 'There she goes.' We watched her go down, stern first, her bow away up in the air, and then she went down and disappeared. There was no show of emotion, and we were all quiet. I expect the others, like myself, were wondering what would happen to us.

We picked up more survivors as the night wore on, and by the first light of dawn the boat was full. There were still people on the rafts we could see with the daylight, and in the distance were other lifeboats. We rowed around picking up more people, among them Mr Sydney Britt, the chief officer, and quartermaster Bob Ironside, who was in No. 3 boat with me when the second torpedo struck. Bob's back had been injured, and one of his hands had been cut rather badly. We picked up others, then rowed to the other boats to see what decision had been made about our future. Mr Britt had, naturally, taken over command of our boat, and now he had a conference with Captain Rogerson, who was in another boat. They decided we would make for the nearest land, the island of St Helena, lying five hundred miles due north. We transferred people from boat to boat so that families could be together. Mr Britt suggested that, as our boat was in a bad way, with many leaks and a damaged rudder, and at least half its water-supply lost, all the children should shift to a dry boat and a few adults take their places in our boat.

When everything was settled we set sail and started on our long voyage. Our boat was now overcrowded with fifty-four persons on board – twenty-three Europeans, including three women, and thirty-one lascars. There was not enough room for everyone to sit down, so we had to take turns having a rest. The two worst injured had to lie down flat, so we made a place in the bows for Miss Taggart, a ship's stewardess, and cleared a space aft for my mate, quartermaster Bob Ironside. We did not know exactly what was wrong with Bob's back. We had a doctor in the boat, Dr Taskar, but he was in a dazed condition and not able to attend to the injured, so we bandaged them up as best we could with the first-aid materials on hand. The youngest person among us, Mrs Diana Jarman, one of the ship's passengers, and only about twenty years of age, was a great help with the first-aid. She could never do enough, either in attending to the sick and injured, boat work, or even actually handling the craft. She showed up some of the men in the boat, who seemed to lose heart from the beginning.

Once we were properly under way Mr Britt spoke to us all. He explained all the difficulties that lay ahead, and asked every one to pull their weight in everything to do with managing the boat, such as rowing during calm periods and keeping a look-out at night. He also explained that as we had lost nearly half our drinking water we must start right away on short rations. We could get two tablespoonfuls a day per person, one in the morning and one in the evening. He told us there were no passengers in a lifeboat, and every one would have to take turns baling as the boat was leaking very badly.

Before noon on that first day we saw our first sharks. They were enormous, and as they glided backward and forward under the boat it seemed they would hit and capsize us. They just skimmed the boat each time they passed, and they were never to leave us all the time we were in the boat.

The first night was quiet and the weather was fine, but we didn't get much rest. A good proportion of us had to remain standing for long periods, and now and then someone would fall over in their sleep. I was in the fore-part of the boat attending to the sails and the running gear, helped by Robert Watts from Reading, whom we called 'Tiny' because he was a big man. He didn't know much about seamanship, as he was an aeronautical engineer, but he said to me that first day, 'If you want anything done at any time just explain the job to me and I'll do it.' His help was very welcome as we did not have many of the crew available for the jobs that needed to be done. From the very beginning the lascars refused to help in any way, and just lay in the bottom of the boat, sometimes in over a foot of water.

On the second day the wind increased, and we made good speed. Sometimes the boats were close together and at other times almost out of sight of each other. Our boat seemed to sail faster than the others, so Mr Britt had the idea that we might go ahead on our own. If we could sail faster than the others, and as we were leaking so badly, we should go ahead and when we got to St Helena we could send help to the others. Mr Britt had a talk with Captain Rogerson when our boats were close, and the captain said that if the mate thought that was the best plan then go ahead. So we carried on on our own.

During the hours of darkness the wind rose stronger, and, as we could see the running gear was not in the best of condition, we hove to. As it got still worse, we had to put out a sea anchor to take turns at the steering-oar to hold the boat into the seas. We had a bad night, and two or three times sea broke over the heavily laden boat and soaked us all to the skin. It was during the night that we noticed Dr Taskar was failing mentally. Every now and then he shouted, 'Boy, bring me coffee,' or, 'Boy, another beer.' He had a rip in his trousers, and in the crowded boat during the night he cut a large piece out of the trousers of the ship's storekeeper, Frank Stobbart. I noticed the doctor with the knife and a piece of cloth in his hand. He was trying to fit the cloth over his own trousers. I pacified him and took his knife, a small silver knife with a whisky advertisement on the side. I had the same knife all through the years I was a prisoner in Germany, and only lost it after the war while serving in another Ellerman liner.

At noon on the third day the wind abated, and we set sails again and went on. We had lost sight of the other boats now and were on our own. We all expected to see a rescue ship or plane at any time, but nothing turned up. On the evening of the fourth day the doctor got worse, and rambled in his speech. He kept asking for water, and once Mr Britt gave him an extra ration, although there was not much to spare. During the night the doctor slumped over beside me, and I knew he was dead. That was the first death in the boat. We cast the body overboard at dawn while Mr Britt read a short prayer. We all felt gloomy after this first burial, and wondered who would be next.

Later in the day I crawled over to have a yarn with my mate Bob, and he said, 'Do you think we have a chance, Angus?' I said, 'Everything will be all right, Bob. We are bound to be picked up.' Bob hadn't long been married, and he was anxious about his wife and little baby in Aberdeen. He couldn't sit up, and I was afraid his back was broken or badly damaged.

Day and night the lascars kept praying to Allah, and repeating 'Pani, sahib, pani, sahib,' and they would never understand that the water was precious and had to be rationed out. On the sixth morning we found three of them dead in the bottom of the boat. The old engine-room serang read a prayer for them, and Tiny and I pushed them overboard, as the lascars never would help to bury their dead. The only two natives who helped us at any time were the old serang, a proper gentleman, and a fireman from Zanzibar, and they couldn't do enough to help.

We were getting flat calms for long periods, and we lowered the sails and used the oars. We didn't make much headway, but the work helped to keep our minds and bodies occupied. I know that doing these necessary tasks helped to keep me physically fit and able to stand up to the ordeal that lay ahead. There were a few Europeans who never gave a helping hand, and I noticed that they were the first to fail mentally. They died in the first two weeks.

I was worried about Miss Taggart's sores, as they had now festered and we had nothing to dress them with except salt water. With her lying in the same position all the time her back was a mass of sores. Tiny knew more about first-aid than the rest of us, and with the aid of old life-jackets he padded her up a bit. But on the seventh night she died and slipped down from her position in the bows. As she fell she got tangled up with another passenger, a Mr Ball from Calcutta, and when we got things straightened out they were both dead. A few more lascars died during the same night, and we had to bury them all at daybreak. The sharks were there in shoals that morning, and the water was churned up as they glided backward and forward near the bodies. Things were now getting worse on board, and a good few of the people sat all day with their heads on their chests doing and saying nothing. I talked to one young engineer, and told him to pull himself together as he was young and healthy and to take a lesson from Diana, who was always cheerful and bright. She had told us, 'Please don't call me Mrs Jarman; just call me Diana.' The young engineer did pull himself back to normal but within two days he dropped back and gave up hope and died. As we buried the bodies the boat gradually became lighter and the worst leaks rose above the water-line, so there was not so much water to bale out, although we had still to bale day and night.

Our own ship's stewardess, Annie Crouch, died on the tenth day. She had been failing mentally and physically for a time, and persisted in sitting in the bottom of the boat. We shifted her to drier places, but she always slid back. Her feet and legs had swollen enormously. Her death left only one woman among us, Diana. She was still active and full of life, and she spent most of her time at the tiller. Mr Britt was beginning to show signs of mental strain, and often mumbled to himself. If I asked him a question he would answer in a dazed sort of way. I worried about him a lot, for he was always a gentleman, and every one thought the world of him. On the twelfth day he was unable to sit up or talk, so we laid him down alongside Bob Ironside, who was also failing fast. Bob called me over one day, and asked me if I thought there was still a chance. I said certainly there was, and urged him not to give up hope as he would soon be home. He said, 'I can't hang on much longer, Angus. When I die, will you take off my ring and send it home if you ever get back?' There were only a few able-bodied men left among the Europeans now, and Tiny Watts, my right-hand man, died on the fourteenth morning. He hadn't complained at any time, and I was surprised when I found him dead. We buried seven bodies that morning: five lascars, Tiny, and Frank Stobbart. It took a long time to get them overboard, and I had to lie down and rest during the operation.

On the fifteenth morning at dawn both Mr Britt and Bob were dead, also three other Europeans and a few lascars. A few more lascars died during the day. One of the firemen said that if he couldn't get extra water he would jump overboard, and later in the day he jumped over the stern. He had forgotten to take off his life-jacket, and as we were now too weak to turn the boat round to save him, the sharks got him before he could drown. The remaining survivors voted that I should take over command. On looking through Mr Britt's papers I could see the estimated distances for each day up to about the tenth day, but after that there were only scrawls and scribbles. When I checked up on the water I found we had enough only for a few days, so I suggested cutting down the issue to one tablespoonful a day. There were plenty of biscuits and malted-milk tablets, but without water to moisten the mouth the biscuits only went into a powder and fell out of the corner of the mouth again. Those people with false teeth had still more trouble as the malted-milk tablets went into a doughy mess and stuck to their teeth.

The boat was now much drier, and there was not so much baling to do as we rode higher in the water and most of the leaks were above the surface. The movement, however, was not so steady as when we were heavier laden, but about the middle of the seventeenth night the boat appeared to become very steady again. I heard Diana cry out. 'We're full of water,' and I jumped up and found the boat half-full of water. I could see the plug-hole glittering like a blue light, and I started looking for the plug. I put a spare one in place, and a few of us baled out the water. There were two people lying near the plug-hole, and they seemed to take no interest in what was happening. About an hour later I discovered the plug gone again and water entering the boat. I put the plug back, and this time I lay down with an eye on watch. Sure enough, in less than half an hour I saw a hand over the plug pulling it out. I grasped the hand and found it belonged to a young European. He was not in his right mind, although he knew what he was doing. When I asked him why he tried to sink the boat he said, 'I'm going to die, so we might as well go together.' I shifted him to the fore part of the boat, and we others took turns in keeping an eye on him, but he managed to destroy all the contents of the first-aid box and throw them over the side. He died the next day, with seven or eight lascars, and a banker from Edinburgh, a Mr Crichton. Mr Crichton had a patent waistcoat fitted with small pockets, and the valuables we found there we put with rings and other things in Diana's handbag. Among Mr Crichton's possessions were the three wise monkeys in jade and a silver brandy flask that was empty.

At the end of the third week there were only eight of us left alive in the boat: the old engine-room serang, the fireman from Zanzibar, myself, Diana, Jack Edmead, the steward, Joe Green from Wigan, Jack Oakie from Birmingham, and a friend of his, Jack Little. Two of them had been engineers working on the new Howrah bridge at Calcutta.

There was still no rain, we had not had a single shower since we started our boat voyage, and the water was nearly finished. Only a few drops were left on the bottom of the tank. About the middle of the fourth week

I was lying down dozing in the middle of the night when the boat started to rattle and shake. I jumped up, thinking we had grounded on an island. Then I discovered a large fish had jumped into the boat and was thrashing about wildly. I grabbed an axe that was lying handy, and hit the fish a few hard cracks. The axe bounded off it like rubber, and it was a while before I made any impression, but when it did quieten down I tied a piece of rope round the tail and hung the fish on the mast. It took me all my time to lift the fish, as it was about three feet long and quite heavy. I lay down again, and at daybreak examined the fish closer. It was a dog-fish. During the struggle with it I had gashed a finger against its teeth, and as we now had no bandages or medicine all I could do was wash the cut in sea water before I proceeded to cut up the fish. I had heard and read about people drinking blood, and I thought that I could get some blood from the carcase for drinking. I had a tough job cutting up the fish with my knife, and only managed to get a few teaspoonsful of dirty, reddish-black blood. I cut the liver and heart out, and sliced some of the flesh off. By this time all hands were awake, although every one was feeling weak. I gave the first spoonful of blood to Diana to taste, but she spat it out and said it was horrible. I tried every one with a taste, but nobody could swallow the vile stuff. I tried it myself, but couldn't get it down. It seemed to swell the tongue. We tried eating the fish, but that was also a failure. I chewed and chewed at my piece, but couldn't swallow any and eventually spat it into the sea.

The day following my encounter with the big dog-fish my hand and arm swelled up, and Diana said I had blood-poisoning. The following day it was much worse, and throbbed painfully. I asked Diana if she could do anything for it, as we had no medical supplies left. She advised me to let the hand drag in the water, and later in the day she squeezed the sore, and all sorts of matter came out. I then put my hand back in the water, and that seemed to draw out more poison. At intervals Diana squeezed the arm from the shoulder downward, and gradually got rid of the swelling, although the sore didn't heal for months, and the scar remains to this day.

There was no water left now, and Jack Oakie, Jack Little, and the Zanzibar fireman all died during the one night. It took the remainder of us nearly a whole day to lift them from the bottom of the boat and roll them overboard. The serang was now unconscious and Joe Green was rambling in his speech. There were a few low clouds drifting over us, but no sign of rain, and I had lost count of the days. I had written up Mr. Britt's log-book to the end of the fourth week, but after that day and night seemed to be all the same. Diana had the sickness that nearly every one in turn had suffered: a sore throat and a thick yellow phlegm oozing from the mouth. I think it was due to us lying in the dampness all the time and never getting properly dry. The sails were now down and spread across the boat as I was too feeble to do anything in the way of running the boat. Against all advice, I often threw small quantities of sea water down my throat, and it didn't seem to make me any worse, although I never overdid it.

One night Joe Green would not lie in the bottom of the boat in comfort, but lay on the after end in an uncomfortable position. When I tried to get him to lie down with us he said, 'I won't last out the night, and if I lie down there you will never be able to lift me up and get me over the side.' The next morning he was dead. So was the serang. Two grand old men, though of different races. There were only three of us left now. Jack Edmead was pretty bad now, and Diana still had the sore throat. But we managed to get the bodies over the side. The serang by this time was very thin and wasted, and if he had been any heavier we would not have managed to get him over.

By this time we were only drifting about on the ocean. I had put the jib up a couple of times, but discovered we drifted in circles, so I took it down again. One day I had a very clear dream as I lay there in the bottom of the boat. I dreamed that the three of us were walking up the pierhead at Liverpool, and the dream was so clear that I really believed it would happen. I told Diana and Jack about the dream, and said I was sure we would be picked up. There wasn't a drop of water in the boat now, and the three of us just lay there dreaming of water in all sorts of ways. Sometimes it was about a stream that ran past our house when I was a child, another time I would be holding a hose and spraying water all round, but it was always about water. Jack was getting worse, and was laid out in the stern, while Diana was forward where it was drier. Sick as she was, she always used to smile and say, 'We still have a chance if we could only get some rain.'

Then one night rain came. I was lying down half asleep when I felt the rain falling on my face. I jumped up shouting, 'Rain, rain', but Jack wasn't able to get up and help me. Diana was in a pretty bad condition, but she managed to crawl along and help me spread the main sail to catch the water. It was a short sharp shower and didn't last long, but we collected a few pints in the sail and odd corners of the boat. We didn't waste a drop, and after pouring it carefully into the tank we sucked the raindrops from the woodwork and everywhere possible. Diana had trouble swallowing anything as her throat was swollen and raw, but I mixed some pemmican with water, and we had a few spoonfuls each. The water was very bitter as the sail had been soaked in salt water for weeks, but it tasted good to us. We all felt better after our drink, and I sat down in the well of the boat that day and poured can after can of sea water over myself, and gave Diana a bit of a wash. She was in good spirits now, although she could only speak in whispers. She told me about her home in the South of England: I think she said it was Windsor, on the Thames. She was very fond of horses and tennis and other sports, and she said, 'You must come and visit us when we get home,' which showed that like myself she had a firm conviction that we would get picked up.

The three days after the rain were uneventful. Diana was a bit better, but Jack was in a bad way, and lying down in the stern end. On the third day I had another shower-bath sitting down in the boat, as it had livened me up a lot the last time. Afterwards I set the jib and tried to handle the main sail, but couldn't make it, so I spread the sail and used it as a bed. I had the best sleep in weeks. In the early hours of the morning Diana shook me, and said excitedly, 'Can you hear a plane?' I listened, and heard what sounded like a plane in the distance, so I dashed aft and grabbed one of the red flares and tried to light it. It didn't go off, so I struck one of the lifeboat matches. It ignited at once, and I held it up as high as I could, and immediately a voice shouted, 'All right, put that light out.' It was still dark, but on looking in the direction of the voice we could see the dim outline of a ship, and hear the sound of her diesel engines. The same voice shouted, 'Can you come alongside?' God knows how we managed, but manage it we did. Even Jack found enough strength to give a hand, and with Diana at the tiller he and I rowed the boat alongside the ship. A line was thrown to us, and I made it fast. A pilot ladder was dropped, and two men came down to help us on board. They tied a rope round Diana, and with the help of others on the ship hauled her on board. I climbed up unaided, and the men helped Jack. The

I held the lifeboat match up as high as I could.

first thing I asked for was a drink, and we sat on a hatch waiting to see what would happen. We thought we were on a Swedish ship at first, but I saw a Dutch flag painted across the hatch. Then I heard a couple of men talking, and I knew then we were on a German ship, as I had a slight knowledge of the language. I told the other two, and Diana said , 'It doesn't matter what nationality it is as long as it is a ship.'

A man came to us soon and asked us to go with him and meet the captain. Two of the crew helped Diana and Jack, and we were taken amidships to the doctor's room, where a couch had been prepared for Diana. The captain arrived, and asked us about our trip in the boat and inquired how long we had been in it. I told him our ship had been torpedoed on the 6th of November, and that I had lost count of the days. He said this was the 12th of December, and that we were on board the German ship *Rhakotis*, and we should be well looked after. I remembered the bag of valuables in the boat, and told the captain where Diana's bag was. The bag was found and passed up, and given into the captain's charge. It was probably lost when the ship was sunk three weeks later. The lifeboat was stripped and sunk before the ship got under way again.

We were given cups of coffee, but were told that the doctor's orders were for us not to drink much at a time, and only eat or drink what he ordered. Diana was lying on the doctor's couch, and when the three of us were left alone for a while she bounced up and down on the springs and said, 'This is better than lying in that wet boat.' Later Jack and I were given a hot bath by a medical attendant, and my hand was bandaged, as it was still festering. We were taken aft to a cabin, and Diana was left in the doctor's room. The crew had orders not to bother us and to leave us on our own, as we had to rest as much as possible. When I looked at myself in the mirror I didn't recognise myself with a red beard and haggard appearance. There didn't seem to be any flesh left on my body, only a bag of bones. Jack looked even worse with his black beard and hollow cheeks.

We had been given some tablets and injected, and were now told to go to bed. Before I did so I asked one of the crew to fetch me a bottle of water. Although this was against the doctor's orders the man did so, and I hid the bottle under my pillow. Then I asked another man to bring me a bottle of water, and in this way I collected a few bottles and I drank the lot. Jack was already asleep when I turned in after drinking the water, and

I turned in on the bunk above him. We slept for hours and when I awoke I found I had soaked the bedding. Later I discovered I had soaked Jack's bed too. He was still asleep. I wakened him and apologised, but he only laughed. The steward brought us coffee at 7 am and when I told him about my bladder weakness he didn't seem annoyed, but took the bedclothes away to be changed. It was over a year before I was able to hold any liquid for more than an hour or so.

We were well looked after and well fed on the German ship, and from the first day I walked round the decks as I liked. Jack was confined to bed for a few days. We were not allowed to visit Diana, but the captain came aft and gave us any news concerning her. She couldn't swallow any food, and was being fed by injections. When we had been five days on the ship the doctor and the captain came along to our cabin, and I could see they were worried. The captain did the talking, and said that as the English girl still hadn't been able to eat, and couldn't go on living on injections, the doctor wanted to operate on her throat and clear the inflammation. But first of all he wanted our permission. I had never liked the doctor and had discovered he was disliked by nearly everyone on board, but still, he was the doctor, and should know more about what was good for Diana than I could. So I told the captain that if the doctor thought it was necessary to operate he had my permission as I wanted to see Diana well again. Jack said almost the same, and the captain asked if we would like to see her. We jumped at the chance, and went with the doctor. She seemed quite happy, and looked well, except for being thin. Here hair had been washed and set, and she said she was being well looked after. We never mentioned the operation to her, but noticed she could still talk only in whispers.

That evening at seven o'clock the captain came to us, and I could see that something was wrong. He said, 'I have bad news for you. The English girl has died. Will you follow me, please?' We went along, neither of us able to say a word. We were taken to the doctor's room where she lay with a bandage round her throat. You would never know she was dead, she looked so peaceful. The doctor spoke, and said in broken English that the operation was a success, but the girl's heart was not strong enough to stand the anaesthetic. I couldn't speak, and turned away broken-hearted. Jack and I went aft again, and I turned in to my bunk and lay crying like a baby nearly all night. It was the first time I had broken down and cried, and I think Jack was the same. The funeral was the next day, and when the time came we went along to the foredeck where the ship's crew were all lined up wearing uniform and the body was in a coffin covered by the Union Jack. The captain made a speech in German, and then spoke in English for our benefit. There were tears in the eyes of many of the Germans, as they had all taken an interest in the English girl. The ship was stopped, and after the captain had said a prayer the coffin slid slowly down a slipway into the sea. It had been weighted, and sank slowly. The crew stood to attention bareheaded until the coffin disappeared. It was an impressive scene, and a gallant end to a brave and noble girl. We had been through so much together, and I knew I would never forget her.

A LONG SWIM
Joyce Stranger

Khazan, a thoroughbred English racehorse, is being taken by boat to Ireland by his owner, Dan, and his trainer, Joe.

Khazan was a curious horse, interested in the world around him. He enjoyed being taken to strange places, and was quite unafraid of the horse box. Dan had sometimes used him to steady a younger animal, putting Zan (Khazan) in the box first. Zan's patient eyes watched the youngster, and the aura of calm emanating from him helped to quieten nerves.

The horse had also been used to steady a windy pony. Zan was quite unafraid of traffic. Dan rode him when he was breaking a new horse for the road, and the older horse turned himself sideways if the young one panicked, interposing his body between the frightening monster that was roaring up to them, shielding the youngster. No one taught him to do so. He took it on himself to teach that cars stayed on the road and were harmless. He had never been hurt by a vehicle and trusted them all, blindly.

He had followed Joe without fear, recognising that this man knew horses. It was not the first time he had gone away from Dan. Nor the first time he had left the stables and stayed in a strange place overnight. He watched the Shire horses in the brewery stables with interest and nosed the mare in the next stall, liking the scent of her.

He had not liked entering the boat. The docks were noisier than anything he had encountered before. There were cranes lifting huge packs above him, and he was afraid that something might drop on him. He did not like the wet slippery weedy jetty, or the waves that broke over his hooves, but he trusted Joe and followed him quietly, bracing himself against the unexpected uneasy movement of the boat.

The doors in the hold had clanged shut behind him, leaving him in the dark. Someone switched on a light, and the horse had stared about him, nostrils working overtime at the sea scent, eyes rolling as the boat tossed. The engine sound was strange and he did not like that either, but Joe was beside him, telling him that he was safe, that it did not matter, that there was nothing to fear. The soft voice soothed him; the gentle hand was comfort; so long as the man was there, nothing would go wrong.

The rending sound panicked the horse. Joe had been flung across the boat and vanished, and then, mysteriously, Joe was gone and Zan was alone, and the gate of his stall open, swinging wildly to and fro. Water was pouring in; water that spilled round his feet, water that splashed and soaked him.

He was surrounded by noise; the wild shriek of the wind; the surge and roar and bellow of the rolling waves, the grinding, creaking noise of the huge doors in front of him. They had been struck by the wreckage of another ship, which had been abandoned an hour before, as she too was flooding. Waterlogged, she had rocked dangerously, a menace to all other boats. The hold doors had been hit with a sideways bang that had unseated the bolts that held them. The great ram across the doors had snapped, as if made of matchwood.

The lights went out.

The engine died.

The *Daisy May* was wallowing clumsily, rolling on the waves. Zan panicked. His flailing hooves struck the doors, which were already creaking open with the weight of the water inside the boat.

The doors flung wide.

The boat rolled.

Khazan lost his footing and was in the water, was outside the boat, was trapped beneath it, was sinking down, struggling for breath, his lungs crying out for air. Water filled his eyes and ears and nostrils. It was bitterly cold, and he was drowning, sucked into a swirl that he could not fight.

The *Daisy May* rolled away from him.

The suck of water had gone. He rose to the surface, long legs flailing wildly, his tortured lungs taking in great gulps of air.

The need to live, the need to fight the terror that engulfed him, was all that he had left. He began to swim, his powerful legs striking out automatically, although he had never been in water before.

It was blind instinct, fighting for survival. Fighting for the safe land beneath his hooves. Fighting against the waves that swamped him, against the wind that tossed the water, against the objects floating around him that hit him and bruised his body.

He had no sense of time.

He swam.

The wind died, all the waves were quieter, and the night was succeeded by the gleam of grey at dawn; Khazan could see the waves that tossed him, could see the deep troughs between them, could see the sky brighten and lighten and the sun shine through.

He was alone in a waste of water, bruised, weary, and very hungry. If he went on there would be men and there would be food. There always had been men and there always had been food, every day of his life. It could not end now. Somewhere men were waiting. He only had to find them. They were not thinking thoughts in his head; only feelings; instincts that told him to go on, not to give up, to fight against this horrible creature that was trying to kill him. He would always fight; if he were wild he would fight other stallions; if he were put with rivals he would fight to the death, because it was in him never to give up, always to go on, always to face a challenge.

He had faced the jumps, even higher and higher.

He had run a race when his heart was pounding in him and breath bursting in him, and the ground rock-hard and the other horses pressing him. But he had to win, had to go all out, whatever he did, always. He had all the arrogance of all the winners that made up his heredity; of the great Miller himself, who had always given his best. He had to go on, even when lightning lanced the sky and wild thunder rolled across the sullen waves, and the crash in his ears seemed endless and no hope was left.

He swam.

He was a small speck in a vast wasteland. He was flotsam, floating on the water. Only one man saw him, and did not realise that he was looking

171

at a horse. He had been on watch for all of the night, and he saw a small speck disappear between the waves, and thought it was a block of wood. Khazan was unaware of the boat that had almost run him down.

He swam.

His legs ached with effort. His breath rasped in his throat. His lungs were sore. He had swallowed an ocean of water. He did not know where he was going, or why he was there, or why men had deserted him. He did not know why he was swimming. He did not know he could stop, give up and sink beneath the waves. Instinct had taken over. Instinct that made him go on, and on, and on. That forced his weary body into ever more effort, breasting each wave more slowly now, almost drifting down into the trough, and then up again.

He did not know that he was being helped by a current that set to the shore when the tide had turned.

He did not know what would happen to him.

He was an automaton, going on relentlessly, even though his efforts were feebler. He was nearing exhaustion and the time would come when even he could not conquer the wind and the sea and the cold.

The time had not come yet.

The sun had risen in the sky. He was aware of hunger; he longed for food and for clean fresh water; for hay, and for a soothing hand to say, 'It's all right, old boy. Not to worry. It'll soon be over.'

Nobody came.

He was alone for ever in a millrace, where the waves broke white over his sodden head, and the water took him like a toy and pushed him about and he could master nothing.

He swam.

The tide was flooding, the current was faster, helping him, but Khazan was not aware of that. He was aware of nothing but the need to go on, to breast the waves, to keep his legs moving, striking out ever more feebly, aching with exhaustion, beyond hunger. Almost beyond caring.

He had been in the water for over ten hours. Far behind him, the *Daisy May* lolled, waterlogged, rocking on a sea now much calmer. Joe had reported that they were safe, over the radio, and asked for the horse to be rescued. The rescue ship arrived. The hold doors had closed again, but the hold was flooded deep. No horse floated on the water. Either he was trapped there, dead, or had somehow been flung into the heaving seas.

Either way, there was no hope for him.

Joe was bitterly disappointed. The horse was insured, but that wasn't the point. He had failed Matt and although the loss wasn't his fault, as the storm had been unpredicted and quite exceptional, he never forgave himself.

No one looked for the horse.

Khazan was no longer swimming. He was floating, drifting with the tide, sinking under the water and struggling wearily to the surface again, refusing to accept water that choked him and hurt his lungs; that stung his eyes, that flooded into his ears. He tried to shake his head. He could not see clearly, because he needed to keep his eyes closed against the stinging salt.

He could not go on.

His legs would not work any more. He was a feeble piece of flotsam, drifting with the seaweed.

The wind from the land strengthened. It blew towards the horse.

The smells around him changed.

There was salt and weed and the sharp sea tang, but there was grass, and cattle and woodsmoke. There was a smell like the smell of the stables in Ireland; there were people, somewhere near him. There was hope.

The will to survive strengthened him and he struck out again, with bolder movements of his legs, towards the shore. The tide was full, and soon would turn. The sea had quietened. There were rocks all around him, with fierce fangs that threatened him, but he was unaware of danger, even though one spike raked his leg, cutting it. He was not conscious of the blood that flowed into the water, and did not even notice the sting of the sea in the wound.

There was land.

There was grass, and he would be able to feed.

There were gulls winging about him, calling, diving to look at this unlikely swimmer, wondering if it was food. They annoyed him, and he tried to change direction, away from the insistence of swooping wings and beaks he was afraid might stab at his eyes. He had never seen sea birds before.

He was rocking with the water. He was heading towards a narrow cove, high cliffs shielding it on either side from the weather, trapping the sun, so that it was warm and a favourite place for some of the village

173

He came through the waves soaked and bedraggled.

children, and for some of those older too, to bask and swim, and lie against the rocks, lazing. Few of them bothered, but there were a small number who knew the cove. Summer visitors never found it. Shallow steps led down the steep cliff, to the rocks that were tumbled around at the head of the beach.

Khazan touched bottom. He could walk, instead of swimming. He moved slowly, almost done for. He stumbled wearily among rocks that trapped him, and tried to swim again, but the water was too shallow now. He came through the waves, soaked, bedraggled, defeated, his head hanging low, too heavy to lift. Once he fell, and lay for a while with the water creaming over his body, while he breathed deeply. A wave came and covered his head, and he struggled up again and walked on, now picking his way delicately among the rocks. There was some sand; that was kind to his hooves.

He was out of the water and on the beach and the sun was setting behind the cliffs. The sky rioted with colour. Dark clouds were slashed with crimson and the light reflected in the water, dying it red.

The light changed the colour of Zan's soaked coat. He was a glowing horse for one moment as he stood, sniffing.

He moved uncertainly, stumbling, pausing between each step. He reached the edge of the cove, where sparse grass grew on the banks of a stream that tumbled down the cliffs. He bent his head to the water.

It was sweet, clean, and fresh.

It was elixir, as he drank, washing away the salt in his mouth and throat. He stood in it, feeling it clear and cold round his hooves.

He cropped at the grass but he had no energy to feed.

He had no energy left at all.

He stretched himself on the sand beneath the cliffs, and lay like a dead horse, sleeping soundly, totally exhausted. The breath that moved his chest was uneven, and fluttered. He did not know that if no one came he would die there, needing food and warmth. The blood still oozed from the cut in his leg.

The birds watched him, waiting, knowing what he did not know.

A small wind needled his mane, but he did not even open his eyes. He had fought to the last, and time was running out for him, fast.

The wild birds knew. The hungry gulls perched on the cliffs all night.

THE WRECK OF THE 'FORFARSHIRE'
Iain Finlayson

Oh, I am weary. I am not well, and it is tiresome to be gawped at by the stream of sightseers who trail endlessly, with great difficulty, to this place simply to catch a glimpse of me. They are evidently disappointed by what they see – a young woman of twenty and six years, not remarkably beautiful or as romantic as they have been led to suppose by popular reports. I look, indeed, rather peaky. Illness has made my face pale, I am now and again convulsed by shivers, and I cough incessantly. The cough is not, perhaps, strictly fair to my audience because I exaggerate it to keep visitors at a distance. Soon I will go to Wooler with one of my sisters. The air at the foot of the Cheviots will do me good. For four years I have been public property. There have been so many people, such excitement, travel, so much well-intentioned fuss, that I might almost regret my impulse . . . but, no. The deed was right. Only the aftermath of my adventure seems increasingly to distort and overwhelm the actual events of that dawn.

The beginning of it all was a letter written by a public-spirited gentleman to the Duke of Northumberland enclosing a copy of a report of their rescue by two survivors of the wreck of the 'Forfarshire'. The report reads simply enough, outlining only the barest facts: '. . . when the 'Forfarshire' Steam Vessel was wrecked at 4 o'clock on the Morning of Friday the 7th of September, 1838, on the Harker Rock, three-quarters of a mile from the light house on the Long Stone at the Farne Islands on the Coast of Northumberland, the After-part of the Vessel having been swept away by the violence of the Sea, and the Forepart being left with nine Persons on the Rock, William Darling the Keeper of the Light House did, at Day-break on that Morning, with the assistance of his Wife and Daughter (being the only persons then with him at the Light House) launch the Light House Boat; and he, and his Daughter Grace Darling, about 22 years of age (who insisted on sharing her Father's danger) did, notwithstanding the Force of the Tempest, which was still raging, succeed in reaching the rock, and bringing those nine Persons to the Light House in safety . . .'

The letter reached the duke about two weeks after the rescue, and that kindly man immediately decided to investigate the report. He wrote, moreover, to the Duke of Wellington, who was Master of Trinity House (the society that employs my father as lighthouse keeper), and to the Royal Humane Society in London. The first my father and I knew of these great doings was a visit from reporters representing the Berwick & Kelso Warder. They wrote about us soon afterwards, describing the lighthouse and myself in highly colourful terms:

'. . . as we approached the lighthouse, the heroine, Grace Darling herself, was described high aloft, lighting the lamps, whose revolving illumination has warned so many an anxious mariner of the rocks and shoals around. At the side where we alighted, a bold cliff is to be ascended ere you reach the lighthouse. Having gained its summit we were soon at the door of the hospitable tower, and received a hearty welcome from old Mrs Darling and her dauntless daughter.'

The 'dauntless daughter' indeed! And I was no lady of the lamp when the reporters arrived, but down on my knees cleaning some brasses. They go on, in their article, to describe me in terms that still made me blush. Perhaps they discovered in my face only what they wanted to find and what best suited their purpose. It was the first chapter in the legend:

'But Grace is nothing masculine in her appearance, although she has so stout a heart. In person she is about the middle size, of a comely countenance – rather fair for an islander – and with an expression of benevolence and softness most truly feminine in every point of view. When we spoke of her noble and heroic conduct, she slightly blushed and

177

appeared anxious to avoid the notice to which it exposed her; she smiled at our praise but said nothing in reply – though her look indicated forcibly that the consciousness of having done so good and generous an action had not failed to excite a thrill of pleasure in her bosom which was itself no mean reward. Her conscious heart of charity was warm . . .'

It takes no warm heart of charity to want to rescue poor drenched wretches clinging to a sea-bound rock in the cold light of morning, and if the gentlemen of the Press were surprised to find me feminine in manner and form, what did they expect? Was I to sit about my home like Britannia with a stern and noble expression wearing a wreath of laurels on my head? What I did to help my father in his duty was no more than anyone would have done. My brothers were not at home, and my mother could scarcely have ventured out in the boat! There was nothing for it, and my father and I had worked together before, tending the light, so he knew my capabilities. I am the daughter of a lighthouse keeper, and there was work to be done, lives to be saved from the element that has pounded in my ears since the day I was born and which I fear and love. I am no highborn, noble heroine. I am Grace Darling.

The Farnes are savage, inhospitable rocks that break ships as a man might break the neck of a bird. Brownsman Island was the first to have a lighthouse and it was there I spent my childhood. I'm not one to sigh in rapture over the stern mysteries of Nature, but I loved the isolation of my surroundings. The fact that I had eight brothers and sisters to play and laugh with meant that I could be solitary when I wished, but never lonely. In a book of travels published recently, a Mr William Howitt describes for the curious public the particular nature of my environment.

'There is a row of square isolated rocks rising out of the sea near the island cliffs called the Pinnacles, the tops of which were covered by sea-fowl. It was one of the most curious and beautiful sights that I ever saw. They were chiefly guillemots and puffins. They seemed all to be sitting erect as close as they could crowd and waving their little dark wings as if for joy. . . On the sides of the cliffs on the little projections sat gulls looking very white and silvery against the dark arch . . .' Mr Howitt goes on to describe the rocky terrain as 'all of dark whinstone, cracked in all directions and worn with the action of winds, waves and tempests since the world began.' He speaks of wrinkled hills of black stone and dismal dells, of seaweed like great round ropes, and everywhere the sun-blotting cloud of wheeling and mewing gulls. There was rarely silence – though I scarcely noticed the breathing, sighing wind and the endless slapping of breakers against the dark shore. But the birds, screaming, yelling, rushing and quarreling were forever in my ears.

My father was a determined, methodical man, a conscientious keeper with a true and profound Christian spirit. He was pursued at all hours of the day up and around the tower by his children and he himself saw to our education. Quarters were cramped, naturally, and as soon as any of us were able to fend for ourselves, he saw us securely settled on the mainland until only I and the twins were left. These twins grew to be strong, manly, brave, duty-bound to life saving like my father. There were many wrecks – the brig 'Monkhouse' (crew saved and all materials), for instance, and the 'Thomas Jackson', a barque of 300 tons which foundered with the loss of the Captain's wife, two boys and two men. It was after this disaster, in 1825, that the Elders of Trinity House began surveying the site of a new lighthouse, our new home, on Longstone. Just three quarters of a mile from Brownstone Island.

It was a perilous place to be. Father drew up a long list of taboos for us children and to be caught breaking any of them was to court his immediate wrath and punishment. Mother lived in daily terror of each and every one of her family coming to some violent death through carelessness. But we survived, happy enough in that desolate place. Again, the rock was seething with birds, their squabbles and screams a constant chorus on land and on sea. My father's Journal records some of the first emergencies we had to deal with. Two days after Christmas, at midnight, the sloop 'Autumn' struck the east point of Knavestone rock and immediately sank. The entry simply reads:

'Crew of three men; two lost, one saved by the lightkeeper and three sons, namely William, Robert and George, after a struggle of three hours. Having lost two oars on the rock, had a very narrow escape. P.S. The man saved, James Logan, stood near ten hours, part on the rock, part on the masthead; the mate lying dead beside him on the rock the last three hours, having perished from cold.'

That was the wreck I noticed at eight o'clock in the morning. I am often in the habit of looking out over the sea. Even in fine weather there are strong currents, running like ribbons through the tossing sea, around the Knavestone. High, flowing tides and strong gales are a wicked combination and ships can be caught like twigs in a stream, borne helplessly to jar against jutting rocks. This time my father and three of my brothers had a narrow escape themselves. I have the Journal here, and I read what it says:

'. . . two oars broke in the attempt to get away. Robert and George Darling, the only two who could swim, had to quit the boat and help her off from the rock . . . it was a miracle that the boat was not destroyed and that all five did not perish.'

So you understand, a little, the life and death struggle with the sea that was in our blood. We could never take for granted a full night's sleep, nor relax for a moment the vigil that the lighthouse kept. The burning eye high above the rocks was an unblinking, perpetual warning to mariners of danger. Danger, yes, but also a hope of rescue. We knew when to expect high tides, and on such nights my father would rouse me in the early hours of the morning to help him make all secure against the flood. On the night of 7th September 1838 I was called, and I dressed quickly. A cloak around my shoulders and a straw bonnet on my head, I helped my father carry all the small moveable gear inside lest it be washed away and made fast the coble to stanchions. I took over the watch in the lantern room while my father slept below, and settled to look out over the sea. At a quarter before five, I sighted a vessel in difficulties over by the Harker rock. It was almost dawn and I could not see clearly the exact nature of the ship's distress, but I took my lantern and hurried to wake my father. And *that*, if you like, was the *real* beginning. The ship was the 'Forfarshire'.

Straining our eyes through the glass, we could make out no survivors on the wrecked ship until, about two hours later, the tide having fallen, we observed three or four people clining to the rock itself. I saw them myself, as I had seen others before. It would be a risky business to attempt a rescue, but my father thought there might be a chance and he is a cautious man who weighs matters carefully before coming to a decision. He is not a rash or a foolhardy sailor. He knows the sea as well as he knows his light and his family, and he has a healthy respect for all of these. But none of my brothers, experienced hands in the coble that we used for rescue, were at home. Only my father, my mother and myself.

The coble needed three men to run her in rough weather, but by about three or four hours after dawn the tide on the reef was at half ebb and the

Harker rock was jutting high enough, about fiften feet, out of the sea for a rescue attempt to be made despite the fierce gale blowing around it. The 'Forfarshire', we reckoned, had broken its back. The sea had poured over her and I thought how the ship must have reared and plunged, crashing like a rising whale, splitting and breaking. It was a miracle that anyone at all had survived the disaster – from the size of the ship it was likely that she would have been carrying about fifty to sixty people all told and the survivors, all that we could see, numbered but four at the most.

I am strong in body and just as strong in will. If my father was of the opinion that a rescue could be attempted, he could not be allowed to go alone. At a pinch, two people could handle the coble and there was little argument about the matter. My mother wailed a great deal at the idea, but somehow or other I got in the little boat, pinned my hair securely lest the wind should lash it across my face, and set my face towards my father who clambered in after me. Looking back, I cannot imagine what I thought at the time. There was nothing to think about except keeping the coble steady. She was a sea-seasoned and sea-wise old lady, a little over sixteen feet long in the keel and something over twenty one feet overall. Amidships, she measured five and a half feet and she lifted in the swell like a seagull. There were five benches, one of them astern. I sat firmly on the midships as we approached the rock the long way round from the south. Our course was to pass southwards through an opening between the Longstone and an island known as the Blue Caps, a route that would shelter us a little from the high, beating storm.

The principal danger would be our exposure right at the start. We'd have to cut through Craford's Gut, which separated Longstone from the reef – a passage swollen by water that rushed through, whipped by a shrieking, driving blast of wind that howled along the passage tearing up the water, lashing it and tumbling the waves that beat along frothing and bubbling like water boiling in a cauldron. We came through, by God's mercy, and by the strength of our arms pulling on the oars, forcing back the weight of water. A middle-aged man, experienced enough but scarcely with the strength of youth, and his twenty two year old daughter. We were courageous, I suppose, but there was no time for anything other than instinct and a healthy sense of self-preservation to occupy our minds. My mother later admitted to having watched us from the lantern room and, at one point, thinking us to have been

The sea was whipped up by a shrieking wind.

overwhelmed by the waves, she thinks she fainted from sheer terror. We reached the rock.

In a pitiable state, clutching at the unyielding stone and huddling together, were nine people. Nine alive, that is. A clergyman lay lifeless high on the rock, and two small children had died in their mother's arms. Eight men and one woman survived, their eyes desperate with hope at our approach. The coble could hold five of them. Four must remain. We would take the woman first, of course, but the eight men madly tried to scramble to the boat all at once with such violence that my father had to spring out on the rock itself to prevent them from crowding into the coble and overwhelming it. I had some difficulty in keeping the boat close to the rock, but finally the woman, one injured man and three others were helped down and we prepared to make our way back to the lighthouse, leaving the rest of the survivors to wait for our return. The woman sat dazedly for'ard with her head resting against the side of the boat as she was in no fit condition to sit upright on a seat. We put a blanket around her and also covered one of the men who lay aft in the same position. We left both the dead children in the wreck. It was easier to get back to Longstone as we now had four hands at the oars, but still the gale – cold and northerly, numbing and shrieking – whipped our wet clothes, slapping them against our soaked bodies.

The tide mercifully continued to fall, and we rowed past the sheltering rocks exhausted but high in spirits that poured energy through our arms and fired our determination to complete the adventure we had begun. The second trip out to the rock was easier than the first as the storm had abated somewhat and two of the men we had rescued volunteered to man the oars. We safely brought off the remaining survivors and returned to Longstone. Later, local people arrived to congratulate us on the rescue and they were particularly attentive to me, praising my courage and generally demonstrating, however kindly, their amazement that a woman should have had strength and will enough to undergo such an adventure. They called it an ordeal, but to be honest I have rarely felt so completely alive, so wholly at one with myself and the elements, as I felt during that long day. I felt a wild and energising exhiliration, a joyousness that all but rendered me insensible to petty questioning and solicitude. I felt like taking wing with the gulls, soaring and crying out with wild shouts of sheer pleasure in being alive and feeling my body exalt in the hot aches that possessed it.

I'm told that I blushed modestly and smiled a great deal. I looked pleased and bright-eyed, and laughed when someone promised me that I'd get a silk gown for my trouble. Joy spiralled upwards in the Longstone lighthouse that day like the very steps up the lantern. I never experienced an excitement and a pleasure like it; no, not in all the days and weeks, months and years that followed. For one day my spirits had been freed, and it is the memory of that high and wheeling joy that I secretly treasure as the most enduring gift of God. The gifts of mankind poured in later, and I am grateful for the interest that people have shown in the endeavour that my father and I put into the rescue. But, Lord, it is too much. I at first took not the slightest notice of the public's attempts to crown me with a heroine's laurels. Truth to tell, the brouhaha bewildered me. But nobody owed me anything. I did my duty as I saw it, and there was an end of it. The gift of a silk dress would have been enough. But I never saw that, though I saw much more: medals, portraits, public meetings, donations of money, newspaper articles, books about me, silver cups from great lords and ladies, even requests for snippets of my hair to put in gold lockets. For a time, I was swept away, carried off from my tall and windswept tower, even came to believe in my personal triumph. The Royal Humane Society presented by father and myself with gold medals – for which there was no precedent: no other persons had ever been awarded such a thing by the Society. They engrossed an address to me on vellum and had it framed. The words read:

'That the singular intrepidity, presence of mind, and Humanity which nobly urged

GRACE HORSLEY DARLING

to expose her life in a small Boat to the impending danger of a heavy Gale of wind and a tremendous Sea, in her intense desire to save nine of the sufferers who were wrecked in the 'Forfarshire' Steam-vessel on the Harker Rock, Coast of Northumberland on the 7th of September 1838, and the extraordinary fortitude which she heroically displayed throughout the whole of that hazardous undertaking has called forth the most lively approbation of this Special General Court, and eminently entitles that brave Girl to the highest Honorary distinction that this Society can bestow – namely, the Gold Medallion which is unanimously awarded her.'

It was kind of them, and I appreciate the honour. The language is very fine, very high-sounding, and no doubt conveys the essence of what the Society considers to be heroism: some noble and selfless attitude that transcends simple pity for those in distress.

I appreciate that it endeavours to describe in its sentiments the girl I was that day. I don't know her, this exalted creature. I know only of that woman, Grace Darling, who was once for a few hours at one with herself, her fellow men and with the wind and the sea.

IN THE MEDITERRANEAN
John Winton

The SS Barsetshire *is on a Mediterranean cruise with a crew of officer cadets including the sophisticated Paul Vincent, the fumbling Ted Maconochie and George Dewberry who seems intent on drinking as much wine as possible at every port of call. These three and the other cadets are all under the watchful eye of Lieutenant-Commander Badger, known to all on board as the 'Bodger'.*

Barsetshire was an elderly lady who needed more time and care than most to make up her face and complete her toilette. Each cruise she retired to a secluded spot to paint ship; in the Mediterranean cruise she anchored in a remote Sardinian bay.

The bay was a desolate spot, with bare brown hills on either side, empty of life or habitation of any kind. In the afternoons the water stretched as smooth as sheet glass and the outline of the shore was distorted by dancing heat vapours. *Barsetshire* lay at anchor, still and motionless, like a painted ship upon a painted ocean. Here, the ship's company settled down to paint ship, or rather, the cadets painted, and the ship's company settled down to watch.

The junior cadets, in their innocence, could not have imagined that there was more to Paint Ship than merely taking paint from a pot and applying it to the ship's side. But they were to learn better. There is more to the art of cosmetics than the mere taking of cream and colour from bottles and putting it on to the skin. Paint Ship in H.M.S. *Barsetshire* was attended with all the rites and ceremonies of a Pompadour's levee.

Able Seaman Froggins and the other lockermen marshalled an awe-inspiring parade of scrapers, buckets and scrubbers (Paint Ship was for them the high moment of a cruise, just as Mr Piles' was a Gun Salute).

The Bosun and his party provided a forest of stages, bosun's chairs and ropes. The Painter mustered bundles of brushes and drew off pot after pot of grey paint. The Ship's Band filled a motor cutter and cruised round and about playing excerpts from the operas of Wagner, the Bandmaster conducting from the sternsheets while the Commander, surrounded by a retinue of divisional officers, captains of tops, the Mate of the Upper Deck and the Chief Bosun's Mate, drove round the ship in the Captain's Motorboat pointing out weak patches in the ship's side with the pomp and authority of a Doge going out to wed the Adriatic.

Before actual painting, there was scrubbing. Stages were lowered over the ship's side, two cadets were lowered on to each stage, and two buckets and two scrubbers were lowered down to each pair of cadets. Every scrubber was attached to a cadet by a lanyard. It might have been assumed that the lanyards were provided so that the scrubbers might in some measure act as marker buoys for cadets who fell from the stages into the sea. Nothing could have been further from the truth. The cadets were intended to act as marker buoys for the scrubbers.

When the ship's side had been scrubbed, bad patches were rubbed with brick and rust marks taken off with scrapers. The canvas was then ready for the paint.

Most of the cadets enjoyed painting. It was one of the few creative pieces of work they were called upon to do in the training cruiser. They found it pleasant to hang over the side on a stage in the sunshine and watch the area of gleaming new paintwork growing overhead.

It was while painting ship that Paul first came into contact with the cadet disciplinary authorities. He was sharing a stage with Maconochie, which was perhaps the root of the trouble. Misfortune hovered over Maconochie as a halo over a saint.

'Don't you feel a certain – how shall I put it? – *atavistic* pleasure in painting, Trog?' asked Paul, of Maconochie.

'Don't call me that,' growled Maconochie.

'But don't you feel something carnally satisfying about it? Dip the brush in, twirl it around, scrape it on the edge, two strokes up, two strokes down, rub it well in and finish on the upward stroke. Don't you sense something vaguely sexually stimulating in it?'

'No,' said Maconochie.

Paul had confirmed early in the cramped space of *Barsetshire* what he had suspected at Dartmouth. Maconochie had no sense of humour. He took everything said to him at its face value. He made a perfect foil for Paul in whimsical mood.

'Like the last lascivious kisses of a dying love, don't you think? The brush moving up and down like the drooping of silken eyelashes against a satin cheek'.

'It's nothing like that.'

'Nor like the caress of a fingertip trailed in tranquil water and sprinkled on a lily-like breast beneath the waving willows?'

'No.'

'Not even the waving willows, Trog?'

'I've told you before, *don't* call me that.'

'You will live to a great age, Trog. I prophesy it. Others may come, dwell their little hour or so, worry a little, and then go. But not Trog. Trog the inscrutable. The Great Trog, the great-nephew of the Great Chang. Have you ever tried to unscrew the inscrutable, Trog?'

'No.'

'Try it. You will find it as rewarding as that wretched band are finding their rendering of The Ride of the Valkyries with the Commander bellowing like a mad thing next door to them. Have you ever ridden with the Valkyries, Trog?'

'Oh, go and get knotted.'

'Tut tut.'

Just then the Captain's red setter, Owen Glendower, looked over the ship's side. Owen Glendower normally enjoyed Paint Ship as much as anyone. There were always interesting pots and cans to sniff at, the decks were always filled with bustle and excitement, there were always ropes and lanyards to gnaw at, and above all there were always more, and more senior, feet to trip over him. Since the day Maconochie had inadvertently trodden on him, Owen Glendower had disliked him; as far as Owen Glendower was concerned, Maconochie's name might as well have been Dr Fell. When Owen Glendower looked over the ship's side and saw Maconochie, his day was spoiled. He seated himself on the beading which ran round the upper deck, immediately above Maconochie's head.

'There's that bloody pooch,' said Maconochie.

Paul looked up and saw Owen Glendower projecting over the sill.

'He doesn't seem to like us very much.'

'It's mutual,' said Maconochie sourly.

Paul looked up at Owen Glendower again. A great temptation seized him. He struggled with it for a time and then gave in. After all, Paul thought, was it not Oscar Wilde who said that the only way to get rid of temptation was to yield to it?

'What would Oscar Wilde have done?' asked Paul rhetorically.

Owen Glendower gave a yelp of rage and vanished.

★　★　★　★

The Cadet Training Officer's Requestmen and Defaulters were held in a special office just off the cadets' messdeck. It was used for nothing else and the inference was that there were normally so many requestmen and defaulters that a separate room was required to hold them. When Paul arrived the only other cadet there was Peter Cleghorn but because he was a requestman and not a defaulter like Paul, Peter Cleghorn was ordered to stand on the other side of the passageway.

Inside the office, the Bodger stood behind a table with Mr Piles at his side to call out the names of the cadets as they were summoned to call out the names of the cadets as they were summoned into the presence of the Cadet Training officer.

'Cadet Cleghorn!'

'Sir!'

Peter Cleghorn sprang to attention and doubled inside. At the door he caught his foot on the sill and fell in a praying attitude in front of The Bodger.

'Get-off-your-knees-Cadet-Cleghorn! Cadet Cleghorn, sir, request to discontinue shaving.'

The Bodger beetled his eyebrows.

'So you want to grow a set, Cleghorn?

'Yes sir.'

'Think you can manage it?'

'Yes sir.'

'How often do you have to shave?'

'Once a day, sir.'

'Quietly confident, eh?'

'Yes sir.'

'Well, I'm not! Furthermore, even if you did succeed in growing a set, which I doubt, I'm not going to have one of my cadets going about the place looking like a gingerbread Saint. Not granted. Get your hair cut.'

'Not granted. Salute! A-bout turn, double march, get our hair cut!' Peter Cleghorn doubled away. Mr Piles cleared his throat.

'Cadet Vincent!'

'Sir!'

'Cadet Vincent, off – cap! Cadet Vincent, sir, first charge, did on the third of October, commit an act prejudicial to good order and naval discipline in that he did improperly paint the rectum of one male red setter dog, the property of Captain Sir Douglas Mainwaring Gregson, Royal Navy, Kennel Club Number 426692L. Second charge, did, on the third of October, improperly use one pot of Admiralty pattern grey paint.'

The Bodger studied the charge sheet. 'Mr Piles?' he said.

'I investigated this case, sir. Cadet Vincent was sharing a stage with Cadet Maconochie, sir, while painting ship. They were painting ship, sir, when the dog made his appearance on the upper deck above them. On seeing the dog, Cadet Vincent reached up and painted the dog's rectum, sir, with Admiralty paint. This action was witnessed by Petty Officer Moody, the Captain of Top. When I asked Cadet Vincent if he had anything to say he was in a very excited state, sir. Kept talking about someone called Oscar Wilde, sir. There is no cadet on board with that name sir. I've checked.'

'Thank you, Mr Piles. Have you anthing to say, *now*, Vincent?'

'Well, no sir, except that it was purely in self-defence.'

'Self-defence?'

'The dog attacked me, sir.'

'*Attacked* you? What, *arse* first?'

'It was a most threatening attitude, sir.'

'I never heard anything like it. If you go around like this, Vincent, you're going to be a menace to society and I hope I never have to serve with you. Lieutenant du Pont, how does Cadet Vincent do his duty?'

Pontius the Pilot had hurried from the wardroom on hearing that one of his cadets was charged with committing an unnatural offence. He was baffled by the reference to Admiralty paint which he had heard as he came through the door.

'Vincent is generally reliable, sir,' he said. 'I can't say I've noticed any signs of aberration before.'

'Hardly an aberration,' said The Bodger. 'I would call it more of a decoration. Though it was hard luck on the dog.'

'Dog!'

'The Captain's dog.'

'The *Captain's* dog!'

'Yes, yes, the Captain's dog,' The Bodger said impatiently. 'Now look here, Vincent. You'd better remember this. You can do what you like with a senior officer's wife but keep clear of his dog, his car and his yacht. Get it?'

'Yes sir.'

'Five days Number Eleven punishment.'

'Five days Number Eleven punishmen! *On*-cap! A-bout turn, double march!'

Outside, Paul was met by a deputation.

'How did you get on?' asked Michael.

'Five days number elevens.'

'You were lucky,' said Peter Cleghorn. 'You know how the old man feels about his dog. I'm surprised he didn't personally call for your head on a silver salver.'

'Oh, The Bodger seemed to think it was jolly funny. He gave me a Bodgerism and five days number elevens.'

'Tough luck.'

'The only person I'm annoyed with is Maconochie. I reckon it was all his fault anyway.'

'It normally is.'

Paul's punishment was inconvenient rather than arduous. It curtailed his spare time but did not impose any undue hardships. It consisted mainly of extra work which normally devolved to picking cigarette end and rubbish up from the upper deck. Paul was shaken a quarter of an hour earlier in the morning and spent the time picking up cigarette ends; during the dog watches he picked up cigarette ends for half an hour and did half an hour's drill under the supervision of the Duty Regulting Petty Officer Cadet; and he mustered for evening rounds outside the Cadet Office, having picked up cigarette ends for the last fifteen minutes.

After two days Paul became as expert as a truffle hound. He knew all the likely places for cigarette ends and visited them periodically, as a hunt draws likely coverts for fox. On the third day there were very few cigarette ends to pick up and Paul was forced to ask the other members of his gunroom to stub out their cigarette ends on the upper deck to give him some employment; even so he frequently found himself faced with endless stretches of deck barren of cigarette ends and he made an arrangement with the gunroom sweepers that they emptied their gunroom spitkids on to the upper deck as soon as they heard the defaulters call sounded off. On the fifth and last day of his punishment Paul had a fellow defaulter to keep him company and, when he went, to assume his mantle. It was Maconochie, who was given three days Number Eleven punishment by The Bodger for emptying his spitkid on to the upper deck instead of down a gash-shute.

Paul's punishment lasted until *Barsetshire* had finished painting ship and sailed to her next port, on the Côte d'Azur.

The bay where *Barsetshire* anchored was cupped in hills which were studded with villas and groves of trees. The small town was built of narrow, red and yellow houses which mounted the hillside to the Corniche above. The harbour was filled with yachts and *Barsetshire* was surrounded by tiny floats paddled by bronzed and near-naked Frenchmen. Monte Carlo lay a few miles to the east, Nice a few miles to the west and the Alpes Maritimes rose up in the blue background.

Michael's first special duty was Main Signals Office messenger. The duties of M.S.O. Messenger, as described by the Chief G.I., were to deliver signals to the officers addressed, make the tea for the watch, and keep out of the Chief Yeoman's way.

When Michael reported, he found the office deserted but a murmur of voices led him out on to the Flag Deck where several signalmen were gathered round the largest telescope in the ship. Their attention was so close and unwinking that Michael thought that a signal of unusual interest was being passed. Perhaps England had declared war on France, or the Commander been promoted.

'Coo!' said the nearest signalman. 'That's what I want for Christmas, mother dear.'

'Let's have it over here a minute, Johno. I think I can see a good one.'

'You go and get stuffed. This is all mine. Keep your filthy fingers off while I look at what makes the world go round.'

Michael picked up a pair of binoculars, followed the signalman's line of sight, and saw a young woman sunbathing in the garden of a villa. She was wearing a very short bathing costume.

'Left a bit,' said a voice at Michael's elbow.

Michael shifted left and saw another young woman, wearing an even briefer costume; it seemd to Michael that she was not so much wearing it as lying near it.

'Now look right and down a bit at five o'clock,' said the voice.

Michael again obeyed and understood the signalmen's absorption. For there lay a third young woman. There was no costume, merely the young woman. Michael had always thought that the Communications Branch led a dull and miserable existence, but he now saw that they, like everybody else, had their compensations.

'Not bad at all,' said the voice.

'Would you like a look?'

'Yes please.'

Michael took the binoculars from his eyes and handed them over.

'Thank you,' said the Communications Officer.

★ ★ ★ ★

Meanwhile, Ted Maconochie was having difficulty with his special duty. He was bowman of a motor boat.

When a boat approached the gangway, the bowman was required to climb on to the forepeak with his boat-hook and there perform a series of exercises known as boat-hook drill.

'Thump your boat-hook twice on the deck,' said the Chief G.I., 'to give your sternsheetsman the tip. Throw your boat-hook up, catch it at the point of balance, swing it horizontal, and then shift your grip to catch the boatrope.'

It was not a series of movements which lent itself to grace; Maconochie, even after considerable practice, still looked like a drum-major on stilts.

The coxswain of the boat was an Indian named Rorari who was not a good coxswain.

'The best thing you can do,' said Maconochie to Rorari, 'is fall overboard and let someone else have a go who knows what he's doing.'

Maconochie's advice was apt when Rorari next brought his boat alongside the gangway. Rorari was lying off when the Officer of the Watch, the Gunnery Officer, came out on to the platform of the gangway to motion him with his telescope to come alongside.

Rorari's boat leapt forward, struck the gangway, and bore up on it, goring it like a savage bull. The gangway swayed under the impact like a reed in a storm and a violent shiver passed up its length. The Gunnery Officer lost his balance and plummeted down into the sea. Rorari opened his throttle wide and accelerated so swiftly that the sternsheetsman, who had been gazing compassionately at the spot of bubbling sea where he had last seen the Gunnery Officer, was caught unawares and silently vanished away over the stern. Maconochie laughed scornfully.

Rorari, who was looking for a scapegoat, heard the laugh.

'Mac'notchee!' he screeched. 'I see you! I see you! You say you are not doing anything while all the time you are doing something! All the time you are laughing, joking say 'Fall overboard!' You ball me up I ditch you!'

Maconochie gave another scornful laugh. Rorari wrenched the wheel hard over. The boat tilted in a tight circle and Maconochie flew off at a tangent.

The third member of the crew, the stoker, a Sikh named Singh, realized that every man who sailed with Rorari was, like the men who sailed with Hawkins, doomed to a watery grave, kept his eye down and studied his gauges and was still on board when Rorari came alongside again, which he did by driving the boat at the gangway and allowing the gangway to stop the boat. The Gunnery Officer was waiting on the step.

'Rorari, Rorari, you're an incompetent, dangerous, criminal, nitwitted, blockheaded, thick-skulled, homicidal, bloody idiot!'

'Please sir, it was not my fault! It was not my fault, sir! The bowman balled me up, sir!'

'Who was your bowman?'

'Mac'notchee, sir!'

'Ah yes.'

Later in the evening The Bodger went ashore to Jimmy's Bar with the Communications Officer. They drank Dubonnet and watched the passers-by.

'Talent's not bad here at all, eh Bodger?'

Rorari wrenched the wheel and Maconochie flew off at a tangent.

'Not bad.'

'Not a bad figure at all, that last one.'

'Not bad. Bit shop-spoiled.'

The Bodger looked gloomily into his glass.

'Oh come, Bodger. Since when this looking of the gift-horse in the mouth?'

'Gift-horse?'

'My dear old Bodger, if you haven't learnt the signals by now, you've no right to call yourself an officer in charge of cadets' training. It's the first thing you should teach them.'

'What are you burbling about, Chris?'

'Forget it.'

The Communications Officer returned to his scrutiny of the local talent. The Bodger looked at his glass.

'Bolshie lot of cadets this cruise, Bodger?'

'Eh?'

'Bolshie this cruise?'

'Who?'

'*Cadets*. Oh, for Pete's sake, Bodger, snap out of it! What's troubling you?'

'Sorry, I was just thinking of all those cadets we've got on board.'

'What about them?'

'There they all are, just out of the egg, mad keen, anxious to learn and do well. Most of them, anyway. We encourage them, all of us from Admirals downwards, to *be* keen. And for what? For why? What's going to happen to them all?'

'Well, they'll all grow up and either be promoted and become admirals, or be passed over and grow onions.'

'That's not what I meant at all. We talk to them about officer-like qualities, we tell them all about word of command, lecture to them about leadership, fill them up with bull and they appear to believe it. Or if they don't believe it, they're polite enough to conceal it. Sometimes I think those cadets on board are laughing at us, humouring us as though we were a lot of fat uncles playing bears, and other times I think they believe every word and everything we do or say has the most frightful significance for the future. It's the second alternative which scares me, because not only are we deluding them, we're deluding ourselves.'

'Oh, everybody knows the whole thing is a colossal confidence trick,' the Communications Officer said. 'No cadet could do all he's expected to do in that vessel and come out alive, and anyone of us who tried to watch all of them all of the time would go straight round the bend.'

'I mean something much more serious than that. If we go on as we are now, in ten years' time there won't *be* any leaders or anyone whom we can draw on for officers. I don't mean to be snobbish in the least little bit but there used to be a class of people in the country who could be relied on to lead. They may have been queers, they may have seduced all the village girls and barred themselves up in their houses for years. They may have been megalomaniacs, or mad, or obstinate, or eccentric, or downright scoundrels but at least they knew how to *lead.*'

'Bodger, you sound like a curate with doubts! Don't you realize this is blasphemy! Don't you know there is but one God to be worshipped and the First Lord is his prophet and his address is Whitehall?'

The Bodger thumped his fist on the table. 'They're not doubts, they're *certainties.* Look at that cadet sitting over there. I used to know his family when we lived in their part of the world. Dewberry. They used to own a good part of the British Isles and one of his family have represented them in every war the country's had since Agincourt. And look at him. Do you think he wants to be in the Navy? Do you think he wants to lead men? Does he hell! He probably doesn't know what he wants but I'm damned certain he doesn't like what he's got! I can see the day coming in twenty years' time when most of these lads will be coming up for Captain, when the Navy will be run by the people, for the people, on behalf of the people. It's my favourite nightmare. Until there's a war, of course. When that happens command will be left in the hands of a few blokes who know what they're doing and do it without having to account for it, simply because there just isn't the time to check up on them. But the minute the shouting and tumult's over, and the captains and kings have departed, every Tom, Dick and Harry gets a chance to think twice about things and we go back to the good old days of 'For why did you do this when you knew so and so had happened?' and 'for what did you give that order when surely you were aware of the grave consequences of any continued deterioration in the so on and so on *ad nauseum?*' then when a war comes along the first thing you've got to do is sack all the peace-time admirals and promote new ones. The wretched fellows have got used to a state where they can't move a finger because one, they haven't got the money, and two, they have to answer for *everything* to the politicians. If a rating wants anythig to happen in a hurry all he's got to do is write to his M.P. and then sit back and watch the fur fly. Did I ever tell you about a very great friend of mine called Jimmy Forster-Jones?'

The name registered immediately upon the Communications Officer. 'The character who gassed the ship's company's canary?'

The Bodger thumped the table again.

'That's *exactly* what I'm getting at! Now Jimmy's known as the character who gassed the ship's company's canary. In spite of the fact that Jimmy was probably the finest clearance diver the Navy's ever had. He did more for good publicity for the Navy in those films about under-water warfare than anyone since Noël Coward. Do you know what actually happened about that canary?'

'Well, there were various yarns going about. The one I heard . . .'

'Jimmy's a friend of mine and I heard the whole story from him and from some of the other blokes who were in the ship at the time. Jimmy was a junior two-striper in a cruiser and he had a chap in his division who had a bucket-bird. You can buy them ashore in the Far East. When the bird's hungry it rings a little bell in its cage and you put the grub in a small basket and the bird hauls it up. Quite clever, in a monotonous sort of way. This particular bird didn't sing, dance or recite, it just rang the bell and hauled the bucket up. Well, one day this bird's owner, who was a bit of a bird himself, slapped in a request to see Jimmy about his bucket-bird. This character said his bird was not thriving on the messdeck. The fumes from some machinery space or other under the messdeck were making the bird cough and he wanted permission to hang the cage on the upper deck. Jimmy said O.K. but not until next week. There was an admiral's inspection coming off in a couple of days and the cage would be in the way of cleaning so Jimmy suggested that the bird should be put in the Sick Bay until the inspection was over and then it could go on the upper deck. The bird had been on the messdeck about a year already and a couple more days wouldn't do it any harm. But the character wouldn't have it. He said bucket-birds needed constant care and attention and they'd probably poison it in the Sick Bay or slit its throat or something. So the cage went back on the messdeck. As luck would have it the bird pegged out the very next day. When they looked at it the next morning, there it was, dead. It was probably just old, but there was the most terrible uproar about it! You know what Jolly Jack is like when he thinks the awficers are not respecting his rights.'

'You needn't tell me.'

'They all nattered about it so much that they eventually came round to the idea that Jimmy had actually got up in the middle of the night and poisoned the thing. You know how these things get going once they start. The owner of the bucket-bird wrote to his wife and she wrote to their M.P., complaining of the treatment her husband had received, you know, why couldn't sailors keep their pets like everyone else and what brutes the awficers were, starving and poisoning the sailors' dumb friends. This was just at the time when all the Marshals of the Royal Air Force were sounding off about how redundant the Navy was and this letter was just up the M.P.'s street. He wrote to the First Lord, who tackled the Board of Admiralty about it, who wrote to Jimmy's Captain and before Jimmy could say 'bucket-bird' he was up in his best bib and tucker before the Old Man.'

'Poor old toff.'

'Then the newspapers got hold of it. Front page headlines. 'Simple Humanities Unknown in Navy.' 'What Would Nelson Have Said?' 'Bucket-Bird Bloodbath.' 'Canary Carnage.' You probably saw them.'

'Yes I remember them.'

'Clergymen started writing for the Sunday newspapers about it and the *Daily Disaster* ran a special feature about the Navy bringing in everything from Captain Bligh to the Invergordon Mutiny. They even unearthed some cracked old retired commander living in Leicestershire and psycho-analysed him. The poor old sod found he'd been a sadist all his life and hadn't known anything about it. The Navy got beaten by the Army at Twickenham the next day and the *Daily Disaster* ran a special jubilee *edition* with all the print running sideways. Then the R.S.P.C.A. chimed in and old ladies began to hiss poor Jimmy in the street. Well, inside a week there was a full scale nausea. Chaps coming down from the Admiralty and Jimmy getting into swords and medals every time the bell struck. The part that really hurt Jimmy was when an old lady who ran an aviary wrote him a letter saying that she didn't think he was as bad as everyone said he was and would he come for a day and see over her aviary and see for himself that tiny defenceless birds could be charming companions – what the hell are you laughing at?'

The Communications Officer was leaning back in his chair with an expression of pain on his face. He had some difficulty in speaking.

'Oh . . . Bodger . . . I . . . I'm sorry,' he spluttered, 'but the idea of an N.O. being shown round an aviary by an old lady who thinks he's a monster . . . it's too much!

'Ha, ha,' said The Bodger nastily. 'It's finished Jimmy. I shall be very surprised if he ever gets promoted now. The trouble with a thing like that is that once it starts it gets bigger and the more it goes on, the more people hear about it, the more other people hear about it and the bigger the stink gets. That little episode went on and on until everybody was heartily sick of it. And it didn't do any good either. Jimmy is now known as the Scourge of God in the bird-fanciers' world. That rating certainly did not get recommended for leading hand and will have the reputation of being a sea-lawyer all the time he's in. And the First Lord was shifted to the Ministry of Agriculture. There wasn't even an enquiry into conditions on the messdeck. Apparently it never occurred to anyone that the fumes which gassed a bucket-bird might also do the same to human beings.'

'Ah well,' said the Communications Officer. 'That's life.'

★ ★ ★ ★

In spite of The Bodger's remarks about him, George Dewberry was enjoying the Mediterranean. It was providing a new and enchanting range of drinks to sample. George Dewberry sampled the local wines so fully that he was almost always drunk on shore. Many of the cadets were confused by the rush and excitement of the new places they visited; frequently their only memory of a town or port was the kind of liquor on which George Dewberry was drunk.

There was Sorrento, a town set in orange and olive trees, monastic calm and cliffs along the sea, where George Dewberry drank Orvieto; Pompeii, where Paul sported amongst buildings and statues, and George Dewberry drank Lacrima Cristi; Vesuvius, where, the funicular having been swept away by an eruption and not yet rebuilt, a guide rushed on up the mountain ahead of the cadets with bottles of vino rosso, which nobody bought at the price except George Dewberry; Capri, where the funicular broke down for half an hour and left the cadets seemingly suspended in a violet sky amongst the scents of jasmine, bougainvillea and poinsettia, and where George Dewberry took the opportunity of finishing a whole flask of Capri wine; and Naples, a city of high buildings on hills and tenements underneath, where George Dewberry drank a bottle and a half of Chianti and slept through an entire performance of 'I Pagliacci' (including two encores of 'Vesti la giubba' and one of 'No, Pagliaccio non son') by the San Carlo Opera Company.

A kindly providence watched over George Dewberry ashore. He was never robbed, nor did he ever lose the way back to some other cadets, nor did he ever fall and hurt himself. Only once was he in the hands of the police.

In Sorrento, George Dewberry was found sitting by himself on a seat late at night trying to sing the soprano part of 'Bella Figlia.' Two men in uniform lifted him to his feet and started walking him back to the ship. As soon as he understood what was happening to him, George Dewberry thrust them away.

'Take your hands off me,' he said. 'You can't do this to me. I'm a British citishen. Take your hands off me this minute or I'll call the Carabinieri.'

'We are the Carabinieri,' said the larger of the two men.

THE BATTLE OF THE RIVER PLATE
Dudley Pope

During the Second World War, three British ships, Achilles, Exeter *and* Ajax
are on the trail of the German ship Graf Spee.

When the lookout in the *Achilles* had called out 'Smoke bearing Red one
double-oh, Sir,' Captain Parry and Lt Washbourn had walked
unhurriedly over to the port wing of the bridge. Both of them had heard
scores of similar reports before, and each time a merchant ship had come
into sight. There was no tension, only boredom . . .

Captain Parry levelled his binoculars at the smoke and Washbourn
looked through the Principal Control Officer's sight – powerful
binoculars mounted on a moveable arm.

There was, however, no mistaking what they saw. There was a thin
feather of orange-brown smoke hanging low on the horizon. Beneath it
they could see a gunnery control tower and a mast; but it was a gunnery
control tower and a mast of a peculiar and unmistakable design.

They both turned to each other.

'My God,' said Captain Parry, 'it's a pocket battleship. Sound the
alarm, Pilot. Warn the engine room that we will be going on to full speed
shortly, and are going into action.'

He wrote later: 'I remember a rather sickening feeling in the pit of my
tummy as I realised we were in for an action in which the odds were
hardly on our side. Luckily there wasn't much time to think about that.'

As Washbourn started to climb back to the DCT the Chief Yeoman of

Signals, Lincoln Martinson, reported: '*Exeter* has hoisted Flag N, Sir . . . "Enemy in sight".'

On the bridge Cowburn had automatically taken over from Washbourn as officer of the watch and from now on would give all helm and engine orders (Captain Parry would give him all the instructions, addressing him as 'Pilot').

The first order had come very promptly.

'Open out to about three or four cables from the *Ajax*, Pilot, and keep loose formation. Weave when the pocket battleship fires at us, but don't use too much rudder.'

By that time the ship's company were racing to their Action Stations. Having fallen out at 0550, almost every one of them not at Defence Stations had turned in again. Sleep was very precious in wartime, and the forty minutes before 'Call the hands' at 0630 was not to be missed.

As the alarm rattlers had sounded, followed by a bugle's urgent doh soh-soh, doh soh-soh calling them to 'Action' (which was not preceded and followed by the 'G' indicating 'exercise'), they tumbled out of their hammocks and ran to their quarters in all sorts of garb – pyjamas, underclothes, shorts or anything they could grab on the way.

Down in the engine room Lt Jasper Abbott, a small, precise man with a neatly-trimmed black beard, worked under the Commander (E) in the ever-present task of using sluggish fuel oil to turn water into super-heated steam – a transformation undreamt of by ancient alchemists intent on changing base metals into gold, but far more valuable. It was steam which at 700 degrees Fahrenheit was invisible, yet three times hotter than boiling water; steam which could strip the flesh from a man's body within seconds.

Each pair of the *Achille's* six boilers supplied steam to an engine room, forming a self-contained unit. If one unit was damaged and flooded, another could keep the ship moving at a reasonable speed.

While the men in the engine room were hard at work providing more steam for the ever-hungry turbines, the guns' crews were getting ready. Lt Washbourn had climbed into his seat in the Director Control Tower and pulled on headphones and the microphone transmitter. In a moment he would be in communication with all the gun turrets and the Transmitting Station. He was preparing to unleash more destructive power in one minute than a medieval emperor dreamt of in a lifetime.

He switched on the microphone.

'Control, TS. Testing communications . . . Report when closed up . . . Enemy in sight bearing Red nine oh . . . All quarters with CPBC[1] and full charges load!'

These orders, repeated with loud shouts in the gun turrets, caused an exchange of meaningful glances: the men, in their hurried dash to their positions, had no time to glean any news. Now they realised something was very definitely in the wind.

By this time the whole Director Control Tower had trained round towards the enemy, like an owl with many eyes. Washbourn was looking through sterescopic binoculars at the *Graf Spee* on the horizon. Between his knees was the gun-ready lamp box with eight indicators on its face. Each of these would glow red as the gun it represented was loaded and ready to fire.

Sitting on Washbourn's right was the Spotting Officer, Sergeant Samuel Trimble. This big, red-faced Ulsterman was better known as 'Baggy' Trimble, and his job was spotting the fall of the *Achille's* shells and reporting them to the Transmitting Station.

On Washbourn's left was the Rate Officer, Mr Eric Watts. Rotund, placid and very competent, he was the Gunner. He had the difficult job of estimating the *Graf Spee's* course and speed, and any alterations she might make, and reporting constantly to the Transmitting Station.

Behind these three men were Telegraphist Frank Stennett, who would be the link with the *Ajax* when the two ships' gunfire was concentrated, Telegraphist Neville Milburn, who would pass on flank-marking reports from the *Exeter*, and Boy Dorsett, a young New Zealand lad who operated the telephones to the turrets.

Above the telegraphists, was the Position-in-Line (PIL) Rangetaker, Able Seaman Shirley, a New Zealander. Using a special instrument, and with his head stuck out of the DCT, he was taking the range of the *Ajax* to get the correction for the position in line when gunfire was concentrated and the *Achilles* was using the *Ajax's* fire orders.

In the forward section of the DCT, sitting lower than the others, were

---

[1] Common Pointed Ballistic Capped: the then latest six-inch armour-piercing shell. The 'ballistic cap' was a light steel nose fitted on the shell to streamline it and so increase the range for a given charge.

four more men. Two of them operated the Director Sight, the master eye by which all the ship's guns were aimed. And they were men hand-picked by Washbourn: men who had keen eyes and keen minds, who would not get flustered or frightened, and who could be relied on, whether the ship was rling or pitching in a heavy sea, zig-zagging, burning or sinking, to go on turning the hand wheels which would keep the Director Sight, and, in turn, the guns aimed at the chosen enemy.

Working at the left side of the sight, an eye glued to a stabilised telescope, was the Director Layer, Petty Officer Alfred Maycock. He was responsible for laying the guns vertically on the enemy (elevation) and, when ordered, pressing the trigger which would fire them simultaneously. On his right was the Director Trainer, Petty Officer William Headon, who trained the guns horizontally.

The other two men with them were the Range to Elevation and Deflection unit Operator, Able Seaman Shaw, and the Cross-Level Operator, Ordinary Seaman Rogers.

Below the DCT was the rangefinder. It worked like a pair of vast human eyes except that Chief Petty Officer William Bonniface and a New Zealander, Able Seaman Gould, focused them; and instead of a brain to register the range, there were dials which were repeated in various parts of the ship.

But although the DCT and the rangefinder were the ship's eyes and the kingdom of the Gunnery Officer, a mechanical 'brain' several decks below, protected by armour, worked out all the complicated mathematics which would ensure that the shells, if Headon and Maycock aimed the Director Sight correctly, arrived on the target.

This 'brain' was officially called the Admiralty Fire Control Table and it was situated in the Transmitting Station. It was a fantastic product of scientific designing, and when it had certain information fed into it, it transmitted a series of answers, or corrections, to the guns.

When the enemy position (from the Director Sight), range (from the rangefinders), speed and course (from the Rate Officer), and fall of shot (from the Spotting Officer), were fed in, it–

Indicated how much the guns had to be trained left or right;

Gave the correct angle of elevation for them;

Worked out precisely where the *Achilles'* shells had to fall, allowing for the problem that she and the *Graf Spee* would each be going in different directions at upwards of twenty-five knots, and the shells would be in the air for almost a minute, and applied the necessary correction;

Allowed for the fact that the right-handed spin given to the shell by the rifling of the gun made it wander to the right;

Allowed for the effect of wind on the shell while it was in flight, and for the temperature and barometric pressure;

Caused the aim of each gun to converge on the target (if the guns were aimed in the same direction they would shoot on parallel lines and the shells would fall the same distance apart as the guns were in the ship. This spread would be far too great);

Allowed for the fact that, when firing over the bow, each gun would be at different distances from the enemy and would require slightly different elevations.

Thus, as Maycock and Headon aimed the Director Sight at the *Graf Spee*, the enemy's elevation and bearing were transmitted to the 'Table' and also to the guns, which trained round in the same direction.

But the Director Sight was aimed directly at the enemy. Since the shells would be in the air for a minute, the guns would have to be aimed at where the *Graf Spee* would be in a minute's time. This 'aim off', called 'deflection', was worked out by the Table and sent electrically to the guns.

But in far less time than it took you to read this, Washbourn was giving his next order:

'Broadsides.'

Every gun in A and B turrets forward and X and Y turrets aft was now loaded with a 112-lb shell and a 30-lb cordite charge. Breeches were closed, and in each breech was placed a small tube like a rifle cartridge with the bullet removed. In the base of the tube – which was filled with explosive – was a thin iridio-platinum wire, and when the Director Layer pressed the trigger an electric current would flow across and fuse it, firing the explosive which would in turn explode the cordite charge.

Quickly the gun-ready lamps in the box between Washbourn's knees flickered on – one, two (X turret, manned by the Royal Marines, was the first to be ready), three, four, five . . .

Washbourn leaned over and spoke into the voicepipe to the bridge. 'Captain, Sir.'

'Yes, Guns?' replied Captain Parry.

'Ready to open fire.'

'Open fire.'

Washbourn glanced at the gun-ready box: all eight lamps were glowing.

He spoke into the microphone:

'Shoot!'

The fire going in the DCT sounded its 'ting ting' and Petty Officer Headon, his left hand automatically spinning the elevating hand wheel to keep the Director Sight aimed at the base of the *Graf Spee's* foremast, squeezed the trigger and completed the circuit.

Electricity flowed across the iridio-platinum bridges – far more than their resistance of 0.9 ohm could take – and fused them. Spurts of flame leapt out to explode the 30-lb charges of cordite, packed like long strings of macaroni in silk bags, and turn it into gas – far more than the chambers could hold without bursting. Something had to give way – the shells.

They were thrust up the barrels, spinning one and a half times as they engaged in the thirty-six grooves of the rifling, and leaving at more than 2,000 miles an hour. They would rise nearly 19,000 feet into the atmosphere before plunging down 60.89 seconds later; and they would burst between twenty-two and twenty-seven millionths of a second after striking with a velocity of 1,500 feet per second.

But once the shells left the barrels the guns' crews were concerned with the next broadside. Each gun, weighing six and three quarter tons was flung back by the enormous power of the cordite and stopped after thirty and a half inches by the recoil cylinder, and then thrust into position again by the run-out springs.

Another shell and another charge came up the hoists to each gun from the magazines, which were hidden behind armour well below the waterline; the breeches were flung open and blasts of compressed air automatically cleared the cordite chambers of any burning residue; soaking-wet rammers – better known as 'woolly 'eaded bastards' – were thrust up the chambers to clean them and cool the mushroom head of the breech block; shells were swung into the chambers and rammed home; charges were slid in after them; the tubes were changed and the breeches closed.

One after another the eight gun-ready lamps in front of Washbourn flicked on again.

Maycock and Headon were still keeping the Director Sight on the *Graf Spee*; Sergeant Trimble was still waiting for the shells to land and Watts was reporting on the pocket battleship's course and bearing. The Deflection had come up from the Table to train the guns round slightly.

'Shoot!' said Lt Washbourn in the *Achilles*.

'Shoot!' said Lt Desmond Dreyer in the *Ajax*.

'Shoot!' said Lt-Cdr Richard Jennings in the *Exeter*.

The *Achilles* had opened fire at 0622, and the *Ajax* at 0623. The range was just over 19,000 yards. The *Ajax's* first broadside fell short. This was signalled to the Transmitting Station, and the Table did many more calculations so that the next salvo would fall where the *Graf Spee* should be sixty seconds after the shells left the guns.

When Lt Dreyer, the Control Officer, ordered 'Up ladder, shoot', the elevation of the guns was adjusted up the scale and the guns fired again. The shells burst over. The range was corrected and a zig-zag group – the guns being so elevated that the salvoes would fall in a zig-zag pattern – fired.

A rapid group was being fired when suddenly the *Ajax* was straddled by a salvo of 11-inch shells from the *Graf Spee*. Immediately Commodore Harwood ordered a thirty-degree turn to starboard to dodge the next salvo and the *Ajax*, steaming at twenty-five knots, heeled as she swung round, followed by the *Achilles*.

The guns of both the cruisers were thrown out by this sudden alteration of course; but rapidly the DCTs and Transmitting Stations brought the turrets round again. Two minutes later the Commodore altered back to the original course, and Captain Parry, whose orders were to conform loosely with the *Ajax's* movements, brought the *Achilles* round again.

From the *Graf Spee's* log: 'The light cruisers pulled rapidly ahead so that at 0625 from their twenty-eight-degree to twenty-five-degree relative bearing there was a danger of torpedo attack. The Captain decided . . . to slowly turn away on to a northerly course. At the same time he ordered a change of target on to the left, light cruiser . . .

'At 0631 the main batteries had another target change to the *Exeter*. At the same time the light cruisers opened fire against the *Graf Spee* without at first scoring any hits.[1]

'The *Exeter* turned to starboard on to a westerly course (and) *Graf Spee* turned with rudder hard to port to a course of 270 degrees. The light cruisers were now quartering off to port and turning slowly to port.

'About 0634 the *Exeter* turned sharply away after heavy hits – only Turret C was still firing – making heavy smoke and for the time being was out of sight.

'The light cruisers were travelling at full speed off the starboard quarter. They could be brought under fire with B turret and secondary batteries several times, but only for short periods because of their use of smoke and fog'.[2]

As soon as he saw the *Graf Spee* swinging round to port at 0637, Commodore Harwood ordered Captain Woodhouse to steer first north and then west to close the range again. As she moved north-westward, away from the three British ships, the pocket battleship started making smoke. Billowing black and brown clouds soon hid the ship for long periods.

The rate officers could see she was zig-zagging violently to avoid the salvoes of the three cruisers; and there was the satisfaction that it threw off the *Graf Spee's* gunners more than it did the British.

Lt Lewin, the pilot of the *Ajax's* Seafox, was anxious to get into the air. After the *Graf Spee* had opened fire he asked Captain Woodhouse: 'Can I take off?'

The aircraft would be useful for spotting; but X and Y turrets were firing within a few feet of the aircraft as it stood on its catapult. At this stage Captain Woodhouse was more concerned with the rate of fire. 'If you can,' he said, 'but I'm not going to hold fire for you.'

That was enough for Lewin. With Kearney, his observer, he went aft to the Seafox which had been prepared for catapulting by Pennefather and Warrant Engineer Arthur Monk. Blast from the muzzles of the guns in X and Y turrets was shaking the aircraft as the two men climbed into their seats. The catapult was trained round and, with her engine at full throttle the tiny Seafox was flung into the air.

---

[1] In fact the *Achilles* opened fire at 0622 and the *Ajax* at 0623.

[2] The cruisers were not deliberately making smoke at this stage.

Just before this, Kearney discovered that the Seafox's wireless was tuned into the reconnaissance wave of 230 kcs instead of the spotting wave of 3800 kcs. To save time he decided to use 230 kcs instead of re-tuning the set, and made a visual signal to the flagdeck telling them to warn the W/T office. This message was never passed on, and the omission was to have a serious result in the early part of the action.

While Lewin climbed to 3,000 feet, the *Achilles* was concentrating her gunfire with the *Ajax* and after thirteen broadsides a salvo of 11-inch shells from the *Graf Spee* erupted in the sea along her port side. Hundreds of splinters spun into the air, several of them cutting through the light plating round the bridge. Six sliced through the 1-inch armour of the DCT, making it look like a tin savaged by a large tin opener.

Captain Parry woke up to find himself prostrate on the deck with Martinson, the Chief Yeoman of Signals, lying nearby and moaning.

He stood up, conscious that all the *Achilles's* guns had stopped firing. Then he saw that they were pointing in the wrong direction . . . Previously, when the *Graf Spee's* gunfire had been getting unpleasantly close, he had told Cowburn: 'Alter *towards* the splashes, Pilot. That will probably upset his gunnery more than anything else we can do.'

Cowburn had been playing this game very skilfully – Captain Parry was later to attribute the *Achilles'* apparent invulnerability to this – and as soon as the salvo landed along the port side Cowburn had ordered a high-speed turn to port.

The idea behind this was that the *Graf Spee*, spotting her own salvoes, would make an 'up' correction for 'shorts' and a 'down' correction for 'overs'. By steering the *Achilles* towards the splashes, Captain Parry would always be steering away from where the second (and correct) salvo would fall.

Realising the Gunnery Control was not functioning Captain Parry went to the voicepipe and called up to the Director Control Tower. There was no reply.

At that moment someone said: 'Look at your legs!' Captain Parry glanced down. Blood was streaming down the back of one of his calves. He sat down on the edge of the monkey island, the platform round the two compasses, and within a few moments the first-aid party arrived.

They found that Martinson's left leg had been hit with splinters and he had a compound fracture of the tibia. Splints were tied on and he was taken away on a stretcher – still asking whether 'my boys' were all right.

The Sick Berth Petty Officer bandaged one of Captain Parry's legs and then said, 'Now the other leg, please, Sir.' Preoccupied with the battle, Captain Parry said, 'Oh, what's wrong with that?' Looking down he saw that it, too, had been badly cut with splinters.

Up in the DCT the situation was far worse. Washbourn – in his official report he wrote 'I was conscious of a hellish noise and a thump on the head' – came round to find the tiny compartment in a shambles. There were several jagged holes in the armour and the wind whistled in.

Behind him both the telegraphists, Milburn and Stennett, had collapsed, killed outright. One of the bodies had fallen through into the tiny rangefinder compartment below (CPO Bonniface was later to report 'A good bit of vibration was set up inside the rangefinder by our own speed and gunfire. Ranging was otherwise comfortable bar the fact of having a corpse at the back of the neck most of the time made it unpleasant. A B Gould kept calm during the action and did not take any notice of the extra ventilation we were getting. He got a bit peeved over a foot sticking in his ear, but soon settled down after it was removed . . .').

The Concentration Link Rangetaker, Edgar Shirley, had dropped off his stool and was bleeding badly from wounds in his thighs and face. Sergeant Trimble had been severely wounded in the back but he said nothing and carried on with his job so that no one would know he had been hit.

Shaw, the R to ED Unit Operator, was dead from multiple wounds in his chest; but he had slumped over his instrument in such a way that no one knew he had been hit. Washbourn saw that both Headon and Maycock were still all right at the Director Sight, and Boy Dorsett was still alive.

Mr Watts, the Rate Officer, spoke quickly into his microphone: 'DCT has been hit. After Control take over.'

Then he stood up and said to Washbourn:

'Come on, Sir. Running repairs.'

Washbourn, still rather dazed, did not understand. 'What's up? I'm all right.'

He put his hand to his head, and it came away sticky. He climbed off his stool as Watts took down a first-aid bag, extracted a bandage, and tied up the scalp wounds.

Climbing back into his seat, Washbourn called down the voicepipe: 'Control; bridge.'

Cowburn answered almost immediately.

'Tell the Captain that the DCT has been hit and the After Control is now controlling. Send up first-aid parties.'

That dealt with, he called out to the surviving DCT crew: 'What's out of action?'

Headon turned from his telescope to say: 'Director seems all right, Sir.'

Meanwhile the *Achilles* started shooting again, but the gunfire was extremely ragged because the After Control position was very ineffective. The two men manning it had been experiencing the continous blast from the muzzles of X turret guns and were completely deafened and nearly stupid from concussion. Although they were also being sick from time to time they carried on as best they could.

Washbourn, realising it was essential that the DCT started operating again as soon as possible, said:

'We'll see what happens. Switch to DCT controlling.'

Everything seemed to work all right, and while Watts deftly tied a tourniquet on Shirley's leg to stop some of the bleeding, Washbourn went to work.

'DCT controlling,' he said into the microphone. 'Broadsides . . . Shoot!'

Nearly a dozen broadsides had been loosed off before Petty Officer Maycock turned round from the Director Sight and reported: 'Archie's had it, Sir.'

Washbourn stooped in his seat and looked down into the forward part of the DCT. He saw that Shaw, sitting at his instrument in a natural position, was in fact dead.

He called to the cross-level operator: 'Rogers, take over Shaw's job.'

It was fortunate that Washbourn, in the previous weeks of practice, had made sure that all the men in the DCT could do every job. Rogers, who took over his new task without a word, could not move Shaw's body; and he had to sit on it to operate the instrument until later in the action.

It was about this time that Boy Dorsett, who had escaped unscathed, could be heard talking angrily into the telephone to the turrets.

Somehow the rumour had got around that he had been killed. 'I'm *not* dead', he said. 'I tell you I'm not *dead*. It's me who's speaking to you.'

When the DCT was hit all wireless communications with the *Ajax* failed and concentrated gunfire was impossible. It is unlikely that Washbourn was very upset by this – no self-respecting Gunnery Officer likes to have the control of his guns taken away from him.

From Captain Bell's report: '. . . At 0620 A and B turrets opened fire at a range of 18,700 yards, Y, turret joining in two-and-a-half minutes later, having been given permission to disregard the aircraft. At this time the ship was being straddled. At 0623 a shell bursting just short amidships killed a tube's crew, damaged communications, and splinters riddled the searchlight, funnels and starboard aircraft . . .'

★ ★ ★ ★

The *Exeter* had been steaming with four boilers in B boiler room, and as the alarm was sounded all the boilers in A boiler room were flashed up and connected. At 0620 Captain Bell ordered full speed, and by that time the Damage Control Headquarters in the Engineer's Workshop was closed up and the majority of the outlying parties had reported correct.

The Gunnery Officer, Lt-Cdr Jennings, had straddled the *Graf Spee* with his third salvo of 8-inch shells. The prospects looked promising and he ordered a zig-zag group.

At that moment one of six 11-inch shells from a broadside fired by the *Graf Spee* landed in the water close alongside the *Exeter*, just short of amidships. A shower of splinters spattered the ship like a handful of rubble flung at a window.

Some spun aft, cutting down, and killing most of the crew of the starboard torpedo tubes; others pierced the thin steel plating of the ship's side and killed two of the decontamination party waiting in the Chief Stoker's bathroom and started a small fire among clothing and towels.

Still more sprayed the searchlights, the two funnels and the starboard aircraft. Electric leads were cut and holes pierced in the upper deck. All the gun-ready lamp circuits and the fall of shot hooter went out of action, making Lt-Cdr Jennings' job as Gunnery Officer doubly difficult. Now he was unable to tell when all his guns were loaded, how many splashes to look for, or when his salvoes were falling.

Immediately reports started coming into the Damage Control Headquarters and parties were sent up to start repairing the damage. Men began to douse the fires, plug the holes in the ship's side and upper deck, and shore down hatches in the compartments below. The bodies were dragged away from the torpedo tubes and fresh men took over. Wounded were led or carried to the Medical Stations.

A few moments later the *Graf Spee* scored her first direct hit on the cruiser. An 11-inch shell smashed through the embarkation hatch on deck abaft B turret, ploughed into the Sick Bay, and went outwards through the ship's side into the sea without bursting.

A Sick Berth Chief Petty Officer was walking back from the fore part of the Sick Bay with bottles of morphine sulphate solution when the shell came through and sent splinters flying through the bulkhead. He was knocked unconscious and the precious bottles fell from his hands and smashed. Men in agony from wounds were waiting for the relief that morphine would give them . . .

When he came round he realised what had happened and stumbled back through the smoke and fumes to get more solution. Coughing and half suffocated, he could not find any bottles so he brought back morphine ampoules. But his troubles were only just starting – the task of helping the wounded had to alternate with dealing with the water flooding through the splinter-ridden deckhead, and the *Exeter* was still to be struck by another six 11-inch shells.

But within a minute of this hit the *Graf Spee* was to deliver an almost decisive blow.

From Captain Bell's report: '. . . After the eighth salvo B turret received a direct hit from an 11-inch shell and was put out of action. The splinters also killed or wounded all the bridge personnel with the exception of the Captain, Torpedo Control and Firing Officers, and wrecked the wheelhouse communications . . .'

As mentioned earlier, the *Graf Spee*, after firing four salvoes of base-fused shells, switched over to impact fuses 'in order to obtain the greatest possible damage to the lightly-armoured turrets and superstructure and through hits on its hull to reduce the ship's speed'.[1]

One of these shells landed on B turret just between the two guns, ripping off the front armour plate and killing eight men at the front of the gunhouse.

They had fired seven broadsides and the Number Ones of the two guns were just about to ram home the next rounds when the shell burst. All the lights went out, leaving the gunhouse in darkness, and dense, acrid fumes started to burn the nostrils and throats of the stunned survivors.

Sergeant Arthur Wilde, RM, groped for the Number Ones who should have been either side of him, but they were not in their seats. Then he saw daylight coming in through the left rear door of the gunhouse, which had been blown open, and he made his way out on deck.

'As I was going aft,' Wilde reported later, 'Marine Attwood called for me to assist him with Marine W. A. Russell. I turned and saw Russell had lost a forearm and was badly hurt in the other arm.

'Attwood and I assisted Russell down to the port 4-inch gundeck and as we reached it there was another violent explosion which seemed to be in the vicinity of B turret. I dropped to the deck, pulling Russell with me.

'After the splinters had stopped, I cut off two lengths of signal halyard, which were hanging loose, and put a clove hitch for a tourniquet around both of Russell's arms above the elbows.

'I went to the Sick Bay and told someone that I had left Russell sitting against the funnel casing, port side. I proceeded down to the waist and turned forward, intending to go to B magazine and shell room, but was ordered back as the gangway was blocked by CPO Evans who was attending to a man who was seriously injured around the legs . . .

'Sometime later I collected Marines Camp, Attwood and Thomas, and we went back to B turret to see what could be done. I observed several small fires, some of which were put out by sand, the fire hydrants being dry.

'Marine Thomas drew my attention to a small fire near the left elevating standard, and I sent him for water and sand. Then remembering I had seen water in the starboard waist, I went down for

[1] Later in the action she reverted to base-fueled shells.

some. When I returned Lt Toase, assisted by Marine Thomas, had extinguished the fire and we proceeded to take the cordite from both rammers and pass it overboard . . .'

While this was being done, the badly-wounded Russell, his clothing bloodstained and his arms still bound with signal halyard, walked round making cheering remarks and, in the words of Captain Bell, 'encouraging all by his fortitude'. (He stayed on deck until after the action, when he collapsed.)

While the guns' crews were handling the dangerous cordite charges, Sergeant Puddifoot was dealing with the magazine and shell room below. When the shell burst, 'We heard a violent crash and felt a shock from above, and simultaneously the turret pump stopped', Puddifoot wrote later.

He called the gunhouse several times but there was no reply. Two men just above them told him they were sure it had gone. He ordered two ratings to continue calling the gunhouse, opened the escape hatch to the magazine, and then told everyone to abandon it.

'When this had been done,' Puddifoot wrote, 'I once more challenged the gunhouse and still having no reply I decided to abandon and ordered everybody on to the Boys' and Torpedo messdecks to await further orders . . . When I reached the messdeck the Sergeant-Major informed me that he had reported by phone to Damage Control Headquarters and that we were to await further orders, and acting on instructions from SPO Knight, in command of Fire and Repair Parties in that sector, we lay down clear of the gangways.

'Shortly after this the ship was struck by the shell which damaged the CPOs' flat and I told SPO Knight to use my people as he liked, and I tried to get aft to ascertain the proximity of the fire with reference to the magazine. Owing to the intense heat and glare it was impossible at that time to enter the CPOs' flat and in view of the fact that the magazine was immediately below I decided to flood, and went below to the handling room.

'The lights were out but ERA Bond, equipped with a torch, followed me down, and together we unshipped the hopper guards, battened down the doors, flung what cordite we could find through the escape door, battened that, and then opened up the flood and seacock . . .'

But although the shell had hit B turret, the worst damage was done on the bridge just above: a withering shower of splinters, like spray from a big sea, had been flung up at more than the speed of sound and cut through the thin armour and window openings, ricocheted down from the metal roof and killed or wounded nearly every man on the bridge.

Within a fraction of a second the *Exeter* was changed from a perfectly-handled fighting ship to an uncontrolled machine. The wheelhouse was wrecked; all communications to the engine room and Lower Steering Position were cut. Captain Bell had been wounded in the face. Among the dead were the Navigating Officer, plotting staff and the men standing either side of Captain Bell.

It took Captain Bell only a few seconds to realise that, with all controls gone, he could not fight the ship from the bridge any longer, and he would have to take over from the After Conning Position. He gave his orders and with the survivors made his way aft as quickly as possible.

The *Exeter's* guns – with the exception of B turret – were still firing; but with no one on the bridge to con the ship she was slowly turning to starboard.

Just after Captain Bell and the rest of the survivors had left the bridge to hurry aft, Sub-Lieutenant Clyde Morse, who was in the Air Defence Officer's Position, happened to look down at the bridge and saw no one there – except for dead and badly-wounded men lying about in grotesque attitudes among the wreckage.

Realising the ship was out of control and seeing the wheelhouse was wrecked, yet not knowing quite what had happened, he jumped down and ran to the buckled voicepipe communicating with the Lower Steering Position. Above the thunder of A and Y turrets' guns and the cries of the wounded he managed to shout down 'Steer 275 degrees'.

In the meantime the Torpedo Officer, Lt-Cdr Charles J. Smith, who had been knocked down by the blast of the bursting shell, was on his way aft to join Captain Bell. He had not gone far before he saw that the *Exeter* was turning to starboard, away from the enemy: in a minute or two, he realised, she would be so far round that the 'A arcs'[1] would close and A turret would not be able to fire.

Running back to the bridge he found Morse had managed to get one message through to the Lower Steering Position, and he was able to pass

[1] The bearings on which the main armament could fire.

A withering shower of splinters ricocheted down from the roof.

the order 'Port 25' to bring her round again.

Captain Bell, wounded in the face, arrived at the After Conning Position to find the steering-order transmitter and the telephone had been put out of action, so that the whole position was isolated. Midshipman Bonham, whose action station was the After Control Position ran down to the After Steering Position with helm orders while a chain of ratings was being formed to repeat Captain Bell's orders.

As soon as this was done, Captain Bell sent Bonham forward to the bridge to hoist the Not-under-control balls.[1] He reached the bridge safely despite splinters flying up from near misses, and with the help of Yeoman Harben, who was wounded in the thigh, hoisted them on one of the few remaining halyards. They had been up only a few seconds when the halyard parted.

Stoker John Minhinnet had previously been ordered by Captain Bell to go to the engine room and tell them to change over to the After Steering Position. He made his way down to the control platform and, above the din of the turbines, now spinning at full speed, passed the message.

He was told to go on to the After Steering Position and give the order direct to the Engine Room Artificer in charge; but on the way there a shell bursting close alongside wounded him. A first aid party took him to the after medical station, but Minhinnet refused any treatment until he was sure his message was delivered.

But the *Exeter* was hitting back at the *Graf Spee*. Mr Cook, the Director Gunner, reported: 'I think it was with our fifth or sixth salvo that we straddled and obtained a hit near the funnel. In different salvoes after this I saw several hits, while the whole of one salvo appeared to burst just along the waterline. The Control ordered an up correction, having taken this as a short. Soon after the fall of this salvo the enemy made smoke and altered course.'

About this time the Chief Quartermaster, Petty Officer William Green, was seriously wounded. Green was at the Upper Steering Position when the bridge was wrecked, and at once went below to make

---

[1] Two black balls which, when hoisted vertically, indicated that a vessel is not under control.

sure that the Lower Steering Position was undamaged and fully manned. Finding everything all right there he started to make his way aft when he was hit.

Meanwhile the two aircraft had been riddled with splinters and twisted by blast. The one on the port side had been fuelled at dawn and petrol was by now spurting from the tanks and blowing aft over the deck and the After Conning Position.

The triatic stay linking the two masts had been cut by blast or splinters, and the heavy wire had fallen across the starboard aircraft. But Leading Seaman Shoesmith realised that both the planes would have to be jettisoned very shortly.

Without waiting for orders, and despite the fact that the blast from Y turret's guns and the enemy shells dropping round the ship might set alight his petrol-soaked clothes or explode the fuel in the tanks, he climbed up on to the wing and dragged the heavy wire clear.

The Gunner, Mr Shorten, had been round to try and help the men wounded at the torpedo tubes when he met Cdr Graham, who had already been wounded. He ordered Shorten to get the charges for firing the catapults to get rid of the two damaged aircraft. The Gunner had already made them up the night before and he collected them and took them along to the catapults. But the catapults had been damaged and were not yet ready.

Less than five minutes had elapsed since the hit on B turret. Captain Bell was successfully conning the ship from aft, using a chain of messengers, and heading north-west at high speed. The *Graf Spee* was by now about 13,000 yards away on the starboard bow heading on a parallel but opposite course.

From Captain Bell's report: '. . . The ship had received two more hits forward and some damage from splinters set up by shells bursting short . . .'

The first of these two shells burst on the sheet anchor, tearing a hole six feet by eight feet in the *Exeter's* side above the waterline. Splinters ripped into the paint store – where a fire started – and Bosun's store and riddled No. 10 watertight bulkhead.

Stoker Petty Officer Albert Jones had immediately started taking his No. 1 Fire Party forward to deal with the damage, but more shells from the *Graf Spee* burst in the water nearby. A splinter hit him and he collapsed; but he realised the next salvo would probably be even nearer, and his men were in a dangerously exposed position. He shouted to them to shelter behind A turret. It was his last order before he died, and it saved their lives. A few seconds later a shell burst on the deck ahead of them, ripping open a twelve-feet-square hole abaft the cable-holder. Again splinters did a great deal of damage, and soon fires were burning.

The Fire Party then ran forward, avoiding the blast from the two guns of A turret, to plug up the holes with hammocks, deal with fires, and examine the watertight bulkheads.

Engine Room Artificer Frank McGarry had been up forward since the beginning of the action, and without waiting for orders he had flooded the petrol compartment – where one spark, let alone a flash from a shellburst, would cause an explosion.

Then the shell had hit the anchor, only a few feet from him. Dense fumes from the explosion had streamed in; men had fallen, killed or wounded by splinters. He was trying to see how much damage had been done when the other shell burst on deck abaft the cable-holder and the blast flung him against the bulkhead and temporarily stunned him. Then, half suffocated by the acrid smoke of the shell bursts, he set about getting shipwrights to investigate the damage, organise stretcher parties and deal with fires.

Sub-Lieutenant Morse, who had jumped down to the bridge when he had realised it was deserted, now saw a fire burning on the fo'c'sle after the shell bursts, and and ran down to organise a party of men to deal with it. He quickly realised he had too few men to tackle it and ran aft to collect more. He found Midshipman Cameron, who was in charge of the 4-inch guns. Cameron, since his guns were not wanted at the moment, had used his men for rigging hoses to the forward part of the ship, but after B turret was hit it had been reported to him that there was no water coming through them and a fire was burning on the fo'c'sle.

Cameron had immediately sent half his guns' crews forward to help while most of the remainder struggled to get the hoses patched up and the water flowing. At that moment Morse arrived, asking for more men and water. Cameron told him that all the men he could spare had already gone forward, and the others were doing the best they could with the hoses.

Morse hurried back to the fo'c'sle to supervise the men. Then the second shell exploded very close to him. He was never seen again, and it is believed that his body was blown over the side.

By now the forward part of the ship was slowly flooding. Water streamed out of a shattered fire main and from hoses pouring water on to the fo'c'sle fire; and the sea was spurting in through splinter holes caused by the hit on the anchor and the many near misses. The flow was increased by the forward thrust of the ship, which was now steaming at full speed.

From Captain Bell's report: '. . . At 0631 the order to fire torpedoes was correctly anticipated by the Torpedo Officer and he fired the starboard torpedoes in local control . . .'

After passing the order to the Lower Steering Position which brought the *Exeter* round to starboard again, Lt-Cdr Smith, the torpedo officer, realised that the *Graf Spee*, on her present course, would very soon be a good torpedo target. But there was no time for him to wait for orders from Captain Bell.

Many of the torpedo tubes' crew had been wounded by the near miss at the beginning of the action. Among them was the Torpedo Gunner's mate, Petty Officer Charles Hallas. However, he was in charge of the tubes and as soon as they were trained he stood by waiting for the order from Lt-Cdr Smith.

Smith waited as the ship slowly swung round; then he gave the order to fire. Compressed air thrust the torpedoes over the side into the sea, and gyroscopes inside took over to keep them on a straight course as they sped at more than forty knots towards the pocket battleship.

But the *Exeter's* luck was out: they had been running only two minutes when the *Graf Spee* suddenly swung round 150 degrees to port, away from the three British cruisers – and away from where she was to have had a rendezvous with the torpedoes. At the same time she started laying a thick smoke screen to hide her movements and confuse the British gunners.

Immediately Captain Bell, passing his orders through the chain of messengers, swung the *Exeter* round to starboard towards the *Graf Spee* so that the port torpedoes could be fired; but as she turned, the pocket battleship struck twice more.

From Captain Bell's report: '. . . Two more 11-inch hits were received, one on A turret putting it out of action, and one which penetrated the Chief Petty Officers' flat where it burst, causing very extensive damage . . .'

Just before the Chief Petty Officers' flat was hit another shell, not mentioned in the above report, hit the Navigating Officer's cabin, passed through the Armament Office, killed five telegraphists and went on for sixty feet before bursting on the barrel of 'S-one' (Starboard one) 4-inch gun, killing or wounding several more men.

The foremost ready-use locker, containing 4-inch shells, immediately caught fire and the ammunition started bursting, sending up showers of debris and splinters. At that moment a man ran up to Midshipman Cameron, in command of the 4-inch guns, and warned him that the fore topmast was just about to fall down.

'I gave the order to clear the fore end of the gun deck,' Cameron reported later. 'As it did not appear to be coming down immediately I started the crews working again.'

The men on A turret had fired between forty and fifty rounds when, at this moment, an 11-inch shell hit the right gun. Once again the explosion tore at the armour plate on the front of the turret. Inside all the lights were put out and fumes streamed in.

Petty Officer Pierce tried to get through to the bridge by telephone, but it was wrecked. Ordering the telegraphists to stay at their posts, he climbed out of the gunhouse to go up to warn the bridge, but finding it had already been wrecked he went back to the gunhouse to tell the men to abandon it.

By this time an 11-inch shell had burst in the Chief Petty Officers' flat and started a bad fire above the 4-inch magazine. After checking that it was being dealt with, Midshipman Cameron returned with Ordinary Seaman Gwilliam to find the 4-inch ready-use ammunition locker still burning from the earlier hit.

'There were still several live shells in the bottom of the locker. Without any hesitation Gwilliam removed his greatcoat and attempted to smother the flames with it,' Cameron reported later. 'At the same time somebody else threw a bucket of sand over it. The flames were extinguished and we proceeded to throw over the side what was left in the locker.

'Gwilliam reported to me there were still several cans of petrol underneath the port catapult. These were threw overboard.

'As the fire on the messdecks was still raging I got more hands on to the job of carrying buckets to it. At the same time Lt Kemball and I kept the remainder occupied in breaking up blocks of holystone in an effort to make sand out of them . . .

'At this time an effort, which subsequently proved to be successful, was being made to get the planes over the side, they having been badly holed and showering out quantities of petrol.'

The shell which burst in the CPOs' flat did so much damage that the *Exeter* later had to discontinue the action. It penetrated the light plating of the ship's side amidships, as if it were cardboard, cut through three bulkheads and then burst on the lower deck above the 4-inch magazine and the torpedo gunner's store, blasting a hole measuring sixteen feet by fourteen feet.

The explosion was felt all through the ship, as though she had been punched in her solar plexus. Blast and fumes thrust back along the starboard passage; one bulkhead door was blocked with debris and bodies, and another with the wreckage of kit lockers; the Chief Petty Officers' flat was in darkness and filled with dense fumes and steam escaping from a punctured heating pipe.

A fierce fire broke out in the lower servery flat, and the crews of the switchboard and forward dynamo rooms were trapped, the whole space filling with fumes, steam and water spraying out from a burst fire main.

Splinters from the shell cut a large number of electric leads, among them vital ones supplying power to the Transmitting Station, the main armament's 'brain'. Because the Fire Control Table could work no longer, the Transmitting Station was abandoned.

More splinters pierced the lower deck and slashed the fire hoses. Water poured into the Lower Steering Position and the Number One low-power room below. Generators and compass alternators were flooded and this put the compass repeaters out of action.

Other splinters sliced through a bulkhead into A boiler room; but fortunately the boilers were saved by spare firebricks which had been stacked up out of the way – otherwise it is probable that every man in the boiler room would have been killed by superheated steam.

The immediate task for the Damage Control parties was to get at the men trapped in the forward dynamo room and the switchboard.

Number Four Fire Party were the first to try. Smoke and fumes would have suffocated any man along the starboard passage in a few moments, so they pulled on their anti-gas respirators and started dragging their hoses towards the fire. But debris and the bodies of seamen killed by the explosion blocked the way.

It seemed impossible to force an entrance into the Chief Petty Officers' flat to see exactly what had happened and what was on fire, so another party was sent up on deck to try to break in from forward: every minute counted now because the trapped men were being badly affected by the fumes.

In the meantime, however, Stoker Patrick O'Brien was trying to break through alone to the main switchboard. In darkness, tripping over twisted metal, bodies and smashed equipment, and almost suffocating from the high-explosive fumes and steam, he managed to clamber and crawl through the apparently impenetrable Chief Petty Officers' flat and shout a message down the main switchboard hatch, which was blocked by debris.

After that he crawled to the hatch over the dynamo room. This, too, was blocked by twisted metal and all sorts of debris; but O'Brien managed to call to the Engine Room Artificer, Thomas Phillips, who was in charge of the trapped party.

Phillips had been struggling in the thick fumes and smoke to get a dynamo going. It had stopped as the shell burst above, and the exhaust fan had broken down. Having made contact with the trapped men, O'Brien then crawled and scrambled out on to the upper deck, and ran back to his fire party and led them into the reeking flat.

In the meantime Petty Officer Herbert Chalkley, who had also been in the forward dynamo room, had managed to force open the door in the escape trunk and crawl over the wreckage of the switchboard hatch. It was jammed, with a good deal of wreckage piled on top of it.

Amid the swirling smoke and barely able to see what he was doing, Chalkley pulled and pushed at the wreckage, trying to lever pieces off to free the hatch. But he could not move it.

Realising he would not be needed again in the dynamo room, he guessed his best move would be to get out on to the upper deck so that he could then guide fire parties to his trapped shipmates. He carefully made his way back through the smoke and steam to the escape trunk and climbed up it. Once in the open air again he found the fire parties and went back to help fight the fires in the servery and CPOs' flat.

By now the blaze in the servery flat was raging fiercely and almost out of control. The 4-inch magazine, bomb room, and the magazine of B turret were in danger from the heat and fumes.

The 50-ton pump supplying water for the hoses forward had failed four or five times and it was at this point that, as mentioned earlier, Sergeant George Puddifoot, in B magazine, realised the fire overhead was getting out of hand and, with ERA Frank Bond, decided to flood the magazine.

Bond then went to the main centre of the fire to check up how much damage had been done – and found that the flooding valve spindle had been shot away and the fire main shattered. However, there was sufficient water from the burst mains pouring into the magazine through shell and splinter holes, so he went on to help fight the fires.

This was proving a difficult task: the ship was so badly riddled with splinters by this time that many hoses and fire mains had burst. Midshipman Robert Don, for instance, was having great difficulty in running hoses to the burning Marines Barracks and also in fighting the fire over the Lower Steering Position. He was one of several men searching for the wounded lying amid the smoke and debris, and dragging them to safety.

The *Exeter's* tall topmasts were still in danger. Flying splinters had cut through many of the wire shrouds supporting them, and when finally the triatic stay joining the heads of the two masts was severed they had started to whip so violently that all the main aerials parted and the ship's wireless link with the Commodore was cut. As soon as the sets had gone dead Chief Petty Officer Telegraphist Harold Newman began the dangerous and laborious job of rigging jury aerials.

The topmasts were so tall that they undoubtedly helped the *Graf Spee's* gunners in finding the range; and had the weather not been exceptionally calm they almost certainly would have toppled down.

As mentioned earlier, the Transmitting Station and the Fire Control Table were out of action. Mr Dallaway, the TS Officer, reported that when communications with B Turret ceased he did not know it was because it had been hit. 'Thinking B turret may have some mechanical trouble,' he wrote, 'I decided to send the Ordnance Artificer from the TS to 'B' to see if he could be of any assistance, realising that he would not have far to go, and also that while everything was running smoothly in the TS he was wasting his talent.

'With the object in view I ordered the TS hatch to be opened so that he could get out of the TS. Before I had time to tell him what to do there was a slight blast effect felt and the TS started to fill with dust and fumes. The TS crew, with the exception of the TS Officer and Communications Number, put on their gasmasks and carried on with their jobs.

'Lights in the TS then went off with the exception of two which remained burning dimly . . . The effect was that the TS was practically in darkness, and combined with the dust it was hardly possible to see anything.

'Everything appeared to happen at once . . .' he added. 'A turret reported they were going on to "local" firing, the range receiver unit stopped working, and then the compressed air working the Fire Control Table failed.

'I did manage to see the Ordnance Artificer playing around with the air valves, but still no air was available on the Table. To work hunters by hand in the existing light was impossible, and that combined with the report from A turret that pointers were not working forced me to the conclusion that the TS was useless. I reported this fact to the Gunnery Officer and then the order to go into local control was passed. Communication to A turret was then lost.

'I then asked permission for the TS crew to go on the Marines' messdeck in order to use them for work. This was agreed to by the Gunnery Officer. The crew could not get out of the TS as they were told that the upper hatch was closed. I went up to investigate the possibility of opening the hatch and found it open. The crew then came up. Everywhere was in complete darkness, but I tried to get into the servery flat, which I soon discovered to be in a shambles.

'Realising that a gangway through there was impossible, I shouted back to the remainder to work their way forward, which they did. For some reason or other I could not get out of the flat by the same way that I had entered, and I have recollections of being lost among the debris.

Eventually I managed to make the starboard waist where I found the TS crew and other ratings.'

★　　★　　★　　★

Despite all the bitter punishment the *Exeter* had taken in forty minutes of battle, she was still in action: Y turret, right aft, was still firing in local control. Lt-Cdr Richard Jennings, the Gunnery Officer, had gone aft to see what was happening, and while standing outside the After Control Position talking to the After Control Officer, Y turret trained round on to an extreme forward bearing and fired. Both men were badly shaken by the blast. Jennings then sent Sub-Lt Wickham, the After Control Officer, to take charge of Y turret while he stationed himself on the roof of the turret, where he could see better, and, ignoring the blast and flying splinters, shouted spotting corrections down through a manhole.

The position at 0700, therefore, was that:

1. A and B turrets were out of action from direct hits;
2. Y turret was still firing in local control;
3. The bridge, DCT and Transmitting Station were out of action;
4. A fierce fire was raging in the CPOs' and servery flats;
5. Minor fires were burning on the Marines' messdeck and in the paint shop;
6. There were no telephone communications – orders could be passed only by messengers;
7. The ship was down by the bows by about three feet because of flooding forward, and had a list of from seven to ten degrees to starboard – due to about 650 tons of water, which had flooded in;
8. Only one 4-inch gun could still be fired;
9. Both aircraft had been jettisoned;
10. Wireless communications had completely broken down.

But mercifully the engine room was undamaged and the ship was steaming at full speed. The heat was so great in the furnaces that the floors were becoming almost fluid, and because of the list the molten brickwork had run over to the starboard side.

Many gallant actions in those forty minutes went almost unnoticed; it needed bravery to carry out even normal duties in the ravaged cruiser. An order to take a message to a position twenty yards away could mean sudden death from an invisible rain of shell splinters; young ratings were making split-second decisions which meant life or death to many of their shipmates. But fortunately months of drill under keen and able officers paid dividends.

Already more than fifty officers and men had been killed and others were so seriously wounded they would die before the day ended; more than twenty others had been badly hurt.

There was, for instance, the cold-blooded gallantry of Captain Bell, one of the few men left alive in the ship who knew all the facts and dangers. Despite the damage caused by the almost undivided attention of a pocket battleship which could match each of his 8-inch shells with an 11-inch shell at the beginning of the action, and now still had six 11-inch guns firing to his two 8-inch (and one of them had stopped firing for a short while), the *Exeter's* Battle Ensigns were still flying and the ship continued in action against the *Graf Spee.*

From the After Conning Position Captain Bell was having to steer the ship with the help of a compass taken from a whaler – the compass repeaters had been damaged some time earlier. But the compass needle was so badly affected by the magnetism of the steel all round that it did almost everything except spin round like a Catherine wheel.

There was the gallantry of Chief Shipwright Anthony Collings, who, although seriously wounded and badly burned, continued to supervise and direct the work of the shipwrights repairing damage in the forward part of the ship. He only stopped when he fell unconscious. A few moments before that he had been asking for a report on the condition of a damaged hatch.

There was Commander Robert Graham, who was wounded in the face and leg early in the action. Yet despite that he cheerfully carried on walking round the ship seeing what was damaged or on fire and giving orders to deal with it.

There was Midshipman Bonham. After hoisting the 'not under control' balls he had been ordered to find some flexible voicepipe so that Captain Bell could communicate with the engine room.

He took two ratings and unrigged the flexible lead from the bridge to the armament office, and while doing this he found a man lying outside Captain Bell's sea cabin. He had both legs blown off but was still alive, so Bonham sent a rating to warn the sick bay.

After searching various places in the ship for more voicepipe he went back to the After Conning Position. He saw that some more had been found and was being rigged, and he was sent forward to the fire still raging amidships.

'I went down through the sick bay flat into the Marines' messdeck where I met Midshipman Don,' he reported later, 'and together we got a hose in, and we were getting it down through the hatch outside the bookstall when he fell through the hatch and vanished. I heard voices below so assumed he was all right, and continued getting more hose and switching on the water. I had to go outside several times as the smoke was very bad . . .'

From the Exeter's *log: '. . . 0729, Y turret ceased firing owing to failure of electricity supply. 0730, Broke off action. 0750, Enemy disappeared to westward pursued by* Ajax *and* Achilles *. . .'*

Strangely enough, it was not the *Graf Spee's* hits which forced Captain Bell to break off the action, but her near misses. As long as he had a gun which worked, Captain Bell was determined to keep the *Graf Spee* under fire, but at last water flooding in through splinter holes in the *Exeter's* side abreast of No 216 bulkhead stopped the power supply.

With his last turret out of action, and only a boat compass to steer by, Captain Bell was now able to devote all his attention to keeping his ship afloat.

WILLIAM AND THE SPY
Richmal Crompton

The members of William's family were having their annual holiday by the sea. They were staying in the boarding-house in which they generally stayed. The Browns chose it because it did not object to William. It was not enough for the Browns to go to a boarding-house that did not object to children. It had to be one that did not object to William. This boarding-house was of a philosophical, if pessimistic nature and took it as in the natural course of things that William's crabs should make their home in the hatstand drawer, that 'pieces' from William's collection of seaweed should make the hall into a sort of skating rink, and that William himself should leave a trail of sand and shells and jelly-fish wherever he went. William, however, was enjoying this holiday less than the other members of his family. Though indulging to the full in the delights of the seaside, he considered them to be greatly overrated. Paddling was a pastime whose possibilities were soon exhausted. He could make it exciting by pretending that he was wading into the sea to rescue shipwrecked sailors or pull to shore a boat of smuggled goods, but he always entered too wholeheartedly into these games and arrived home soaked to the neck. Paddling was generally forbidden by his mother after the third day at the seaside, because, as she said, he only had three suits, and, when he got them all soaked in one day, there was nothing to fall back on.

It happened to be too cold for swimming, for which Mrs Brown was thankful, because last year the other swimmers had grown so tired of rescuing William that they had threatened to let him drown the next time he got into difficulties.

When paddling was forbidden, William took to exploring the rocks with results even more disastrous than those of paddling, for there were pools of water among the rocks into which he was always falling, as well as jagged surfaces down which he was always sliding. His mother's attitude to this annoyed William almost beyond expression.

'How d'you think I'm ever goin' to be able to have any sort of adventure when I grow up if I don't try'n' get a bit of practice now?' he protested passionately.

'How d'you think Hereward the Wake 'd ever have been a hero if his mother had gone on at him like what you do at me whenever he got his suits wet?'

'I don't know how many suits Hereward the Wake had,' said Mrs Brown firmly, 'but, if he only had three and had soaked two and torn the third, I don't see what his mother could have done but make him stay indoors till one of them was fit to wear.'

And so it came about that William was sitting in the drawing-room of the boarding-house in his dressing-gown, while two of his suits dried before the kitchen fire, and the third was at the tailor's having a new seat put in.

William had never patronised the drawing-room before, and the novelty of the situation rather intrigued him. There was an old lady in an arm-chair by the fire who had already requisitioned him to hold her wool for her to wind. William disliked holding wool for people to wind, and with a skill born of long practice had managed to get it into such a tangle without apparently moving his hands at all, that the old lady had given up the whole thing in despair and gone to sleep. On the other side of the fire sat another lady, tall and thin and middle-aged, engaged upon a piece of crochet work and wearing a pair of pince-nez balanced on the very end of her nose. Between her and the sleeping old lady was a circle of other ladies, all middle-aged and thin and spectacled and engaged upon needlework of some sort. William, clad in his dressing-gown and forming part of the circle though completely ignored by it, gazed around at them with deep interest. He had had no idea that all these women were different. He always came in to meals when everyone else had finished, and, meeting these visitors occasionally in the passages, he had thought that there was only one of them.

Now he looked round at them with the thrill of the discoverer . . . One, two, three, four, five, six, and so much alike that he had thought they were all the same.

The one by the fire was talking. Her name was Miss Smithers. She had lived an utterly uneventful life and had never had anything to talk about till the war came. She hadn't yet realised that most people had stopped talking about the war.

'Of course,' she was saying, 'the country had been *full* of their spies for *years* before the war began. They'd come over as tourists or students or even professors – and they'd pass as Englishmen *anywhere,* you know, they're such clever linguists – and they'd each take a tiny bit of the coast line and *study* it till they knew every *inch* of it. *Riddled* with spies, the country was. And what they've done once they can do again . . . We're never on our guard.'

The others, who had heard it all before, were not taking any notice, but William was sitting forward, eyes and mouth wide open, drinking in her words. The war had been over before William was born, and William's immediate circle was one that lived in the present. He had never heard anything like this before . . . Most thrilling of all was the 'And what they've done once they can do again.'

He was just going to demand further details, when his mother opened the door to tell him that one of his suits was dry now and he could go and put it on. He followed her into the hall. There stood an elderly man with a short, white beard talking to the proprietress. He held a suit-case in his hand and had evidently just arrived. He was saying, 'I'm a geologist, you know. I've come here to study this part of the coast.'

And then, of course, William knew beyond a shadow of doubt that he was a German spy who had come over to prepare for the next war.

★　★　★　★

'What's a geologist?' William asked his mother as he struggled into his suit that, though dry, was still strongly perfumed with seaweed.

'A man who studies rocks,' said his mother.

William uttered an ironic laugh.

'That's a *jolly* easy way to do it,' he said.

'What are you talking about?' said his mother, who was looking doubtfully at his suit and wondering whether it had been as much too small for him as that before its immersion in sea water.

But William merely repeated his ironic laugh.

The next morning William set off to a withdrawn spot among the rocks that had already served him as a Red Indian camp and a pirate's ship, and there he held a meeting of the secret service men under his command. They all saluted him respectfully as he entered – a magnificent figure in a blazing uniform with jingling spurs. He informed them curtly of the danger (there were, of course, innumerable Germans studying each a mile or so of the coast) and warned them that the work on which he was sending them would probably mean death (he was a ruthless man with no compunction at all in sending his men to their death, but he went to his own so bravely and so continually that they could not resent it). Then, after ordering them each to dog one spy and report to him daily, he gave them the secret code and password, and explained the complicated system of signals by which they were to communicate with each other and with him. He warned them to expect no mercy from him if they failed. That, of course, was part of his ruthlessness, for which nevertheless they all adored him. An ordinary passer-by would have seen nothing of this. He would merely have seen a small boy in a suit that had obviously suffered as the result of frequent immersion in sea water, playing by himself in a hollow among the rocks. Ordinary passers-by, of course, never see things as they really are.

At the end of the meeting William changed his rôle to that of one of the secret service men (the best and most promising of them, whose courage had already been tried in many a desperate adventure) and, saluting the magnificent figure in the resplendent uniform, emerged from the rocks after making elaborate precautions to escape detection. With his collar turned up, and his head sunk into it so deeply that nothing of his face could be seen but the tip of his nose, he set off in order to shadow his victim.

★　★　★　★

Professor Sommerton was not at all surprised to find himself dogged throughout the morning by a small boy. He had learnt that, wherever one was and whatever one was doing, small boys always hung about to watch and if possible annoy one. This small boy was rather odd in his behaviour (for instance one could see nothing at all of his face, as he kept his cap pulled down and his coat collar turned up, and he followed one in an extraordinary fashion, sidling along by the rocks), but then the professor considered all small boys to be odd in their behaviour, differing only in degrees of oddness, and he disliked them all uniformly. This boy, however, really began to get on his nerves as the morning wore on, and he returned to the boarding-house earlier than he had meant to, only to discover to his annoyance that he had lost the sheet of paper on which he had been making his shorthand notes. At that very moment William was entering the hollow in the rocks still with elaborate precaution of secrecy – gazing round on all sides to see that the coast was clear and then pulling up his coat collar so high that one of the sleeves gave audibly beneath the strain – and handing the sheet of paper to the chief in the magnificent uniform.

'Here's his code what I've got at deadly peril,' he was saying. 'If he'd seen me he'd've killed me. He'd gotter special pistol in his pocket made to look like a fountain-pen an' I bet if he'd've seen me I'd've been dead by now.'

The magnificent chief read the paper with many a low whistle and exclamation of 'Gosh!'

He said that none of the others had done so well and promoted William to be second-in-command.

'When you hear of me bein' killed by crim'nals,' he said, 'what I'm likely to be any minute, you jus' carry on here. Seems to me you're the bravest man I've ever come across – next to me, of course.'

William went home well satisfied by his morning's work. The professor was less satisfied.

'Most tiresome,' William heard him say at lunch. 'I lost the paper on which were the results of my whole morning's work.'

He met William's eye – a completely blank eye – and sighed. He did not connect William with the boy who had haunted him all the morning, but he felt vaguely that the world would be a more peaceful place if there were no small boys in it.

After lunch he went out to the rocks and set to work again. He had a tape measure and a little hammer, and he worked hard, stopping every now and then to make notes or to add to the contours of a rough map that he was making. Again the boy was there, peering at him between the buttonholes of his coat (which was pulled up till the collar was on a level with the top of his head, and which now showed a large rent round the sleeve), crawling after him on hands and knees, watching him from inadequate hiding-places among the rocks, sidling around him in a way that distracted the professor indescribably. And then when he reached the boarding-house he found that he had lost the map that contained the results of his afternoon's work.

William was seated in the hollow among the rocks. He had grown tired of the magnificent chief and had had him killed by criminals. He was holding a meeting of the other secret service men and telling them that the chief had been killed by criminals and that he was now in sole charge. He told them that he had got both the code and the map from his spy, and asked how they had been getting on. They had, of course, no results at all to show him, and he was very stern with them.

★　★　★　★

The professor set out the next morning with a firm determination to send that boy about his business – by force if needs be. The whole situation was getting on his nerves. He was sure that he would never have lost those papers if it hadn't been for that boy's distracting his attention by his antics.

He went a longer way down the coast than usual. William followed him as before, slipping from rock to rock. William was blissfully unaware that his quarry had even caught a glimpse of him. He imagined that, thanks to his methods of secrecy, he had been completely invisible to him all the time. It was therefore an unpleasant surprise when, as he was engaged on watching his victim on hands and knees from the shadow of a rock, his victim turned on him savagely and said:

'I've had enough of your monkey tricks, my boy. Clear off and be quick about it.'

William rose to his feet with dignity. He thought it best now to reveal himself in his true colours.

'Yes,' he said, 'I bet you'd like me to clear off. I bet you don't know who I am?'

'Who are you then?' said the professor irritably.

'I know all about *you*,' said William darkly. 'I know what you're doin' an' where you've come from an' I've got your code so it's no use tryin' to send any secret messages, an' my men are all surroundin' you so it's no use trying to escape an' –'

'Clear off,' roared the professor angrily, 'and don't give me any more of your impudence.'

William was slightly nonplussed by this attitude. The man should have been cowering at his feet and begging for mercy by now. Suddenly the professor made a threatening gesture with his hammer and roared again, 'Clear off.' William lost no time in clearing off. He told himself when he reached the promenade that his life was of too great service to his country for him to risk it unduly. He stood on the promenade wondering what to do. His afternoon's dogging of his victim had not improved his never-very-spruce appearance. His grown-up sister passed him at that moment with an immaculate youth in tow. She passed him with bated breath and eyes staring glassily in front of her, in fear lest William should see and recognise her. William was too much engrossed in his problem to have eyes for Ethel and her escort. In any case he cherished a healthy contempt for Ethel's idea of pleasure. He went down to the beach and threw stones idly into the sea while he pondered what was best to do. Some people who were swimming came out of the sea to remonstrate, and William moved away with dignity to an unattended boat, in which he sat trying to look as if it belonged to him and continuing his mental wrestling with his problems.

He might, of course, go to the hollow in the rocks to report, but he was growing tired of the hollow in the rocks. He had that morning, as he dressed, sent a messenger to dismiss all the other secret service workers so that he needn't be bothered with them any more. There was no doubt at all, however, that the man was a spy and that it was his duty to bring him to justice. He sat up and looked about him. Along the promenade a policeman was coming with slow and measured tread. That was the best thing to do, of course. Tell a policeman about it and leave him to catch the spy and put him in prison. William realised suddenly that there were a lot of interesting things he wanted to do, and that it would be quite a relief to get rid of his spy by handing him over to justice. He made his way up to the promenade and followed the policeman, dodging in and out of people's legs till he caught him up.

'Please!' he said breathlessly.

The policeman turned. He had a fierce moustache, and eyebrows that were fiercer still. William looked at him and decided to find one who looked a little more sympathetic before he told his tale.

'Well,' the policeman had snapped, 'what d'you want?'

'What's the time please?' said William meekly.

'Use your eyes,' said the policeman, pointing to the Tower Clock a few yards away.

Then he continued his walk with slow dignity.

William stood staring after him sternly. In imagination he had reassumed the character of the late magnificent chief in order to deal with the policeman, and the policeman was pleading abjectly to him for his life. William treated the policeman to some of his famous ruthlessness, before he finally pardoned him. His self-respect restored by this proceeding, William went on down the promenade. He met Ethel again with the immaculate youth and pulled his most hideous grimace at them. The immaculate youth drew himself up, outraged and affronted, and Ethel passed on with an angry, glassy stare. William knew that Ethel would disclaim all knowledge of him and then would live in terror of the immaculate youth's discovering that he was her brother. Between William and Ethel there existed a state of continual warfare. What Ethel gained in the authority that accrued to her added years she lost by that respect for appearances that frequently laid her at William's mercy, and so they were about equally matched as adversaries. Up-lifted in spirit by this encounter, William turned off the promenade into one of the crowded streets that led to it. At the end of it he saw a policeman regulating the traffic. He was the policeman of one's dreams. He radiated kindness and sympathy in every glance and movement. William felt that this was the one policeman of all the policemen in the world in whom he must confide his story of the spy. Narrowly escaping death beneath the wheels of several cars, he crossed the road to the middle, where the policeman, waving on one line of traffic and holding up another, looked down at him and said, 'You'll cross the street like that once too often one day, my lad.'

William, however, had not come to discuss his methods of crossing streets.

'There's a spy down on the beach,' he said breathlessly, 'he's measuring it out an' making a map ready for the next war. You'll catch him if you're quick.'

The policeman looked down at him, still kindly and amused.

'Now, my lad, don't try any of your funny work on me, because I haven't time for it.'

Whereupon he held up the traffic for William to continue his passage of the street. Disconcerted, William continued it. He stood doubtfully on the further pavement, wondering what to do next. He was convinced that, if this policeman wouldn't believe him, none would. And the responsibility of bringing his spy to justice had begun to weigh heavily upon his spirit. He wandered slowly back to the shore, climbed into the unattended boat again and sat there thinking. As he scowled out over the sea, his head between his hands, he uttered his famous sardonic laugh. He knew why they wouldn't believe him. They thought of him as a child. They'd no idea what he really was. If he could get a grown-up to see what the spy was doing, it would be all right. The policeman would believe a grown-up. They always believed grown-ups.

'Now then!' said a voice behind him, 'nip out o' this an' look sharp.'

William turned. The boatman to whom the boat belonged had come upon him unawares. He was a large man with a red face and a twinkle in his eye that belied his fierce voice.

'Less of course,' he went on with obvious sarcasm, 'you're wantin' a row an' willin' to pay for it.'

And then suddenly the idea came to William. Here was his witness, the grown-up who should catch the spy red-handed and give him over to the police. The spy would be keeping a look out upon the land, of course, but he worked with his back to the sea and he wouldn't be prepared for any one coming upon him from that quarter.

'If you found a spy spyin',' said William, 'would you give him up to the police?'

'You bet,' said the man, winking at the breaker for want of anything else to wink at. 'Why, I've caught dozens of 'em in my time.'

William felt in his pocket. There reposed in it a sixpence that his father had given him that morning.

'Yes, I'll have a sail,' said William, 'a sixpenny one, please.'

'How far d'you think you'll get for sixpence?' said the man scornfully.

'I'll get as far as I want to get,' said William, 'an' I'll jolly well show you somethin' that you din't know was there.'

There seemed to be no other prospective customer in sight, so the man good-naturedly pushed off his boat and jumped into it. William watched him with envy. He had often wanted to do that. Once he got this spy business over, he'd see if he could learn how to do it. It probably wasn't as hard as it looked. There were lots of unattended boats along the beach that he could practise on.

'Well, where d'you want to go?' said the man.

'Keep close along the coast,' said William, 'it's jus' round that big rock – the bit you can't see from here.'

The boatman, thinking rightly that William would be a credulous audience, began to tell him about the sea serpents he had seen in his youth, but William's response was half-hearted. He was living for the moment when they should steal upon the spy from behind, and catch him engaged upon his nefarious work. Then there was that next and just-as-thrilling moment to think about, when the burly boatman should hand him over to the police, and William should tell how he had shadowed him and finally caught him.

'Round this 'ere point, did you say?' asked the boatman.

'Yes.'

'You can't land there, you know, now,' said the boatman, 'it's high tide.'

At that moment they rounded the point, and there, clinging in terror to the rocks, waist high in water, was the professor. As soon as he saw William and the boat, he gave a shout of joy.

'My rescuer!' he cried, 'my noble rescuer!'

★   ★   ★   ★

It was the next day. William was walking along the sea coast to the line of rocks beyond the beach. He had spent last evening in a blaze of glory. The professor had told the story eloquently to everyone in the boarding-house. 'This boy was playing about near me while I was working, and I sent him away because it worries me to have boys playing

The professor was clinging to the rocks in terror.

about near me when I'm working. He went away and later on he noticed that I had not returned, and, knowing that it would be high tide and that the rocks where I had been working would be covered (a fact that I had foolishly omitted to ascertain), the brave boy quietly hired a boat to come to my rescue. He saved my life . . .'

William, who was beginning to have a dim suspicion that the professor was not a spy after all, saw no reason to contradict the story. If the notoriety of having captured a dangerous spy were denied one, that of having rescued a celebrated professor of geology was better than nothing. He received the plaudits of the boarding-house with modest nonchalance.

'Oh, that's nothin',' he said, 'I'd do that for anyone any time. Savin' a person from drownin's nothin'.'

To mark his gratitude the professor presented William with a ticket to a lecture that he was giving in the town that evening on Geology. William went to it, and it confirmed his suspicions that the professor was not a spy, because he was sure that no spy could make quite as dull a speech as the professor made. Further to mark his gratitude, the professor gave William's mother five pounds to add to William's post office savings account. William thanked him perfunctorily. William looked upon his post office savings account as a deliberate scheme of his parents to divert from him any money that might come his way.

But it was now the next morning, and everyone, William included, was beginning to forget that he had saved the professor from a watery grave the day before. William was tired of being a secret service agent. He had decided to be a spy. He was an English spy in a foreign land. He had a piece of tape, stolen from his mother's work bag, and a piece of stick to represent a hammer. With them he measured and tapped the rocks, stopping occasionally to scrawl hieroglyphics on a piece of paper. Sometimes imaginary natives of the place would pass, and William would slip the tokens of his trade into his pocket and talk to them volubly in their own language, explaining that he was a professor of geology. He brought all the foreign words he knew into these conversations. 'Hic, hæc, hoc,' he would say, *Je suis, tu es, il est, mensa mensa mensam, la plume de ma tante, dominus domine dominum –*'

He was perfectly happy . . .

'FROM FALMOUTH'
Robin Knox-Johnston

Robin Knox-Johnston was an entrant in the Sunday Times Round-The-World Race. His book A World Of My Own *describes his voyage in full: this extract follows the last part of his journey back to Falmouth.*

On March 17th I celebrated my thirtieth birthday. The temptation to philosophize in my diary upon passing this milestone was irresistible:

March 17th, 1969   *Day 277*
Firstly all those sevens are obviously propitious, but I still doubt if we can get home by April 17th as I had hoped. I'm feeling very lethargic. Quite frankly I think I have been on my own long enough and am getting stale. I need something to break the monotony, and getting home is the best cure I can think of. After finding our noon position, the big time of the day is 2100 when I listen to the BBC News. I occasionally scribble a bit, thinking ahead to the book I shall have to buckle down to when I get home, and over the last few days I have described the business in the Foveaux Strait and off Otago. It won't do for the book as it stands, but it's still fresh in my mind now.

It does not depress me that this decade is past. I have enjoyed it and managed to do more than most poeple. Certainly I do not regret a day of it, although perhaps I would like to mark time at this stage for a few years. There seems to be so much left to do in life and I'm itching to get on with something new. This voyage is about played out as far as I'm concerned. Barring accidents we'll be home in a month and that will be an anti-climax for me, however the race has turned out.

It's rather depressing to think that in another ten years I shall be forty, which seems middle-aged from my present position; however, I can remember feeling the same about thirty, ten years ago. I think this is an ideal age actually, young and fit enough for sports, and yet with ten years of adult experience behind one. (I hope in ten years time I am as content). Perhaps the most interesting thing that has occurred in the past ten years is the change of outlook of people. When I was twenty I had difficulty in identifying with people of thirty, and yet before I sailed I found I could identify more easily with people of twenty than those of forty. These are generalizations, but I wonder why this is. I suppose better education is the answer.

Now that I have got over my indigestion, apart from a recurrence today as a result of cooking a mixed grill for a celebration lunch, I feel well, but I have noticed that my fingers are becoming less sensitive. The other day when the deck bolt on the starboard runner sheared, I had to rig a tackle on the runner. I transferred a shackle pin from my left to right hand, and despite directions to the contrary, the pin slipped from the hand and fell overside. I was angry about this at the time as I am running short of shackles now and cannot affort to lose any more.

I called Dick [my brother in the Royal Signals in Germany]; we had arranged this schedule before I sailed; on 16 Mc/s at 1300 and 1400 GMT as arranged, but could hear nothing except Latin American stations in reply.

Tried to set the Big Fellow today. Each time it twisted up into a ball, and on the last occasion managed to wrap itself round the forestay which took some sorting out. As usual it was torn when I took it in so that is that until I get some repairs done.

Usually on the run north in the North-East Trades, one finds the winds veering round towards the east the farther north one gets. For some reason the winds decided not to co-operate with me, or so it seemed at the time, and continued to blow from north of north-east. Then when they at last began to veer, they dropped strength; we had reached the Horse Latitudes. To put it mildly, this was frustrating. The Horse Latitudes usually commence about twenty to twenty-three degrees north of the Equator; we ran into them at eighteen degrees North, about level with the Cape Verde Islands. By this time I had come to consider any light winds from an awkward direction a personal insult, deliberately designed to hold me up, and the only way I could let off steam was by swimming until I exhausted myself and then trying to find an absorbing job to keep me occupied. It may seem incredible that I got out paint and grease and began to overhaul all the rigging screws, deliberately putting new servings on the threads and the splices, but I did it to stop the feeling of helplessness that would have built up otherwise.

March 23rd, 1969   *Day 283*
Oh God, this is hopeless. 67 miles to noon and we are still heading N.W., the best I can manage with a N.N.E. wind, a heavy northerly swell, and northerly, N.E. and easterly seas. I feel bloody dispirited. I can do no more than we are doing in these conditions. Despite the good conditions yesterday we in fact made less northing than when we were all but becalmed. What the hell can I do? This is what gets me, the answer is absolutely nothing, but sit and hope for more average conditions.

Yet, as usual in the Variables, the weather could change suddenly:

March 25th, 1969   *Day 285*
Well, today beats everything. It got up to a full gale by lunchtime and I've spent most of my time reducing sail. I raced as long as I dared, feeling that if it's going to blow a gale from the S.S.E. I might as well take full advantage of it, but the seas were confused and I had to ease her to stop the pounding. By 2000 it was Force 9.
I don't mind gales in this weather; at least it's warm.

Our position at this time was approximately 24° North, 41° West and we were beginning to meet small clumps of Sargasso weed floating on the surface. When at school, collecting cigarette cards, I remember seeing on one of them a picture of a Spanish Galleon covered with long, trailing tentacles of weed in the Sargasso Sea. Columbus was the first to sight the Sea, and the seamen of the day were convinced that they were on the border of a vast malignant ocean of weed, that would trap their ships and keep them there until they starved or were killed by the primeval sea-monsters that lurked there. The thought of this picture fascinated me for years, and I visualized a vast number of nautical antiques just waiting to be collected by an enterprising adventurer.

The reality was disappointing. If you take a tea tray and drop five grains of rice onto it you will have an idea of the proportion of weed to water in the Sargasso Sea. The weed is broken off the coasts of the Caribbean by storms and is carried into the Sargasso Sea by the Gulf Stream. It propagates by fragmentation. It grows on the surface of the sea and only in a few tangled clumps does it go deeper than nine inches. The fascinating thing about the weed is the life it supports, most of which is normally found only along the sea coasts. I used to drag clumps of the weed aboard and shake out the small yellow crabs and shrimps that hide in the leaves, always hoping that I might find a Sargasso fish, a small, cleverly disguised fish found only amongst this weed. I have yet to find one, but on one occasion as I was picking over a lump of weed, an eel or snake about five inches long sprang clear and shot off very quickly with a jerky, sinuous movement. It had the same dull yellow colour as the weed, but moved too quickly for me to get a close look. I tried to find some reference to this creature in the books I carried with me, but there was no mention of it. As all sea snakes are venomous I was rather careful how I picked weed out of the water after that; I did not want to take any unnecessary risks even with what appeared to be a small edition of something. But I collected about sixteen crabs and rather more shrimps and periwinkles and put them with some of the weed in a perspex box aquarium that I made. The crabs' favourite food appeared to be tinned sardines, so from then on these figured prominently on my menus. I also tried bully beef but their opinion of it seemed to coincide with my own. The fatality rate was high amongst my passengers, and every day I had to pick out and bury a few corpses. The most robust crab hung on until four days from Falmouth, by which time I think the water had become a bit too cold – or he had become allergic to sardines.

The Variable winds in the Horse Latitudes nearly drove me round the bend. It was hopeless trying to leave the tiller untended as *Suhaili* would yaw and gybe so I had to steer the whole time, discontentedly watching pieces of weed drifting slowly past. When I grew tired in the evenings I would leave the tiller lashed, but I generally had to get up three or four times during the night to gybe back onto course, or as on this occasion:

March 29th, 1969   *Day 289*

Awoke for the news at 0200 G.M.T. Ike is dead. Well, he has been ill for a long time now and has been fading recently, but I still have a slight feeling of personal loss. I can still remember the excitement when we went back into France in 1944 and although, of course, Monty was 'our man', he had to share the honours with Ike. It is never pleasant for a proud nation to have to admit it is no longer the biggest power and to place its armies under a foreign leader; few men could have handled the situation with such tact and understanding.

The only break in the monotony of the days was when we crossed a shipping lane, as apart from the hope of sighting a ship and getting a report through, the lane was usually well marked with rubbish such as bottles, dunnage, and even hatchboards, that littered the sea. Some of this rubbish is a real threat to a small boat. A hatchboard may weigh as much as a person and they are bound at either end with heavy metal bonds. If a boat hits one of these when travelling at speed the hull could easily be stove in. Even more menacing farther north are the pitprops that litter the sea lanes. *Suhaili* might have survived a collision with one of these but she is much more strongly built than the ordinary boat. A fibreglass or plywood hull would not stand a chance.

On April 2nd, at 2 p.m., when about six hundred miles south-west of the Azores, we sighted a Norwegian cargo vessel ahead and immediately hoisted *Suhaili's* signal letters and *MIK,* the International Code for 'Please report me by radio to Lloyd's, London.' As the ship came closer I got out the rifle and fired three shots into the air. When it was a mile away and through binoculars I could see no one on the bridge, I fired two more rounds. We passed about 150 yards apart, close enough for me to read the name and home port, Tonsberg, but it was not until we were abreast the bridge that the O.O.W. appeared to take a lookout. By the time he had found his binoculars he had moved past and he did not bother to turn and answer my signal lamp. You can take as many precautions as you like, have the brightest lights and the biggest radar reflector ever made, but if the O.O.W. is not doing his job, you've had it.

Four days later, after drifting with still only occasional bursts of wind from the south-west, we crossed another shipping lane; a busy one as there were ships in sight all afternoon. I spent the whole time trying to signal them but all ignored me until the B.P. tanker *Mobil Acme* appeared.

I quote the conversation from my signal logbook:

Sent: British *Suhaili*. Round the world non-stop.
Received: Please repeat name.
Sent: Suhaili. Please report me to Lloyd's.
Received: Will do. good luck.
Sent: E.T.A. Falmouth two weeks.
Received: R(oger).

I was jubilant. At last after four months I had managed to get a report through. I started to imagine the effect at home and at the *Sunday Mirror* when the news got through. I knew that my family would not have given up hope for me; I had pictured my father shifting a pin on the chart in the hall and telling everyone quite categorically where I was within a couple of days. I did not know then that Bruce had already been out in the Azores helping to organize a close lookout for me by the American, Canadian and Portuguese Air Force units there, and by the local fishing fleets; although on occasions I heard aircraft, I did not see any until I was nearly in British waters.

Later that night I switched on the radio for the BBC News, thinking that there might be a mention which would confirm that I had been reported, but there was no comment. I began to think that perhaps the *Mobil Acme* had not reported me after all, although of course it was quite on the cards that Moitessier had already arrived and there was little interest in those who followed him.

In fact, the *Mobil Acme* must have cabled London immediately, as within two-and-a-half hours of the sighting, Lloyd's had phoned my family and told them that I had been sighted off the Azores. This was highly efficient work on everyone's part and brought an end to the anxious waiting at home. What pleased me was that I later heard that the *Mobil Acme* had added to their message to Lloyd's, 'Standard of signalling excellent.' This helped reassure people that I had not gone barmy and was also, from a professional point of view, a pretty compliment. I can say the same for the officer on the bridge of the *Mobil Acme* at the time, but then of course we probably went to the same signal school down London's Commercial Road.

We were due west of the Azores with 1,200 miles to go to Falmouth when we met the *Mobil Acme*. If the prevailing westerly winds held we should have had no trouble reaching Falmouth in two weeks. But that very night the wind swung round to the north and there it stayed for the next forty-eight hours, keeping us down to 89 and then 79 miles in the day's runs. The excitement of meeting the *Mobil Acme* and the thought that I was so close to home had led me into the yachtsman's trap of calculating an ETA based on the last good run, but the unfavourable winds and apparent silence of the BBC combined to bring about a feeling of anti-climax.

April 7th, 1969   *Day 298*
Up at 0400 when the wind arose from the S.W. I took a reef to ease her and help her reach, and went back to bed for a couple of hours. Steered all day.

I saw land to the S.E. during the early part of the morning. It faded as soon as the sun got high. This will be Corvo and Flores – 'where Sir Richard Grenville lay!' My sights put us 30 or so miles off at noon and I steered a course to pass well to the north. I'll visit the scene of the battle some other time.

The glass is dropping and as the wind is now S.W., we can expect a cold front and northerly winds shortly. I am heading *Suhaili* well north at present in order to gain sea room, as if we get a bad blow I'll have to run like last time we passed here, and I want as much room between me and the islands for this as possible. We're reefed down at present and running with a bias to port. Going comfortably at about 4 knots. I would steer her but I cannot see any stars and I have a shocking headache; anyway she is doing very well by herself at present.

This headache developed and I was sick the next day, probably due to food poisoning; anyway I did not eat anything for a day and felt better for my fast.

This good burst of south-westerly winds gave us a nice push homeward, but on 11th April, after three days and 359 miles, they eased.

Great, it's 2200. We are completely becalmed and there are ships all around so I dare not sleep – not that I could with the booms banging as they are. I feel completely licked. I don't think, even in the Variables, I have felt so low the whole voyage. Just sitting here, unable to do anything. There is some malignant being watching over me which takes a delight in playing with my hopes and frustrating my wishes.

This was heartbreaking; so close to home, as far as I knew unreported and unable to make radio contact to report myself, and now the winds had deserted me. But the next day, Saturday, 12th April, another sighting broke my solitude at last. From then on I found myself thinking of myself as a sailor rather than a sea creature. The spell which when I had rounded the Horn had made me want to sail on was finally broken. The sea was not now my environment but an obstacle between me and home. I suddenly wanted to see my own people and my own country – and the sooner the better.

I was sitting quietly in the cockpit repairing some flags when a ship came up over the horizon astern. I rushed to hoist my signal letters and got out the Aldis, but although she came close enough for me to read her name, *Mungo* of Le Havre, she motored by before I could finish signalling a message.

April 12th, 1969   *Day 303*
I took down the flags and began to do a few repairs when about five minutes later I looked up and saw the ship returning. This was very unusual and rather encouraging and when he started signalling my hopes rose. I received: 'What do you want?' and sent that 'I am non-stop round the world reported missing.' They asked what name and when I told them they began to wave so I knew I was recognized. I was by this time signalling with the fog horn and I sent R.T. 2182. This was acknowledged and I switched on the radio. For an agonizing minute the transmitter refused to work, but then we were through.

Now the news. Moitessier is apparently going round for a second time. I am thought to be 'Le Premier' and was reported missing some time ago. I asked him to send a message to Cliff Pearson [of the *Sunday Mirror*] for me and he agreed and when I told him to send the account to Marconi's he laughed and told me there would be no charge for this sort of message. I think at one point he doubted if I really was not a hoaxer and he asked my name and when I told him I heard him say 'Yes, that's right.' We spoke in a mixture of English and French. I was pretty excited at the thought of getting a message home at last and my English was scarcely coherent, so I don't know how he understood my French.

He asked me if I wanted a position and I told him I was in approximately 44°30′N, 22°00′W. He said I was exactly 44°25′N, 21°58′W. Any seaman will agree that as I had not yet got my Meridian Altitude I was pretty close. It's reassuring.

We chatted for a bit. I said I would be glad to get home and he said he could understand that!

At 1630 another French ship appeared, a tanker, *Marriotte*. She came over and gave three blasts which I acknowledged, so it looks as if the news is out. I'm sitting up for the BBC news at present.'

That night, with the bit now well between my teeth, I kept the Big Fellow set, and although the wind died away to a whisper I stayed up with him, steering, and we made 98 miles to noon on Sunday, April 13th.

That evening, I switched on the radio for the BBC's 6.00pm News and when it was over spun the dial through the frequencies as usual. I picked up the GPO High Frequency station at Baldock and decided to give him a shout. This had been a pretty fruitless exercise for three months, but my luck had changed at last and to my delight my call was immediately acknowledged. This was wonderful and after we had chatted for a bit the operator asked if I wanted to speak to anyone by phone. I asked for my home number. Mike answered and I'm told that he nearly went through the roof. Father was out, so I then spoke to Mother and Diana. The Chief Engineer in charge at Baldock, Mr Johnston, has since very kindly presented me with a tape of the conversation. It sounds a pretty exciting moment, as indeed it was, but the best news was that all the family were well. It is often forgotten that the worrying is not only confined to those left at home. I had had no news of my family for five months and I had had plenty of time to think of them.

Mike confirmed that Moitessier in *Joshua* had sailed on round the Cape of Good Hope and into the Indian Ocean, and I was able to discard the unworthy thought that the *Mungo* might have been misleading me and that Moitessier was right on my heels. Certainly I had expected him to be close and the Indian Ocean was the last place where I imagined he would be; as we now know, Moitessier eventually sailed on into the Pacific, where after 307 days at sea, he dropped anchor in Tahiti. So of the nine who had set out, only three of us were left, all British, which I thought to be a Good Thing.

Nigel Tetley in his trimaran *Victress* was off the coast of Brazil and Donald Crowhurst in *Teignmouth Electron,* the other trimaran, was thought to have just rounded the Horn. Mike also told me that Mother and Father and Diana would be coming out from the Scilly Isles in *The Queen of the Isles,* and that Ken, Bruce and Bill would be coming out in Guy Crossley-Meates's ex-air-sea-rescue launch, *Fathomer,* from Falmouth, where they had already installed themselves in the Marine Hotel. I only hoped that Bob and Di had remembered the specific details of my postcard booking from Australia and were keeping the best room for me! The rest of the family was already moving in on Falmouth, so it looked as if we were going to have quite a party.

Just the same, when I had finished writing up my diary, I got out the whisky bottle. Barring last minute accidents, *Suhaili* was going to be the first boat ever to sail round the world non-stop and I went on deck and poured a dram over her stern. As an afterthought I sacrificed another dram as a libation to Shony, one of the old British Gods of the Sea, before I took a good long swig myself. In the circumstances I thought he would have approved, but for the next two days my diary contains only 'Steered all day' and 'Steered all day, but it's getting very calm.'

On the following day, Wednesday, April 16th, I got through to Cliff Pearson at the *Sunday Mirror* and told him that I just might arrive in Falmouth on Sunday, April 20th, but as I was almost becalmed even while I spoke to him, it was very difficult to be more definite. Cliff told me that the Supporters Club in *Fathomer* intended to make contact on the Friday or at dawn on Saturday. He asked me to give any future positions in the code Bruce and I had worked out before I sailed and which had been approved by the GPO. The *Sunday Mirror,* as one of the sponsors for my voyage, naturally wanted as much exclusive copy on my return as they could get and they thoroughly deserved it. But already, Cliff told me, other newspaper boats were in the Scillies watching *Fathomer's* every move. From my vantage point it all sounded good fun, and I wished I was a hound rather than the hare. I arranged to make a contact with Bruce on the Saturday morning and signed off.

I went on deck and poured a dram over the stern.

With all these carefully laid plans on the boil, the wind dropped completely, and at the same time my long suffering battery charger gave up the ghost, which put me in a spot as my batteries were no longer taking a full charge and would not last for long. Once again I started to take the charger to pieces, but with the Big Fellow, staysail, main and mizzen set in the light airs, *Suhaili* needed my constant attention, and in the event I never was able to fix it. On Friday the batteries were further drained when I received a message via Land's End Radio from B.I. and spoke to George Martin of the *Sunday Mirror* in London.

April 18th, 1969   *Day 309*
George told me to watch out for a Beechcraft G–ASDO, which might be out looking for me. He also said *Fathomer* was being 'tagged' – real cloak and dagger stuff this – most enjoyable!

I am a little worried about my position as I did not get good sights today and I met a whole crowd of trawlers just before noon. These would, I think, be on the 100 fathoms line which, according to my sights, we were 30 miles short of at noon. There are some humps so maybe that's where they are, but I'd like to get stars tonight if the sky clears. 280 miles to Falmouth at noon . . .

It's 1830 and a most remarkable thing has happened. I was sitting on the containers reading *Timon of Athens* when I heard a scuffling in the starboard bunk and there, in the medical box, was a small grey bird with a slender pointed beak. It was the size of a wren. I have let it out.

That evening we were getting up amongst shipping and I could see navigation lights all round so I did not like to sleep; I kept watch from the cockpit, fortifying myself with coffee laced with whisky. Shortly after midnight a well-lit ship that had been overtaking, slowed down astern of us and appeared to be taking up station half a mile away. At the same time I noticed a smaller boat which I had assumed to be a fisherman coming in fast and taking up station. After watching both rather anxiously for some time, I decided to challenge the larger with the Aldis lamp. Back came the reply: *'Queen of the Isles'.* They closed in with flash bulbs popping and I was able to speak directly to Mother and Father for the first time for 309 days. It was a wonderful moment, but conversation was difficult in the rising wind and sea, and all too soon I had to give up trying to make myself heard and concentrate on reducing sail. The smaller boat closed soon afterwards and identified herself as *Fathomer*. They then stood off for the night, and with two watchdogs on guard I felt it safe to turn in.

When I awoke the next morning there was nothing in sight. My watchdogs had lost me. Visibility was down to two miles and the wind was up to Force 7. At 0815 I switched on the radio and made immediate contact with Bruce; he asked me 'Where the hell' I was and I had to reply that I did not really know. I could almost hear him groan at this but there was nothing we could do about it. The sun was hidden and I could not get a sight. By 1000 the wind had risen to Force 8 from the south–east and rather than strain *Suhaili* this close to home, I handed all sail, streamed the warp and hove-to. I spent the next two hours standing in the hatchway keeping a lookout for boats and hoping for a glimpse of the sun, which eventually rewarded me just before noon. I took a sight and worked out our latitude and radioed it out to Bruce. By this time all the newspapers were working together trying to locate us and it did not matter if anyone else knew my position.

I was tired and depressed. There was nothing I could do until the wind changed or eased and I turned in. This was the limit; to come this far and then get a contrary gale just when I could almost smell home, was too much. I did not sleep for long though. At 2.30pm I drifted awake to the sound of a siren. I leapt out of my bunk, imagining some vessel bearing down on us, but the sound came from the *Queen of the Isles*. I waved to my parents and then looked around at the sea. Whether it was because I had had a rest or because there was a ship close up I don't know, but the wind and sea seemed to have eased, and rather shamefacedly I went about setting some sail and getting in the warp. *Fathomer* appeared just as I got under way again, riding the sloping seas incredibly comfortably for such a small boat. As she closed I picked out Ken, Bruce and Bill waving wildly on her foredeck, Bill, as usual, covered in cameras.

Apparently the three of them had been discussing the best way to handle this meeting. From my radio messages they assumed that I was still perfectly sane but they were a little concerned that after all these months of solitude I might be under some tension at the prospect of getting amongst people again, for they had a better idea than I did of the plans that were being made to greet me in Falmouth. They agreed not to say anything to me until I had spoken and they had had a chance to gauge my reactions. For my part I was waiting for them to speak first. The boats closed to within fifteen yards as we grinned owlishly at each other, and Ken later swore that I then ruined a Moment in History when I at last shouted to him, 'I see you're still wearing that same bloody silly hat!' He promptly took it off and flung it into the Atlantic.

Fathomer and *Queen of the Isles* kept station with me all Saturday night. Following the gale the wind stayed stubbornly in the south-east, and as we would be pushed north towards the Bristol Channel if we stayed on the starboard tack, I went about and stood south. It seemed that the wind and weather were determined to give the lie to any E.T.A. I gave Cliff Pearson in Falmouth, but as before I sailed I had given April 14th as the date round about which I expected to be home and I was only six days out in my reckoning now, I did not think he would complain if a couple more went astray.

At 7.15 on Sunday morning I tacked round and headed north-east towards Land's End, 150 miles away. After a large plate of porridge I took a sight and shouted my position to Captain Evans of the *Queen of the Isles,* who had done the same thing: although in shouting distance we agreed that in practice we were two miles apart. In the afternoon *Fathomer* shot off for the Scillies to refuel and bring out fresh bread, newspapers and cigarettes for the *Queen.* I had not had a cigarette for over six weeks, and although I certainly felt the better for it and had not really missed them, to talk of them in such casual terms had a far more disturbing effect upon me than I could have imagined. As I drank my after-lunch coffee, I felt an addict's craving coming over me.

With the *Queen of the Isles* acting as my temporary Nanny, I was looking forward to a last good night's sleep before I closed the land. *Suhaili,* with reefs in the main and mizzen to reduce the pounding, was sailing comfortably to the Force 5 south-easterly winds, and with the prospect of some light rain during the night I turned in. I was too excited to sleep, which was just as well, because when I went on deck at 10.30pm with a cup of cocoa, the horizon ahead was dotted with the lights of a French fishing-fleet. From seeing too few ships I was now seeing far too many. Navigating through a fishing fleet at any time is a tricky business, but to do it at night can be positively nerve-racking, particularly for a small boat under sail. By the very nature of their work, fishing boats are constantly changing course, and as fast as you work out the course to steer to avoid one vessel, the last one you observed has completely changed its mind and is bearing down on you with every intention of maintaining its legal right of way. Multiply this process by thirty or forty boats and the sea suddenly becomes a very small and dangerous place.

I went about and headed south to try to sail round the fleet, but when a couple of hours later I made up towards Land's End again, they were still square-dancing in my path. At this rate I could have gone on dodging about all night without making any progress at all, so I said 'To hell with it,' held my course, and four exhausting hours later found myself in clear water at last. The *Queen of the Isles* had uncomplainingly sat on my tail throughout all these manoeuvres, and although she received greater respect from the fishermen because of her size, she was as relieved as I to be clear of them.

At 5.00am on Monday, April 21st, the wind went round to the south-west, and leaving *Suhaili* running under reefed main, heading at last for the Lizard, I turned in.

I was up again in three hours. *Suhaili* had followed the wind as it backed slightly, so I had to gybe again to be sure of clearing Bishop's Rock off the Scillies, and Land's End. I also wanted to keep well clear of the strong tidal stream that runs between the two. At 1135 I picked up Bishop's Rock lighthouse, bearing 100° True, my first sight of home for 312 days. I suppose that seeing the slim silhouette of the Bishop on the horizon should have been an emotional moment. Over the centuries it has been the last and first sight of Britain for generations of seamen, but my recollection is that I noted the sighting in the log simply as a navigational mark. My emotions, more prosaically, were concerned with a pint of beer, a steak, a hot bath and clean white sheets.

Fathomer rejoined at 2.00pm and took over from the *Queen of the Isles*. As if this were a signal the party started. A couple of helicopters clattered overhead with cameramen hanging crazily out of the open doors, and craft of all shapes and sizes joined us, one of them a tiny red skiboat from St Mary's. He probably had an easier time looking for me than I would have done looking for him, because most of the time he was completely hidden from me by the waves. A Coastal Command Shackleton appeared on the scene and made half a dozen low-level runs over the little convoy, scattering the helicopters out of its path like startled chickens.

Ahead of me I could see the grey shape of a minesweeper closing rapidly over the horizon. This was something I had been waiting for. HMS *Warsash*, an RNR ship, commanded by Lieutenant-Commander T. A. Bell, had been deputed by Rear Admiral B. C. G. Place, VC, DSC, RN, Admiral Commanding Reserves, to escort me in. This was a wonderful choice of ship in view of my RNR connections, and when I saw her I would not have changed her for a dozen aircraft-carriers. She swept round to my stern keeping properly to leeward, flying *QKF*, the International code for 'Welcome.'

Tom Bell came right in, handling his ship beautifully. There was a cheer from the deck and as I acknowledged it I saw standing amongst the crew my three brothers. We exchanged the usual family ruderies and then *Warsash*, who like her sisters is not designed for slow speed work, pulled off to one side and thereafter kept station ahead of me until I began the run into Falmouth.

That night I advanced the ship's clock for the last time to bring us into British Standard Time. I was pretty well exhausted. I had had little sleep for the past few days, and I knew that the next day, if it was to be my last at sea, would be very tiring. Already my voice was hoarse from three days of shouting messages to other ships, and if one discounts my singing it had probably had as much work in that time as in the previous 308 days.

I turned in at 1000 with Wolf Rock and Tater Du lights in sight, getting up at 3.00am on Tuesday morning to gybe round towards the Lizard, which was well in view. By dawn I had passed through the overfalls off the Lizard (to the annoyance of my watchdogs) and with a good westerly was heading up under full sail towards the Manacles buoy. Falmouth was then eight miles away and I could clearly identify Pendennis Point and St Anthony Head, which mark the entrance to the harbour.

The convoy was growing hourly. Off the Manacles we were met by the Falmouth lifeboat and the tug *St Mawes*, both dressed overall and looking as smart as paint. The lifeboatmen were in their full rig of seaboots, oilskins and distinctive red 'cap comforters'. I took an immediate fancy to their headgear and after I got into Falmouth, John Mitchell, the mate of *Fathomer*, presented me with his: it has now become one of my prized pieces of sailing gear.

The *St Mawes* was originally the *Arusha*, a B.I. tug stationed on the East African coast, and for this day the Company had chartered her and put her into her old livery, her black funnel with its distinguishing two white bands gleaming in the early morning sunshine. She bustled in flying an enormous Company house flag and I hoisted my own, together with the burgees of the Ocean Cruising Club and Benfleet Yacht Club, and for good measure I hoisted *Suhaili*'s signal letters *MHYU* on the port yardarm.

On board the *Arusha* I could see Captain Lattin and Captain Ben Rogers, who had been my first captain at sea on the *Chindwara*, and many other familiar faces. The Company had been my home since I left school, I had learned my seamanship in it, and they had given me every possible encouragement in preparing for my voyage. To be greeted like this was wonderful.

I was six miles – less than two hours – off Pendennis Point when at 9.00am the wind swung suddenly to the north-north-west and rose sharply. I was forced away to the east, reducing sail progressively as I went and the wind rose to Force 7 and 8. This was when I got really angry. *Suhaili*'s inability to sail close to the wind isn't an unduly worrying factor at sea, but for close work like this it was infuriating.

As I drove to the north-east away from Falmouth and towards Dodman Point, the helicopters and light aircraft which had been fluttering around disappeared. I imagine that with the prospect of a full day's tacking before them, they wisely decided to refuel and leave me with my seaborne escort of yachts and small craft, which stuck gamely and wetly to me for the rest of the day.

At least the wind was offshore and by creeping in towards the land I was able to keep to smoother water and a higher speed. I threw in another tack towards Porthmellon Head and out again to Dodman. It was cold and wet, but nothing was going to stop us now. *Suhaili* and I had been away for 313 days and covered over 30,000 miles together; heaving-to at this stage was unthinkable. Off Dodman we wore round and began the tack towards St Anthony Head. We raced across the harbour entrance until I was clear for the run in. I wore round for what I thought would be the last time, easing the sheets to give us a fast and comfortable finish. As we neared Black Rock, which lies between Pendennis Point and St Anthony Head, there seemed little for me to do except wave to the bustling fleet of small boats that was closing in round us. On Pendennis Point I could see the sunlight reflecting on the lines of parked cars, and on the front, people were waving to us. We were nearly there, and that pint of beer was almost in my hand when the Harbour Master's launch came bursting through the mêlée and I was told that the *Sunday Times* had established the 'finishing line' between Pendennis Point and Black Rock. At that moment another competitor nearly dropped out. I had left Falmouth between Black Rock and St Anthony Head and saw no reason why I should not take the same route coming in, and I said so in terms that were unfortunately picked up by the BBC TV microphones at the time. Nevertheless, showing more forbearance than I usually do, I wore round to make another tack to the west. Half an hour later, at 3.25pm I crossed the finishing line and a cannon fired.

The first people to board were Her Majesty's Customs and Excise officers from Falmouth. As they jumped across, the senior officer, trying to keep a straight face, asked the time-honoured question:

'Where from?'

'Falmouth,' I replied.

THREE INCIDENTS FROM ROBINSON CRUSOE
Daniel Defoe

Alexander Selkirk, 1676-1721, Scottish sailor, was the prototype of Robinson Crusoe. He joined Dampier in May 1703, in a privateering expedition to the South Seas as sailing master of the Cinque Ports *galley. In September 1704 the* Cinque Ports *put in on Juan Fernandez Island, west of Valparaiso; here Selkirk had a dispute with his captain, Thomas Stradling, and at his own request was put ashore with a few ordinary necessities. Before the ship left he begged to be taken back on board, but this was refused. Selkirk remained alone in Juan Fernandez until January 31, 1709, when he was found and taken on board the* Duke *privateer commanded by Captain Woodes Rogers with Dampier as pilot. Selkirk was made mate of the* Duke *and afterwards given command of a prize the* Increase. *Selkirk returned to the Thames on October 14, 1711. He died on December 12, 1721, as master's mate of* H.M.S. Weymouth.

WRECKED

. . . A second storm came upon us, which carried us away with the same impetuosity westward, and drove us so out of the very way of all human commerce, that had all our lives been saved as to the sea, we were rather in danger of being devoured by savages than ever returning to our own country.

In this distress, the wind still blowing very hard, one of our men early in the morning cried out 'Land!' and we had no sooner run out of the cabin to look out in hopes of seeing whereabouts in the world we were, but the ship struck upon a sand, and in a moment, her motion being so stopped, the sea broke over her . . . The mate . . . lays hold of the boat, and with the help of the rest of the men, they got her slung over the ship's side, and getting all into her, let go, and committed ourselves, being eleven in number, to God's mercy and the wild sea.

And now our case was very dismal indeed, for we all saw plainly that the sea went so high that the boat could not live, and that we should be inevitably drowned. As to making sail, we had none; nor, if we had, could we have done anything with it: so we worked at the oar towards the land, though with heavy hearts, like men going to execution; for we all knew that when the boat came nearer the shore she would be dashed in a thousand pieces by the breach of the sea. However, we committed our souls to God in the most earnest manner, and the wind driving us towards the shore, we hastened our destruction with our own hands, pulling as well as we could towards land . . .

After we had rowed or rather driven about a league and a half, a raging wave, mountain-like, came rolling astern of us, and plainly bade us expect the *coup de grace*. In a word, it took us with such a fury that it overset the boat at once, and separating us as well from the boat as from one another, gave us not time hardly to say, 'O God!' for we were all swallowed up in a moment.

Nothing can describe the confusion of thought which I felt when I sank into the water; for though I swam very well, yet I could not deliver myself from the waves so as to draw breath, till that a wave, having spent itself, went back, and left me upon the land almost dry, but half dead with the water I took in. I got upon my feet, and endeavoured to make on towards the land as fast as I could before another wave should return and take me up again. But I soon found it was impossible to avoid it; for I saw the sea come after me as high as a great hill, and as furious as an enemy which I had no means or strength to contend with. My business was to hold my breath and raise myself upon the water if I could, and so by swimming to preserve my breathing and pilot myself towards the shore if possible, my greatest concern now being that the sea, as it would carry me a great way towards the shore when it came on, might carry me back again with it when it gave back towards the sea.

The wave that came upon me again buried me at once twenty or thirty feet deep in its own body and I could feel myself carried with a mighty force and swiftness towards the shore . . . but I held my breath and assisted myself to swim still forward with all my might. I was ready to

A mountain-like wave took us with a great fury.

burst with holding my breath . . . when . . . to my immediate relief I found my head and hands shoot out above the surface of the water . . . I struck forward against the return of the waves and felt ground again with my feet. I stood still for a few moments to recover breath, and till the water went from me, and then took to my heels and ran with what strength I had further towards the shore. But neither would this deliver me from the fury of the sea, which came pouring in after me again, and twice more I was lifted up by the waves and carried forward as before . . . The last time . . . the sea dashed me against a piece of rock . . . I held my hold till the wave abated, and then fetched another run, which brought me so near the shore that the next wave, though it went over me, yet did not so swallow me up as to carry me away; and the next run I took I got to the mainland, where, to my great comfort, I clambered up the cliffs of the shore and sat me down upon the grass, free from danger, and quite out of the reach of the water . . . and began to look up and thank God that my life was saved . . .

I walked about on the shore lifting up my hands, and my whole being, as I may say, wrapped up in the contemplation of my deliverance, making a thousand gestures and motions which I cannot describe, reflecting upon all my comrades that were drowned, and that there should not be one soul saved but myself; for, as for them, I never saw them afterwards, or any sign of them, except three of their hats, one cap, and two shoes that were not fellows.

A FOOTPRINT IN THE SAND

It happened one day, about noon, going towards my boat, I was exceedingly surprised with the print of a man's naked foot on the shore, which was very plain to be seen in the sand. I stood like one thunderstruck, or as if I had seen an apparition. I listened, I looked round me, I could hear nothing, nor see anything. I went up to a rising ground, to look farther. I went up the shore, and down the shore, but it was all one; I could see no other impression but that one. I went to it again to see if there were any more, and to observe if it might not be my fancy; but there was no room for that, for there was exactly the very print of a foot — toes, heel, and every part of a foot. How it came thither I knew not, nor could in the least imagine. But after innumerable fluttering thoughts, like a man perfectly confused and out of myself . . . terrified to the last degree, looking behind me at every two or three steps, mistaking every bush and tree, and fancying every stump at a distance to be a man . . . when I came to my castle – for so I think I called it ever after this – I fled into it like one pursued. Whether I went over by the ladder at first contrived, or went in at the hole in the rock which I called a door, I cannot remember; no, nor could I remember next morning, for never frighted hare fled to cover, or fox to earth, with more terror of mind than I to this retreat.

MAN FRIDAY

He was a comely, handsome fellow, perfectly well made, with straight strong limbs, not too large, tall and well shaped, and as I reckon, about twenty-six years of age. He had a very good countenance, not a fierce and surly aspect, but seemed to have something very manly in his face; and yet he had all the sweetness and softness of a European in his countenance too, especially when he smiled. His hair was long and black, not curled like wool; his forehead very high and large, and a great vivacity and sparkling sharpness in his eyes. The colour of his skin was not quite black, but very tawny, and yet not of an ugly yellow nauseous tawny, as the Brazilians and Virginians and other natives of America are, but of a bright kind of a dun olive colour, that had in it something very agreeable, though not very easy to describe. His face was round and plump; his nose small, not flat like the negroes; a very good mouth, thin lips and his fine teeth well set and white as ivory. After he had slumbered, rather than slept, about half an hour, he waked again, and . . . he came running to me, laying himself down . . . his head flat upon the ground, close to my foot, and sets my other foot upon his head . . . to let me know he would serve me as long as he lived. I understood him in many things, and let him know I was very well pleased with him. In a little time I began to speak to him and teach him to speak to me. And first, I made him know his name should be Friday, which was the day I saved his life . . . and I let him know I would give him some clothes; at which he seemed very glad, for he was stark naked.

THE END OF THE COMPASS ROSE
Nicholas Monsarrat

The Compass Rose *was one of the ships that took part in 'the Battle of the Atlantic' that raged throughout the Second World War. After safely escorting four ships to Reykjavik, the ship sets out to rejoin the rest of the convoy a long way ahead. Night fell . . .*

The torpedo struck *Compass Rose* as she was moving at almost her full speed: she was therefore mortally torn by the sea as well as by the violence of the enemy. She was hit squarely about twelve feet from her bows: there was one slamming explosion, and the noise of ripping and tearing metal, and the fatal sound of sea water flooding in under great pressure: a blast of heat from the stricken fo'c'sle rose to the bridge like a hideous waft of incense. *Compass Rose* veered wildly from her course, and came to a shaking stop, like a dog with a bloody muzzle: her bows were very nearly blown off, and her stern was already starting to cant in the air, almost before the wave was off the ship.

At the moment of disaster, Ericson was on the bridge, and Lockhart, and Wells: the same incredulous shock hit them all like a sickening body-blow. They were masked and confused by the pitch-dark night, and they could not believe that *Compass Rose* had been struck. But the ugly angle of the deck must only have one meaning, and the noise of things sliding about below their feet confirmed it. There was another noise, too, a noise which momentarily paralysed Ericson's brain and prevented him thinking at all; it came from a voice-pipe connecting the fo'c'sle with the bridge – an agonised animal howling, like a hundred dogs going mad in a pit. It was the men caught by the explosion, which must have jammed their only escape: up the voice-pipe came their shouts, their crazy hammering, their screams for help. But there was no help for them: with an executioner's hand, Ericson snapped the voice-pipe cover shut, cutting off the noise.

To Wells he said: 'Call *Viperous* on R/T. Plain Language, Say —' he did an almost violent sum in his brain; 'Say: "TORPEDOED IN POSITION OH-FIVE-OH DEGREES, THIRTY MILES ASTERN OF YOU".'

To Lockhart he said: 'Clear away boats and rafts. But wait for the word.'

The deck started to tilt more acutely still. There was a crash from below as something heavy broke adrift and slid down the slope. Steam began to roar out of the safety-valve alongside the funnel.

Ericson thought: God, she's going down already, like *Sorrel*.

Wells said: 'The R/T's smashed, sir.'

Down in the wardroom, the noise and shock had been appalling; the explosion was in the very next compartment, and the bulkhead had buckled and sagged towards them, just above the table they were eating at. They all leapt to their feet, and jumped for the doorway: for a moment there were five men at the foot of the ladder leading to the upper deck – Morell, Ferraby, Baker, Carslake, and Tomlinson, the second steward. They seemed to be mobbing each other: Baker was shouting 'My lifebelt – I've left my lifebelt!' Ferraby was being lifted off his feet by the rush, Tomlinson was waving a dish-cloth, Carslake had reached out above their heads and grabbed the hand-rail. As the group struggled, it had an ugly illusion of panic, though it was in fact no more than the swift reaction to danger. Someone had to lead the way up the ladder: by the compulsion of their peril, they had all got there at the same time.

Morell suddenly turned back against the fierce rush, buffeted his way through and darted into his cabin. Above his bunk was a photograph of his wife: he seized it, and thrust it inside his jacket. He looked round swiftly, but there seemed nothing else he wanted.

He ran out again, and found himself already alone: the others had all got clear away, even during the few seconds of his absence. He wondered which one of them had given way . . . Just as he reached the foot of the ladder there was an enormous cracking noise behind him: foolishly he turned, and through the wardroom door he saw the bulkhead split asunder and the water burst in. It flooded towards him like a cataract:

quickly though he moved up the ladder, he was waist-deep before he reached the top step, and the water seemed to suck greedily at his thighs as he threw himself clear. He looked down at the swirling chaos which now covered everything – the wardroom, the cabins, all their clothes and small possessions. There was one light still burning under-water, illuminating the dark-green, treacherous torrent that had so nearly trapped him. He shook himself, in fear and relief, and ran out into the open, where in the freezing night air the shouting was already wild, the deck already steep under his feet.

★　★　★　★

The open space between the boats was a dark shambles. Men blundered to and fro, cursing wildly, cannoning into each other, slipping on the unaccustomed slope of the deck: above their heads the steam from the safety-valve was reaching a crescendo of noise, as if the ship, pouring out her vitals, was screaming her rage and defiance at the same time. One of the boats was useless – it could not be launched at the angle *Compass Rose* had now reached: the other had jammed in its chocks, and no effort, however violent, could move it. Tonbridge, who was in charge, hammered and punched at it: the dozen men with him strove desperately to lift it clear: it stuck there as if pegged to the deck, it was immovable. Tonbridge said, for the fourth or fifth time: 'Come on, lads – heave!' He had to roar to make himself heard; but roaring was no use, and heaving was no use either. Gregg, who was by his shoulder, straining at the gunwale, gasped: 'It's no bloody good, Ted . . . she's fast . . . It's the list . . .' and Tonbridge called out: 'The rafts, then – clear the rafts!'

The men left the boat, which in their mortal need had failed them and wasted precious minutes, and made for the Carley floats: they blundered into each other once more, and ran full tilt into the funnel-guys, and shouted fresh curses at the confusion. Tonbridge started them lifting the raft that was on the high side of the ship, and bringing it across to the other rail; in the dark, with half a dozen fear-driven men heaving and wrenching at it, it was as if they were already fighting each other for the safety it promised. Then he stood back, looking up at the bridge where the next order – the last order of all – must come from. The bridge was crooked against the sky. He fingered his life-jacket, and tightened the straps. He said, not bothering to make his voice audible:

'It's going to be cold, lads.'

Down in the engine-room, three minutes after the explosion, Watts and E.R.A. Broughton were alone, waiting for the order to release from the bridge. They knew it ought to come, they trusted that it would . . . Watts had been 'on the plate' when the torpedo struck home: on his own initiative, he had stopped the engine, and then, as the angle of their list increased, he had opened the safety-valve and let the pressure off the boilers. He had followed what was happening from the noise outside, and it was easy enough to follow. The series of crashes from forward were the bulkheads going, the trampling overhead was the boats being cleared away: the wicked down-hill angle of the ship was their doom. Now they waited, side by side in the deserted engine-room: the old E.R.A. and the young apprentice. Watts noticed that Broughton was crossing himself, and remembered he was a Roman Catholic. Good luck to him tonight . . . The bell from the bridge rang sharply, and he put his mouth to the voice-pipe:

'Engine-room!' he called.

'Chief,' said the Captain's far-away voice.

'Sir?'

'Leave it, and come up.'

That was all – and it was enough. 'Up you go, lad!' he said to Broughton. We're finished here.'

'Is she sinking?' asked Broughton uncertainly.

'Not with me on board . . . Jump to it!'

D plus four minutes . . . Peace had already come to the fo'c'sle; the hammering had ceased, the wild voices were choked and stilled. The torpedo had struck at a bad moment – for many people, the worst and last moment of their lives. Thirty-seven men of the port watch, seamen and stokers, had been in the messdecks at the time of the explosion: sitting about, or eating, or sleeping, or reading, or playing cards or dominoes; and doing all these things in snug warmth, behind the single closed water-tight door. None of them had got out alive: most had been killed instantly, but a few, lucky or unlucky, had raced or crawled for the door, to find it warped and buckled by the explosion, and hopelessly jammed. There was no other way out, except the gaping hole through which the water was now bursting in a broad and furious jet.

The shambles that followed was mercifully brief; but until the water quenched the last screams and uncurled the last clawing hands, it was as Ericson had heard it through the voice-pipe – a paroxysm of despair, terror, and convulsive violence, all in full and dreadful flood, an extreme corner of the human zoo for which there should be no witnesses.

★　★　★　★

At the other end of the ship, one peaceful and determined man had gone to his post and set about the job assigned to him under 'Abandon Ship Stations'. This was Wainwright, the leading-torpedo-man, who, perched high in the stern which had now begun to tower over the rest of the ship, was withdrawing the primers from the depth-charges, so that they could not explode when the ship went down.

He went about the task methodically. Unscrew, pull, throw away – unscrew, pull, throw away. He whistled as he worked, a tuneless version of 'Roll out the Barrel'. Each primer took him between ten and fifteen seconds to dispose of: he had thirty depth-charges to see to: he reckoned that there would just about be time to finish . . . Under his feet, the stern was steadily lifting, like one end of a gigantic see-saw: there was enough light in the gloom for him to follow the line of the ship, down the steep slope that now led straight into the sea. He could hear the steam blowing off, and the voices of the men shouting further along the upper deck. Noisy bastards, he thought, dispassionately. Pity they hadn't got anything better to do.

Alone and purposeful, he worked on. There was an obscure enjoyment in throwing over the side the equipment that had plagued him for nearly three years. The bloody things all had numbers, and special boxes, and check-lists, and history-sheets; now they were just splashes in the dark, and even these need not be counted.

Someone loomed up nearby, climbing the slope with painful effort, and bumped into him. He recognised an officer's uniform, and then Ferraby.

Ferraby said: 'Who's that?' in a strangled voice.

'The L.T., sir, I'm just chucking away the primers.'

He went on with the job, without waiting for a comment. Ferraby was staring about him as if he were lost in some terrible dream, but presently he crossed to the other depth-charge rail and began, awkwardly, to deal with the depth-charges on that side. They worked steadily, back to back, braced against the slope of the deck. At first they were silent: then Wainwright started to whistle again, and Ferraby, as he dropped one of the primers, to sob. The ship gave a violent lurch under their feet, and the stern rose higher still, enthroning them above the sea.

★　★　★　★

D plus seven . . . Ericson realised that she was going, and that nothing could stop her. The bridge now hung over the sea at an acute forward angle, the stern was lifting, the bows deep in the water, the stern itself just awash. The ship they had spent so much time and care on, their own *Compass Rose*, was pointed for her dive, and she would not be poised much longer.

He was tormented by what he had not been able to do: the signal to *Viperous*, the clearing of the boats, the shoring-up of the wardroom bulkhead, which might conceivably have been caught in time. He thought: the Admiral at Ardnacraish was right – we ought to have practised this more . . . But it had all happened too quickly for them: perhaps *nothing* could have saved her, perhaps she was too vulnerable, perhaps the odds were too great, and he could clear his conscience.

Wells, alert at his elbow, said: 'Shall I ditch the books, sir?'

Ericson jerked his head up. Throwing overboard the confidential signal books and ciphers, in their weighted bag, was the last thing of all for them to do, before they went down: it was the final signal for their dissolution. He remembered having watched the man in the U-boat do it – losing his life doing it, in fact. For a moment he held back from the order, in fear and foreboding.

He looked once more down the length of his ship. She was quieter already, fatally past the turmoil and the furious endeavour of the first few minutes: they had all done their best, and it didn't seem to have been any use: now they were simply sweating out the last brief pause, before they started swimming. He thought momentarily of their position, thirty miles astern of the convoy, and wondered whether any of the stern escorts would have seen *Compass Rose* catching up on their Radar, and then noticed that she had faded out, and guessed what had happened.

That was their only chance, on this deadly cold night.

He said: 'Yes, Wells, throw them over.' Then he turned to another figure waiting at the back of the bridge, and called out: 'Coxswain.'

'Sir,' said Tallow.

'Pipe "Abandon ship".'

He followed Tallow down the ladder and along the steep iron deck, hearing his voice bawling 'Abandon ship! Abandon ship!' ahead of him. There was a crowd of men collected, milling around in silence, edging towards the high stern: below them, on the black water, the two Carley floats had been launched and lay in wretched attendance on their peril. A handful of Tonbridge's party, having disposed of the Carleys, had turned back to wrestle afresh with the boat, but it had become locked more securely still as their list increased. When Ericson was among his men, he was recognised; the words 'The skipper – the skipper' exploded in a small hissing murmur all round him, and one of the men asked: 'What's the chances, sir?'

Compass Rose trembled under their feet, and slid further forward.

A man by the rails shouted; 'I'm off, lads,' and jumped headlong into the sea.

Ericson said: 'It's time to go. Good luck to you all.'

Now fear took hold. Some men jumped straight away, and struck out from the ship, panting with the cold and calling to their comrades to follow them; others held back, and crowded farther towards the stern, on the high side away from the water; when at last they jumped, many of them slid and scraped their way down the barnacled hull, and their clothes and then the softer projections of their bodies – sometimes their faces, sometimes their genitals – were torn to to ribbons by the rough plating. The sea began to sprout bobbing red lights as the safety-lamps were switched on: the men struck out and away, and then crowded together, shouting and calling encouragement to each other, and turned to watch *Compass Rose*. High out of the water, she seemed to be considering the plunge before she took it: the propeller, bared against the night sky, looked foolish and indecent, the canted mast was like an admonishing finger, bidding them all behave in her absence.

She did not long delay thus: she could not. As they watched, the stern rose higher still: the last man left on board, standing on the tip of the after-rail, now plunged down with a yell of fear. The noise seemed to unloose another: there was a rending crash as the whole load of depthcharges broke loose from their lashings and ploughed wildly down the length of the upper deck, and splashed into the water.

From a dozen constricted throats came the same words: 'She's going.'

There was a muffled explosion, which they could each feel like a giant hand squeezing their stomachs, and *Compass Rose* began to slide down. Now she went quickly, as if glad to be quit of her misery: the mast snapped in a ruin of rigging as she fell. When the stern dipped beneath the surface, a tumult of water leapt upwards: then the smell of oil came thick and strong towards them. It was a smell they had got used to, on many convoys: they had never thought that *Compass Rose* would ever exude the same disgusting stench.

The sea flattened, the oil spread, their ship was plainly gone: a matter of minutes had wiped out a matter of years. Now the biting cold, forgotten before the huge disaster of their loss, began to return. They were bereaved and left alone in the darkness; fifty men, two rafts, misery, fear, and the sea.

★ ★ ★ ★

There was not room for them all on the two Carleys: there never had been room. Some sat or lay on them, some gripped the ratlines that hung down from their sides, some swam around in hopeful circles, or clung to other luckier men who had found a place. The bobbing red lights converged on the rafts: as the men swam, they gasped with fear and cold, and icy waves hit them in the face, and oil went up their nostrils and down their throats. Their hands were quickly numbed, and then their legs, and then the cold probed deep within them, searching for the main blood of their body. They thrashed about wildly, they tried to shoulder a place at the rafts, and were pushed away again: they swam round and round in the darkness, calling out, cursing their comrades, crying for help, slobbering their prayers.

Some of those gripping the ratlines found that they could do so no longer, and drifted away. Some of those who had swallowed fuel-oil developed a paralysing cramp, and began to retch up what was poisoning them. Some of those who had torn their bodies against the ship's side were attacked by a deadly and congealing chill.

There was a muffled explosion and the Compass Rose *began to slide down.*

Some of those on the rafts grew sleepy as the bitter night progressed; and others lost heart as they peered round them at the black and hopeless darkness, and listened to the sea and wind, and smelt the oil, and heard their comrades giving way before this extremity of fear and cold.

Presently, men began to die.

★　★　★　★

Some men died well: Chief Petty Officer Tallow, Leading-Seaman Tonbridge, Leading-Torpedo-man Wainwright, Yeoman of Signals Wells; and many others. These were the men who did all things well, automatically; in death, the trick did not desert them.

Tallow died looking after people: it had always been his main job aboard *Compass Rose*, and he practised it to the last. He gave up his place on Number One Carley to a young seaman who had no lifebelt: when he saw the man's plight, Tallow first reprimanded him for disobeying standing orders, and then slipped down off the raft and shouldered the other man up. But once in the water, a fierce cramp attacked him, and he could not hold onto the ratlines; even as the man he had rescued was grumbling about the 'bloody coxswain never giving them any peace', Tallow drifted away and presently died of cold, alone.

Tonbridge overspent his strength trying to round up people and guide them towards the Carleys. He had already brought in half a dozen men who were too far gone to think or act for themselves, when he heard another choking cry from the farther darkness, another man on the point of drowning. He set off, for the seventh time, to help, and did not come back.

Wainwright, having decided that it would be better if the two Carleys kept close together, set himself the job of steering and pushing one towards the other. But it was heavier than he thought and he was not as strong as he hoped; he soon lost his temper with the sea that kept forcing the rafts apart, and the cold that robbed him of his strength, and he wrestled with the task to the point of exhaustion, and died in a fierce rage.

Wells died making lists. He had been making lists nearly all his seagoing life: lists of signals, lists of ships in convoy, lists of code-flags. Now it seemed to him essential to find out how many men had got away from *Compass Rose*, and how many were left alive: the Captain was sure to ask him, and he didn't want to be caught out. He swam round counting heads, for more than an hour; he got up to forty-seven, and then he began to be afraid that some of the men he had counted might have died in the meantime, and he started to go round again.

It was much slower work, this second time, and presently, as he swam towards a dark figure in the water, a figure who would not answer his hail, the man seemd to draw away instead of coming nearer. Wells approached him very slowly, unable to manage more than one stroke at a time, resting for long pauses in between, and within a few minutes of finding that the man was dead, he died himself, calling out a total which was now far from accurate.

★ ★ ★ ★

Some men died badly: Chief Engine-room Artificer Watts, Able-Seaman Gregg, Petty Officer Steward Carslake; and many others. These were the men whose nature or whose past life had made them selfish, or afraid, or so eager to live that they destroyed themselves with hope.

Watts died badly: perhaps it was unfair to expect him to do anything else. He was old, and tired, and terrified; he should have been by the fire with his grandchildren, and instead he was thrashing about in oily water, bumping in the darkness against men he knew well, men already dead. He never stopped crying out, and calling for help, from the moment he jumped from *Compass Rose*: he clung to other men, he fought wildly to get onto one of the Carleys which was already crammed with people, he got deeper and deeper into the grip of an insane fear. It was fear that killed him, more than anything else: he became convinced that he could stand no more, and that unless he was rescued immediately he would perish. At this, a last constricting terror began to bind his weak limbs and pinch the brittle arteries of his blood, until abject death itself came to rescue him. It had nothing about it that the death of an old pensioner should have had, and both his service and his normal spirit deserved far better than the last prayerful wailing that saw him out. But that was true of many other people, at this fearful ending to their lives.

Gregg died badly, because he clung to life with ferocious hope; and on this account he met death in a curious way. Just before the ship sailed, Gregg had got another letter from his friend in the Army. 'Dear Tom,' it said, 'you asked me to keep an eye on Edith when I got home on leave. Well . . .' Gregg found it hard to believe that his wife could have gone straight off the rails again, the moment he had left her and returned to his ship; but even if it were true, he felt sure that he could fix it all up in a couple of days. Just let me get back to her, he thought: she's only a kid, all she needs is a good talking-to, all she needs is me to make love to her . . . For that reason, he felt that he could not die: it was a feeling shared by many of his shipmates, and the competition to stay alive was, in out-of-the-way corners, spiteful and violent.

It took Gregg an exhausting hour to jostle and force his way to a place alongside one of the Carleys: he saw that it was hopeless to try to get on top of it, but his immense determination drove him to do all he could to see that he did not lose his place. He finally squeezed his body between the side of the Carley and the ratline that ran round it, so that he was fastened to the raft like a small parcel tied to a larger one; and there, securely anchored, he aimed to pass the whole night, dreaming of home and the wife who must surely love him again as soon as he got back . . . But he had been too greedy for his life: as the night progressed, and he weakened and grew sleepy with cold, the rope slipped from his shoulders to his neck – the rope which ran, through loops, all the way round the raft, and was being drawn tight by a score of desperate men clinging to it. He woke suddenly, to find it pressing hard on his neck; before he could struggle free, the raft lurched upwards as a man on top fell from one side to the other, and the rope bit deep under his chin and lifted him from the water. It was too dark for the others to see what was happening, and by that time, Gregg's strangled cries might have been any other strangled cries, the ordinary humdrum sounds of drowning. His wild struggles only shortened the time it took to hang himself.

Carslake died a murderer's death. The small baulk of wood which floated near him during the darkest hour of the night was only big enough for one man, and one man was on it already, a telegraphist named Rollestone. Rollestone was small, bespectacled, and afraid; Carslake matched him in fear, but in nothing else, and the fact that he had not been able to get a place at one of the Carleys had inflamed in him a vindictive frenzy to preserve his life. He saw Rollestone's figure, prone on the plank of wood, and he swam over slowly, and pulled at one end of it so that it went under-water. Rollestone raised his head.

'Look out,' he said fearfully. 'You'll have me over.'

'There's room for both of us,' said Carslake roughly, and pulled the wood under-water again.

'There isn't . . . Leave me alone . . . Find another piece.'

It was the darkest hour of the night. Carslake swam slowly round to the other end of the plank, and went to work with his hands to loosen Rollestone's grip.

'What are you doing?' whimpered Rollestone.

'I saw this first,' said Carslake, panting with the effort to dislodge him.

'But I was *on* it,' said Rollestone, nearly crying with fear and anger. 'It's mine.'

Carslake pulled at him again, clawing at his fingers. The plank tipped and rocked dangerously. Rollestone began to shout for help, and Carslake, shifting his grip, raised an arm and hit him in the mouth. He fell off the plank, but immediately started to scramble back onto it, kicking out at Carslake as he did so. Carslake waited until Rollestone's head was clearly outlined against the dark sky, and then raised both hands, locked together, and struck hard, again and again. Rollestone only had time to shout once more before he was silenced for ever. It was the darkest hour of the night.

But the murderous effort seemed to weaken Carslake. His body, hot for the moment of killing, now grew very cold; when he tried to climb onto the plank, he found that he was too heavy and too awkward in his movements, and he could not balance properly. Presently he rolled off it, and sank back into the water, breathing slowly and painfully. The plank floated away again, ownerless.

★　★　★　★

Some men just died: Sub-Lieutenant Baker, Stoker Evans, Lieutenant Morell; and many others. These were the men who had nothing particular to live for, or who had made so fundamental a mess of their lives that it was a relief to forfeit them.

In the abandoning of the ship, Baker had swum about for some minutes and then found a place on Number Two Carley; but the slow drying of his body after he had climbed out of the water had been horribly painful. He had fidgeted and altered his position continuously, without relief, for several hours, and finally, driven to desperation, he had slipped off the raft and into the sea again. He died as quickly as would any other man who welcomed the cold, at a moment when a single degree of temperature, one way or the other, could make the difference between a blood-stream moving and a blood-stream brought to a dead stop.

Stoker Evans died for love: indeed, there had been so much of it, in one form or another, in his life, that it had long got out of hand. By this stage of the war, Evans had acquired two nagging wives – one in London, the other in Glasgow; he had a depressed young woman in Liverpool, and a hopeful widow in Londonderry; there was a girl in Manchester who was nursing one of his children, and a girl in Greenock who was expecting another. If the ship went to Gibraltar, there would be a couple of Spanish women gesticulating on the quay: if it went to Iceland or Halifax or St John's, Newfoundland, some sort of loving or threatening message would arrive on board within the hour. All his money went to meet half a dozen different lots of housekeeping-bills, or to satisfy affiliation orders: all his spare time in harbour was spent in writing letters. He was rarely inclined to go ashore, in any event; the infuriated husbands or brothers or fathers who were sure to be waiting for him outside the dock-gates, were not the sort of welcome home he relished.

Evans had arrived at this deplorable situation by a fatal process of enterprise. He was not in the least good-looking; it was just that he could never take 'No' for an answer.

But recently there had been a new and more serious development. Just before *Compass Rose* had sailed, the two official 'wives' had found out about each other: the ship had in fact only just cleared harbour in time for him to escape. But he could guess what would happen now. The wives would combine against the other women, and rout them: they would then combine again, this time against himself. He saw himself in the police-court for breach-of-promise, in the dock for seduction, in prison for debt, in jail for bigamy: he could imagine no future that was not black and complicated, and no way out of it, of any sort.

When, towards three o'clock in the morning, the time came for him to fight for his life against the cold, he felt only lassitude and despair. It seemed to him, in a moment of insight, that he had had a good run – too good a run to continue indefinitely – and that the moment had come for him to pay for it. If he did not pay for it now – in the darkness, in the cold oily water, in private – then he would have to meet a much harsher reckoning when he got home.

He did not exactly surrender to the sea, but he stopped caring much whether he lived or died; and on this night, an ambiguous will was not enough. Evans did not struggle for the favour of life with anything like the requisite desperation; and that potent region of his body which had got him into the most trouble seemed, curiously, the least determined of all in this final wooing. Indeed, the swift chill spreading from his loins was like a derisive snub from headquarters; as if life itself were somehow, for the first and last time, shaking its head and crossing its legs.

Morell died, as it happened, in French, which was his grandmother's tongue: and he died, as he had lately lived, alone. He had spent much of the bitter night outside the main cluster of survivors, floating motionless in his kapok life-jacket, watching the bobbing red lights, listening to the sounds of men in terror and despair. As so often during the past, he felt aloof from what was going on around him; it did not seem to be a party which one was really required to join – death would find him here, thirty yards off, if death were coming for him, and in the meantime the remnant of his life was still a private matter.

He thought a great deal about Elaine: his thoughts of her lasted as he himself did, till nearly daylight. But there came a time, towards five o'clock, when his cold body and his tired brain seemed to compass a full circle and meet at the same point of futility and exhaustion. He saw now that he had been utterly foolish, where Elaine was concerned: foolish, and ineffective. He had run an antic course of protest and persuasion: latterly, he had behaved like any harassed stage husband, stalking the boards in some grotesque mask of cuckoldry, while the lovers peeped from the wings and winked at the huge audience. Nothing he had done, he realised now, had served any useful purpose: no words, no appeals, no protests could ever have had an ounce of weight. Elaine either loved him or did not, wanted him or could do without, remained faithful or betrayed him. If her love were strong enough, she would stay his: if not, he could not recall her, could not talk her into love again.

It was, of course, now crystal clear that for a long time she had not given a finger-snap for him, one way or the other.

The bleak thought brought a bleaker chill to his body, a fatal hestitation in the tide of life. A long time passed, with no more thoughts at all, and when he woke to this he realised that it was the onset of sleep, and of death. It did not matter now. With calm despair, he stirred himself to sum up what was in his mind, what was in his life. It took him a long and labouring time; but presently he muttered, aloud;

'*Il y en a toujours l'un qui baise, et l'un qui tourne la joue.*'

He put his head on one side, as if considering whether this could be improved on. No improvement offered itself, and his slow thoughts petered to nothing again; but his head stayed where it was and presently the angle of enquiry became the congealing angle of death.

★　★　★　★

Some – a few – did not die: Lieutenant-Commander Ericson, Lieutenant Lockhard, Leading Radar Mechanic Sellars, Sick-Berth Attendant Crowther, Sub-Lieutenant Ferraby, Petty Officer Phillips, Leading-Stoker Gracey, Stoker Grey, Stoker Spurway, Telegraphist Widdowes, Ordinary-Seaman Tewson. Eleven men, on the two rafts; no others were left alive by morning.

It reminded Lockhart of the way a party ashore gradually thinned out and died away, as time and quarrelling and stupor and sleepiness took their toll. At one stage it had been almost a manageable affair: the two Carleys, with their load of a dozen men each and their cluster of hangers-on, had paddled towards each other across the oily heaving sea, and he had taken some kind of rough roll-call, and found that there were over thirty men still alive. But that had been a lot earlier on, when the party was a comparative success . . . As the long endless night progressed, men slipped out of life without warning, shivering and freezing to death almost between sentences: the strict account of dead and living got out of hand, lost its authority and became meaningless. Indeed, the score was hardly worth the keeping, when within a little while – unless the night ended and the sun came up to warm them – it might add up to total disaster.

On the rafts, in the whispering misery of the night that would not end, men were either voices or silences: if they were silences for too many minutes, it meant that they need no longer be counted in, and their places might be taken by others who still had life in their bodies.

'Christ, it's cold . . .'
'How far away was the convoy?'
'About thirty miles.'
'Shorty . . .'
'Did anyone see Jameson?'
'He was in the fo'c'sle.'
'None of *them* got out.'
'Lucky bastards . . . Better than this, any road.'
'We've got a chance still.'
'It's getting lighter.'
'That's the moon.'
'Shorty . . . Wake up . . .'
'She must've gone down inside of five minutes.'
'Like *Sorrel*.'
'Thirty miles off, they should have got us on the Radar.'
'If they were watching out properly.'
'Who was stern escort?'
'*Trefoil*'
'Shorty . . .'
'How many on the other raft?'
'Same as us, I reckon.'
'Christ, it's cold.'
'Wind's getting up, too.'
'I'd like to meet the bastard that put us here.'
'Once is enough for me.'
'Shorty . . . What's the matter with you?'
'Must be pretty near Iceland.'
'We don't need telling that.'
'*Trefoil's* all right. They ought to have seen us on the Radar.'
'Not with some half-asleep sod of an operator on watch.'
'Shorty . . .'
'Stop saying that . . .! Can't you see he's finished?'
'But he was talking to me.'
'That was an hour ago, you dope.'
'Wilson's dead, sir.'
'Sure?'
'Yes. Stone cold.'

'Tip him over, then . . . Who's coming up next?'
'Any more for the Skylark?'
'What's the use? It's no warmer up on the raft.'
'Christ, it's cold . . .'

At one point during the night, the thin crescent moon came through the ragged clouds, and illuminated for a few moments the desperate scene below. It shone on a waste of water, growing choppy with the biting wind: it shone on the silhouettes of men hunched together on the rafts, and the shadows of men clinging to them, and the blurred outlines of men in the outer ring, where the corpses wallowed and heaved, and the red lights burned and burned aimlessly on the breasts of those who, hours before, had switched them on in hope and confidence. For a few minutes the moon put this cold sheen upon the face of the water, and upon the foreheads of the men whose heads were still upright; and then it withdrew, veiling itself abruptly as if, in pity and amazement, it had seen enough, and knew that the men in this extremity deserved only the decent mercy of darkness.

Ferraby did not die: but towards dawn it seemed to him that he *did* die, as he held Rose, the young signalman, in his arms, and Rose died for him. Throughout the night Rose had been sitting next to him on the raft, and sometimes they had talked and sometimes fallen silent: and had recalled that other night of long ago, their first night at sea, when he and Rose had chatted to each other and, urged on by the darkness and loneliness of their new surroundings, had drawn close together. Now the need for closeness was more compelling still, and they had turned to each other again, in an unspoken hunger for comfort, so young and unashamed that presently they found that they were holding hands . . . But in the end Rose had fallen silent, and had not answered his questions, and had sagged against him as if he had gone to sleep: Ferraby had put his arm round him and, when he slipped down farther still, had held him on his knees.

After waiting, afraid to put it to the test, he said: 'Are you all right, Rose?' There was no answer. He bent down and touched the face that was close under his own. By some instinct of compassion, it was with his lips that he touched it, and his lips came away icy and trembling. Now he was alone . . . The tears ran down Ferraby's cheeks, and fell on the open upturned eyes. In mourning and in mortal fear, he sat on, with the cold stiffening body of his friend like a dead child under his heart.

Lockhart did not die, though many times during that night there seemed to him little reason why this should be so. He had spent most of the dark hours in the water alongside Number Two Carley, of which he was in charge: only towards morning when there was room and to spare did he climb onto it. From this slighly higher vantage point he looked round him, and felt the cold and smelt the oil, and saw the other raft nearby, and the troubled water in between; and he pondered the dark shadows which were dead men, and the clouds racing across the sky, and the single star overhead, and the sound of the bitter wind; and then, with all this to daunt him and drain him of hope, he took a last grip on himself, and on the handful of men on the raft, and set himself to stay alive till daylight and to take them along with him.

He made them sing, he made them move their arms and legs, he made them talk, he made them keep awake. He slapped their faces, he kicked them, he rocked the raft till they were forced to rouse themselves and cling on; he dug deep into his repertoire of filthy stories and produced a selection so pointless and so disgusting that he would have blushed to tell them, if the extra blood had been available. He made them act 'Underneath the Spreading Chestnut Tree', and play guessing games: he roused Ferraby from his dejected silence, and made him repeat all the poetry he knew: he imitated all the characters of ITMA, and forced the others to join in. He set them to paddling the raft round in circles, and singing the 'Volga Boatmen': recalling a childhood game, he divided them into three parties, and detailed them to shout 'Russia', 'Prussia', and 'Austria', at the same moment – a manoeuvre designed to sound like a giant and appropriate sneeze . . . The men on his raft loathed him, and the sound of his voice, and his appalling optimism: they cursed him openly and he answered them back in the same language, and promised them a liberal dose of detention as soon as they got back to harbour.

For all this, he drew on an unknown reserve of strength and energy which now came to his rescue. When he climbed out of the water, he had felt miserably stiff and cold: the wild and foolish activity, the clownish antics, soon restored him, and some of it communicated itself to some of the men with him, and some of them caught the point of it and became foolish and clownish and energetic in their turn, and so some of them saved their lives.

Sellars, Crowther, Gracey and Tewson did not die. They were on Number Two Carley with Lockhart and Ferraby, and they were all that were left alive by morning, despite these frenzied efforts to keep at bay the lure and sweetness of sleep. It was Tewson's first ship, and his first voyage: he was a cheerful young Cockney, and now and again during the night he had made them laugh by asking cheekily: 'Does this sort of thing happen *every* trip?' It was a pretty small joke, but (as Lockhart realised) it was the sort of contribution they had to have . . . There were other contributions: Sellars sang an interminable version of 'The Harlot of Jerusalem', Crowther (the Sick-Berth Attendant who had been a vet) imitated animal noises, Gracey gave an exhibition of shadow-boxing which nearly overturned the raft. They did, in fact, the best they could; and their best was just good enough to save their lives.

Phillips, Grey, Spurway, and Widdowes did not die. They were the survivors of Number One Carley, with the Captain; and they owed their lives to him. Ericson, like Lockhart, had realised that sleep had to be fought continuously and relentlessly if anyone were to be left alive in the morning: he had therefore spent the greater part of the night putting the men on his raft through an examination for their next higher rating. He made a round-game of it, half serious, half childish: he asked each man upwards of thirty questions: if the answer were correct all the others had to clap, if not, they had to boo at the tops of their voices and the culprit had to perform some vigorous kind of forfeit . . . His authority carried many of the men along for several hours: it was only towards dawn, when he felt his own brain lagging with the effort of concentration, that the competitors began to thin out, and the clapping and shouting to fade to a ghostly mutter of sound: to a moaning like the wind, and a rustling like the cold waves curling and slopping against the raft, the waves that trustfully waited to swallow them all.

The Captain did not die: it was as if, after *Compass Rose* went down, he had nothing left to die with. The night's 'examination' effort had been necessary, and so he had made it, automatically – but only as the Captain, in charge of a raftful of men who had always been owed his utmost care and skill: the effort had had no part of his heart in it. That heart seemed to have shrivelled, in the few terrible minutes between the striking of his ship, and her sinking: he had loved *Compass Rose*, not sentimentally, but with the pride and the strong attachment which the past three years had inevitably brought, and to see her thus contemptuously destroyed before his eyes had been an appalling shock. There was no word and no reaction appropriate to this wicked night: it drained him of all feeling. But still he had not died, because he was forty-seven, and a sailor, and tough and strong, and he understood – though now he hated – the sea.

All his men had longed for daylight: Ericson merely noted that it was now at hand, and that the poor remnants of his crew might yet survive. When the first grey light from the eastward began to creep across the water, he roused himself, and his men, and set them to paddling towards the other raft, which had drifted a full mile away. The light, gaining in strength, seeped round them as if borne by the bitter wind itself, and fell without pity upon the terrible pale sea, and the great streaks of oil, and the floating bundles that had been living men. As the two rafts drew together, the figures on them waved to each other, jerkily, like people who could scarcely believe that they were not alone: when they were within earshot, there was a croaking hail from a man on Lockhart's raft, and Phillips, on the Captain's, made a vague noise in his throat in reply.

No one said anything more until the rafts met, and touched; and then they all looked at each other, in horror and in fear.

The two rafts were much alike. On each of them was the same handful of filthy oil-soaked men who still sat upright, while the other men lay still in their arms or sprawled like dogs at their feet. Round them, in the water were the same attendant figures – a horrifying fringe of bobbing corpses, with their meaningless faces blank to the sky and their hands frozen to the ratlines.

Between the dead and the living was no sharp dividing line. The men upright on the rafts seemed to blur with the dead men they nursed, and with the derelict men in the water, as part of the same vague and pitiful design.

Ericson counted the figures still alive on the other Carley. There were four of them, and Lockhart and Ferraby: they had the same fearful aspect as the men on his own raft: blackened, shivering, their cheeks and temples sunken with the cold, their limbs bloodless; men who, escaping death during the dark hours, still crouched striken in its shadow when morning came. And the whole total was eleven . . . He rubbed his hand across his frozen lips, and cleared his throat, and said:

'Well, Number One . . .'

'Well, sir . . .'

Lockhart stared back at Ericson for a moment, and then looked away. There could be nothing more, nothing to ease the unbearable moment.

The wind blew chill in their faces, the water slopped and broke in small ice-cold waves against the rafts, the harnessed fringe of dead men swayed like dancers. The sun was coming up now, to add dreadful detail: it showed the rafts, horrible in themselves, to be only single items in a whole waste of cruel water, on which countless bodies rolled and laboured amid countless bits of wreckage, adrift under the bleak sky. All round them, on the oily, fouled surface, the wretched flotsam, all that was left of *Compass Rose*, hurt and shamed the eye.

The picture of the year, thought Lockhart: 'Morning, with Corpses.' So *Viperous* found them.

IN THE HANDS OF GOD
Captain Marryat

Peter Simple describes how as a young man aboard the sailing ship Diomede *the vessel and the lives of all on board are put in jeopardy by a storm which threatens to drive the ship onto a rocky lee shore . . .*

We cruised along the coast, until we had run down into the Bay of Arcason, where we captured two or three vessels, and obliged many more to run on shore. And here we had an instance showing how very important it is that a captain of a man-of-war should be a good sailor, and have his ship in such discipline as to be strictly obeyed by his ship's company. I heard the officers unanimously assert, after the danger was over, that nothing but the presence of mind which was shown by Captain Savage could have saved the ship and her crew. We had chased a convoy of vessels to the bottom of the bay: the wind was very fresh when we hauled off, after running them on shore; and the surf on the beach even at that time was so great, that they were certain to go to pieces before they could be got afloat again. We were obliged to double-reef the topsails as soon as we hauled to the wind, and the weather looked very threatening. In an hour afterwards, the whole sky was covered with one black cloud, which sank so low as nearly to touch our mast-heads, and a tremendous sea, which appeared to have risen up almost by magic, rolled in upon us, setting the vessel on a dead lee shore. As the night closed in, it blew a dreadful gale, and the ship was nearly buried with the press of canvas which she was obliged to carry: for had we sea-room, we should have been lying-to under storm staysails; but we were forced to carry on at all risks, that we might claw off shore. The sea broke over as we lay in the trough, deluging us with water from the forecastle, aft, to the binnacles; and very often, as the ship descended with a plunge, it was with such force that I really thought she would divide in half with the violence of the shock. Double breechings were rove on the guns, and they were further secured with tackles; and strong cleats nailed behind the trunnions; for we heeled over so much when we lurched, that the guns were wholly supported by the breechings and tackles, and had one of them broken loose, it must have burst right through the lee side of the ship, and she must have foundered. The captain, first lieutenant, and most of the officers remained on deck during the whole of the night; and really, what with the howling of the wind, the violence of the rain, the washing of the water about the decks, the working of the chain-pumps, and the creaking and groaning of the timbers, I thought that we must inevitably have been lost; and I said my prayers at least a dozen times during the night, for I felt it impossible to go to bed. I had often wished, out of curiosity, that I might be in a gale of wind; but I little thought it was to have been a scene of this description, or anything half so dreadful. What made it more appalling was, that we were on a lee shore, and the consultations of the captain and officers, and the eagerness with which they looked out for daylight, told us that we had other dangers to encounter besides the storm. At last the morning broke, and the look-out man upon the gangway called out, 'Land on the lee beam!' I perceived the master dash his fist against the hammock-rails, as if with vexation, and walk away without saying a word, and looking very grave.

'Up there, Mr Wilson,' said the captain to the second lieutenant, 'and see how far the land trends forward, and whether you can distinguish the point.' The second lieutenant went up the main-rigging, and pointed with his hand to about two points before the beam.

'Do you see two hillocks inland?'

'Yes, sir,' replied the second lieutenant.

'Then it is so,' observed the captain to the master, 'and if we weather it we shall have more sea-room. Keep her full, and let her go through the water; do you hear, quarter-master?'

'Ay, ay, sir.'

'Thus, and no nearer, my man. Ease her with a spoke or two when she sends; but be careful, or she'll take the wheel out of your hands.'

It really was a very awful sight. When the ship was in the trough of the sea, you could distinguish nothing but a waste of tumultuous water; but when she was borne up on the summit of the enormous waves, you then looked down, as it were, upon a low, sandy coast, close to you, and covered with foam and breakers. 'She behaves nobly,' observed the captain, stepping aft to the binnacle, and looking at the compass; 'if the wind does not baffle us, we shall weather.' The captain had scarcely time to make the observation, when the sails shivered and flapped like thunder. 'Up with the helm; what are you about, quarter-master?'

'The wind has headed us, sir,' replied the quarter-master, coolly.

The captain and master remained at the binnacle watching the compass; and when the sails were again full, she had broken off two points, and the point of land was only a little on the lee bow.

'We must wear her round, Mr Falcon. Hands, wear ship – ready, oh, ready.'

'She has come up again,' cried the master, who was at the binnacle.

'Hold fast there a minute. How's her head now?'

'N.N.E., as she was before she broke off, sir.'

'Pipe belay,' said the captain. 'Falcon,' continued he, 'if she beaks off again we may have no room to wear; indeed there is so little room now, that I must run the risk. Which cable was ranged last night – the best bower?'

'Yes, sir.'

'Jump down, then, and see it double-bitted and stoppered at thirty fathoms. See it well done – our lives may depend upon it.'

The ship continued to hold her course good; and we were within half a mile of the point, and fully expected to weather it, when again the wet and heavy sails flapped in the wind, and the ship broke off two points as before. The officers and seamen were aghast, for the ship's head was right onto the breakers. 'Luff[1] now, all you can, quarter-master,' cried the captain. 'Send the men aft directly. My lads, there is no time for words – I am going to *club-haul*[2] the ship, for there is no room to wear. The only

---

[1] Turn the head of the ship to face the wind.

[2] To tack a ship by letting the lee-anchor down as soon as the wind is out of the sails, by which her head is brought to the wind. A last resort (in a very dangerous situation) to change the ship's direction.

chance you have of safety is to be cool, watch my eye, and execute my orders with precision. Away to your stations for tacking ship. Hands by the best bower anchor. Mr Wilson, attend below with the carpenter and his mates, ready to cut away the cable at the moment that I give the order. Silence, there, fore and aft. Quarter-master, keep her full again for stays. Mind you ease the helm down when I tell you.' About a minute passed before the captain gave any further orders. The ship had closed-to within a quarter-mile of the beach, and the waves curled and topped around us, bearing us down upon the shore, which presented one continued surface of foam, extending to within half a cable's length of our position. The captain waved his hand in silence to the quarter-master at the wheel, and the helm was put down. The ship turned slowly to the wind, pitching and chopping as the sails were spilling. When she had lost her way, the captain gave the order, 'Let go the anchor. We will haul all at once, Mr Falcon,' said the captain. Not a word was spoken. The men went to the fore brace, which had not been manned; most of them knew, although I did not, that if the ship's head did not go round the other way, we should be on shore, and among the breakers, in half a minute. I thought at the time that the captain had said that he would haul all the yards at once. There appeared to be doubt or dissent on the countenance of Mr Falcon; and I was afterwards told that he had not agreed with the captain; but he was too good an officer, and knew that there was no time for discussion, to make any remark; and the event proved that the captain was right. At last the ship was head to wind, and the captain gave the signal. The yards flew round with such a creaking noise, that I thought the masts had gone over the side, and the next moment the wind had caught the sails; and the ship, which for a moment or two had been on an even keel, *careened*[1] over to her gunnel with its force. The captain, who stood upon the weather-hammock rails, holding by the main-rigging, ordered the helm amidships, looked full at the sails, and then at the cable, which grew broad upon the weather bow, and held the ship from nearing the shore. At last he cried, 'Cut away the cable!' A few strokes of the axes were heard, and then the cable flew out of the hawse-hole in a blaze of fire, from the violence of the friction, and disappeared under a huge wave, which struck us and deluged us with water fore and aft. But we were

---

[1] To heave over to one side.

now on the other tack, and the ship regained her way, and we had evidently increased our distance from the land.

'My lads,' said the captain, to the ship's company, 'you have behaved well, and I thank you; but I must tell you honestly that we have more difficulties to get through. We have to weather a point of the bay on this tack. Mr Falcon, splice the main-brace, and call the watch. How's her head, quarter-master?'

'S.W. by S. Southerly, sir.'

'Very well; let her go through the water'; and the captain, beckoning to the master to follow him, went down into the cabin. As our immediate danger was over, I went down into the berth to see if I could get anything for breakfast, where I found O'Brien and two or three more.

'By the powers, it was as nate a thing as ever I saw done,' observed O'Brien: 'the slightest mistake as to time or management, and at this moment the flatfish would have been dubbing at our ugly carcases. Peter, you're not fond of flatfish are you, my boy? We may thank Heaven and the captain, I can tell you that, my lads: but now, where's the chart, Robinson? Hand me down the parallel rules and compasses, Peter; they are in the corner of the shelf. Here we are now, a devilish sight too near this infernal point. We knows how her head is?'

'I do, O'Brien: I heard the quarter-master tell the captain S.W. by S. Southerly.'

'Let me see,' continued O'Brien, 'variation 2¼ – lee way – rather too large an allowance of that, I'm afraid, but, however, we'll give her 2½ points; the *Diomede* would blush to make any more, under any circumstances. Here – the compass – now we'll see'; and O'Brien advanced the parallel rule from the compass to the spot where the ship was placed on the chart. 'Bother! you see it's as much as she'll do to weather the other point now, on this tack, and that's what the captain meant when he told us we had more difficulty. I could have taken by Bible oath that we were clear of everything, if the wind held.'

'See what the distance is, O'Brien,' said Robinson. It was measured, and proved to be thirteen miles. 'Only thirteen miles; and if we do weather, we shall do very well, for the bay is deep beyond. It's a rocky point, you see, just by way of variety. Well, my lads, I've a piece of comfort for you, anyhow. It's not long that you'll be kept in suspense, for by one o'clock this day, you'll either be congratulating each other upon your good luck, or you'll be past praying for. Come, put up the chart, for I hate to look at melancholy prospects; and, steward, see what you can find in the way of comfort.' Some bread and cheese, with the remains of yesterday's boiled pork, were put on the table, with a bottle of rum, procured at the time they 'spliced the mainbrace'; but we were all too anxious to eat much, and one by one returned on deck to see how the weather was, and if the wind at all favoured us. On deck the superior officers were in conversation with the captain, who had expressed the same fear that O'Brien had in our berth. The men, who knew what they had to expect, were assembled in knots, looking very grave, but at the same time not wanting in confidence. They knew that they could trust to the captain, as far as skill or courage could avail them; and sailors are too sanguine to despair, even at the last moment. As for myself, I felt such admiration for the captain, after what I had witnessed that morning, that, whenever the idea came over me, that in all probability I should be lost in a few hours, I could not help acknowledging how much more serious it was that such a man should be lost to his country. I do not intend to say that it consoled me; but it certainly made me still more regret the chances with which we were threatened.

Before twelve o'clock the rocky point which we so much dreaded was in sight, broad on the lee-bow; and if the low sandy coast appeared terrible, how much more did this, even at a distance. The captain eyed it for some minutes in silence, as if in calculation.

'Mr Falcon,' said he, at last, 'we must put the main-sail on her.'

'She never can bear it, sir.'

'She *must* bear it,' was the reply. 'Send the men aft to the main-sheet. See that careful men attend the buntlines.'

The mainsail was set, and the effect of it upon the ship was tremendous. She careened over so that her lee channels were under the water; and when pressed by a sea, the lee-side of the quarter-deck and gangway were afloat. She now reminded me of a goaded and fiery horse, mad with the stimulus applied, not rising as before, but forcing herself through whole seas, and dividing the waves, which poured in one continual torrent from the fore-castle down upon the decks below. Four men were secured to the wheel – the sailors who obliged to cling, to prevent being washed away – the ropes were thrown in confusion to leeward, the shot rolled out of the lockers, and every eye was fixed aloft,

The danger was more dreadful than the noise of the sea.

watching the masts which were expected every moment to go over the side. A heavy sea struck us on the broadside, and it was some moments before the ship appeared to recover herself; she reeled, trembled, and stopped her way, as if it had stupified her. The first lieutenant looked at the captain, as if to say, 'This will not do.' 'It is our only chance,' answered the captain to the appeal. That the ship went faster through the water, and held a better wind, was certain; but just before we arrived at the point, the gale increased in force. 'If anything starts, we are lost, sir,' observed the first lieutenant again.

'I am perfectly aware of it,' replied the captain, in a calm tone; 'but, as I said before, and you must now be aware, it is our only chance. The consequence of any carelessness or neglect in the fitting and securing of the rigging will be felt now; and this danger, if we escape it, ought to remind us how much we have to answer for, if we neglect our duty. The lives of a whole ship's company may be sacrificed by the neglect or incompetence of an officer when in harbour. I will pay you the compliment, Falcon, to say, that I feel convinced that the masts of the ship are as secure as knowledge and attention can make them.'

The first lieutenant thanked the captain for his good opinion, and hoped it would not be the last compliment which he paid him.

'I hope not, too; but a few minutes will decide the point.'

The ship was now within two cables' lengths of the rocky point. Some few of the men I observed to clasp their hands, but most of them were silently taking off their jackets and kicking off their shoes, that they might not lose a chance of escape, provided the ship struck.

' 'Twill be touch and go, indeed, Falcon,' observed the captain (for I had clung to the belaying-pins, close to them, for the last half-hour that the mainsail had been set). 'Come aft; you and I must take the helm. We shall want *nerve* there, and only there, now.'

The captain and first lieutenant went aft, and took the fore-spokes of the wheel, and O'Brien, at a sign made by the captain, laid hold of the spokes behind him. An old quarter-master kept his station at the fourth. The roaring of the seas on the rocks, with the howling of the wind, were dreadful; but the sight was more dreadful than the noise. For a few moments I shut my eyes but anxiety forced me to open them again. As near as I could judge, we were not twenty yards from the rocks at the time that the ship passed abreast of them. We were in the midst of the foam, which boiled around us; and as the ship was driven nearer to them, and careened with the wave, I thought that our main yard-arm would have touched the rock; and at this moment a gust of wind came on, which laid the ship on her beam-ends, and checked her progress through the water, while the accumulated noise was deafening. A few moments more the ship dragged on, another wave dashed over her and spent itself upon the rocks, while the spray was dashed back from them, and returned upon the decks. The main rock was within ten yards of her counter, when another gust of wind laid us on our beam-ends, the foresail and mainsail split and were blown clean out of the bolt-ropes – the ship righted, trembling fore and aft. I looked astern; the rocks were to windward on our quarter, and we were safe. I thought at the time that the ship, relieved of her courses, and again lifting over the waves, was not a bad similitude of the relief felt by us all at that moment; and, like her, we trembled as we panted with the sudden reaction, and felt the removal of the intense axiety which oppressed our breasts.

The captain resigned the helm, and walked aft to look at the point, which was now broad on the weather quarter. In a minute or two he desired Mr Falcon to get new sails up and bend them, and then went below to his cabin. I am sure it was to thank God for our deliverance: I did most fervently, not only then, but when I went to my hammock at night. We were now comparatively safe – in a few hours completely so; for strange to say, immediately after we had weathered the rocks, the gale abated, and before morning we had a reef out of the top-sails. It was my forenoon watch, and perceiving Mr Chucks on the forecastle, I went forward to him, and asked him what he thought of it.

'Thought of it, sir!' replied he; 'why, I always think bad of it when the elements won't allow my whistle to be heard; and I consider it hardly fair play. I never care if we are left to our own exceptions; but how is it possible for a ship's company to do their best when they cannot hear the boatswain's pipe? However, God be thanked, nevertheless, and make better Christians of us all! As for the carpenter, he is mad. Just before we weathered the point, he told me that it was just the same 27,600 and odd years ago. I do believe that on his death-bed (and he was not far from a very hard one yesterday), he will tell us how he died so many thousand years ago, of the same complaint. And that gunner of ours is a fool. Would you believe it, Mr Simple, he went crying about the decks, "Oh my poor guns, what will become of them if they break loose?" He appeared to consider it of no consequence if the ship and ship's company were all lost, provided that his guns were safely landed on the beach.'

Acknowledgements

The publishers would like to extend their grateful thanks to the following authors, publishers and others for kindly granting them permission to reproduce the copyrighted extracts and stories included in this anthology.

DISASTER from *The Poseidon Adventure* by Paul Galico. Reprinted by kind permission of Hughes Massie Ltd and Coward, McCann and Geoghegan Inc. © Paul Galico and Mathenata Anstalt.
FIRST DAYS AT SEA from *Doctor At Sea* by Richard Gordon. Reprinted by kind permission of Curtis Brown Ltd and Michael Joseph Ltd.
THE MARY CELESTE by Jean Morris. Reprinted by kind permission of the author.
MATTERS MARINE from *The Loud Hallo* by Lilian Beckwith. Reprinted by kind permission of Curtis Brown Ltd and Hutchinson Publishing Group Ltd. © Hutchinson and Co Ltd 1964.
THE RETURN TO ITHAKA by Iain Finlayson. Reprinted by kind permission of the author.
PROBLEM AT SEA by Agatha Christie. Reprinted by kind permission of Hughes Massie Ltd and Dodd, Mead and Co.
A LONG SWIM from *Khazan* by Joyce Stranger. Reprinted by kind permission of William Collins, Sons and Co Ltd.
THE WRECK OF THE 'FORFARSHIRE' by Iain Finlayson. Reprinted by kind permission of the Author.
IN THE MEDITERRANEAN from *We Joined The Navy* by John Winton. Reprinted by kind permission of Michael Joseph Ltd.
THE BATTLE OF THE RIVER PLATE from *The Battle of the River Plate* by Dudley Pope. Reprinted by kind permission of Campbell Thomson and McLaughlin Ltd. © 1956, 1974 Dudley Bernard Egerton Pope.
WILLIAM AND THE SPY by Richmal Crompton. Reprinted by kind permission of William Collins, Sons and Co Ltd.
'FROM FALMOUTH' from *A World of My Own* by Robin Knox-Johnston. Reprinted by kind permission of John Farquharson Ltd.
THE END OF THE COMPASS ROSE from *The Cruel Sea* by Nicholas Monsarrat. Reprinted by kind permission of Campbell, Thomson & McLaughlin Limited and Alfred Knopf Inc.

Every effort has been made to clear copyrights and the publishers trust that their apologies will be accepted for any errors or omissions.